The
DESIRES *of* HER HEART

By Lyn Cote

THE DESIRES OF HER HEART
BLESSED ASSURANCE

The
DESIRES *of* HER HEART

TEXAS: *Star of Destiny*

BOOK ONE

LYN COTE

AVON

INSPIRE

An Imprint of HarperCollins*Publishers*

Interior text designed by Diahann Sturge

ISBN-13: 978-1-60751-904-1

Dedicated to my faithful readers.
Your e-mails and letters inspire me. Thank you!

"I am free and not bound by marriage or slavery."

Isabel de Olvera, a free *mulatta* (*sic*), in Queretaro, Mexico, in a signed affidavit before Don Pedro Lorenzo de Castillo and Baltasar Martinez, royal notary

January 8, 1600

The
DESIRES *of* HER HEART

Prologue

New Orleans, early August 1821

With tiny sharp teeth, worry ripped and gnawed at Dorritt Mott's peace of mind. Her stepfather, Mr. Kilbride, had been up to something for months. But what exactly? And how would it affect Dorritt's private plan? Today the colorful and chaotic gathering of the crème de la crème of New Orleans society buffeted Dorritt like the whirlwinds of a hurricane. But she'd come because attending the amateur race at the horse track outside the city would give her a chance to pick up a few more clues, to see what Mr. Kilbride was doing away from their plantation.

Scanning the elegant assembly for her stepfather, Dorritt saw that the race had drawn more than just the gentry. Westerners in buckskin with long rifles slung over their backs and sailors who might be pirates in Jean Laffite's crew dotted the crowd. Then she glimpsed a knot of beaver-hatted gentlemen—some jovial and all excited—gathered around a bookmaker who was taking bets near the horse stable. Of course, Mr. Kilbride was in the midst of them. The man never learned.

She began moving through the crowd, nodding and smiling when addressed. Present but apart. Ever since she had debuted, she had watched New Orleans society in a detached manner, as if watching an absurd, sometimes aggravating, play.

Two overly perfumed ladies in feathered bonnets—one gray and one brown—stepped in front of Dorritt, blocking her. Behind their fans, they were of course gossiping. Gray bonnet said, "Did you hear about the Dorsey chit marrying the Hampton heir?"

"Didn't her father forbid him to court her?" the brown bonnet objected.

Dorritt didn't blame the father. The Hampton heir was a rake. But of course, to some, wealth covered a multitude of sins.

"Hampton lured the girl away and took her driving in a *closed* carriage—" Gray bonnet lowered her voice. "—and they didn't come home until well into the night."

"Well into the night? Didn't her mother warn her about such indiscreet behavior?" Brown bonnet sounded aghast.

Dorritt started to move away. Some women embraced the calculated destruction of reputations as their lifework. Dorritt had no doubt the Hampton heir had ensnared a green girl who would put up with his dubious behavior. All to give him an heir. Men must have their sons at all costs. *And people wonder why I've chosen to remain a spinster.*

Pushing ahead, Dorritt managed to navigate within hearing distance of the men around her stepfather. They were discussing the merits of the horses scheduled to run today. From the corner of her eye, she noted that a few of the Westerners were coming up to put down bets too. Mr. Kilbride was touting the merits of his entry in today's race and placing a bet on it to win. The staggering amount he'd just wagered with a smile made Dorritt blanch. She kept the books for the plantation. If their horse lost, which of their people would he have to sell to recoup this bet?

Feeling panicky, Dorritt turned blindly and nearly walked into her half-sister's admiring all-male court. Fifteen-year-old Jewell, with her curly black hair, large brown eyes, pale complexion, and graceful figure knew exactly how to enthrall men. Her most favored and fervent admirer at the moment was sole heir of a wealthy family.

Dorritt edged away as her sister purred, "I do hope no one will be hurt today. Horse races can be so perilous." Jewell was fluttering her white egret feather fan against the heavy air already smothering them, the reason that the races were held early in the morning.

"Will you favor me with one of your ribbons to wear?" the wealthy young heir named André asked Jewell. "I'm sure I will win if you bestow your favor on me."

Dorritt felt the urge to gag. Most of the conversations she overheard were romantically exaggerated, devoid of any content. But she had a sudden insight. While most girls didn't debut until sixteen, Mr. Kilbride had insisted Jewell debut this year. Why? Was this part of his scheming?

Hastily, Dorritt turned, came face-to-face with the man she should have been watching out for. A recent widower with two children still in leading strings, he thought Dorritt was the answer to his need for a wife and stepmother. But she didn't want to get tangled up in those long ribbons on the toddlers' dresses. She tried to smile, repressing the urge to pick up her skirts and run.

Before he'd lost his wife, Dorritt had hoped she could persuade him to back her financially in her secret plan for independence. But now he viewed her as the quick solution to his problem of raising children alone. After all, Dorritt, at twenty-five, was on the shelf, a spinster. How could she afford to refuse an honest man's proposal?

She was saved by the horn announcing the start of the first race. She turned toward the track and hoped she could drift away from the widower before she was forced again to discourage him.

The persistent worry over what her stepfather was up to, the worry that had begun waking her up nights, tried to catch her, clench her again within its sharp teeth. She hurried forward, her pulse racing. *I can't think of that now.*

One

Belle Vista Plantation
New Orleans, late August 1821

"You wish to marry well? By that, Jewell, you mean marry a wealthy man?" Dorritt sat in her stepfather's lavish ivory and gilded parlor, the heavy afternoon heat weighing her down.

"There can be no other meaning, sister." Fanning herself, her younger half-sister took another promenade around the parlor.

Dorritt ignored her mother's shocked disapproval. She sensed that today was the climax of months of planning by her stepfather.

Dorritt's tambour frame and stand sat in front of her at hand level. Placing tiny artful stitches helped her conceal how her heart skipped and jumped. How would it all play out today? Dorritt looked up at her half-sister, her opposite in everything, from Jewell's olive skin and wavy blue-black hair to Dorritt's fair skin and straight golden hair. "I believe love is necessary to marry well."

Jewell made a sound of dismissal, her high-waisted white dress swayed with her wandering. "These odd humors, your peculiar comments all come from books. You read too much, Dorritt. Father always says so and mother agrees."

"Then it must be so." The heat of the afternoon was squeezing Dorritt like a sodden tourniquet. She put down her needle and pinched the bridge of her nose. Over the past months, she had stood back and read the signs of her stepfather's devious manipulation of facts and circumstances. Of course, Jewell had no idea that the culmination of these might come today. But Dorritt knew well what red ink in a ledger meant.

With a handkerchief, her mother blotted her rosy, perspiring face, which still retained a faded beauty. "Please, Jewell, you must sit down and relax; compose yourself."

"Why hasn't André come yet?" Jewell attacked the lush Boston fern sitting on the stand by the French doors. She pulled off a frond and began stripping it. "He told me he would be asking my father's permission today."

There is many a slip between the cup and lip. "Perhaps he has been delayed." Dorritt set another tiny stitch with rigid concentration.

Would her stepfather manage to work his trickery once more, bend reality to his selfish and greedy will? And more important, could Dorritt use it in her favor? Her hands stuttered and she had to pull the needle back out.

The sound of an approaching horse drew Jewell to the French doors that led to the garden. "I can't see the rider. He has already dismounted under the porte cochere. That doesn't look like André's horse," she added fretfully, and tossed the mangled frond back into the pot.

They all turned their heads to listen to the swishing of the grand front doors being parted, the murmur of their butler, the hum of another man's voice, footsteps down the hallway to her stepfather's den. If it wasn't André, who could it be?

"It could be Philippe." Jewell beamed and gave a little skip. "Maybe I will receive two offers of marriage today."

One proposal would achieve your doting father's goal, dear sister. Dorritt took a deep breath and began an intricate French knot.

"Do you think it might really be Philippe Marchand?" Their mother sounded awestruck. "Why he is worth nearly half a million."

Jewell did a pirouette and swirled her hands in the air. "And I would be mistress of Marchand Plantation and eat blancmange every day."

Dorritt imagined herself decorating her sister's face with the white jellied dessert. She bent farther over her embroidery so neither her sister nor mother would see her unaccountable amusement. More of her odd humors.

"Come away from the window, Jewell," her mother said in a low voice. "You must not appear as though you're aware of any of this."

For once, her younger half-sister obeyed. Jewell went and sat in the Chippendale chair beside Dorritt, lifting the needle from Dorritt's hand and moving the tambour frame in front of herself.

Their mother uttered a soft scold for Jewell's theft. But Jewell ignored it as usual.

Dorritt stopped to blot her face with her hankie. She could only hope that André had come to propose. If not André, then Philippe. If Jewell were married, this might ring the first bell of freedom for her.

"Don't you dare take one stitch," Dorritt ordered in an undertone, holding her own nervousness in strict check.

"I embroider just as well as you do," Jewell lied with a mocking smile. Her bitter chocolate eyes flashing, she boldly stuck the needle into the design.

Dorritt stood up. *You need your face slapped, Jewell. But not by me.* "I have work to do." She strolled the length of the room, fanning herself with a woven palm fan. Glancing out the windows, she glimpsed the horse hitched in the shade of the porte cochere. She halted in midstep on her way to the hall. Surely it wasn't *he* who had come and gone into her stepfather's den. Surely not.

Just as she reached the door of the room, she heard footsteps coming toward the parlor. It was what she feared. The widower who was pursuing her, Job Wilkinson, strode beside her stepfather. Job looked like a white crane, and her stepfather waddled like a balding, plump self-satisfied gander. Not a good sign. The urge to flee nearly overcame her. But she composed herself, arranging her face into a sweet false smile. "Good day, Mr. Wilkinson. Won't you come in and I will order tea to be served." She turned in time to see her sister's flushed, irritated face.

If only Dorritt could have enjoyed this experience of for once flouting her sister's conceit. *But I thought I made myself clear . . .* How like a man to ignore her stated wishes.

"No tea," her stepfather ordered. "Jewell and Mrs. Kilbride, come with me. We will leave these two young people alone."

Pouting, Jewell threw down the needle and rose. Their mother quickly led Jewell out. Her stepfather closed the pocket door to the parlor, and they were alone.

Dorritt watched her abandoned needle sway, dangling on its silk thread tether. "Tell me that you didn't. . . ." She faced Mr. Wilkinson and read the truth. Her voice faded.

"Yes, I did seek your stepfather's permission to pay my addresses to you. I thought it over many times since our last conversation. Dorritt, you are just the wife I need. And just the mother I need for my little orphans. You are thrifty and good with children."

Dorritt knew that she should be flattered by these words, but she wasn't. *You've just insulted me and you don't even know it.* "I told you, dear sir, that I don't really wish for marriage." *Not a marriage of convenience.* She knotted her hands together to keep from slapping his earnest face.

"Dorritt, I'm afraid that you may decide that you should change your mind." He hesitated a moment. "I've heard some disturbing news about your stepfather's . . ."

I've heard rumors too. And she knew more than the rumor-mongers did. "Talk is cheap and gossip is untrustworthy." She turned away dismissively, trying to ignore the way her pulse suddenly galloped as if over rough turf.

"Belle Vista is about to be foreclosed."

She stopped where she was. She wasn't good at avoiding the truth. But she had been trying hard to avoid this partic-ular truth, which had been bearing down on her for weeks. Cold liquid desolation trickled through her heart and then on through each vein.

"I am not unaware of my stepfather's financial difficulties." Her murmured words were so inadequate to the situation.

The widower laid a gentle hand on her shoulder. "Dorritt, I know you're not in love with me. And my sweet wife has only been gone for about nine months. But I'm certain there's no one who will look askance if we married."

She stiffened herself bit by bit against her sudden weakness. "You know I don't consider marriage as my purpose."

"You don't need to think of it. Just say yes. Dorritt, we are old friends. I'll be a kind and indulgent husband."

From outside, Dorritt heard another horse arrived. No doubt André was arriving to offer for Jewell—she hoped. The fingers of despair slipping around her heart, Dorritt looked at her suitor. He was an honest man. But marry him? She couldn't ignore how she felt . . . a sense of wrongness, that this wasn't the path God had for her. "Thank you. But I just can't." Dorritt was aware of a new arrival at the door, now speaking to their butler.

"I feared that you would give me that reply. But I will merely say that my offer stands." He stepped forward, lifted her hand to his lips and kissed it. "You need only send me a message."

She accepted his homage with a curtsy and a soft *"Merci."* He left her and clutched in a terrible lethargy; she returned to her chair and the tambour frame. The needle still hung by the thread, tethered just as she was to this place, these people. But she had barely lifted her needle to set a new stitch when the butler showed André, Jewell's suitor, into the parlor.

André greeted her with a bow. She rose again, trying to look pleased. "I'm sure, sir, that you haven't come to see me. *Ah,* I hear my sister's footsteps." Dorritt walked to the door and started to pass her sister. Jewell was entering the room, her face sparkled with welcome.

"Don't leave us, Miss Dorritt," André said, "I can only stay a moment. I've come to say farewell."

"Farewell?" Jewell echoed him, shock vibrating in her tone. "Where are you going?"

"I only learned today that *you* will be leaving New Orleans. You will be sorely missed," André said these words in a rush as if he'd rehearsed them over and over.

Dorritt almost pitied her sister. Of course, Jewell had not noticed anything, not picked up any troubling clues from her father's behavior over the last critical month.

"Leaving New Orleans?" Jewell looked and sounded stunned.

"I'm sure I wish you well in Texas. And I have brought you a token to remember me by." He pulled a small red velvet box from his coat pocket and handed it to Jewell. Smoothly he lifted her free hand to his lips. And then he disappeared. Taking a large income, acres of bottom land, and nearly one hundred slaves away with him. Ringing the death knell to more than Dorritt's hope of emancipation.

Dorritt and her sister didn't move. Then Jewell turned slowly and stared at Dorritt. "What has happened?" Jewell's voice was low, harsh, and accusatory.

Dorritt had known how precarious their finances were ever since the bank Panic of 1819. But she was saved from answering by her stepfather hustling into the room.

"Why did André leave so suddenly?" Mr. Kilbride asked, for once looking surprised, troubled.

Jewell didn't move; she merely held the velvet box in her open palm.

"That's odd," her mother said, entering the room at her husband's elbow. "Surely he couldn't have proposed and given you the ring in those few moments."

Jewell still said nothing.

Dorritt actually pitied her. "André came to bid us farewell." The words flowed from her lips as if she memorized them to recite, "We will be sorely missed but he wishes us well in Texas."

Dorritt's words brought Jewell out of her trance. "Texas!" she threw the word at her father. "Never!"

Her stepfather turned his glare to Dorritt. "He said Texas? How could he know?" He frowned and then said, "I feared that. His father must have overheard me when I was discussing the new settlement . . . ." Then he cursed softly.

Dorritt could only stare, feeling disconnected from them, from their emotions. Her own shock had broken her silence. She'd expected that news of their financial troubles would come to light. She even planned how to use it to escape her unhappy situation. But Texas? She found she could no longer keep up the charade of behaving as if she didn't know how bad things were. "I knew we were close to ruin, but Texas? Why Texas?"

"You know how our finances stand," he said, sounding angry at her. "I tried but couldn't recoup our losses gaming over the last months, and instead of winning big, I lost money at the races. Everything went against me." Mr. Kilbride took a menacing step toward her as if he were going to slap her.

Dorritt stared him down.

"We're ruined?" Jewell blurted out. "We can't be. We own this plantation and slaves and . . . This is insane."

Mr. Kilbride took a hasty turn around the room. He halted in front of the fireplace. He pounded one hand into the other. "Since neither of you could do your duty to your parents and marry well, we'll be leaving for Texas in ten days. I've done all I can to save our fortune, but the Panic of 1819 put us into deep debt. And there's no way out. When a man needs a run of luck, it never comes."

Dorritt knew that this was part of the truth. They had along with almost everyone else lost money in the Panic. But her stepfather's penchant for gambling deep was what had ruined them. How could he have fooled himself into thinking that wagering would put them into the black? This accusation crawled up and pushed against her throat, clamoring to be voiced. She walked away and looked out through the white sheers.

"This is all your fault!" Mr. Kilbride declared.

The injustice of this made Dorritt whirl around. "I—"

But Mr. Kilbride shook his finger in Jewell's face, not hers. "If you hadn't kept André dancing on your string so long, he would have proposed a month or two ago. Texas is all your fault."

Jewell visibly shook with fury. She threw the velvet box at her father's chest. It bounced off him, landing on the floor. "Why didn't you tell me we were in danger?"

Their mother stooped, picked up the velvet box, and opened

it. "André gave you a lovely silver locket." This inconsequential comment was so out of tune with everyone else in the room that they all swung to look at her. "He didn't have to come at all or give you a parting gift, dearest." With a tremulous smile, their mother showed the locket nestled in the velvet.

Dorritt closed her eyes. Her mother strolled through life in a vague haze.

Jewell ignored their mother. "Father, we *can't* leave New Orleans."

"Stephen Austin has struck a bargain with the Spanish Crown to let Americans immigrate to the Texas territory. We will be given free land. And I have won a small herd of mustangs and longhorns we'll pick up in Nacogdoches in a little over a month. Then we head to the Brazos River."

"I'm not going to Texas," Jewell declared, her hands fisted.

"You don't think I want to go, do you?" her father shot back. "Texas was my backup plan. I hoped you'd marry André and that the widower would take Dorritt off my hands. Then I'd take what was left from selling Belle Vista and with the generosity of my sons-in-law, your mother and I would have lived comfortably in the city." Mr. Kilbride glared and then turned to Dorritt. "We leave in ten days. See to it." He marched out the door.

Jewell stomped one of her feet. "I won't. I won't."

Numb with shock, Dorritt watched her sister's impotent rage. It was as if Jewell were expressing Dorritt's anger as well as hers. Their mother went to Jewell and tried to comfort her. Jewell snatched the velvet box with the locket from her mother's hand, dashed it to the floor, and stomped on it. Then she turned her fury onto Dorritt's sampler, ripping it from the tambour frame and throwing it to the floor too. "André loved me. He did."

"I'm sure he did." Their mother patted Jewell's shoulder. "Depend on it, his parents made him cry off. They are filled with their own consequence."

And they knew that if André offered for you, Jewell, that he'd end up supporting your parents too. And I was to marry the widower. Dorritt knew her stepfather well enough to believe this. She wondered if any of this even crossed her mother's mind. Dorritt had hoped her stepfather's plan would work but would set her free too. If André had married Jewell and Belle Vista had been sold, Mr. Kilbride wouldn't need Dorritt to run the plantation that should have been his job. And Dorritt had hoped Mr. Wilkinson could be persuaded to bankroll the school for young ladies she'd hoped to open. And then she would have been set free.

But now what? Texas? Dorritt tried to think what to do in light of this. Their mother was holding a sobbing Jewell in her arms and stroking her back. "There, there. Someone will love you and marry you for yourself."

Someone will love you and marry you for yourself. Dorritt went over to her chair, stooped and picked up her mishandled embroidery. She wondered if it even occurred to her mother to ask her if Wilkinson had indeed proposed to her. Of course not. Wilkinson proposing hadn't meant as much to her stepfather because Wilkinson was not wealthy enough or foolish enough to support all the Kilbrides. He was only important if he would take Dorritt off Mr. Kilbride's hands. Mother would never say to her, "Someone will love you and marry you for yourself."

We leave in ten days. See to it. It had not been a request. There had been no discussion of how to take care of this overwhelming task. *See to it.* And he marched out. What would he do in ten days if nothing had been done? What if she just sat down and worked on her sampler for ten days? And did nothing?

Ignoring Dorritt completely, their mother led Jewell out the door, still supplying sympathy and comfort. Dorritt rose and stepped out the French doors. The garden was a riot of lush green, pink, and red. She looked up at the blue sky overhead, feeling herself shrinking from what lay ahead. "Oh, Father of the fatherless," she murmured, "bless me."

She'd been only a small girl in Virginia when her father had died. The pastor at the funeral had comforted her with the promise that God was the Father to the fatherless. Now she curled her hands around her embroidery as if clinging physically to Him. Her stomach rolled and clenched. Only one person would understand, comfort her. And Dorritt needed to tell her what had happened. She marched over the cobblestone path, around the house to the detached kitchen. She entered, and in a sudden passion, moved to toss her sampler into the low fire.

Her maid, Reva, who was helping the cook shuck corn, grabbed Dorritt's wrist just in time and took the sampler. "What you doing? You been working on those azaleas for months."

Dorritt faced her. "We're leaving for Texas in ten days. I won't have time for embroidery." She ignored the loud shocked reaction that this announcement brought, and letting go of the cloth, Dorritt rushed back outside.

Still holding the embroidery, Reva hurried out behind her. "Miss Dorritt."

Dorritt didn't reply, just rushed farther along the cobblestone path, past the smokehouse and by the chicken yard to their private place. There she and Reva were shielded from the house by a windbreak of popple trees near the stream that flowed through a marsh into the Delta. A vast low marshland, it was the place they always went to talk where no one could overhear. Her only true friend, Reva had been with her since they were babies.

Sounding winded, Reva halted beside her. "Didn't that André propose to Miss Jewell?"

"No." Dorritt quivered from shock that was turning into anger.

"Why not? And what you talking about Texas for?"

Dorritt tried to calm herself. Reva was counting on her. "We're ruined. André bid us a fond farewell. And we're going to Texas where there is free land."

Reva gawked at her. "Texas? I can't believe it."

"Believe it." Dorritt's throat was filling up, making it harder to speak.

"What're we going to do?" Reva asked, and gripped Dorritt's elbow.

Dorritt blinked her eyes to hold in tears. "I'll think of something."

"The widower came today too," Reva probed politely.

Dorritt gave a sharp, mirthless laugh. "He proposed because I'm thrifty and would make a good mother for his little orphans. He promised to be a kind and indulgent husband."

"Oh." Reva sounded uncertain.

Dorritt finally looked into Reva's pretty face, the color of coffee with cream and with large nearly black eyes. "You think I should have accepted him?"

"Well, we would get away from your stepdaddy and we wouldn't be going to Texas."

Resentment swelling inside her, Dorritt folded her arms. "I'd hoped Mr. Wilkinson would back me financially to start our finishing school. I've told him that repeatedly, but it wasn't what he wanted to hear so he ignored me." *Just like men do. They only hear what they want to and a woman is easy to disregard.* "It would have freed both of us. I would have shamed Mr. Kilbride into giving you to me as a gift. And if André had married Jewell, my stepfather would have. Then we'd have been free. Or as free as two unmarried women in New Orleans can be."

Reva patted her shoulder. "Could you be happy with Mr. Wilkinson? He not a bad man."

Dorritt looked down, her chin quivered with the insult he'd

given her. "I won't be a convenience to any man. I can't, won't, marry unless I trust a man and love him. And that will never happen." She looked to Reva. "I can leave a stepfather, but I can't *leave* a husband."

Dorritt admitted that she truly longed to be loved by a man, just like Jewell. If only the widower had said anything about his feelings for her. But no. He'd had some respect for her talents, that was all. *Will there ever be a love like that in any man's heart for me?* "No," she whispered, "I will never marry."

With her usual practicality, Reva asked, "But how're we going to leave your stepdaddy in Texas?"

"I'll think of a way." Dorritt began to gather her scattered wits, pulling herself together. "I am a well-educated lady of good family. That is respected anywhere. We'll stay together, Reva. I promise you."

Reva looked down. "If Mr. Kilbride is ruined, he might sell me."

Dorritt constricted inside, so tight, so painful. "If it comes to that," she forced out the words, "your going on the block, I'll accept Mr. Wilkinson's offer and ask him to buy you as my maid." Dorritt took Reva's hand. "We won't be parted. I promise."

Reva squeezed Dorritt's hand. "I hear there no slavery in Texas."

"Yes, I know." Dorritt tried to take a deep breath, but couldn't yet.

"Maybe I go to Texas and find freedom. *We* find freedom."

Dorritt pulled Reva's hand closer and gazed out over the vast green marshland in front of them. Could they be free in Texas? She stared at the summer sky, still pure blue and cloudless. Sometimes it seemed as though God waited just behind the sky, the blue curtain. She murmured her favorite verses from Psalm 37, the ones that gave her and Reva strength in hard times.

Trust in the Lord, and do good; so thou shall dwell in the land. . . .

Delight thyself also in the LORD; *and he shall give you the desires of thine heart.*

Dorritt blinked back tears. *Father, no one but Reva knows me or sees me or loves me but You.*

Leaving New Orleans for Texas terrified her. Suddenly, she felt so much apprehension and excitement it was as if she were standing on the edge of a cliff about to step off. She whispered, "Maybe we can be free in Texas."

Her whisper was swallowed up by the squawk of a snowy egret. It lifted off its spindly legs and flew low over the water first and then higher, higher.

And then she saw it. If the ungainly egret could fly . . . maybe they could be free in Texas. Somehow . . . some way.

Dorritt took a deep breath and stepped off the cliff.

Two

Natchitoches, Louisiana
September 1821

From inside the inn on the outskirts of the village, Quinn heard the arrival of a large party—human voices, horses neighing, oxen bellowing. He ambled to the doorway to see who'd come—stranger, friend, or foe. Looking across the small clearing within the piney woods, he saw a black gig with unusually stout wheels, two Conestoga wagons drawn by oxen, a thoroughbred stallion, a young colt and pregnant mare, a mule, a few cows, chickens, and goats, and nearly a dozen slaves—men, women, and children. Then he froze in place.

Why would *she* be here? He'd immediately recognized the tall lady from her slender form and the way she walked. And her voice. It was low like the call of a mourning dove, though richer and stronger. He stepped outside to see her better. Her slight hesitation and stiffness announced that she was bone weary. But she still walked very straight, not giving in. He liked the way she moved. Tall, assured, with no wasted movement. And he'd not forgotten her milk-white skin and corn-silk hair.

With sudden hot anger, Quinn also recognized the barrel-chested Kilbride. Fortunately Kilbride completely ignored Quinn and walked past him, leading two other women, one younger and one older, who must be Kilbride's wife, into the inn. What was the tall lady's connection to Kilbride? Another daughter? He took a deep breath. He shouldn't be surprised at Kilbride showing up here. After all, they were headed for the same place at the same time. But seeing the plump bald weasel in the flesh brought it all back. It still galled Quinn.

Dorritt ached all over. From many miles away, she had noticed the smoke from different chimneys and had hoped for an inn they could reach before dark. When they had approached the clearing just before sundown, she nearly embraced the inn-keeper in the stable yard. He was one of those wiry gray-haired men who could have been anywhere from forty to seventy. His weather-beaten face hid his thoughts, opinions of his guests. With a few sparse words, he told her that there was a loft where visitors could sleep with their own bedding and that there was still some squirrel stew left.

Dismissed, Dorritt glanced around the clearing once more and spied a Westerner, dressed all in fringed buckskin with moc-casins on his feet. He wore a leather hat pulled down low on his forehead and a tail of sun-bleached dark hair trailed down his left shoulder. He wasn't a man to ignore. *And he is watching me.* She stopped, suddenly winded, and then shook herself men-tally. In the past on the streets and wharves of New Orleans, she had seen Westerners, both traders and explorers. Why did this man make her uncomfortable? Perhaps it was his unwavering attention. It made the hair on the back of her neck prickle. She couldn't decide if he was being rude or merely inquisitive. But what did it matter, anyway?

She turned away and walked toward the two Conestoga wagons and the gig Jewell had insisted on driving against everyone's prediction that it wouldn't make it to Texas. Dorritt approached the two ox drivers, both seasoned slaves. "You know what to do," she murmured to them. Nodding politely, they went about unhitching the oxen. Trying to ignore the Westerner's gaze as it lingered upon her, Dorritt turned to the cook, who was already getting out dried meat and sea biscuits, and thanked her.

Reva came up, holding one of the slave babies. Dorritt turned to her and said, "Please take the family bedding to the loft inside the inn. Then would you get the orphan children fed and settled down in the stable or in the wagons?" Reva nodded and bustled away. One of the younger boys, tall for fourteen years, Amos, volunteered to set possum traps for tomorrow's meals. Dorritt patted his bare shoulder, thanking him.

Dorritt sighed. Standing still had been a mistake. Her fatigue nearly paralyzed her. After ten days of sorting, selling, buying, and packing and over a week on the road, she longed to just sink down and go to sleep right here and right now. Instead, she turned and faced the man who had not ceased to track her every movement. She walked briskly toward the inn door even as her muscles complained. As she passed the Westerner, he pulled at the front of his hat, a somewhat polite gesture. *I will ignore him,* she told herself, her traitorous pulse dancing through her veins. Still, she glanced at him. A mistake—he was a handsome man, a very handsome man.

Quinn stayed where he was and went over what he had just observed. The tall lady had been doing everything that Kilbride should have seen to. That was odd. Quinn had watched parties of Americans before, and the men—not the women—always took care of the animals and servants. The women always walked inside inns and sat down. Or if there were no inn, they began preparing a meal and tending to children.

When the tall lady had come toward Quinn and paused, he had searched her face. Her nearness had washed over him in an unusual wave of sensitivity. Something similar to the awareness that he experienced when he sensed someone was tracking him. Within the confines of her bonnet, he found a pretty face but a firm chin, large gray eyes, and a direct gaze. This was the tall lady, the one who had snared his notice in New Orleans. Then she passed him and was inside.

He stayed outside in the dusk, letting this sharp turn at seeing her again flow through him and away. He rarely felt any draw to a stranger. And she had not remembered seeing him in New Orleans. She was barely aware of him here and now. She was, after all, a lady. A lady he would ignore.

* * *

Later that evening in the shadows under the loft, Dorritt waited until her stepfather walked outside. Her mother and half-sister were already up in the loft, chattering, preparing to sleep. She should be with them in the loft's stifling heat. But before Mr. Kilbride returned, she needed to do something. Seeing the Westerner had given her an idea, one that might save all their white skins and scalps.

He was sitting beside the hearth, his long legs stretched out in front of him. She hurried to him and then cleared her nervous throat. "I was wondering if I might have a word with you, sir." He turned toward her. She waited for his response, searching his suntanned face with high cheekbones and large deep-set eyes, blue eyes. Oh, he was a half-breed.

Once again, he pulled at the brim of his hat, evidently his sign of courtesy. "Miss?"

Her words rushed out, "I was wondering if you have traveled across the Sabine into Texas recently."

"I have."

"How many days from here until we reach the Sabine?" She kept her voice low and watched for her stepfather. If he found her talking to this Westerner, he'd be angry. But she had to get the information she needed and Mr. Kilbride wouldn't "lower" himself to ask this man anything.

"A party your size goes slower than me alone. How many days since you left New Orleans?"

"We've been. . . ." She stopped. "How did you know that we're from New Orleans?" Earlier he had gawked at her. But he couldn't have followed them. He'd been here when they arrived.

To her mind, he waited just a second too long before he replied, "Just a guess. Most people come up the trace from New Orleans. How many days?"

Still rattled, she went on. "Nine days."

"You have another three or four before the Sabine."

"That long?"

He gave a slight nod.

"So far there has been a clear trace to follow. Will that continue until the river?"

"Yes. The illegal trade of cattle and other goods between the Spanish colony of Texas and the U.S. in New Orleans made that trace."

He was givng her the information she so needed, but too slowly. She wished she could just draw it out in a long unbroken thread. "Is the Sabine easy to ford?"

"Depends." A mule brayed in the distance.

"On what?" she asked, glancing over her shoulder at the doorway.

"Storms."

"How far is Nacogdoches in Texas from the Sabine crossing?" Warm perspiration trickled steadily down her spine like teardrops.

"Dorritt, get away from that half-breed!" Her stepfather's voice boomed in the small one-room inn.

So the tall lady's name was Dorritt. Quinn watched as she turned to face her father. Had her face gone even whiter?

"Mr. Kilbride, I was just—"

"Get upstairs where you belong! Don't you know better than to speak to a common stranger in an inn?"

The man's face turned red. The tall lady bent her head in embarrassment and gave Quinn a slight nod. Then she hurried to the ladder to the loft and mounted it.

Kilbride gave him a haughty look and followed her. Quinn hadn't liked the man in New Orleans and liked him less now. *Bully.* Quinn tried to let go of the burning sensation that Kilbride gave him. He couldn't. Probably nothing would convince him that Kilbride had not cheated him.

* * *

Listening to everyone breathing in sleep, Dorritt thought she would die of the heat. How did people survive in these small cabins without windows? The heat of the day had gathered, swelled in the loft. Since the four of them were together, she was sleeping in her sweat-soaked day clothing on a cotton blanket on the hard pine floor. The stench of her own perspiration filled her with distaste, which was growing to revulsion. *I have to get some air. Or I'll smother.*

Below on the main floor of the cabin slept the innkeeper and the Westerner. Would she be able to slip outside without anyone being the wiser?

Quinn woke at the sound of movement, the creak of a ladder rung. Who was up? Now the cabin door stood open and full moonlight flowed inside. He didn't shift but his eyes followed the movement. Then the figure was passing out the doorway. It was the tall lady. Miss Dorritt. Quinn lifted himself soundlessly and followed her. He hung back in the doorway. Where was she going?

She slipped into the thick pine forest around the clearing. Unable to fight against his curiosity and his deep-rooted duty to protect a female, he tracked her as a doe. Soon she reached the creek which flowed into the Sabine River. After thought, he'd figured out why she'd been asking him about crossing the Sabine. She must be the one who was in charge.

But then again, that couldn't be right, could it? She'd obeyed Kilbride when he'd told her to go to bed. And why would a woman be in charge? White men didn't let women lead a party.

And why was she outside in the night alone? Decent white women didn't wander alone at night whether they were in a city or the wilderness. Especially not white American women. He hadn't known any such women to talk to, but he had been in cities and seen them.

Then again, this lady was not the usual white woman. That much he knew.

Ahead in the moonlight, he watched her slip off her shoes and white stockings and then begin to lower her white panta-loons. He sucked in air. He turned and rested his back against a wide-trunked old oak. So she had come out to bathe. Suddenly the idea of getting wet washed over him—-almost overpower-ing. Water flowing over his hot grimy skin, washing away the sweat, refreshing, cooling . . .

He imagined her slipping her dress off her shoulders. They would be ivory in the moonlight . . . *Stop*, he ordered himself. He had not been raised to be the kind of man who would hide in the trees and secretly eye a woman while she bathed. And imagining her undressing would be just as rude. Just as disrespectful. But he shouldn't leave her alone. Besides 'gators, there were many animals that hunted at night. Bear. Wild cat. Wolf.

He tried to ignore the sound of her hushed splashing in the water. A sad trial. He kept erasing images of her that the tantalizing sound brought to mind. At last, the splashing stopped. He heard her loud, long satisfied sigh. It made him more miserable and sticky than ever. And then she was moving through the trees, rustling the feathery pine branches. She passed him without realizing he was there. He whispered, "You shouldn't be outside alone and unarmed at night." He hadn't meant to speak, but she had to be warned. His heart pounded like a war drum.

She stopped, whirled around, and stared. Finally, she whispered, "Who's there?"

From the cover of fir trees, he replied in a low tone, "I followed you from the inn."

"You watched me?" Though speaking quietly, she sounded bothered.

"No," he said. He couldn't see her expression. *I should have stayed silent*. His face warmed. Silence.

"Why did you follow me?" Her tone was laced with mistrust.

Then just before he stepped out where she could see him, he remembered he'd taken his shirt off. White men usually remain covered around white women. Would she take this as a slight too? He remained hidden. "No one should swim alone or go out unarmed into the wilderness at night."

She started walking away. Then she paused. "I believe you. I thank you."

She believed him? About what? That she shouldn't be out alone? Or that he hadn't watched her? It was important to him to know.

* * *

The Westerner led them all the next day—unseen. Dorritt was certain that she was the only one who read the signs, who sensed they weren't alone on the trail. At a few spots, new trails veered off from the one they were taking. At first, the Westerner had left a few scraps of cloth on branches to alert her and later bent branches on fir trees, showing the way to go. Following the signs, she'd kept the ox drivers on track. Why was he helping her? Or was he keeping track of Jewell? Jewell's pretty face had turned more than one male head.

Of course, her stepfather wasn't aware that she, Dorritt, was directing the party. He rode at the head of the party and gave directions to the drivers who nodded and said, "Yes, sir."

But during the long, sweltering day, the drivers watched her as she walked near the head, showing the way at forks. Did her stepfather realize this? Probably not. He was so puffed up in his own regard that he couldn't see anything but himself. Sometimes she wondered if anyone in her family ever saw what was really going on under their up-tilted noses.

The end of the dreadful day finally came. Dorritt was suffering prickly heat rash under her arms. And that was exactly how she felt—hot and prickly. Along the narrow heavily wooded trail, they arrived at a lone cabin with a fenced paddock but no barn. Would the Westerner be here waiting? Dorritt tried to hold back the rise of anticipation.

With a baby still in leading strings on one hip, the young woman of the house dressed in a simple homespun dress and dingy apron hailed them eagerly. Eyeing Jewell's deep violet bonnet, she said, "Oh, but you're fine folk. Whatever brought you out this way?" Dorritt smiled at the woman but let her mother, who got down from the gig to *coo* and *ahh* over the baby, do the pleasantries. Dorritt glanced around but saw no one else. Then a man dressed in homespun came around the cabin. With him was the Westerner. Dorritt ordered her pulse to return to its normal pace. In vain.

Mr. Kilbride scowled, but went forward to ask for shelter for the night at least for his "ladies." The farmer welcomed them and said that the womenfolk could sleep in the loft. The men would make do on the floor.

While her stepfather was watching, Dorritt made certain that she didn't look toward the Westerner. An unaccustomed disquiet stirred her. There were plenty of reasons for uneasiness but she couldn't lie to herself. It was the stranger who had roused her, made her feel different. But why?

* * *

The evening meal was eaten outside, where they might catch any stray breeze. A bright red sunset colored the sky above the tall pine tops. While the slaves gathered around the ox wagons and made a meal of roasted grain and raccoon, the whites sat around a long homemade trestle table, eating venison stew and cornbread. Dorritt sensed the Westerner was being as careful as she not to trade glances, not give her stepfather any excuse to insult the Westerner as he had the night before. But she needed to talk to him again. Why hadn't she asked him his name last night? She'd hoped their host or hostess would address him by his name, but they merely called him *sir*. And each time the couple used this term with the Westerner, Kilbride's lip curled. Her stepfather's ill-concealed contempt for those he deemed his inferiors always grated on her nerves, especially since he classed her with the inferiors.

By sitting between her and the Westerner, Mr. Kilbride isolated Dorritt. Why didn't he want her to speak to the Westerner? The two men couldn't have met before. Mr. Kilbride prided himself on making only advantageous social connections. No matter what, Dorritt must have a word with the Westerner to find out what she needed to know. Every day now, their people turned to her with worried eyes and an unspoken plea for her to protect them. They knew well the unreliability of their master and his blind but mistaken belief in his own invincibility. So in spite of her stepfather, she must gain knowledge about the trail to Texas. So many lives depended on her. This thought lay like a paving brick over her heart. What did she know of Spanish Texas? Who was this Stephen Austin?

Had Mr. Kilbride gotten all the facts right? Where was the Brazos River? How much farther west from the Sabine? And would the present trail lead them to Nacogdoches? These questions with their sharp claws scared her. And here sat the Westerner who had the answers she needed for their survival. But how to find a moment alone to ask him? Last night, she had met the Westerner after everyone was asleep. Could she do that again?

At this thought, a strange thrill traced up her spine. Though she hadn't spoken to the Westerner, she couldn't ignore his presence. She tried to parse why this was, but failed. He said little and moved with quiet ease, but she'd been as aware of him as she would of a storm gathering.

At long last the night came. The women bedded down in the loft with the wife and the fretful baby while the men settled down on the dirt floor. Dorritt heard Mr. Kilbride grumbling. She fought to stay awake, but worry and fatigue defeated her and she fell asleep.

Later she awoke, shock rushing through her in waves. She sat up. Someone, something nudged the bottom of her foot in the darkness. She couldn't even see her hand. But then she heard his barest whisper, "Come out."

It was the Westerner. She slid over the rough planks, feeling them rasp her skin through the thin cotton of her dress and pantaloons. She was more than usually aware of her physical self. Carefully, carefully she let herself down rung by rung. At the bottom, she turned. The door opened silently on the leather hinges and moonlight pooled in the doorway. The Westerner preceded her outside. By the silvery light, she was able to tiptoe around the sleeping men.

Outside, the heat and humidity still hung in the air, heavy and cloying. But at least outside, she could draw a deep free breath. Dorritt wished that there was a creek nearby so that she could again cool herself in its waters. She paused. Last night, this stranger had listened to her bathe. Her face burned at this intimacy. Willing herself to behave naturally, she tiptoed around the side of the cabin and to the back corner, which shielded her from the yard.

The Westerner waited there. "We must whisper," he warned, leaning close.

She didn't pull back from his nearness, though it heightened her awkwardness at this situation. "I am Miss Dorritt Mott," she introduced herself, offering him her hand as she curtsied.

He stared at her for a moment. The moonlight picked up the gold threads in his long dark hair, tied back into a single tail, and his clear blue eyes. He took her hand and squeezed it once. "I'm Quinn. I woke you to tell you a storm is coming."

His unexpected comment made her dumb for a moment. "A storm? You mean a hurricane?" Even though they were miles north of the Gulf, a hurricane's wind and rain could still wreak havoc here.

"Yes. Did you see the red sunset?"

She nodded, her cheek accidently brushing his shoulder. They were so near it made her face warm. "But a red sunset doesn't always mean a hurricane. It could just mean another hot, miserable day tomorrow."

"You are right. But I saw many high thin clouds all this day." He raised his hand high in a natural gesture, which caused his hair to flicker soft against her arm. "And it has been wetter in the air."

"I see." *I feel it.* Perspiration had beaded on her upper lip.

"This is the Gulf of Mexico storm season."

With these simple words, despair sifted through her. How

like her stepfather to set them out on a trip in the midst of hurricane season.

"You must stay here," the Westerner said closer to her ear.

The short baby fine hair on the side of her face and along the rim of her ear quivered at his nearness. She swallowed to moisten her suddenly dry mouth. "I'll try. But I'm sure my stepfather won't listen."

"Kilbride is your stepfather?"

"Yes." It seemed as if she were in a waking dream—standing here in the dark speaking in barely audible whispers within inches of this stranger. "Thank you for leading us today." As if there were a sudden shortage of air, his presence pressed in around her. She turned to the question she'd come to ask. "If you please, are you going to Texas too?"

"Yes."

She hesitated. He was a stranger. But she was in desperate need of help. And perhaps he was the Lord's provision. She nearly reached out to press her hand to his leather shirt. "Would you . . . would you continue to lead me, us?"

"I do not understand. You are a woman."

Her lungs constricted. She should have expected this response. Quinn was after all a man. "Yes, I am a woman."

"Then why do *you* ask me, not your stepfather? Why do *you* lead your party?"

Crickets brought the darkness alive with their endless chant. This man's insight was acute. But perhaps living outside civilization forced one to observe closely. Still, she couldn't—even in this private moment—tell the truth. No man accepted a woman as leader. And she needed this man's help. Desperately. "My stepfather is the leader. I merely take care of many duties for him."

"Then why do *you* ask me to guide your party?" he repeated.

She grumbled the true answer to herself, *Because my stepfather isn't wise enough to recognize that we need help.* Again, she couldn't voice that. This man was too perceptive, the complete opposite of her stepfather. "It is difficult for my stepfather to ask for help," she muttered.

"Then how can I give what he will not ask for?"

Of course, she should have realized that. She'd been so worried that she'd forgotten this very important detail. "You're right." She tried to keep the quaver from her voice. "You helped me today, but that won't work for long." All she could foresee was disaster. She'd hoped for assistance from this man, but she admitted now she'd actually been wishing more than expecting. She cleared her mind and asked for what help she could. "Is there anything, any hazard, besides the coming storm, that you could give me warning of?"

He shrugged. "No more inns till well into Texas. Do you speak Spanish?"

"I know a few words." She'd known Creole ladies in New Orleans, descendants of the Spanish colonial elite who'd controlled New Orleans for a time. How much good would *"Buenos días"* do her?

"You must stay here tomorrow," he reiterated. "Or be caught in the storm."

The starch went out of her. She imagined herself slumping to the ground. "Mr. Kilbride will insist on our leaving in the morning. Unless the hurricane breaks before daylight." *And if it were going to, the wind would have already started to rise.*

Quinn stepped back, signaling their talk was over. "You should go back in first. Leave the door open so you can see your way in." He moved away, his fringe swaying.

For just one bereft moment, she wilted against the rough log wall. She'd been able to talk to Quinn about her concerns. But expressing worries wasn't the same as finding help. As usual, only God remained her ever-present help in time of trouble. *Dear Father, help us.*

Lifting herself slowly, she tiptoed back inside. She skirted the snoring men and made it to her blanket in the loft without disturbing anyone. Within a few moments, the door closed, the moonlight vanished with a whisper of movement below. Quinn had returned. She lay then in hot, stuffy darkness. A hurricane. What could a hurricane do to their caravan out in the open? Dorritt feared that she would find out in stark detail on the morrow. While her mother and sister slept on, troubled tears rolled down Dorritt's cheek onto the floor. *Lord, help, help.*

* * *

On the humid already scorching morning, the breakfast table again was set outside. Dorritt sat near Quinn, who also sat drinking chicory coffee and gazing at the gloomy sky. Trying to hint at the truth, Dorritt said to the woman of the house, "I think I've read the signs that a storm is approaching. Have you?"

The woman looked up at the sky overhead. "It does look hazy up there—"

"Nonsense," Mr. Kilbride snapped. "It's going to be a fine day. A few days more and we will be near the Sabine crossing."

"You really going to settle in Texas?" their host asked.

"There are fortunes to be made in Texas," Kilbride said, his chest expanding as if he were the one who had discovered Texas. "And free land for Americans."

Dorritt stared at him in disbelief. How could a man as full of himself have survived so long? They were heading into a hurricane. The signs were plain and yet he ignored them. *We could die today. And there is nothing I can do to stop it.*

Three

Quinn was proved right by afternoon. This was no ordinary storm; it must be the northern reach of a hurricane. Wild wind flapped the deep brim of Dorritt's poke bonnet back and forth, making it difficult for her to peer toward the head of their caravan. She cradled one of the slave babies, shielding it. The pine and oak forest, thick on each side of the rugged track, swayed and bowed to the riotous wind.

Reva leaned into the gale, walking beside Dorritt. "What're we going to do? The main storm's going to hit and soon. It'll eat us alive."

Dorritt closed her eyes a moment, drawing in breath as if it could take away the chill panic that rippled up and down her spine.

Dorritt had hoped for a break in the forest where they could drive the cattle in among the trees. But could that be worse than just hunkering down here on the trail? Ahead, her stepfather kept busy grappling with the reins of his high-spirited and expensive young stallion. Wiser than its owner, the horse pranced, agitated and wary. In the animal's movements, she saw her own tension and foreboding over what was coming. If only she could have persuaded her stepfather to stay at the house where they'd spent last night.

The memory of her secret midnight meeting with Quinn heated her neck and face. Rarely if ever had she been completely alone with any man. And Quinn was a different kind of man than she was accustomed to. Still he'd left before them this morning and was probably far ahead by now. This thought brought an unusual feeling of loss, an opening to an empty place inside her. Somehow she had expected better of him. *But he owes me nothing.*

Reva began praying aloud, worry in every syllable.

"Perhaps Mr. Kilbride will see we must take cover," Dorritt said, as if feeling her way in the dark. To get her stepfather to take action to protect them, she would need to get him to think it was his idea. Usually she could think of a way to do this. But her mind had gone blank from fear. In her arms, the little baby stirred. She nestled him closer against her warmth and tucked the blanket around him tighter. *I'll keep you safe, little one.* She hoped she was telling the truth.

Overhead, the sky had become a treacherous, murky gray-green, never a good sign. When the brunt of the storm hit, would they all survive without anywhere to shelter?

The cool wet edge of the storm smacked Dorritt's face like a hand. She gasped for breath and pressed the baby against her. The wind yanked the tightly pulled-down beaver hat from her stepfather's head.

Then the wind slammed her like a fist. She stumbled to the ground. Her worst fear would no longer be denied. They would face a hurricane. Here. Soon. Desperation fired inside her. There was no sense trying to reason with her stepfather. If any of them were going to survive the coming storm, she would have to do her poor best. Reva helped Dorritt up. "Take this child to its mother. And begin gathering up the children. The worst of the storm is nearly upon us."

Reva accepted the child and hurried toward the tail of the caravan, where the children straggled along, trying to keep up. Dorritt ran foward to the first ox wagon. Sudden rain poured down as if someone in heaven had overturned a bucket as large as Louisiana. Dorritt fought for breath as if she were drowning. Her sodden skirts hampered her. "Be prepared to halt and take cover!" she shouted to the driver, rain spraying into her mouth. "Be prepared to unyoke the oxen and head them into the woods!"

"Yes, Mistress!" the first and then the second wagon's driver responded.

She nodded and then raced, holding her skirt out, toward the rear, calling, swallowing more rain, "Keep together! Gather the children!"

The servants and their children cast around wild-eyed glances. Their fright became her own, welling up inside her, threatening to cast her into mindless terror. Still, she tried to reassure them, urging them closer together and hurrying them forward toward the wagons. She scooped up two small children, one after the other, and shoved them into the rear of the nearest wagon.

The rain pounded her relentlessly. But not from above. It was raining sideways now.

A branch flew over her head and she ducked. From ahead, she heard her stepfather bellowing at her sister who was driving the black gig. Dorritt looked skyward, trying to decide what her stepfather would do if she directed the ox drivers to halt and unyoke the oxen and take cover now?

Near her, Amos was dragging at a leash, hauling a quarrelsome and bleating billy goat. She went to help, and between the two of them, though lashed by wind and rain, they managed to keep up with the rest. She glanced around, taking a head count of their people to see if everyone had clustered in and around the wagons. She counted once; she counted twice. Then she called ahead to Reva, "Who's missing? I've come up one short."

* * *

Racing ahead of the oncoming storm, Quinn urged his mount back over the rutted track. His heart beat in time with his horse's hooves. On either side of him, live oaks branches twisted and swayed in the wind, moaning and groaning. Their gray Spanish moss flung high and then low, then high again. Would he reach Dorritt's party and lead them to safety before the main force of the hurricane hit?

He rode around a bend, and there was the gig with the two women. Beside it, Kilbride was fighting to restrain his stallion. Quinn shouted to Kilbride, "Shelter's ahead!" He gestured toward the trail behind him. "Hurry! There is a barn and house! Hurry!" Not waiting for a response, Quinn galloped along the caravan. Where was Dorritt?

Slowing to a canter along the length of the train, he told the ox drivers that a farm lay ahead. "When you get there, unhitch the oxen and drive them and the cattle into the barn!" He shouted, nearly choking on the flying rain. "Take shelter in the barn!"

Holding tight his reins, he cast around for Dorritt. He couldn't see her. He raced down the line until he came to its end. He pulled up on his reins. Where was she? A gust nearly lifted him from the saddle. His horse reared, but he held him in check. Then a black girl ran toward him, waving her arm, shouting, "Miss Dorritt. She went after that poky boy! That orphan child!" She pointed back up the road. Without waiting, Quinn galloped full out. The trees around them were losing leaves, branches, creaking as sturdy boughs danced on gusts like twigs. Around

the next bend, he saw her, scurrying back to the party, huddled
around a dark child.

Just as he met her, the wind flailed like a whip. The tall pines
bent double, their tops brushing the ground. Several snapped
and were sent flying into the air. His horse screamed, lurched.
He forced his mount back down. Then he grabbed up Dorritt
with the child and threw her onto the saddle before him. *Safe.*
Bending low to protect her from flying debris, he heeled his
mount forward. The lady called out near his ear, "You came
back! Thank you! Thank God!"

Within minutes, Quinn caught up with the party, already approaching the farm in the midst of the thick piney wood on the
sheltered side of a rise. Earlier, he'd found it just where he remembered it. Now, he drew up at the front door of the cabin and
let Dorritt slide down onto the muddy ground. The old woman
of the house waved her inside. But he had more to do. In the
downpour and gusting wind, Quinn rode to the barn and helped
the Negro men unhitch the oxen and drive them under the
barn roof. At last, all the slaves and the cattle were in the barn.
Quinn set the bar across its door, barricading them in against the
storm.

On his way to the cabin, Quinn bent into the gale, slipping
in the mud. Dorritt was there at the door to let him in. Fighting
wind gusts, he slammed and bolted it behind him. He turned
to her.

"Thank heavens, you're safe," she murmured, touching his
sleeve. Her concern for his safety startled him and prompted a
vague and unexpected urge to touch her shoulder, her cheek. It
had been a long time since anyone had worried about him. He
didn't know what he should say. Or if he should say anything.

"Is everyone safe under shelter?" she asked, still looking
troubled.

"Yes," he muttered and brushed past her, "all are under cover."

Outside, the tree branches moaned, grunted, creaked in the storm. But the rolling hills and forest around the cabin were a bulwark, affording protection. He glanced around the dark, windowless cabin. Kilbride, his wife, and other daughter were safe inside. Sweeping off his dripping hat, he bowed in thanks to the older man and woman, who'd already offered warming coffee to the drenched-looking Kilbrides.

Kilbride rose and walked over to him with his hand outstretched. "We are in your debt." Kilbride's voice was polite but forced.

Quinn shook the man's hand with reluctance. He didn't like false manners. And he didn't want to shake this man's hand any more than Kilbride wanted to shake his. The younger daughter came forward and offered him her thanks as well, curtsying with a false smile. Quinn nodded to her and to the mother. The gray-haired woman of the house handed him a cup of coffee. He walked to where Dorritt was praying. He caught some of her words, "Save us . . . shelter . . . mother and sister . . . hollow of your hand. Protect our people . . . storm . . . For your glory . . . for your good favor . . ."

Taking a sip of the hot bitter brew, Quinn hoped her God was listening, because this storm had blown up faster and fiercer than he'd expected. How bad was it going to get before it passed over them? The log walls groaned and quivered.

And Kilbride was staring at him. Was he finally remembering who Quinn was? Or had he recognized him all along and was only now deciding whether or not to acknowledge their acquaintance?

Quinn gazed into his cup, not letting himself look at Dorritt, though she was what had drawn him back into the storm.

* * *

The hurricane raged on. Hours and hours went by as Dorritt paced the small cabin. She could not be still. Like fearsome bats, all her smothered worries about this trip now flapped and darted in her mind. Their party had found shelter only because of Quinn's help. What disaster or danger would come next?

Only one tallow candle flickered on the roughhewn mantel. Mr. Kilbride, her mother, and half-sister sat on benches at the narrow split-log table, their heads down on their folded arms. How they could sleep through this she didn't know. But the older couple who owned the cabin had also hours earlier taken to their narrow rope bed in the corner.

Quinn lounged on the halved-log floor beside the door. He sat very still but he wasn't sleeping. She had thanked him when he rescued her and the orphan child. But she wished she could say or do more. *He'd come back for them . . . for her.* That thought gave her a funny scratchy feeling inside. She couldn't remember the last time anyone but Reva had looked out for her without expecting something in return.

I'm making too much out of this. He's just a decent man who wouldn't leave anyone to face a hurricane out in the open. She walked past him again. Wet wind flooded in around the barred door. So far the roof had held secure.

In the dark silent room with the din outside, her eyes repeatedly sought out the glimmer of the gold in Quinn's hair. She envied his evident calm. But he didn't have to worry about tomorrow or the days after that. He was a man. He could live alone, defend himself. He couldn't be forced into a situation like this.

"You should sit down," he said, his voice coming low underneath the unrelenting lashing winds.

He was right. Her pacing didn't help anything. Except that each step she took was like a bead on a rosary like the ones she'd seen the nuns fingering at the Cathedral of St. Louis in New Orleans. Each step had become a plea for protection and courage to go on. She blurted out, "Do you think they are all right?" She knew that all their people couldn't have fit into this one room, but it still upset her that they had been "stabled" with the stock.

"The barn looked well built."

"Good." Being alone with Quinn for the third night in succession was tempting her to a false sense of security, familiarity. She shouldn't, couldn't, count on him.

"Are you still cold from getting wet?" he asked.

"No." She shivered, belying her words. "No," she said, making her subdued voice stronger, "it has been hours since we came here. I've had time to dry out. It was fortunate that you found shelter."

"I have been on this road a few times, and I checked with the man where we stayed last night to inquire if these people still lived here. Even if they'd gone, I hoped the buildings and corral would have remained. You don't think even this far north, with a hurricane brewing, I would set out without making sure of a place ahead to shelter, do you?"

Dorritt didn't respond right away, her stomach had been unsettled before she'd drunk the strong chicory coffee. And his final question underscored her deep uneasiness over this trip, making her stomach roll. The fact was Mr. Kilbride had set them off this morning with only bravado as their protection. She began moving again. The pacing helped her hold in the fearful words that threatened to come pouring forth like the sheets of rain outside. Still, she needed to talk. And Quinn was the only one awake that she could talk to. Further, she admitted she wanted another private conversation with this tall, lean Westerner—to gain more information about Texas; that was all. "You say that you been this way before?" she asked.

"I've been most places a few times."

His wry tone caught her up short. She pressed her lips together, half amused. "I beg your pardon. I didn't mean to pry."

"I didn't mean to be rude. My father was a scout, and I went along with him on many jobs. He died when we were with Zebulon Pike in '05, and I became a scout then."

True or not true? "You seem too young to have done that," she said with caution.

"I *was* young, about thirteen."

Zebulon Pike's explorations ranked second only to Lewis and Clark and their expedition west to the Pacific. This man was definitely her opposite, a man of experience while she was a woman of much book learning. But more than ever, she was confident that if this man was their guide, he could keep them alive. She just needed to come up with a way to prompt Mr. Kilbride to hire Quinn. But what might Quinn expect in payment? They didn't have much cash.

She rubbed the heels of her palms together. The incessant wind was getting on her nerves more and more instead of less and less. With her sense of hearing dulled by the constant wind, she'd become much more aware of Quinn's presence. She distinguished the odor of the wet fringed-leather jacket that he had shrugged off. It hung on a peg beside the door, dripping into a puddle beside him. She imagined that she could feel warmth emanating from him.

"Why don't you sit down and go to sleep?" His voice was low but compelling, like a hand at the small of her back, leading her in a dance. "It is still many hours till morning. And there is no guarantee that the storm will end with daylight. There is nothing for you to do."

His commonsense unruffled voice suddenly grated on her nerves even more than the sound of the wind. How could he stay so composed? "Doesn't anything bother you?" she snapped.

"Scorpions."

She halted in her tracks. She hadn't expected an answer. And now she didn't know whether to laugh or question him. Did Texas abound with scorpions? *No, please, not scorpions.*

Quinn watched Dorritt in front of the cold hearth. He lifted his rifle propped against the wall beside him and laid it across his lap. He needed to work. The storm made it impossible to sleep. Kilbride, who should have taken responsibility for his womenfolk, was snoring. No Cherokee woman would marry such a stupid man. How had Kilbride gotten fine horses, slaves, a wife and family?

From his pocket Quinn pulled a round flat tin of oil and a rag. He began to clean his long rifle. He didn't need to see the gun. He knew it by touch. He could hear Dorritt murmuring to herself. Was she still praying to her God? Would He protect her from her foolhardy stepfather?

Dorritt was a name he'd never heard before, but it fit her—a clean and strong-sounding name. She continued pacing. He couldn't possibly feel her footsteps through the log floor or hear them, yet he thought he did. She was much too light and her shoes were soft-soled. Still, her continuous motion started winding the muscles up the back of his neck. "Why don't you sit down?" The repeated question was out of his mouth before he realized he'd spoken.

In the gloom, the lady's pale golden hair caught what little light there was. His unwilling eyes followed her as she drew near again. He couldn't help asking, "What keeps you awake? Troubles you?"

Suddenly, she scowled. "Does it matter to you, a man? I'm just a woman. And a spinster at that. What I want doesn't ever matter."

Her voice was prickly like a cactus and she looked downcast. "That's not true. Women count . . . sometimes."

She gave him a sad laugh. "Sometimes? No, I don't think so."

He hadn't meant to say that. Women did matter. But they weren't like men. And after his mother died when he was a child, he'd had few women in his life. He didn't know how to talk to them. He hadn't sought a wife; life was too uncertain, too short it seemed to him. Still, he'd insulted Dorritt and that irritated him. "I meant no disrespect."

She paused and gazed at him again. He saw the reflection of her large eyes and the lowlight. She said, "You were probably just being honest, refreshingly honest. May I ask you a question?"

He liked that she waited for permission and didn't just go on and ask. "Yes."

She drew a step nearer to him. "I shouldn't be asking you this, but I find that I can't stop myself. Where are you going in Texas?"

He thought of all he knew about her stepfather. "Nacogdoches."

"But that's where we're headed."

He heard the surprise in her voice. He knew why he and Kilbride were both headed for the same Spanish mission town. But of course, she didn't.

She cleared her throat. "I know we discussed that Mr. Kilbride is the one that must ask you to be our guide. But if he did ask you, how much would you charge?"

He answered truthfully, "I don't need money."

"What do you need?"

"Sit down." He patted the floor beside him. He couldn't deny it. He wanted her near him—even for just a little while. She was a good woman with a good heart. Would she sit and talk with him, the half-breed, one more night?

Finally she sank down on the other side of the door, out of the direct draft and leaned back against the wall. "What do you need?" she repeated.

He liked how she always remained focused on what she

wanted. "I don't need it, but I want a thoroughbred colt. That's what I went to New Orleans to find." Finally he could speak some truth to her.

"A thoroughbred? Why would you need a thoroughbred? If you don't mind my asking."

Her question didn't bother him. He was not a gentleman. A mustang should do for him. "I want to breed it with mustangs."

"I see. We have a colt, as you know, and our mare is breeding too. I don't know if Mr. Kilbride would part with either."

"I doubt he would." *If he said he would, I wouldn't believe him.* "But why have you set out without a guide? This rough trail to Nacogdoches is difficult to follow on the other side of the Sabine. The Camino Real, the King's Highway, is barely a trace, just a track really. Doesn't your stepfather know this?"

"I don't know."

"So we are back where we talked last night. I cannot help you if he does not ask me."

"I'll think of a way."

He went on working on his long rifle. He wondered if Dorritt would come up with a way. And if she did, would he agree to guide Kilbride, the man who'd cheated him? To protect her, he might. She would make some man a good wife. In fact, why wasn't she married by now with children of her own?

Four

The hurricane finally gave up late the next afternoon. Dorritt waited, her hands clasped in front of her, holding onto hope. She hoped and prayed that their people had weathered the storm.

Quinn unbarred the door and stepped outside. Dorritt moved out behind him, followed by the rest of her family and the older couple. She breathed in the fresh clean air. After hours of dim light, Dorritt and everyone else blinked in the sunshine. She shaded her eyes, gazing around. Broken branches, stout and thin, leaves and wooden shakes lay upon the ground in disarray. Much of the paddock fence slumped and dragged on the muddy ground. Water puddled everywhere. During the early hours of the morning, she'd come up with a plan of how she might plant the idea of hiring Quinn as their guide in her stepfather's mind. Now, she just had to wait for the right opportunity.

Quinn and the owner of the farm headed straight for the barn. Jogging on his short legs, Kilbride caught up with them.

Dorritt hung back, waiting with the women around the door of the cabin, watching for Reva. Earlier, after everyone had awakened, Dorritt had kept her distance from Quinn. She wouldn't give her stepfather and sister any cause to suspect she'd even noticed the Westerner. But memories of their hours together— virtually alone—kept coming to mind: the way his strong hands had moved over his long rifle, his low voice, strong and honest. She stiffened herself. She couldn't afford foolish tender feelings or weakness on this journey.

At the barn, Quinn was lifting the bar across the double door, and he along with the older man pushed them back. Their people poured out, and as they looked skyward, they too shaded their eyes as if they were all just waking up after a long dreadful nightmare.

Reva lifted a hand and Dorritt waved back at her, her mood lifting. Knowing Reva was safe, Dorritt moved to her sister. "Jewell," she said in a low voice, "it's fortunate Mr. Quinn found this place and came back for us."

Jewell merely shrugged.

Then Dorritt whispered closer to Jewell's ear, "If we're going to make it alive to Texas, it might be a good idea if your father hired Mr. Quinn as our guide. He is going to Nacogdoches too."

Jewell walked away without replying, not an uncommon response. But Dorritt was depending on Jewell's desire to survive and be well cared for. If Jewell made the suggestion, Mr. Kilbride might listen.

So Dorritt approached the barn, listening to the men discuss repairing the barn roof and paddock fence. Soon Quinn and a few of the slaves were busy gathering or making wooden shakes to replace those blown away and climbing onto the roof to pound them into place. While Mr. Kilbride, the gentleman, watched, leaning against the paddock fence. Dorritt and Reva went into the house to help their hostess prepare an evening meal. Her mother and Jewell took chairs and sat outside, watching the men work.

A few hours later, the men came in for the evening meal. They washed their hands at the basin by the door and then took their places on the benches around the long trestle table. Mr. Kilbride gave a long flowery prayer of gratitude to God and their host and hostess. Dorritt hated it when her stepfather prayed these florid and insincere prayers. She wondered how he had the nerve to think that he could fool God. And of course he didn't mention Quinn's kindness in coming after them and saving them from the storm. One didn't thank a half-breed.

Quinn sat directly across from Dorritt while Mr. Kilbride sat at Dorritt's elbow. She tried to keep her eyes from drifting toward Quinn's. She had to act as if they had not become acquainted over the past three nights. She knew she should be famished but she was too keyed up to feel hunger.

"Mr. Quinn," Jewell said in that flirty, arch way of hers, "we owe you a debt of gratitude, as well as to our kind host and hostess." Ever the gracious lady, Jewell nodded toward the older couple, then turned her gaze back to Quinn. "Dorritt was telling me that you are heading to Nacogdoches too."

Dorritt clutched her fork. This was the worst possible tack Jewell could have taken. Jewell knew better than to mention Dorritt's name in connection with any suggestion to her stepfather. Handling Mr. Kilbride took subtlety. Why was Dorritt the only one who saw reality?

"Yes, I know that Quinn is on his way to Nacogdoches," Mr. Kilbride spoke up with a wide self-satisfied grin. "I didn't say anything before because a man doesn't like to boast. But it was Quinn who told me about Moses and Stephen Austin's agreement with the Spanish Crown to bring American settlers to Texas. And Quinn is the reason that we are going to Nacogdoches in the first place." Mr. Kilbride turned to Dorritt and gave her a taunting look.

Dorritt was confused. What did he mean that Quinn had told him about Austin? The two men couldn't be acquainted. *No.* She refused to speak, afraid that she would say exactly the wrong thing.

Instead, Jewell voiced the prompted question, "Why is that, father?"

"Because Quinn lost ten head of cattle and two mustangs to me in a card game in New Orleans." Mr. Kilbride lifted his tin cup toward Quinn. "Normally I wouldn't mention this. No man likes others to know when he's been bested."

Dorritt betrayed herself with a gasp. Was Quinn truly the one that had started them off to Texas? He had gambled with her stepfather? And worst, he had recognized her father but had not betrayed this knowledge to her? As each of these realizations occurred to her, her heart dropped one more notch. She found that her mouth was open and closed it. She tightened her shaky grip on her fork. There could be no mistake. Jewell must have spoken to her father before the meal and planned to disconcert Dorritt.

Quinn said nothing, nor did he apologize to her. He sipped his coffee.

"Now, Quinn, though our association did not start out as a happy one," her stepfather continued in a smooth charming tone, "perhaps you'd like to travel with us? Isn't it always safer when one ventures into the frontier to travel with a larger party?"

Quinn did not reply. He stared into Mr. Kilbride's face.

"Well?" Mr. Kilbride finally pressed him. "What do you say to my offer?"

"If you want me to guide you to Nacogdoches," Quinn said in an implacable, completely cold tone, "I expect to be paid."

The sudden flush of red that surged up Mr. Kilbride's neck and face broadcast his anger. Dorritt found she couldn't chew. The unmasked animosity between Mr. Kilbride and Quinn was palpable.

"You know you need a guide," Quinn said in the same emotionless voice. "Texas isn't U.S. territory. It's wild and Spanish."

"I'm sure you're just the man for the job too," Dorritt's mother spoke up in a cheery tone, drawing all eyes to her. "I'm sure it's God's providence that we met up with you on the trail. How much is your fee?"

Dorritt put down her fork and clasped her hands in her lap. For once, perhaps her mother's complete indifference to reality might work in their favor. Dorritt prayed silently it would, but with a sour taste in her mouth. She bit her lower lip. She could understand Quinn's not wanting to reveal losing to Mr. Kilbride, but why hadn't he let on that he knew him?

Quinn lifted his fork. "I don't need money. But I would barter my service as your guide for the colt or the mare's foal."

Dorritt could sense her stepfather's jaw clench although she kept her gaze on her plate. She knew he would not willingly part with either thoroughbred.

"What do you think, Mr. Kilbride? Is that a fair trade?" Dorritt's mother asked, as usual out of touch with the tension her words had sparked.

Dorritt watched her stepfather grappling with how to come out on top in this situation. "That sounds fair to me," Mr. Kilbride said at last. "Shall we shake on it?" He offered his hand across the table.

Quinn hesitated. "Just to Nacogdoches or to the Brazos or Colorado? I've heard both rivers mentioned as the place to meet Austin."

"To the Brazos or Colorado Rivers and wherever Stephen

Austin's party is." Her stepfather jerked his outstretched hand, demanding a reply.

"To the Brazos and Stephen Austin's party," Quinn repeated and shook Mr. Kilbride's hand.

Looking down, Dorritt picked up her fork again and began eating. The food was wholesome and nourishing, yet tart disappointment spiced the meal. Hollow inside, she fought tears. She'd thought the man who sat across from her was a rare find, an honest man. But keeping back the truth was as bad as a lie.

* * *

Two days later in midafternoon, the Kilbride party reached Gaines Ferry at the Sabine, separating Louisiana and the Spanish colony. Though the worst of the hurricane had passed, high winds continued. At the head of the party, Quinn viewed the treacherous-looking current, which still carried branches, small logs, and other windfall downriver.

The ferryman puffed on a corncob pipe. "Yessir, that storm has made the river fast. Lucky that it didn't overflow the banks. But the water is high, all right. You can see that."

Quinn nodded, trying to judge whether they should cross today or wait until the morrow. He dismounted and began judging the wide wooden ferryboat, tethered to the shore with strong ropes. The sturdy-looking ferry rode the rapid river current. Spanning the river, thick ropes attached to the bargelike ferry, looped securely around formidable trees in the forest on each side of the river.

Kilbride trotted up on his stallion and looked over the water to the far shore. He ignored the rushing river. "Texas! And in only two weeks."

"This current will make the crossing more dangerous." Quinn turned to face Kilbride. But he looked past the man to Dorritt, standing by the gig. As usual, she carried a slave baby in her slender arms. The brim of her bonnet shielded her face from him, but he could see her firm chin. Since Kilbride had hired him as guide, she had refused to speak to him or even look at him. *I should have told her everything.*

"But this ferry appears quite substantial," Kilbride objected. "Why should the current stop us?"

Were moneylenders chasing this man? Quinn turned away and studied the river again. He couldn't understand this man's hurry. He brushed aside Kilbride and tried to ignore the sensation of Dorritt's disapproval. Why did he care what she thought of him? He was just the hired half-breed scout in her eyes.

Quinn pointed at the river. "If we cross now, we'll have to put fewer people and stock on the ferry for each trip across. I don't want to take the chance of anything or anyone being pitched into that drowning current. I don't dare let the horses or oxen swim across. Even they could be swept away."

Before Kilbride could reply, the grizzled ferryman spoke up, "Your guide's right, mister. Best not push our luck by trying to carry everything across as we would in the normal way. The river's way high. I'll give you a cut on m'fare so you don't pay for the extra trips across. Not your fault that we had a hurricane this week. So don't you worry. And I wouldn't risk my ferry if I thought it wouldn't make the trip back and forth. If we're watchful, all should scrape through."

With this guarantee, Quinn nodded and proceeded to strike the bargain, ignoring Kilbride's interruptions. Quinn shook the ferryman's hand to seal it. Then he started to direct the slow process of unhitching cattle and unloading some of the boxed possessions stowed in each ox wagon. It would be best to take the extra time and get everything safely onto the Texas riverbank.

As Quinn told the Negroes how they would be crossing the river, Kilbride's daughter, Miss Jewell, announced in a good likeness of her father's high-handed manner, "I will cross with my mare. She'll need me to stay calm."

"I'm sorry but I must do what's best for the stock," Quinn told her. "Your mare will need a stronger hand on this crossing."

Miss Jewell began to wrangle. But her mother beckoned her away and then talked to her apart from the rest. The girl didn't look ready to settle down. He'd keep an eye on Miss Jewell. She was her sire all over. He'd leave the women till last. If anything went wrong, they could take shelter in the ferryman's cabin. There was only wilderness on the Texas side.

On the first trip across the swollen river, Negroes traveled across with boxes, which they then unloaded on the Texas shore. The oxen did not trust the unsettled river or the ferry. And it took the strength of two men and rags over the oxen's eyes to still their nerves on the next two trips. The oxen made it safely to the other side, and Quinn's hopes rose.

The people, the possessions, the other cattle were ferried across. Finally only the mare, the colt, and the ladies remained on the Louisiana side.

From the Texas side, Quinn called to them, "Just a few more trips and we will all be in Texas!" The mare and colt would cross ahead of them.

Quinn and one of the slave men came back to Louisiana to finish up the crossing. With a man pushing from behind, Quinn safely got the gig onto the ferry. Then he turned and offered his hand to Dorritt. She gave him a look he couldn't read, but she let him help her onto the ferry. He had never held a woman's hand that was gloved. It copied the way she had withdrawn from him ever since she'd found out he hadn't told her about meeting her stepfather in New Orleans.

Holding the mare's reins, Quinn waited with the other daughter on the Louisiana side. The mare was restless. The gig and

Dorritt reached Texas. And the ferryman brought the ferry back to the Louisiana side.

"I will go across with my mare," Kilbride's daughter repeated with a mulish look.

"I'm sorry," Quinn said, "but the mare is already spooked. It's best I go alone—"

"She'll do much better if I lead her," Jewell insisted with a lift of her chin. "I helped train her."

"No," Quinn said. "You'll stay where you're told." The mare whinnied and danced but Quinn succeeded in leading it onto the swaying ferry.

The ferryman loosed the rope. At the last moment—Kilbride's daughter leaped onto the barge. "I'm not your servant. I will go when I wish!" Jewell's sudden leap caused the ferry to slew slightly on one corner. The ferryman cursed. Quinn clung to the bridle of the startled mare, now stepping high and whinnying. A huge oak branch riding the current came around the bend upriver. It headed right for them.

"Hold on!" the ferryman roared, leaning hard against the tiller.

The huge bough broadsided the ferry railing. The barge lurched. Quinn lost his footing. He heard Jewell scream just as she lost her balance and slid into the rushing river. The mare let out a shrill shrieking of panic. The girl screamed again. He had no choice. He heaved the bridle toward the ferryman. Then Quinn plunged into the high water.

The current was a giant throat sucking him under. He lunged upward. His legs whipped together. His head broke water. Bobbing with each stroke of his legs, he let the relentless current carry him. He blinked, scanning through the watery glaze over his eyes. Another scream.

He saw her then, ahead, flailing in the water. Her skirts. Her skirts would pull like heavy weights wrapped around her legs. With all his force, he propelled his body forward and then dived under. The churning water prevented him from seeing. But the river was carrying them both in the same direction. He made another lunge forward. He bumped a body.

He grabbed her and then pushed upward. Her skirts dragged them down. He flexed his legs like a frog and leaped upward. Again he broke the surface, gasping for air. The skirts tangled him in their web too. He spat water and slashed his legs together with all his strength. The shore was only feet away, but how could a man defy the racing current, carrying them away? The girl was fighting to stay above water. Her breath harsh against his ear, she was losing the battle.

Ahead to the right, a low bush hung over the river. Debris had caught in its lowest branches. Could he boost them into it and gain a hold? There it was—just a few feet to the right. Their chance. He shoved her with all his might toward it. "Catch the branches! Catch hold!" And then the mighty river throat sucked him down.

* * *

After Dorritt lost sight of Quinn and Jewell with the curve of the heavily wooded riverbank, she paced the soggy Texas sand. She tried to block out her stepfather's ranting about losing his only child and the worthless guide who should have stopped her from boarding the ferry. Why wasn't he racing down the shore to save Jewell? She almost shouted this at him, but held back. She'd always thought him a coward. *And I'm not happy to be proved right.*

What to do . . . What to do? She halted abruptly. "Amos!" she called. He came, looking concerned. "Amos, get the mule ready for us. You and I are going ahead to find them."

"Yes, miss!" He ran off toward the mule.

She turned and her stepfather was before her. "What do you think you're doing, girl? Jewell can't have survived—"

"Amos and I will ride downriver along the bank and see if we can find them." She started past him.

"You'll only find their bodies. I can't bear it!" Kilbride moaned.

Jewell and even Quinn might need help now. She didn't have time to cater to her stepfather's dramatics. "I know you want to go," she lied. "But you must stay to protect mother, our people, and possessions. Amos and I will go and find them. Pray God they live."

Hiking up her skirt, she ran toward Amos, who was holding the bridle. She let him toss her up onto the horse blanket and then she motioned for him pull himself up on her arm. She tapped the mule's sides with her heels. She called over her shoulder, "I'll be back no later than nightfall!"

And they were off following a narrow path through the thickly grown brush and pine trees beside the swollen river. Her mother's horrified hysterical voice, both bemoaning the loss of one child and scolding Dorritt for riding astride, followed them. Dorritt ignored it, her heart hammering. How could anyone stay alive in that rushing current?

Damage from the hurricane winds and torrential rain complicated their way downriver. They alternately rode and dismounted, walking over and around downed trees and branches, and picked their way through far-flung debris from miles away. Wooden shakes, shattered glass, broken ox yokes, crushed daisies, and small drowned and battered animals littered the footpath worn along the bank. "Let's just walk," she said. Amos nodded, took the bridle, and fell in step just behind her.

"Jewell!" she called as the bank rose higher. "Quinn!" They picked their way over the rough ground. She stopped. Had she heard someone?

"I hear it too," Amos whispered as if they were acting in secret. "Let's ease down by the bank. Maybe we can see more from there."

Dorritt nodded. She'd chosen Amos because he was clever

and quick. She led him down, gripping branches of bushes and riverside trees as her inadequate shoes slid in the mud. "Jewell!"

Again it came—sounding like a whisper against the frothing, churning current. They worked their way down, and then the bank fell away just before them. Amos gentled the mule as it tried to pull away from the swollen river.

"Help!" It was Jewell's voice, weak and hopeless. Amos made to go to help her sister, but even though he was barely thirteen, he was heavier than she and might lower the branch too much or even snap it. Dorritt motioned him to stay with the mule.

"No, miss, please, let me," Amos objected.

"No, the branch isn't safe for you. If I need help, I'll call." She clung to the branches of the bushes and a downed tree nearest the river. Ahead, she glimpsed Jewell, still buffeted by the current and clinging to its farthest branches. Her heart skipped. Jewell could drive her to distraction. But at this moment, the bond of blood pulled taut. *She's my sister.*

Dorritt hiked her slender skirt and petticoat up to her waist and threw one pantalooned leg over the branch that extended out over the river. "I'm coming, Jewell. Hang on!" Feeling the rough wood bark rasp her thighs, she inched herself out over the river. It sucked at her feet, dragging off one shoe. But the trembling bough held. At last, she reached her half-sister. Gasping from exertion, Dorritt leaned down and tried to pull Jewell farther up. But her sister wouldn't let go. "Jewell, I can't pry your hands off without your help."

"I'm afraid!"

"I'm securely on the bough. I'm going to grasp your wrists and pull you up, and you must grab hold of the bough here."

"You'll drop me!"

Dorritt realized Jewell was beyond reason. But that couldn't stop her. "Very well. I'll go back to shore and leave you—"

"No! Please!"

"Then do—as—I—say," Dorritt commanded. "When I grab your wrists, let go and I'll pull you to me and across the bough. But you must let go! Will you?"

"Yes . . . yes!"

Dorritt made sure she was wedged into a fork of the bough. Then she leaned forward, grabbed Jewell's wrists. "Now!"

She yanked and Jewell's body slued in the current. Her sister screamed. At the last moment, Dorritt jerked again. And Jewell was half on the bough. Dorritt sucked in air and heaved the girl the rest of the way. They clung to each other, gasping.

She'd saved Jewell. But where was Quinn?

Five

Panting, Dorritt half-carried Jewell up the bank to the mule. Amos hurried to help her. Her half-sister was exhausted and drenched, but alive because of Mr. Quinn. "Amos, I want you to put Miss Jewell on the mule and hurry back to our mother. She'll know what to do to keep Jewell from becoming ill." People who survived drowning often developed fatal pneumonia.

"Yes, Miss Dorritt," Amos agreed. "But what about Mr. Quinn?"

What about Mr. Quinn? "He can't be far ahead," she insisted with paper-thin conviction.

"That probably be right. But that a fast river."

Yes, a fast and treacherous river. "I'll go ahead—"

"Miss," Amos objected, "what Mr. Kilbride say about that?"

The question burned like a hot needle. Setting off alone in the wilderness after a man was foolhardy. But if she went back with Jewell, her stepfather was quite capable of forgetting Mr. Quinn's existence and going on without him. *Do I have a choice?*

"Amos, it can't be helped," she said, her tone brisk. "Mr. Kilbride will want you to bring Miss Jewell back as soon as possible. Tell them that I've gone on ahead to look for Mr. Quinn. We will probably meet up soon and come back together." *Please, Father.*

"Yes, miss," Amos said with a dubious expression. He lifted Miss Jewell and set her upon the mule.

"Amos, go ahead and climb up behind her and hold her so she doesn't fall off," Dorritt ordered. "Mr. Kilbride might not like you riding behind her with an arm around her waist, but in these circumstances, it can't be helped."

Worry creasing his forehead, Amos nodded and did as she'd told him. Dorritt watched Amos ride away with her half-sister, limply bobbing in front of him. They were out of sight around a wooded river bend soon, too soon. And she was alone. Dorritt took a deep breath and began again picking her way through the storm debris. Jewell had been swept farther downriver than Dorritt had anticipated. Why hadn't Quinn grabbed the same branch as Jewell? Had he been knocked unconscious or swallowed too much water and sunk . . . ? She stopped her mind.

Holding up her wet hem, she moved forward, one foot bare. She had already walked a hole in each thin sole of her city shoes. She discarded the remaining shoe, and with each step, wet sand squished between her toes. The image of Mr. Quinn lying white and breathless dogged each gritty step. *Father, I need Mr. Quinn. No matter that he's a gambler and a liar.* She called, "Mr. Quinn!" and walked and stumbled and walked.

The sun began lowering, hovering closer, closer to the tops of the pine trees, which hedged in the riverbank. She paused and gazed at the sky, uncertain and uneasy. That funny jittery sensation that Mr. Quinn aroused in her plagued her. The thought of spending the night alone along the river pricked her, nibbled at her nerves. *Go on or not?*

Dorritt couldn't stop until she found Quinn. If she found him injured but was unable to move him and return to their party, her mother would make Mr. Kilbride send someone for her. That much she could expect from her abstracted mother.

Tears tried to start. She forced them back by breathing in and blinking rapidly. But the farther she went, the more she doubted she would find Quinn alive or at all. Thinking of losing him in this way—in an unnecessary accident forced on him by her half-sister's excessive need to always have her way. It was cruel.

Mr. Quinn had taken advantage of her need of a scout to serve his own ends. Yet, he had a way of capturing her attention and worse, her trust. A very dangerous man.

Feeling lonelier than usual, she began reciting the Twenty-third Psalm, clinging to David's words of trusting God and winning through hard times. She halted. Down by the water's edge, caught in the branches of the shrub was Mr. Quinn's leather hat. She stepped, tiptoed through debris until she was able to reach the hat and yank it from the shrub. It told her nothing really about his location. But she could not stop a pulse of hope from lifting her spirits. She shouted, "Mr. Quinn!" She picked her way back up the bank to the path and trudged on.

Hours passed, and then she found him. He lay facedown on the sand. So still. The river turned sharply inward here, form-ing an eddy, or pool. That must have given him a chance to break away from the quicksand-like current. "Mr. Quinn?" she asked, nearing him, her voice quavering. "Are you all right?" He didn't move. She sank to her knees and shook his shoulder. "Mr. Quinn?" When she didn't receive a response, she turned him over. One eye was purpled and swollen shut. His face and neck were scratched and scraped, probably from branches. Diluted blood trickled from his hair down his face. Her breath caught.

She bent and pressed her ear against his chest. She pressed harder against his wet leather shirt. She heard it finally, his faint, slow heartbeat. *Thank you, Father.* The tears she'd been holding back leaked down her face. Ignoring them, she sat back on her heels, scanning the area. Only squirrels and birds were watching them. What should she do? She had seen people being slapped awake when they were unconscious, but she wasn't a slapper. So she again shook one of his shoulders, then both his shoulders. No response. She sat down beside him to wait.

Before the sun went down, Quinn moaned and moved as though in pain. Never was a moan more welcome. "Mr. Quinn? It's me. Dorritt Mott." She got up on her knees beside him, touched his shoulder. "Can you hear me?"

His eyes fluttered open. He stirred, tried to sit up, but wasn't able to accomplish it.

He's alive. Thank you, Father. She slid her arm over the wet sand underneath his shoulders and helped lift him to sit up. Their faces were so close, her cheek brushed his. Some powerful reaction shuddered through her.

He panted as if he'd been running. "Where are we?" he muttered, leaning against her.

She had to stop herself from stroking the head that lay against her shoulder. "Far downriver from the ferry."

"The girl?" He gasped, still panting as if each word cost him pain.

"I found Jewell and sent her back with one of our young men."

"Why are you here?" With obvious effort, he looked into her eyes.

"Because I had to find you. Or at least try to. Where do you hurt?"

He gave a harsh chuckle. "Let me think a moment."

She closed her eyes, waiting, feeling the weight of him on her.

"There's something not right about my ankle. Let's see if I can stand up." He rolled away from her onto his knees. She got up quickly and offered him her hands, palms up. He hesitated and then took her hands, pushing down and letting her help him stand. She had a time keeping steady under his weight. He wobbled and fell against her, nearly taking them both down. But at the last moment she was able to keep her balance.

"Don't move, Mr. Quinn." She stood holding him close to her, feeling his breath panting against her neck and face and the heaving of his chest against her. Standing pressed against him, she savored the solid feel of him as if she were a feather against rock.

"I'm as weak as a baby," he muttered.

"You were in the water for a long time. I'm hoping you didn't get any water into your lungs. That could cause a fever. Can you rotate your ankle?"

"Yes, but it hurts."

"Probably just a sprain." She glanced around in the low light. "Let's move up the bank away from the water. You might start to get chilly soon." With his arms around her shoulders and her arms around his chest, they managed to stagger up the bank. His weight nearly overpowered her, nearly took them down several times. Being this intimate with the man, touching him, unnerved her. Finally the two of them fell into a heap where the sandy soil was drier. She rolled away, righting her skirts, breathless. With one easy motion, he pulled off his leather shirt. "Hang this on a branch to dry. Please." Then he tugged off his high moccasins and cleaned out the sand and pebbles from each.

Dorritt first wrung out his shirt and then hung it up as instructed. "Thanks." He shivered. The evening shadows had faded into darkness. How could she keep him warm in the night? True it was still moderate at night, but he'd been chilled to his bones and his lungs needed warmth and protection. But she'd come without a blanket or even a wrap or shawl. Foolish.

She didn't know what else to do so she sat down beside him. The situation was so foreign she felt exposed. Rarely in her life had she been permitted to be near a man without a chaperone.

Her mind recalled the poor girl in New Orleans who'd been forced to marry because of coming home well into the night from a carriage ride. Thank heavens she was far from where anyone but her family would ever know of this night. And she fought the undertow of emotions being alone with him again was causing. "We should make a fire." She worried her lower lip. "But I don't have a flint and everything is so wet."

He fiddled with a small pouch at his belt and pulled out a flint box. "Can you reach any of the Spanish moss on the trees? And look around up here for driftwood. There might be some that was too high to be flooded. It has been some time since the rain."

Glad for a task, she did as she was bidden. Soon she brought him several handfuls of Spanish moss and driftwood of various sizes and put them in front of him. She sat down beside him again, tucking her skirts around her modestly. Being all alone with the man made her self-conscious. She hoped the fire would catch to keep them both warm from the damp chill of the bank.

Soon he had a small fire started in the moss, to which he added twigs and then slender branches until finally the larger driftwood caught flame. She sighed with relief at the welcome light and warmth. Sitting with her knees bent, she wiggled her bare toes.

Quinn pulled another, larger, pouch on his belt and opened it. She watched as he drew out a wet folded piece of deerskin and what looked like a fish-bone needle with a large eye. "Make a footprint in the sand."

"What?"

"I'm going to make you moccasins to wear."

Dorritt's mouth opened. Moccasins? Wear Indian shoes?

Quinn's jaw firmed. "Do you want to walk barefoot through Texas?"

She obeyed. Soon he double folded the leather and cut out

two soles with ample leather around three sides. Then he cut out two half circles to cover her toes. "Bring me the two longest pieces of fringe from the back of my shirt." She obeyed him, and soon her moccasins took shape before her eyes. She held them in her hands.

He grinned. "After you're done admiring my handiwork, you can try them on."

She chuckled, feeling foolish. But it was so rare that someone did something for her without being asked. It was a happy feeling she tried to suppress. This must have shown on her face.

"I'm sorry I didn't tell you the truth," he said.

His unexpected honesty took her by surprise. Completely. She couldn't find words.

"What I did tell you was the truth. I just left out the fact that I had gambled with your stepfather in New Orleans."

"That was a very important omission." Dorritt wrapped her arms around her knees. What did he hope to gain by this admission?

"Omission?"

"It means you left out something."

"That's what I said." He looked into her face, his blue eyes vivid in the low light. "I recognized your stepfather. And I wondered why he acted as if we hadn't met. So I didn't say anything." He shrugged. "I can't figure out your stepfather."

He's not hard to understand. If you remember that he is the most important person in the world. But of course she didn't say that. *I shouldn't even think it but, Father, it's so hard.*

He searched her face. "Why didn't your stepfather come after his daughter and me?"

His bold question was no more welcome now than a similar one the first time they'd spoken. She didn't know what to say to him. Evidently he was used to straightforward people. She couldn't lie. "Don't ask me that. Please."

"Why?"

She buried her face into her bent knees. "There are some things which women cannot say about men."

He added another piece of driftwood to the modest fire and poked it with a stick. The wet sand and the nearby river made the night chillier than she'd expected. She looked up. He shivered, tried to hide it, and shivered again more violently. Inevitability forced itself on Dorritt. After all, when dancing the waltz, men had held her in their arms. This wouldn't be much different, would it?

"The fire is good, but I need to keep your chest warm. It's the only way we have of warding off a fever."

He looked into the orange fire, stirring it again. "I'm tough. Don't worry about me."

She shook her head. Men were so predictable. She motioned for him to come closer. He stared at her and shivered again. After an inner battle, slowly he approached her. He sat down behind her and stretched his wet buckskin-covered legs along the sides of her skirt. His chest pressed against her back. Inside, a hurricane of sensation roared and rocked her. She closed her eyes, trying to stop his effect on her. He moved against her, settling in. She blushed and was glad that the night had enfolded them. Only the firelight flickered.

Finally he spoke, "My father was an American. My mother was Cherokee. When my mother died, I began traveling with my father with whites. So I have met some Americans, but not many. Your stepfather isn't like the Americans I have met before."

"Yes, he is unique or nearly so." She tried to slow and return to regular breathing, but his nearness made this impossible.

The fire crackled. "Unique?"

"I'm sorry." She sat very still. "One of a kind is the meaning of unique."

"You sound as if you have learned much from books."

She was used to hearing this. But for the first time, this man didn't say it as a criticism. He sounded . . . impressed. "Yes, I like to read." Her voice betrayed her, coming out breathless.

"I have sometimes wished that I learned to read English."

She glanced sideways at his face. Most men who couldn't read or write would not admit it to a man much less a woman. It gave her the courage to ask, "Is there anything else that I should know about your gambling with my stepfather?"

"I don't think so."

Closing her eyes and trying to think of something else, someone else other than Quinn, she'd never guessed that touching a man like this would act upon her so powerfully. But Quinn was still holding something back. She was almost certain.

* * *

Late the next morning, Dorritt and Quinn were making slow progress upstream along the riverbank. Since Quinn could not walk alone on his weakened right ankle, they walked with their arms around each other. Now his buckskin shirt shielded her from the feel of his skin against hers. But the ripple of his muscles and the solid weight of him against her still managed to throw her off-kilter. She thrummed with awareness of him. Dorritt tried not to let the feeling of closeness continue bonding her with this man. Awakening with him lying close behind her hadn't helped. Yet Mr. Quinn had behaved like a gentleman and nothing had happened—outwardly. Inwardly, she knew she was in danger of becoming drawn to him.

"Sister!"

Dorritt looked up and saw Jewell riding her mare toward them. Amos, looking concerned, brought up the rear on the mule.

"Jewell." Dorritt was surprised to feel disappointment. Her private time with Quinn, this rare instance away from her family, had ended.

Soon, Amos gently helped Dorritt up onto the saddle behind

Jewell and then pushed and hoisted Quinn onto the mule and climbed up behind him. Jewell turned her horse and they headed upstream. "What are those on your feet?" her sister asked.

"Mr. Quinn made them for me. My shoes had worn out."

"Well, I guess I shouldn't have worried about you," Jewell said. "I had imagined you lost and Mr. Quinn dead. Instead, you two . . ." Her voice trailed away.

Dorritt had no trouble guessing at what her sister was insinuating. The best tactic was no response at all. And the memory of being alone with Quinn all was too tender, too special to be discussed in the light of day.

"You may end up married, after all," Jewell said with sly derision, "now that you've been compromised."

Dorritt maintained her silence. Still, Jewell was ruining the precious aura lingering from last night.

"Spending the night out in the wild frontier—"

Dorritt interrupted her, "Leave it, Jewell."

Her sister turned and gave her a nasty look. But with pursed lips she fell silent.

Dorritt knew Jewell always found a way to pay Dorritt back for standing up to her. But in Texas, Jewell might finally pay for her recklessness and unkindness. Something told Dorritt that the consequences of foolishness might be even fatal on the frontier. They could have proved fatal yesterday. But there was too much of her father in Jewell to permit common sense.

"Father is champing at the bit to be off. So we must hurry." Jewell urged her mount to pick up the pace. Before Dorritt expected, she saw their party ahead, ready to leave. Reva pressed a cup of hot coffee into Dorritt's and Quinn's hands. Quinn was helped onto his horse, and Dorritt was settled beside one of the ox drivers. The caravan set out. Reva hurried along beside Dorritt and clambered up onto the wagon. She put her arms around Dorritt. "You all right?"

Dorritt nodded, reading in Reva's expression all the unasked questions she would answer later when they were alone. Dorritt took a deep breath. "I snapped at Jewell."

"*Uh-oh*," Reva said, "we better watch out."

* * *

East Texas proved to be so much like Louisiana that Dorritt had a hard time believing that they were not still on American soil. But three days after crossing the Sabine, she was sitting beside the lead ox driver as the train was traversing a break in the piney woods, a small stretch of meadow sprinkled with blue salvia, daisies, and black-eyed Susans. Ahead, she glimpsed a large contingent of men approaching them, scattering jackrabbits and making squirrels in the nearby trees screech. Seeing armed men dressed in blue and white uniforms riding in ranks made her blink. Spanish horse soldiers?

Soon their caravan was overtaken and surrounded by them. Grim-faced and well-armed soldiers hedged them in on all sides. Tremors of distrust shuddered through Dorritt. Had her stepfather got his facts straight? Were Americans really welcome here now? Stories of Americans who had returned to New Orleans after spending time in Mexican prisons flooded her mind.

The soldier with the most gold braid on his uniform and an intimidating saber on his belt approached Quinn. He spoke to Quinn rapidly in unfriendly sounding Spanish. Her stepfather rode up to the soldier and declared, "I am in charge of this party."

Quinn turned to Mr. Kilbride. "Do you speak Spanish?"

"No, but—"

Quinn spoke over Mr. Kilbride's denial, "This is Captain Jose Eduardo Estevan Montoya of the Spanish army in Mexico. He wishes to know by what right you have brought a party of Americans onto Spanish soil."

"Tell him that we are joining Stephen Austin near the Brazos River," Mr. Kilbride answered.

"I have told him that. But he did not know that more parties would be joining Stephen Austin."

Dorritt clenched her hands, praying for safety.

"Tell him that we were delayed," Kilbride went on, sounding glib. "Tell them we are going to pick up some cattle and horses belonging to me at Nacogdoches and then we will head straight to the Brazos to join the main Austin party."

Quinn translated this. The Spanish officer asked more questions.

Dorritt's suspicions danced like sparks inside her. What if they reached Austin's party only to be turned back—unwanted? What if they were turned back here? She gripped the wooden seat to keep silent.

"The captain says," Quinn continued, "that he sees that you have Negroes with you. Are they free laborers or indentured servants? No slaves are permitted to be brought into Spanish territory. King Fernando VII outlawed slavery in 1817."

"They are indentured servants," Mr. Kilbride said.

Appalled by this bald-faced lie, Dorritt nearly swallowed her tongue. Didn't her stepfather ever fear the consequences of his lies being uncovered?

Quinn translated this and the Spanish officer parried with another rapid question. To Dorritt's ear, the Spaniard did not sound convinced. Quinn said, "The captain wishes to see the indenture papers."

"Of course." Mr. Kilbride rode to the ox wagon where Dorritt sat, and moving a panel from the side, he took out a small metal box. He carried it to the Spanish officer and unlocked it. He handed the Spaniard a stack of documents.

After glancing to make sure they were actually indenture agreements, Dorritt looked down, afraid that her utter shock, disbelief, and fear would be seen and give them away.

The Spanish captain took his time looking over the papers. Then he handed them back to Mr. Kilbride. He spoke to Quinn again. Quinn turned to Kilbride. "He wants to know if you all have *bautismo* or *confirmación* papers from a Roman Catholic priest, proving that you are members of the holy Roman Catholic Church."

Dorritt's mouth sagged. They were expected to convert? There was no freedom of religion in Spanish Texas?

"Tell him," Mr. Kilbride said with a smile, "that we're planning on converting when we arrive at our destination. I take it that there will be a mission church near there where we can become communicants."

Dorritt clamped her mouth shut. Only fear kept her silent. Here they were in the wilderness surrounded by armed Spanish soldiers and her stepfather was lying and lying. Anything could happen.

Quinn translated the falsehood about Mr. Kilbride's imminent conversion. The Spanish captain studied Mr. Kilbride for a few moments. He spoke to Quinn. Then he saluted and wished them *"Adiós."* The troop of armed men rode off, heading south.

Quinn turned to Mr. Kilbride and challenged, "You don't really expect to get away with—"

Ignoring Quinn, Mr. Kilbride rode back to the wagon where Dorritt sat. With Quinn behind him, he leaned over and retuned the box to the hiding place behind a false panel in the side of the wagon.

Dorrit could not recall a time when she had been more incensed with Mr. Kilbride. Her white-hot fury radiated from her in intense, invisible waves. He'd brought them into the wilderness without any real agreement with the Austin party, with false papers, and with lies about their religion. Did the man have no fear—even of God? "What do you mean by this?" she demanded, leaning toward her stepfather. "Did you even make contact with this Stephen Austin?"

"How could I, girl? I don't know him from Adam. I just heard about his deal from Quinn and a few others and came ahead. Austin won't turn us away."

Monstrous deception, foolhardy and callous disregard for their safety goaded her to speak. "What was that about our becoming members of the Roman Catholic Church? Why would you tell him we're going to convert? Do you intend to?"

"No."

Liar. "And what was that about indenture papers? When did you decide to make your slaves into indentured servants?" she dared him, her words scorching her throat.

Mr. Kilbride shrugged. "I didn't. I just had these fake documents drawn up in case my having slaves was questioned."

Shaking, Dorritt clung to her self-control only so she wouldn't lose the power of speech. "So you mean that you lied about *everything* to a Spanish officer?"

Mr. Kilbride waved his hand in dismissal. "I'll probably never see him again. If I do, I'll just say the same."

Blistering words exploded from her throat. "Don't you realize those indenture papers can be deemed legal and enforceable? If anyone wants to know if our people are free, I'll say yes. I won't lie. I'll tell the truth. And make it so!"

Mr. Kilbride's hand shot forward.

Quinn caught his wrist. Her stepfather tried to pull from Quinn's grip and could not. Their mounts moved restlessly. "Let me go," Mr. Kilbride hissed.

"You will not strike your daughter."

Six

Quinn's disgust with this cheat and liar nearly made him start swinging his fists. Instead, he clamped down harder on the man's hand and on his own temper. *I didn't like you in New Orleans. And if you think, I'll stand by and let you hurt this lady . . .*

Kilbride tried to wrench himself free. Quinn tightened his grip even more. He knew his grasp must be hurting Kilbride now. And he wanted to hurt this poor excuse for a man. Wanted to make him behave toward Dorritt as he should. She was looking down. Quinn couldn't see her face, shielded by her bonnet brim. *Look at me, Dorritt.*

"Let go of me," Kilbride snarled.

Quinn hung on. "You are a man without sense. And you're a liar. That may have worked for you in New Orleans. It will not work for you here." *Look at me, Dorritt.*

Kilbride paid him no mind, just continued to struggle. In vain.

"Here if you tell lies and people get to know that," Quinn

continued, "no one will trust or have anything to do with you. On the frontier, a man's word, his honor, is everything."

Kilbride was so beside himself that he couldn't form words. He became red with anger. Odd sounds came from his mouth.

"Let go of him!" the younger daughter shouted from her gig.

"I will let go of him when he apologizes to Miss Dorritt. She told him the truth and he raised his hand to strike her. I will not let him." Quinn set his jaw. Why wouldn't Dorritt look at him? Was she too shamed by her stepfather's actions? Or ashamed of him for causing a scene?

Quinn held on. The younger sister got down out of her gig and tried to use her light whip on Quinn. Kilbride continued to strain. Quinn snatched it from her and tossed it away. Mrs. Kilbride began to cry. Quinn stared into Kilbride's contorted face. "You think that just because you are Americans that you can lie to the Spaniards and they won't know it. Do you know what happened to Philip Nolan, the mustanger? To Zebulon Pike when they trespassed on Spanish soil?" Quinn paused for effect.

Then he continued, letting all his scorn flow out in his tone. "Nolan ended up dead with his ears cut off. And the rest of his party is in prison at hard labor for life in Chihuahua. Those of us with Pike were escorted out of Spanish territory under armed guard. Do you understand? The Spanish are not stupid and they do not tolerate outlaws or trespassers."

Kilbride stopped struggling and glared at Quinn. His expression made it plain that he did not believe what Quinn had said. The man was a fool.

Finally, still with downcast eyes, Dorritt spoke up in her low rich voice, "Thank you, Mr. Quinn. But you will not teach my stepfather anything."

Kilbride cursed her under his breath.

Quinn stared at Dorritt. She had intrigued him from the first moment he had glimpsed her. There had been something in the way she carried herself. Today he hadn't been able to make Kilbride show her respect, but Dorritt now showed mercy and good sense. She had the right of it. A fool could not learn. *Very well.*

With his free hand, Quinn pulled the brim of his hat toward her and then flung away Kilbride's wrist. He waited to see if the man would try to strike her again. But Kilbride was too busy cradling his red swollen hand.

Dorritt said, "I thank you, Mr. Quinn."

He nodded and rode on ahead, letting the rhythm of the horse drain away his tight anger.

Dorritt spoke quietly to the driver beside her, telling him to get the ox started forward again. Everyone went on, but all looked away from Mr. Kilbride. She sensed everyone's tension as if it were her own. To whom would Mr. Kilbride direct his revenge?

After the caravan had traveled about a mile, Dorritt slid down from the wagon and walked back to Reva. She fell into step beside her friend.

"Well," Reva said in an undertone, "that was sure something."

"I couldn't believe it. No one has ever stood up for me."

"And you say nothing happened between you two the other night?" Reva looked away as she asked this question.

"Nothing—certainly nothing such as you are intimating." Heat flowed through her, recalling Mr. Quinn pressed close behind her. Then dread washed through her in cold waves, sweeping away any pleasure at the memory. Would everyone jump to this damning conclusion, that something untoward had passed between them? "We just talked."

"That must've been quite the conversation. Can we trust him?" Reva met her eyes now.

"I want to trust him. But . . ." Dorritt opened her arms in a gesture of helplessness. To be defended had filled her with a joy she'd never known, but how would her stepfather seek revenge for this public slight?

"I know, Miss Dorritt. We never had anybody else to trust but each other. Do you think he want something from you? I mean, besides what every man always want from a woman." Reva looked abashed.

This was a disturbing thought. Did Mr. Quinn have "feelings" for her, want something from her? *Oh, no, please.* "I don't know. When we were alone, he didn't make any improper advances—" She was grateful that her bonnet hid her face from Reva. "—and he apologized for not telling me that he knew Mr. Kilbride in New Orleans. I don't know what to think."

"I'm with you there."

Dorritt looked away, still flushed with the intimacy of that night where nothing had happened but perhaps when everything might have changed. Mr. Quinn was the wild card in this move west. Or maybe just the first harbinger of the unexpected challenges ahead.

"Well, maybe Mr. Quinn spoke the truth," Reva said.

"What do you mean?" Dorritt still didn't look into Reva's eyes, keeping her telltale face hidden.

"Mr. Quinn say on the frontier a man's honor is everything. Maybe you were right."

"Right about what?" Dorritt couldn't follow Reva's logic.

"That maybe we find our freedom in Texas," Reva said earnestly. "Maybe we can find honest men, good husbands in Texas."

Dorritt didn't reply to this. When Reva became free in the future—as Dorritt hoped, Reva would likely marry because she'd need a husband's protection and support. But marriage in Dorritt's mind equaled bondage and a bondage harder to escape than the one she lived under now.

It was possible that Mr. Quinn was what he appeared to be, an honest man. Even a good man. But race would always separate them in the eyes of the world. She seemed to be the only white person who saw people as more than the color of their skin. Why this was so she'd never figured out. But a lady like she did not marry a half-breed scout. She—along with Quinn—would be shunned. Her mother would die of the scandal. And in the end, long ago, she'd put away a girl's romantic notions of a fine gentleman who would love her and take her away. No, she must learn to take care of herself here in Texas, not depend on any man.

She shook her head and came back to the present. "Reva, stay clear of my stepfather. I don't want him . . . taking out his anger on you."

Reva nodded. "I hear you."

* * *

The sun was dipping low on the horizon when the party stopped and made camp for the night. Deeply uneasy and wary, Dorritt watched their people, very subdued, go through the routine of settling the horses, cattle, and oxen to graze among the pine trees for the night and getting the evening meal started. Each face looked apprehensive; every one of them afraid of what Mr. Kilbride might do next. A red-shouldered hawk swooped overhead.

Nearby, Jewell walked at her father's side, talking and no doubt stoking his anger. Mr. Kilbride stalked up and down the line, cuffing ears and swearing for no reason. Dorritt resisted the urge to intervene. Her stepfather was in a dangerous mood. She chewed her lower lip. Almost anything could cause a whipping tonight, a vicious one.

Then Amos had the misfortune to trip and drop some kindling wood he'd gathered. Mr. Kilbride swung around and backhanded the boy, cursing him. All the other slaves froze where they were. Dorritt saw the fear in their eyes, felt it shiver through her. Mr. Kilbride scanned the people nearest him and roared, "Get back

to work! You lazy good-for-nothings! When we get to Nacogdoches, I'm going to sell some of you! Worthless! Shiftless!"

"Yes," Jewell loudly agreed with him. And with a pointed
glance toward Dorritt, Jewell added, "That Reva isn't earning
her keep. My maid can do for both my sister and me."

Waves of panic from the slaves flowed to Dorritt. Jewell was
trying to hurt her in her weakest spot, her concern for their
people, especially Reva. Mr. Kilbride held the power of life and
death, slavery or freedom over Reva, the person in the world
Dorritt loved the most. Dorritt turned away as if she hadn't
heard. *Show no fear.* But Jewell's treachery made Dorritt decide
she would pursue her new goal. Yes, she would ask Mr. Quinn.

It was time she did more than tell herself that she would be
ready to take care of herself. And today, Mr. Quinn had protected her from Mr. Kilbride. She already owed Quinn much
and he owed her nothing, but she would still ask. She shut her
eyes for a moment of prayer. *Oh Father, protect us.* Then she
tried to force away the warmth that rushed through her at the
memory of Mr. Quinn defending her.

* * *

As Quinn crouched, starting a fire for the cook, he watched Kilbride's slaves go about their tasks in fear. How did a stupid man
get so much wealth? Was it just that Kilbride was a clever cheat?
Why hadn't someone put a bullet into the man by now? It was
a riddle. And why had Dorritt stopped Quinn from forcing Kilbride to apologize to her? He needed to know. He needed to
talk to her. And there had to be some way to protect her from
her stepfather.

It's not my place. Let it be. Even as Quinn thought this, he
heard a sharp crack and looked toward it. Kilbride had slapped
the young black who'd come on the mule after Quinn and Dorritt. The other slaves all looked away. Quinn rose from near the

fire he'd just started. Even from many feet away, as if his rising were a threat, Kilbride glared at Quinn.

"She too good for this family," the old cook muttered beside him.

Quinn glanced at the woman's dark, lined face.

"Yes, you know who I'm talkin' about." The older woman turned away and began mixing cornbread-cake batter to fry on a cast-iron griddle.

Quinn nodded. More and more he thought that he shouldn't leave Dorritt at the Brazos with her family. He could not think of what to do for her. But he must find another place for her where she would be safe and free of her stepfather. How he didn't know.

* * *

Night had fallen; the camp was quiet when Quinn sensed someone approaching him in the dark. Quinn slipped his knife from its sheath into his hand and rolled up to meet whoever it was.

Dorritt's maid held up both hands. "I'm Reva," she gasped. "My mistress say to come and get you. The mare is foaling."

As he followed the maid and passed the wagons, he heard Kilbride, that worthless man, snoring. Everyone slept, but Dorritt, the true leader, was awake. At the end of the caravan, she walked the mare, stroking her neck, murmuring to the animal. "Mr. Quinn," she greeted him quietly, "things are going apace. This foal might be yours, so I thought you'd like to be here for its birth."

He nodded, still wondering why she oversaw every part of the family's life and property. Then he noticed she wasn't alone attending the birth. Two male slaves hovered nearby over a low fire.

She answered Quinn's unspoken question, "I'm not really needed but I like to watch little ones born. Even kittens. It's such a miracle."

Her voice sounded excited. Sudden hope jolted him too. When he'd lost at cards in New Orleans, he'd thought his chance to own a thoroughbred had ended. And this woman understood that, understood that he'd want to be here for the birth.

"Would you like to walk her?" Dorritt asked him.

He was so pleased he couldn't say a word. But he managed to nod and took the mare's bridle. The birth of a foal wasn't anything new to him. But this would be *his* first thoroughbred foal—unless Kilbride decided to part with the colt. Suddenly Quinn knew that this mare would bear a filly. That had been what he'd wanted most to start his Texas thoroughbred line. A filly, mother to his line of mixed mustang thoroughbreds. He led the mare around and around, listening to her labored breathing. Dorritt walked beside him. He liked her near him.

For the first time in his life, he regretted that he was what and who he was. He was a half-breed and he knew how little whites thought of those with mixed blood. She was a white lady of much learning. And he couldn't even read and write. What did a man without property like him have to offer someone fine like her? But perhaps he could find someone, a white man of honor, who would recognize her worth. That was one solution of how to break Dorritt away from her family. But the idea set his teeth on edge.

Finally, she murmured to him, "Thank you for . . . for what you did for me today. I appreciated it."

Quinn's anger flashed through him afresh. His words rushed out, "He has no right to hit you for telling the truth. Has he hit you in the past?"

"No, at least, not since I became an adult."

"Why have you not taken a man, a husband?" These words also burst out before he could stop them. *Why don't you have someone to protect you?*

She didn't answer him right away. "You mean why did I stay with my family?"

"Yes. Why?" He wanted to know.

"I don't wish to marry."

"But every woman wishes to marry," Quinn said, the words again slipping out with no forethought.

"I've been told that many times." She stopped and stroked the mare's belly with long slow comforting motions. Not looking at him, she asked, "Why haven't you married? Or am I wrong? Are you married already?"

"I have never settled down. I am twenty-eight years. My father died at thirty. And I have nothing to offer a wife."

She did not reply to this, but said, "I have a favor to ask of you."

"What?" He watched her face in the low light.

"I wish to buy a rifle of my own. Will you help me? Will there be guns for sale in Nacogdoches?"

A rifle? He looked at her in the low light, surprised. "You could not handle a rifle."

"Because I'm a woman?"

"No, because you could not hold up a long rifle." He paused and lifted his firearm from his back. "Here. Try to hold it and aim it."

She tried but the nose of the gun ended up in the dirt. "It's too heavy and too long."

Nodding, he took the gun back. "You could learn to shoot a musket. It has a shorter barrel. Why do you want to have a gun?"

She released a loud sigh. "I don't want to shoot anyone, but I think I should be armed—just in case . . ." Her voice faded away.

Just in case what? he thought, but only nodded. Kilbride was no protection for her. The mare was closer now to the birth. He saw the pace speed up.

Dorritt touched his sleeve. "My stepfather will try to cheat you of this foal, you know that?"

Her slight touch made him almost unable to speak. "Yes."

Then their conversation ended. The mare began the final stages of giving birth. He stepped forward and helped the two men with the newborn foal. With old sacking, he rubbed down the little filly. He looked up at Dorritt, grinning. "This is the one I want."

She nodded, but her eyes repeated what she had said earlier: "My stepfather will try to cheat you."

Quinn nodded just barely, grimly. *He may try, but he will not succeed.*

* * *

Their caravan arrived in Nacogdoches the next day. Quinn was familiar with the small sleepy village with its mission church made of mesquite poles and mud at the center of town where the plaza was. Here, instead of the more imposing one in San Antonio de Bexar, the plaza was a large unkempt green with clumps of dandelions and thistle. When he'd told Dorritt that there was a church here, she'd acted like it would be something like St. Louis Cathedral in New Orleans. He'd warned her not to expect much. But right now her expression was easy to read: *We've come all this way for this?*

Quinn led them to the one sad-looking inn. Kilbride dismounted, swaggering inside. Quinn followed him, leaving his reins with Amos. The business didn't take long and Quinn came out of the inn just as his friend, tall and dressed in buckskins, rode up on a fine mustang stallion. He slid from his saddle and met Quinn in the shade under the porch of the inn. "Well, Quinn," the black man drawled in a voice that had a touch of a Spanish accent mixed with an American one, "I see you finally found your way back to Nacogdoches. Later than I expected. I'd almost decided some Louisiana wildcat got you."

"Ash," Quinn greeted him with a smile and an upraised hand, wondering how Kilbride would react when he met Ash, who was almost family to Quinn.

"Did you get what you went to New Orleans for?" Ash scanned the caravan.

"In a way." Quinn gestured toward the end of the caravan where the little foal was nursing her mother. "We're going to have to go southwest to the Brazos first. I'm leading this party to meet up with Stephen Austin."

Mr. Kilbride stepped outside. "Who is this person?" His tone oozed disdain.

Quinn shifted his gaze to Kilbride. Distaste for the man soured his mouth. "This is Ash. My partner."

Ash offered Kilbride his hand and Quinn knew why. Ash always wanted to know where he stood with someone new.

Kilbride just looked at the hand and turned away.

Quinn burned to have it out with this self-important liar.

But Ash just chuckled. And withdrew his hand. "So, Quinn, you signed up to take this party to Austin, then? I didn't count on going that far west. I thought we were going to head down to Santa Roseta way. See about a job."

Kilbride swung back. "Does this Negro have his manumission papers?"

Leaning back against a rough porch post, Quinn let Ash speak for himself. He glanced at Dorritt. He would like to introduce Ash to her. But not now.

Ash casually shoved up the brim of his hat and gave Kilbride a look of mild interest. "I don't need any manumission papers. I was born the son of a *mestizo padre* and free *negro madre*. This is Spanish territory. There's no slavery here."

Kilbride said in a bitter lowered voice, "But there are plenty of runaway slaves here in Texas."

"We Tejanos don't think much of slavery. Or slave owners," Ash commented in the same tone as Kilbride.

The man refused to acknowledge Ash and continued to glare at Quinn. "I won't have any free Negro in my party. It's unnatural."

Quinn grinned suddenly. "If you decide, after our agreement has been struck, that you no longer need me, I still get my foal." It was beginning to almost amuse Quinn to see how easy it was to fire up Kilbride. "Is that what you want?" Out of the corner of his eye, he glimpsed a Spanish soldier strolling through the plaza. And four Mexican *vaqueros* watching them closely.

"I am not breaking our agreement, either of our agreements. You owe me ten head of cattle and two mustangs. But neither agreement mentioned having a free black along. It isn't good . . ." Kilbride pursed his lips as if he just recalled why he shouldn't be calling notice here and now to his owning slaves. Maybe he had noticed the Spanish soldier too? "I don't like it."

"You mean," Ash taunted Kilbride, "that you didn't know that there was no slavery in Spanish territory? Aren't all these people—" he gestured toward the slaves in the caravan, "—free?"

"They are indentured servants," Kilbride snapped, his eyes darting to the soldier who had paused and was eyeing them in turn.

Quinn pushed up his hat brim just as Ash had. And grinned. Leave it to Ash. "That's right. And Mr. Kilbride has the papers to prove it."

"Then unless Mr. Kilbride—" Ash nodded politely toward Kilbride. "—wants to lose his guide and his foal, I guess I'll be going with you to the Brazos."

Quinn enjoyed watching Kilbride try to hide his aggravation. Finally the man gave the barest nod to Quinn and stalked toward his wife and daughter. On his way past Amos, Kilbride cuffed the boy hard enough to knock him down.

Ash made as if he were going after Kilbride, but Quinn stopped him with a shake of the head. It would only cause more trouble for Dorritt. And the slaves. "Not now," Quinn muttered. *But soon.*

* * *

He hadn't expected anything unusual on the way home from Loui-
siana after the cattle drive. Now he stood here in Nacogdoches with
his cousin and two compañeros *watching the plump Anglo be bested*
by the half-breed Quinn and his friend the negro Ash. Both Quinn
and Ash had reputations as men not to be trifled with. Well, he
wasn't planning on trifling with them. But these Anglos—he didn't
like more whites coming into Texas. The Spaniards and Creoles had
lorded it over men like him long enough. Mexico should be for Mexi-
cans. The rumors he'd heard in Louisiana about angloamericanos
who were entering the Spanish territory to become legal residentes
of Texas must be true. What was the government in Mexico City
thinking? But now that the government had changed hands, Mexico
belonged to the Mexicans at last. The Spaniards would leave. And
no Anglos should be welcome. If he could help it.

This trip was supposed to have been just another cattle drive,
one of many. This, however, was the first time his cousin had ac-
companied them. Did his cousin finally suspect how much had been
secretly stolen from him in the past when the cattle had been sold
without his presence at the transaction?

One of the Anglos, a señorita, *walked into the bright sunshine.*
She turned and looked directly at him, and as her bonnet slid to
her shoulders, he glimpsed her face. Her wind-tousled hair fluttered
in the sunlight. And her skin was the palest he'd ever seen. He saw
his cousin staring at her, staring at her in a special way. My cousin
wants her? If so, can I use this attraction to hurt him? I will keep
watch and see.

* * *

Dorritt woke the next morning in a small upstairs room in
the inn and stretched luxuriously like a cat. The bed was not
wide or comfortable but it was a bed. And she'd had a bath the
night before. What a difference these mundane comforts made.
She rose and went to the window and, looking out, prayed her

morning prayer, "Father, let me be the woman you want me to be today."

As she gazed out over the city square, or as the innkeeper had called it, the plaza, the town was just coming to life. It reminded her a bit of the town square, back in her home state Virginia, with its commons where anyone could let their cows, goats, and sheep graze.

A vague and troubling uneasiness plagued her. They were deep in Texas. In a few weeks, they would arrive at the Austin settlement, still deeper into the wild Spanish Texas. Would they be welcomed or turned away? Would she really have the nerve to purchase a weapon and learn how to fire it?

A few Mexicans rode into the plaza and slid off their horses. Though they were still in a piney woods, everything looked different here in the kind of people and their dress. The Spanish evidently preferred more colorful and embellished clothing than Americans. And the differences between those with wealth and those without also showed up more sharply in their clothing. Yesterday, Dorritt had even seen Indians roaming the square, bare-chested and scantily dressed in buckskin. And there had been darker-skinned Mexicans, called *mestizos*, who were of Spanish and Indian blood, alongside the more European-looking Spanish. Down on the street, one of the Mexicans stared up at her window. Could he see her? She stepped back away from the window, embarrassed.

A bell rang in the mission at the end of the plaza. The sound kindled a longing to her heart. She had not been in a house of the Lord for over a month. She knew from living in New Orleans that the priest had rung the bell to call the faithful to matins, morning prayers. The longing inside her to be in a house of worship became a physical pull toward the mission.

She scrambled into her undergarments and the dress that had been laid out over the chair by the bed. She didn't wear a bonnet, wishing to blend in with the peons walking toward church. Instead, she slipped her purse into her pocket, cast a shawl around her shoulders, and hurried downstairs and across the stirring plaza, hoping no one would see her. She felt as if she were going to a long-awaited tea at a friend's house.

Seven

Dorritt entered the church. She pulled the shawl up over her hair, hoping no one would notice her. Though her stepfather attended church only because it was expected, if he found out she'd attended Mass, he would be angry. Still, inside the cool shadowy church, a sigh breathed through her. It was good to be in a house of the Lord again, even one that didn't look like any church she'd ever attended. Catholics genuflected just as the Episcopalians did, so she performed this and then knelt on the cool half-log floor. The priest came out from behind the altar and began the service in Latin, lighting short white candles and exotic incense. Overhead, the few bells rang out once more and then fell silent.

Dorritt understood almost none of the Franciscan friar's Latin liturgy. But even in this rough wood structure, the flickering candles and the statue of the Virgin Mary and Baby Jesus reminded her so much of the St. Louis Cathedral in New Orleans that she shed a few tears of homesickness. Even though her family did not worship there, when in town she had always liked to sit in the back of the solemn cathedral. In her life, now filled with change and danger, this church was a bit of civilization on the wild frontier—a reminder that her Heavenly Father had not been left on the other side of the Sabine.

The prayers ended and she reluctantly rose from the back pew. As she left the cool, dimly lit mission, an elderly Mexican woman whose suntanned face was etched with deep lines stared at her. Dorritt nodded and smiled.

Outside from the shadows around the door, Mr. Quinn moved into the morning light. "Miss Dorritt, do you still want to buy a musket?"

He took her by surprise and she gasped. When she'd left the inn, he must have been watching for her. Had anyone else noticed her coming here? Like Jewell, who would use it to Dorritt's disadvantage? "Yes, I do."

He motioned toward the plaza. "I know a man here who might sell a gun."

Dorritt felt a flash of excitement and fear. Knowing she should really return to the inn, she began walking beside him, unable to withstand the lure of the pleasure of his company. The silent men they passed nodded or tipped the brims of their hats to Quinn. She was not surprised that he was a man who was respected where he was known. She also noted the cast of speculation in the eyes of the men they passed. They were wondering who she was. And why she was with Quinn. Her stomach fluttered with her own daring. Texas seemed to be having this effect on her. "How long will we stay in Nacogdoches?" she asked.

"I think just a few days. Once we leave Nacogdoches, there aren't any towns between here and the Colorado River. I thought you ladies would like a bit of easy living."

She chuckled. In spite of general disapproval, walking beside this man was bit by bit relaxing her, lowering her usual guard. "You aren't wrong. It was wonderful to wake in a bed this morning." She glanced down and saw that his footwear had changed. "You're wearing boots."

"Yes, boots are better when I'm herding cattle."

She looked at her dusty moccasins and wondered what wearing boots would feel like. She went on, "Herding cattle? Do you have cattle?"

"Yes, a few."

"And mustangs, right?"

"A few."

Dorritt smiled. No one would ever call Mr. Quinn talkative or a braggart.

"I see you went to church," he said.

She could perceive no hidden meaning or reproach in his words. "Yes, that felt good too."

"I don't know much about the white man's God. My mother taught me about the Creator of All who lives beyond the sun, the Green Corn festival, and such. My father taught me a little about heaven and hell and what he called the Ten Commandments."

As usual, this man spoke to her without any agenda other than honestly sharing his thoughts. She nodded, but ventured to add, "Then you know more than you think you do. Did he ever speak to you about Jesus?"

"Yes, that is the man on the cross I've seen in the mission churches. The man who died for the sins of all. Do you think that is possible—one to die for all?"

The way he spoke so naturally about God stirred up an odd scratchy feeling inside, like ants running over her skin. "Yes, the Son of God died for our sins. But that's because Jesus was not just a man, but a man and a god."

"My father said that, but I have never understood it."

As they walked, she gazed at Quinn's profile, the assured lift of his chin. A free, confident man. If only all men were as honest and at ease with life. "It is not easy for anyone to understand. But if God is God, then he can do anything, can't he?"

Quinn nodded. "Here is the man's *casa*." Inside the shady doorway of the modest log house, a Spaniard came forward and bowed slightly. Dorritt could tell from the man's lighter complexion that he was a Spaniard, not a *mestizo*. In Spanish, Quinn told him what they needed. Soon, the man brought out a used musket. Quinn looked it over and then handed it to Dorritt. "It's in good shape. Here, get the feel of it."

She took it from him. It was cold and heavy. "How should I hold it?"

He looked pleased by her question. "When you are walking, you carry the musket like this." He showed her how to rest the musket on her arms, its muzzle pointed down. "This is the India Pattern smoothbore muzzle-loader." He patted the butt of the gun.

She nodded, repeating his information to herself. She was aware that the Spaniard was eyeing her with disapproval. Was it because she was a woman holding a musket? Or because she was with Quinn? Or both?

Quinn spent some time haggling over the price of the musket. And finally, at Quinn's word, she handed over the silver pieces for the weapon.

Glancing around the quiet plaza, she decided to steal a few more moments of freedom. "Let's go somewhere you can show me how to load and fire this gun. And I'd appreciate it if you'd start teaching me enough Spanish to get along with the Mexicans." *Because I won't have you for long.*

Quinn nodded, then led her away beyond the plaza. Dorritt resisted the feeling that she was being followed or watched. She glanced around many times, but did not see anyone suspicious, just Mexicans who, of course, looked curious about her, a stranger and an Anglo. She had been called that before, the short form of *angloamericano,* by Creoles, the older New Orleans residents of Spanish or French descent. And they used the term often with disdain. The French and Spanish both considered Americans gauche and crude. But as with anything, money always made the difference. A rich Anglo was still rich and, therefore, acceptable in society.

Soon they approached a small hut made of narrow standing logs with a thatched roof. Nearby was a large rudely fenced paddock. She had seen some of these in Texas already. "What is that kind of house called?"

Quinn nodded toward it and said, "It's a *jacal,* made out of mesquite."

She repeated it after him. It sounded like "ha-call." She wondered how it was spelled.

He waved toward the paddock and said, "And this is called a *potrero.* Here are my mustangs."

"*Potrero,*" she repeated as she drew closer and looked over the horses. "You have done well. Where did you get such fine stock?"

She watched Quinn's deeply tanned face flush at her words. And she was glad she had complimented him.

"Ash and I went northwest through Comanche and Kiowa territory and gathered the wild cattle and mustangs that roam the frontier."

"Aren't the Comanche very dangerous?" she asked, aware of how how feminine she felt standing beside him.

"Yes, but Ash and I know how to pass unnoticed if we want to. We made many trips so we could slip in and out with a few at a time."

She smiled at him. *A brave man and a clever one.* "Where are your longhorns?"

"They're south of here," Ash said, walking out of the hut and joining them. "We branded ours and left them grazing on a friend's land." He shook the hand Dorritt offered him.

"Yes," Quinn added, "we'll pick them up soon."

As Dorritt turned, she brushed against Quinn's shirt. The contact brought memories of their night alone by the river. She scrambled to distract herself. "May I ask about your unusual name? I've never met an Ash before. Or is it short for Ashley?"

Ash laughed with friendly amusement. "No, I'm not Ashley. That name is way too fancy for me. My mother's father was from the Ashanti people in Africa. Or that's what she told me. She named me Ash so I would remember her family."

"That makes sense," she said, wondering at his ability to laugh about his family being enslaved.

"And my family name from my father is Martinez. Just like the governor of Texas." Ash grinned even broader. "I'm afraid he can't claim kinship with me."

She chuckled, liking his lack of pretension. Maybe she'd left behind all the pretentious people in New Orleans, except for her stepfather.

Ash looked around the clearing. "I see you didn't bring along that pretty woman that Quinn told me is your maid."

"Reva?" she asked.

"Reva. Now that's a pretty name. It fits her."

Before Dorritt could reply, Quinn pointed to the new gun. "Ash, Miss Dorritt has just bought this. And I'm going to teach her how to load and shoot it."

"Is that so?" Ash asked with a dubious tone.

This sparked her own uncertainty. "I know it's unusual for a woman to learn to shoot. Maybe too unusual." She moved back as if distancing herself from the musket.

"Well, miss," Ash replied, "it's out of the ordinary. But you might have to shoot, say, a rattler." He grinned.

"A rattler?" she said. "I've never seen one."

"Well, they like Texas." Ash leaned an arm on the top of the fence.

Dorritt took a deep breath. She felt uncomfortable being here with Quinn and Ash without a chaperone. And without her bonnet, her face exposed to the hot sun. Perhaps that explained her sense of unease. Or was God trying to tell her not to do this? But when she imagined one of the slave children disturbing a nest of rattlers, she knew she wanted to be prepared. She nodded twice—firmly.

In the midst of Quinn showing her how to load the musket, the *padre* from the mission shuffled up. *"Buenos días, señorita y señors."* Then he added in heavily Spanish-accented English, "Good morning."

Dorritt curtsied and greeted him in Spanish, a mistake because he started speaking to her in rapid Spanish. She held up her hand. "Pardon me, *padre*. I speak only a little bit of Spanish as yet."

He smiled at her. "I saw you at matins today. So even though you are an Anglo, you must be a faithful daughter of the church."

"I don't to want to mislead you, *padre*—"

He interrupted her with upraised palms. "You need to say nothing. Your actions speak louder than words."

Ash whispered into her ear, "Never blurt out the truth to a Spaniard. They don't like it. Appearances are everything in Spanish society." Then he turned to the *padre*. "Quinn is going to teach Señorita Dorritt how to protect herself from rattlesnakes."

"¡Excelente!" the *padre* approved with another broad smile.

Looking past the priest, Dorritt saw that the same elderly woman she'd noticed in church had followed the priest from the plaza. She came limping toward them, but stopped in the shade of an oak tree and lowered herself onto a tree stump used for chopping wood into kindling. The woman seemed to stare at her. Dorritt imagined nothing much ever happened in the sleepy town. Any stranger, especially an Anglo, would be of interest. She turned and followed Quinn.

Beyond the paddock, he had gone farther toward the remains of a log cabin. One wall had been half torn down. Quinn picked up chunks of wood and sat them like a row of soldiers on the half wall. Then he placed the musket butt into her shoulder, showed her how to extend her left arm to support it, how to close one eye, sight down the barrel, and how to release the flintlock to fire. The wood and metal tucked so close, so intimate, made her stomach jump in odd little skips. Or was it the inadvertent brushing and touching of Quinn's strong tanned hands on her skin?

Quinn's striking blue eyes delved into hers. "You must be careful to place the butt right because of the recoil."

Unable to look away from him, transfixed, she murmured. "Recoil?"

"When it fires," Quinn replied, "expect it to jump back against you."

Oh, dear. That didn't sound like something she wanted to deal with.

"Are you ready to try?" Quinn asked her.

No, I'm not ready. But of course she couldn't say that. *I started this and I must either go through it or stop now. I hope this is from you, Father.* She took a deep breath, adjusted her aim. She released the bolt. To the sound of an explosion. The musket lurched in her arms. Nearly knocked her off her feet. If Quinn hadn't been right behind her and steadied her, she would have fallen. She gasped, leaning back against him. He held her in place with his hands firm on her shoulders.

Raucous laughter finally penetrated her deafened ears. She turned and saw that four Mexicans, all obviously *mestizos,* lounged back against the paddock fence. Three of them were jeering and mocking her. One of them, however, was merely gazing at her as if taking her measure. She studied him. He was a bit taller with a lighter complexion than the others. Two other things set him apart; he wore finely tooled leather boots and silver spurs that glinted in the sun.

Her face flushed with aggravation. This surprise attack, this vulgar intrusion, had shattered this private time. In effect, reality had just slapped her face. Rigid with defiance, she turned her back to them. Her voice gritty and harsh in her throat, she said to Quinn, "Please show me how to load this gun again."

He glanced at the *mestizos* and then back at her. "Don't let them throw you. You did fine for your first time." He helped her reload the musket with ball and powder. A little shaky, she turned her back to the Mexicans and lifted the musket back into place. "That's right," Quinn murmured close to her ear. "Fire when ready."

Set to prove her determination to the mockers, she braced herself and shot the gun. This time she had better luck staying on her feet. And she had the satisfaction of seeing that her shot actually hit the wall, if not the target. She grinned.

"Not bad," Ash said.

The priest agreed in warm tones. Then he added, "You have heard of the trouble here in Mexico, yes?"

Dorritt was reloading the musket with Quinn's help. "What trouble?"

"The revolution." He shook his head. "I am told we are all to say, ¡*Viva Independencia!*"

"What revolution?" Quinn asked for her.

"Word has come that we are no longer a Spanish colony. No longer under the Crown."

"But we just saw Spanish troops on the way here," Dorritt objected, drawing closer to Quinn.

The priest shook his head. "There has been a revolution. This is now the Republic of Mexico, no longer a Spanish colony. But nothing here has changed. You see there are so few of us and we are so far north of Mexico City." He shrugged. "Nearly ten years ago, Padre Hidalgo tried to bring about a revolution—"

"And all it did was get a lot of people killed and him executed," Ash commented with a dark look. "Do you think the new government will care anything for the poor?"

The priest shrugged. "Who can say?"

Ash gave his opinion with a loud snort.

Talk of a revolution gave Dorritt gooseflesh. "Will that affect the Austin settlement? I mean Austin's agreement will hold strong even if the government has changed, won't it?" This was worrying news, since Austin was farther south, much closer to Mexico City and the government. And the army.

The priest held up his hands. "Only God knows. A few other Anglos have come through Nacogdoches on their way to the mouth of the Colorado River. That is where the Anglos are to meet Don Estevan Austin."

Dorritt looked into the eyes of Quinn, who looked as troubled as she felt. "I hope . . ." She couldn't finish her sentence. She didn't want to put into words the fear that they would go all the way to the mouth of the Colorado and then be turned back. As Quinn helped her reload the heavy musket, his hand skimmed her shoulder. Another touch, another instinctive reaction, a heightening of awareness.

One of the *mestizos* jeered her, "Have you given up so soon, *señorita*? You should leave guns to men!"

She quelled the temptation to turn the musket toward the voices. Instead, she hardened her jaw, finished reloading, and lifting the musket to her shoulder, took aim. Quinn leaned close, checking her stance, igniting a fresh tide of sensitivity to him.

"What do you think you're doing, young lady?" her step-father's voice thundered across the clearing.

Dorritt went ahead and fired. After the smoke cleared, she said, "I am learning how to shoot a musket." In spite of a twitch in her throat, she kept her voice cool, as if she were sitting in the parlor, stitching her azalea pattern. Amos was a step behind her stepfather. He'd been keeping the boy with him, so he had someone convenient to vent his irritation on.

Her stepfather's face glowed bright red. "You are not some unlettered leatherstocking woman. You have been raised as a lady. Put that weapon down and return to the inn and your mother. *At once.*"

More and more, her disrespect for the man was making it harder and harder for her to obey him. Or even appear to obey him. She respected this "leatherstocking" Quinn more than him.

But the priest was watching her and all the other men, all whom her stepfather would hold in contempt. If she did not obey, he would retaliate for any slight under these circumstances.

Dorritt glimpsed the old Mexican woman painfully getting to her feet. Across the distance the old woman's eyes met hers. Dorritt was gripped by a sudden feeling of connection. The old Mexican woman bowed her head and then turned to walk away.

"Are you ignoring me?" Mr. Kilbride demanded.

"No, sir." She couldn't risk defiance. She wasn't afraid of what he might do to her, here and now, but she couldn't allow her own feelings to endanger her people, poor Amos, maybe Reva. Any more than they already were, that is. "Of course, Mr. Kilbride. I just thought—"

"Women are not supposed to think. They are supposed to obey."

Outraged, Dorritt was forced to endure his cavalier dismissal of her whole gender in silence. If she hadn't taken over the running of the plantation from his mother when she died, ruin would have come to them years earlier. *If I'd been born a man, he wouldn't treat me with such disrespect.* She swallowed down the outraged words jammed together in her throat. "Yes, Mr. Kilbride." She handed the musket to Mr. Quinn. She saw the understanding in his eyes and it nearly laid her low.

Kilbride snapped at Amos and shoved him. Then her stepfather grabbed Dorritt's arm and turned her toward town. He began a string of insults, spoken just loud enough for her ears.

One of the *mestizos* called out. She didn't understand the word, but she understood the intent. They were letting her know that she had stepped out of bounds that constrained her, a woman, and they would make her pay. Quinn looked shocked and angered, his face tightening. She had left Louisiana behind, but not the strictures upon her as a woman, as a "lady."

Then the tall Mexican, who had studied her but not insulted her, snapped angry words at the others and motioned them to come away with him.

She longed to be free of Kilbride, who was now berating Amos just out of ill humor. Yet at the same time, women who lost their honor in the eyes of men would be deemed fair game for every kind of ill-treatment and scorn, even rape. Why did a woman always have to be in the care of a father, brother, or husband? Why couldn't all men treat her the way Quinn and Ash did? Quinn didn't think she was less because she was a woman. *He treats me like a person.* Then she imagined what Mr. Kilbride would say if he knew what she was thinking. And at that thought, she shuddered.

* * *

Two days later, Ash rode along with Quinn, raising dust, driving their twenty head of bawling cattle to the south end of the plaza. Kilbride had refused to ride out as far as the ranch where Quinn and Ash had left their cattle. Quinn was surprised until Ash pointed out that Kilbride, a dishonest man, didn't trust Quinn, an honest man, away from witnesses. A cheat always expected to be cheated. Ash knew Quinn had dreaded today and so did he. Having to hand over ten head of cattle, which they'd risked their lives to gain, to the man who Quinn believed had cheated him was bad enough. But having to do it in the plaza, where all would stare, made it even harder. Still, honor demanded Quinn live up to his wager.

Kilbride rode up on his showy stallion. "I don't want a lot of bulls. Just one bull and the rest cows."

"What do you plan on doing with these cattle?" Ash asked, delighted to begin goading the man.

Kilbride ignored him and rode around the cattle, inspecting them.

"What are you planning on doing with these cattle?" Quinn repeated Ash's question. "Are you going to start a herd to sell for beef? Or what?"

Kilbride responded with obvious sarcasm, "Who would I sell the beef to in the middle of the wilderness?"

Ash wondered how any man could be this ignorant. Ash answered for Quinn, "Down at Matagorda sometimes you can sell beef. They slaughter some right there and then hang the sides of beef and ship it east to New Orleans by water. Most other southern Tejano ranchers drive herds overland through Natchitoches to New Orleans too."

Kilbride still ignored Ash and spoke to Quinn, "I didn't know ships came into Matagorda. Do the traders pay cash money?"

Quinn remaind silent, just working the cattle, keeping them calm.

"They pay in silver. Go ahead and take mostly cows," Ash said.

"We don't mind bull calves because we're going to turn them into steers, fatten them, and sell them." When a few more of the cattle tried to stray, Ash flicked the end of his lariat.

"I'll stick by my original intent." Kilbride then began to point out the cattle he wanted.

Ash knew this choosing was not part of this bargain. But after some discussion, he and Quinn had decided to let Kilbride make his choice of the cattle and mustangs. Then when Quinn took payment for guiding at the mouth of the Colorado River, he would make his choice of horse. And it would be the foal. If Kilbride objected, Quinn would merely remind Kilbride that he had been allowed to choose the cattle and mustangs he wanted. Quinn was soothing the cattle with soft words and coaxing sounds to keep them from stampeding in the plaza.

Ash glanced around the plaza. This transaction had attracted the curious. The four Mexicans who had taunted Dorritt rode up to watch Kilbride. Ash couldn't deny that one of the four *vaqueros* intrigued him. The one with the silver spurs looked as if he aspired to be more than a cowboy. He had a way of sitting in the saddle with extra pride. Of the four, he had the lightest skin, which meant he had more Spanish blood. And those of Spanish blood alone had ruled here.

Still, this *vaquero* hadn't joined in mocking Dorritt. He'd spent his time watching her and sizing her up. Of course, anyone with eyes could see she was quite the lady, a true lady. No wonder Quinn might be taken with her. But that wouldn't end well. White ladies didn't mix with half-breeds. To do so meant crossing a line that could never be reversed.

As Kilbride finished picking out the cattle he wanted, Ash asked the question that Kilbride obviously hadn't considered, "Who's going to drive your cattle and mustangs?"

Surprised, Kilbride faced Ash, forgetting that he was ignoring him. "Why my slaves, of course. I mean, my indentured servants," he amended, glancing around as if to see if any had overheard his slip.

"Do they have horses to work cattle with? Have they ever herded wild cattle and barely broken horses through wilderness?" Ash asked, amused.

"No." For once, Kilbride looked perplexed. Then he brightened. "Why, Quinn will."

Quinn shook his head. "No, I signed on as your guide, not your *vaquero*. Ash and I have our own cattle to herd."

Kilbride sputtered.

Ash wondered how he'd stomach Kilbride day after day. Quinn rode away from the man and began herding the cattle out of town again. Ash turned the head of his horse to join Quinn.

"Wait!" Kilbride called after them. "Where do I hire *vaqueros*?"

Quinn stopped and turned his horse back. But before he could speak, one of the four Mexicans waved to Kilbride. "You want to hire *vaqueros*?"

Ash turned to look at the man too. It wasn't the one with the silver spurs. This *vaquero* had sun-darkened skin and a long deep scar that ran from the lower lid of one eye down the cheek to his chin. Ash had a feeling he was one who had taunted Dorritt yesterday. The Mexican spoke and moved like a braggart.

"Yes, are you interested in employment?" Kilbride asked, looking eager. Then he changed his expression and made his tone brusque. "I can't pay much."

The scarred Mexican considered this with his arms folded.

The Mexican put Ash on his guard. The fact that he could speak English alone set him apart from the average *vaquero*. And the way he weighed and measured Kilbride with his dark eyes gave Ash more reason for pause. Ash had to admit he plain didn't like the man. He and his friends had insulted Miss Dorritt, and Ash liked the lady. Not to mention her pretty maid he'd seen around town.

"We're headed toward the mouth of the Colorado to join up with Stephen Austin's new settlement," Kilbride explained to the Mexican. "Would you be interested in driving the cattle that far?"

"We were traveling in that direction," this *vaquero* allowed. "How much would you pay?" Then he looked back at the Mexican with the silver spurs who sat frowning on his horse.

"Five dollars American," Kilbride bargained.

Didn't Kilbride know that offering such low pay was an insult? Ash was glad Quinn had struck a better bargain. The foal was growing day by day, and gaining the animal was worth putting up with Kilbride a little longer.

"Ten dollars silver," the scarred Mexican countered as his *compañeros* scowled. The one with the silver spurs watched intently.

"Seven dollars silver and that's my final offer," Kilbride said with a stubborn look.

"*Sí.*" The same Mexican gestured toward his three companions. "And the same for them? I cannot drive so many cattle all by myself."

Ash watched the four Mexicans size up Kilbride. None of them looked happy about the bargaining. The one with the silver spurs appeared especially tense.

Kilbride looked nettled. "I'll pay for two *vaqueros*. The other two can come along, but I'm not paying them."

The Mexican who'd struck the bargain considered this, looked to his friends. Unspoken communication took place. Then the one with the silver spurs nodded, and the others followed him. The scarred Mexican strode over to Kilbride and held up his tanned hand. "It's a deal. I am Eduardo. This is Carlos." Eduardo motioned toward the *vaquero* with the silver spurs.

True to form, Kilbride hesitated, but then grasped Eduardo's hand for a quick shake. "I'm Kilbride. We leave tomorrow. At dawn. Here." Kilbride rode away.

Ash and Quinn urged the cattle out of the plaza. Ash glanced over his shoulder at Carlos with the silver spurs. The man was looking toward the inn, and there was Miss Dorritt.

Dorritt couldn't believe how her luck went from bad to worse. Mr. Kilbride's hiring those insolent men made her stomach burn. Exiting through the inn's back door, she tried to walk off her annoyance, moving from shade tree to shade tree toward the public well, where the women were doing laundry. Reva was there, scrubbing Dorritt's chemises and dresses. The same older Mexican woman, whom she'd seen before, sat in the shade and watched the other women working. Once again the woman bowed her head to Dorritt in greeting. Dorritt responded in kind, then approached Reva and murmured into her ear, "Mr. Kilbride hired those Mexicans I told you about, to herd the cattle he won from Mr. Quinn."

Reva looked up, her expression troubled.

Dorritt pursed her lips and walked to a bench beside the large stone pool near the public well. Texas was full of complications. A revolution, disdainful *vaqueros* traveling with their party, the danger to her reputation because she'd tried to learn to shoot a gun . . . what next?

And over all of this—even if her family ever reached the mouth of the Colorado, she would still be no closer to achieving her goal of freedom for her and Reva. The first step she'd attempted toward independence, learning to protect herself by acquiring a musket, had given her a taste of just what she'd face if she stepped too far from her reputation as a genteel maiden lady of good family. She rubbed her forehead.

Unbidden, her mind brought up the day she and Reva had stood overlooking the marshland at Belle Vista and the snowy egret had taken flight. She'd felt so certain at that moment that God wanted her to step out in faith. Had she just been carried away in a stressful moment?

Jewell appeared suddenly and approached Dorritt with the expression that signaled Jewell was going to see if she could slice off a few ounces Dorritt's flesh. Just for the fun of it. Dorritt had been avoiding her. Now she braced herself.

"So I see you have made a conquest of our half-breed guide," Jewell said, firing the opening shot.

Dorritt behaved as if she hadn't heard her sister.

"I wonder what the people in Stephen Austin's party will think of a woman with your tarnished reputation. Or perhaps a *woman's* honor doesn't matter so much on the frontier."

Dorritt turned away.

"What were you thinking about to be firing a musket? My father has decided once and for all, your wild ways must be curbed."

Dorritt faced Jewell.

Jewell nodded with a false look of sympathy. "He's going to marry you off to the first eligible male at the Austin settlement. White women, American women, will be in short supply, so someone, as long in the tooth as you, Dorritt, will be able to find a husband. Maybe a widower with children to raise."

Dorritt didn't let the inner riot these words caused show. "If I'd wanted to marry, I'd have married in New Orleans."

"In New Orleans, you were given a choice. At the Brazos, you won't." Jewell flounced off, chuckling.

Dorritt's will became as stiff as wrought iron and she murmured, "I wonder, dear sister, how you will like having to manage everything when I leave." As each day passed, Dorritt realized she would have to have more than desire to be free of her family. She needed to come up with a plan that would work.

* * *

So they would travel with the angloamericanos *to the Brazos, not so far from home. As the plump Anglo who'd hired them rode away, he made a joke about the foolish man, causing his cousin to chuckle, the cousin he'd hated since childhood. The chuckle sparked the flames of his own* resentimiento. *Behind his own broad smile, he writhed. If he had been his cousin's heir, he would have already made him meet with death years ago. Yet how many more years could he take his cousin's superior ways? He must find a way to seek revenge. He would wait upon events. He was like the cat that always landed on his feet. He would show his cousin who the smarter man was. But even sweeter would be to destroy his cousin's* reputación, *his good name. And make him live in shame. If only he could find a way.*

Eight

Just before dawn the next morning, the day they would set out on the Camino Real, the King's Highway and the last leg of their journey, Dorritt sneaked out of the inn and hurried to the church in the cool gray light. She didn't know when she would see another church of Christ. God was always with her, but throughout her life, church had been a true sanctuary to her. And she needed to feel that this morning. She could no longer turn to Mr. Quinn, and she felt totally alone, completely unprepared for what might lie ahead, might lie in wait.

Once she left Nacogdoches, there would be little chance of turning back. In the back of her mind, she had cherished the fallback plan that she would travel to the Colorado River and get her family settled there. And then she with Reva would return to New Orleans and perhaps she could become a governess. She saw now that was not possible. Too much danger, too many miles. And at every turn she saw her stepfather forcing them—ill prepared—down a dangerous path. Today, God felt a long ways away from Nacogdoches, Texas.

The mission church was quiet and deserted, cool and dim. With a shawl over her head, she sank to her knees. And then at a loss for words, she let her soul cry out to God. Finally, she calmed enough to open her Common Book of Prayer and begin reading. Then she heard the creak of the old wood doors and the slow slide of leather sandals on the stone floor and looked up. The older woman, who had stared at her over the past few days, was limping up the aisle toward her.

"*Señora, buenos días.*" Dorritt stood and curtsied to the woman so much her elder.

"I've prayed you would come this morning, *mi hija*, my child. There is much that I have wanted to say to you."

Dorritt stared in shock. How did this woman who looked like an uneducated Mexican speak English, beautiful English?

"*Ah*, I have surprised you." The older woman chuckled and wagged a finger. "I am Maria, just Maria. But when I was a young *señorita*, I lived in Mexico City." The woman, lowered herself bit by bit to the pew beside Dorritt.

Maria sighed and smiled. "And my lady, my sweet mistress, was an Englishwoman who had married a Spaniard. Because both their families were not happy with their marriage, they had left Spain. When they set up their house in Mexico City, I was very young. When I saw you in the plaza, you took me back to her. She was fair like you. And my lady taught me to speak English. She didn't have anybody else to speak English with, you see?"

Dorritt had wondered why this woman had been interested in her. Now she knew. With a smile, she said, "I am Dorritt. What may I do for you, ma'am?"

"*Nada.*" Then Maria pointed from herself to Dorritt. "I come to give *you* something."

"What?" Dorritt peered into the woman's pleasantly wrinkled face.

"Courage. You are going into the wilderness." She waved her hand as though directing Dorritt onward. "*Valor* is what you will need there, and that is what I bring."

Dorritt doubted Maria's ability to give her courage. But the fact that this stranger understood she was afraid and of what overwhelmed her. Tears rushed into Dorritt's eyes. "How can you give me courage, *señora?*" *It's not possible.*

"By telling you God is still with you." Maria made the sign of the cross. Then she pushed back Dorritt's shawl and stroked her hair, the woman's rough skin catching the fine strands. "You are going where He wants you to go, *mi hija.*"

Dorritt wanted to believe this, couldn't believe this. "How do you know that?" she asked, fearing what the woman might say.

"I have been watching you—" Maria said, and grinned, lifting all the deeply etched lines of her face. "—listening to you. You have seen me—I know. And I have heard others speak of you. Your *negroes.* When a lady's servants speak well of her, that tells me everything I need to know about her. And that sister of yours, the one with the black hair—what they say, she is a spoiled child and has a nasty temper."

Dorritt nodded. Why try to deny it? "She hates me." The words were out before Dorritt knew it. She pressed her hand to her mouth.

"You did not need to tell me that." Maria nodded twice, whispering "*Sí, sí.* Your sister knows you are a better woman, a finer lady than she is, that you have worth she does not. You earn the respect of those who know you. She is pretty and is flattered by those who know her. But no one respects her. And that digs deep into her heart."

That all made sense. "I never thought she envied me. She's always gotten everything she's wanted."

"And those people are always the most unhappy and the most envious of what they can't get. I have lived nearly ninety years, *señorita*. I have seen much and pondered what I have seen. Perhaps some would call me wise. But I only watch and think." Maria tapped her temple with one finger and grinned.

Dorritt wanted to believe this woman had wisdom, some advice to help her on her way. "Do you have any comfort for me, *señora*?" *Please, Father.*

"I do not know if it will comfort you, but the hand of God is upon you." Maria nodded several times. "I see your love for the Father because you show His love to others."

Tears clogging her throat, Dorritt caught Maria's gnarled hand. "I'm frightened, *señora*. Not only of the journey—" She gave a tight smile and cleared her throat to go on. "—though that does concern me. But also I'm very worried about my life in the Austin settlement. We are strangers, so I can speak to you candidly." Dorritt took a deep breath. "My stepfather is a liar and a cheat."

"I have watched *him* too. A weak man, a boy who was never weaned. He is still throwing *rabietas*, tantrums. His mother should have taken the switch to him." Maria grinned again and then sobered. "He will only cause trouble for those around him. The boy Amos has become his whipping boy. Your slaves fear he will suffer a beating, but can do nothing."

"Yes, all that is true. I can turn to my stepfather for neither support nor courage." *And I need both.*

"I think God has provided support and courage for you. He has sent you that man they call Quinn. And his friend Ash. They are known not only in Nacogdoches. Both are men of *valor*."

Dorritt looked away. "I think you speak the truth." Even though these were matters never spoken out loud, she continued in a lowered voice, "But I'm not supposed to seek help from a man who is half Cherokee and one who is part Negro."

Sudden resentment flashed through her, hot then cold. Her heart pounded. "Because my stepfather's skin is white, society values him more than two men of honor. Why is that? Why do I see what no one else does?"

Maria rocked a little on the old worn pew. "Some see it, others ignore it. You see, *mi hija*, you see people with the eyes of God." The older woman motioned toward Dorritt's eyes again. "God sees through the clothing and the skin to the heart."

These words made Dorritt swallow back more tears. *The eyes of God?* It sounded too grand for her, almost sacrilegious. "How? Why do I see . . . through the eyes of God?"

"It is a gift." Maria said, beaming as if pronouncing a blessing.

Dorritt gave a half chuckle, a half sob. *A gift?* "It does not feel like a gift. I would not want to change it, *señora*. But I see our slaves' pain, their terrible burden of being looked down on, of being classed with the animals. It makes me different. I'm always out of step with everyone around me."

Maria objected, "You are not out of step with those two men, Quinn and Ash."

In her lap, Dorritt creased the edge of her shawl between her fingers, looking down, ready to go on. "*Señora*, there is a price to pay if one steps out of the bounds of society. The other day when I was trying to shoot the musket, you heard those men calling me names." Dorritt looked up. "I do not want to pay the price, to face scorn again. Or to make Quinn or Ash pay a price for my straying."

The old woman took her hand in both of hers. The woman's rough calluses rasped Dorritt's hand. This was a woman who had labored much in her life. "I will pray for you. And ask God to bless your way. There is no church until you reach San Antonio de Bexar and the reports I hear of the priest there . . ." Her voice trailed off and she shook her head. "Not everyone in a robe or a collar serves God. Some serve themselves."

Dorritt nodded. "I know. I'm afraid that every church has its hypocrites. God is more patient—"

"Than we are," Maria finished for her with a smile.

The old church door creaked behind them. And Reva stepped inside. "Miss Dorritt, the family is stirring."

Dorritt rose quickly. "*Señora*, I must wish you farewell."

The woman made the sign of the cross in front of her and, tugging Dorritt closer, kissed both her cheeks. "*Vaya con Dios, mi hija.*"

"Thank you, *señora. Gracias.*" Dorritt hurried out of the church.

Back to the inn with Reva at her side, they clasped hands and then parted. Before Dorritt was able to reenter the inn, her stepfather burst through the door. "Where have you been? Are you just coming back?" He shook her by both arms. "Did you have a rendezvous with that half-breed?"

"You're hurting my arms." Dorritt pulled against his grip. "And no, I have not had an assignation. I went to pray in the church for our journey."

"We're not Roman Catholic."

"Say that a little louder, Mr. Kilbride." She shook free of him, her breath coming shallow and quick. "This is not America with freedom of religion. You are the one who decided we would move to Spanish Texas. So I merely went to the church available to me where you have taken us." She lifted her chin. "Now I must go eat breakfast and prepare for our departure." She walked away, resolute. But his simmering resentment followed her like a bad odor. And then he bellowed for Amos. *Father, protect poor Amos.*

* * *

A few days later, the Kilbride party had left behind the piney woods and entered the rolling prairie of coarse bluestem and buffalo bunchgrasses. There were fields of purple-berried pokeweed and wild petunias in pink, white, and red, with scattered groves of post oak and pecan trees. Bobwhites scurried through the grass, calling out their own name. Leading one of his mustangs with a rope, Quinn rode at the end of the caravan, where the cattle herd ambled along. The cattle grazing, they were slowing the wagon train down.

Quinn felt pulled in opposite directions, like a man tied by the wrists to two different horses. The strain dragged at him, tugging him in two.

On one hand, this slow progress put Quinn on edge. He wanted to be far south, away from this caravan, from Kilbride and his spoiled younger daughter. After he sold most of his cattle and mustangs, Quinn would look to hire on with a boss who would let him raise thoroughbreds on the side. Or perhaps he'd buy a small plot of land, just enough to have a *jacale* for him and Ash and a barn and corral for the horses. He didn't kid himself—that was all he was capable of handling. All he wanted from life was a home and raising horses, fine horses. And he was weary of wandering.

But in another way, he really didn't want this journey to end. Their slow pace gave him more days near Dorritt. Watching her from a distance was like gazing at the stars in the night sky—so beautiful but so beyond his reach. He still carried her musket in his gear and wondered if she would want him to give it to her or take it with him. He hadn't forgotten the name-calling from the four *vaqueros*. Within weeks, they would be near the mouth of the Colorado and he would leave her. When he thought of never seeing her again, an emptiness opened inside him. It threatened to drag him under like the swollen Sabine River had.

Ash rode up beside him. "Look ahead."

Quinn did as he was told and saw a party of Indians in the distance. *Great.* Handing the end of his mustang's rope to Ash, Quinn spurred his horse forward, galloping to the head of the party. As he passed Kilbride, he pointed to the Indian party and waved to him. Quinn lifted his long rifle out of its saddle casing. He saw they were outnumbered, but he had to be ready. At the head of the party, he slowed, still trying to identify if they were a threat or not. Which tribe was it?

Kilbride drew up beside him. "Indians? Shouldn't we take cover?" The man pulled a pistol from his belt.

"Wait." Quinn grabbed Kilbride's hand with the gun in it. The man was foolish enough to try a shot this far out of range. And where could they take cover in this prairie? Quinn narrowed his eyes against the sunlight, peering into the distance. The Indians were ignoring them and even at this range, he thought he glimpsed the paint on their faces. *Comanches*, he thought, but not wearing war paint. "They see us. But I don't think they're going to bother us."

"Why?" Kilbride barked, his voice rough with nerves.

"It's not a war party. They have their women and children with them. They're just moving farther south for the winter." Quinn released Kilbride's hand.

"So they won't bother us?" Kilbride asked, sounding both relieved and uncertain.

"I don't think they will, but they still might sneak back in the night and try to steal our horses."

"What about the cattle?"

"Indians don't like beef. They prefer buffalo," Quinn said.

"I can't afford to lose my horses. We'll have to post guards, then."

Quinn nodded. Then he started back along the caravan to the rear, where the cattle still moseyed. As he passed Dorritt, who as usual was walking with her maid and carrying a small black child, she looked up. "Should we be concerned?"

He halted, keeping his face stiff. "No, it's not a war party." She nodded and walked on.

Quinn couldn't stop himself. He watched her walk away.

Then there was a squawk from Kilbride's younger daughter. Quinn looked back and tried to hide his smile. The tough
yet battered gig had finally broken its last wheel. Miss Kilbride
would now be walking too.

* * *

Long after sunset, with only a sliver of a moon and the stars
for light, the night draped around them, black and treacherous.
Quinn walked his horse from the head of a caravan to its end.
This nearly moonless night was a perfect one for a few young
Comanche braves, itching to prove their manhood, to slip into
camp and steal horses.

As Quinn walked to the rear, he paused to buck up the Negro
men who had been set on watch near the wagons. Since they
were unarmed, he couldn't let them guard the horses. It could
cost them their lives. He hadn't even bothered to point this out
to Kilbride, just told him he wouldn't need the help of his slaves
to guard the stock.

"You think the Indians will really come, sir?" Amos asked, the
bruises on his swollen face plain in the faint light. Kilbride had
slapped and punched the boy for spilling water yesterday.

Quinn touched the boy's shoulder. "Don't worry. Comanche
want horses, not prisoners."

Amos nodded. "Yes, sir."

After squeezing the boy's shoulder, Quinn walked farther
down the wagon train. One of the *vaqueros* was walking on the
other far side of the wagons from Quinn. Why was he there?
Quinn paused and thought about stopping him to ask why the
Mexican wasn't with the cattle, where he belonged. But the man
was probably just stretching his legs. When Quinn had almost
reached the end of the caravan to talk to Ash and the *vaqueros*,
he heard Dorritt's voice in the dark. He could go no farther.

Dorritt and her maid must be standing in the midst of the
small grove of oak trees nearby. Curiosity drew him within lis-

tening distance. He shouldn't of course, but he had kept himself apart from her for days. And he just wanted to hear her low voice again, feel its richness flow through him, fill him like it always did.

"Reva, I've been trying to come up with a plan for us. I don't know how much longer I can bear living with my stepfather."

"That might not be long," Reva said, "if he plan to marry you off to the first man who want you in the Austin settlement."

Quinn's neck muscles tightened at this news. One of the cattle lowed in the darkness. A warning? Was someone slipping closer in the night? He slid his long rifle into his hands and cast around, listening, watching.

"That's only what Jewell said. I have no doubt my stepfather would like to rid himself of me. But it's only talk. He won't force me to marry someone against my will. It would cause a fresh scandal. And after losing everything in New Orleans, he wants to be landed again. Important again."

"I see that," Reva replied. "But you know if you don't do what he say, he'll threaten to sell me. Or worse, make me marry somebody I don't want to marry. And I can't refuse like you can."

"I still think I might be able to buy your freedom or pressure Mr. Kilbride to give you to me."

"How can you do that?"

Intrigued, Quinn stroked his horse's neck to keep him quiet and listened for Dorritt's reply. Still, he had the feeling he was not the only one listening to this conversation. The back of his neck prickling, through the blackness he tried to catch a glimpse of who also must be nearby listening. *No luck*. Maybe it was just because he was alert for a possible raid?

Dorritt continued, "I still have my education, my place in society. I can teach school and not endanger that reputation. I will be thought of as odd to prefer spinsterhood to marriage. But I can just make it seem as if I left my shattered heart with some forbidden man in New Orleans. People will fall for any kind of tragic romantic story. I don't even have to lie. The gossips will write and embroider the tale themselves."

Reva chuckled.

Quinn smiled. Dorritt was nobody's fool.

"If I teach school, I could take you with me to keep house. We wouldn't need much. Just a cabin, which could double as a school and our home. We could plant a garden, keep chickens and a cow, and accept food and wood for payment."

"It sound like it should work. But I just don't know how. What worry me most now is how your stepfather's been treating . . . Amos . . . I mean the boy tries to keep his distance, but Mr. Kilbride . . ."

Quinn nudged his horse and turned him away. He'd been worried about Dorritt's future, but now he needed to get down to business, make sure no Comanche would get one of the mustangs. Or more importantly his foal. He soon found Ash, with the other two Mexican *vaqueros*, Pedro and Juan, waiting for him. "Where are Carlos and Eduardo?"

"*Aquí.* Here." Carlos sauntered out of the darkness, fastening his buttons. And Eduardo at his side stepped into the firelight and nodded.

Quinn said, "I'm putting each of you to watch Kilbride's horses."

"*Sí,*" Carlos agreed.

Quinn still didn't have a good feeling about this man, but maybe that was because many times he'd seen Carlos watching Dorritt. Still something felt wrong about these four. He'd noted Juan and Pedro took orders from both Carlos and Eduardo. But there was still something off about the entire group. He shook off these thoughts and told each Mexican which horses to protect. Since Quinn would patrol up and down, he asked Ash to watch over his foal. He wanted nothing to happen to his little horse. In private, he had named her *Señorita*. "Any questions?" Quinn asked.

"Are we to kill the thieves?" Carlos was loading his musket.

"No, I don't want to kill anyone. They'll just want the horses. I don't want to turn a few young braves into enemies who might follow us, harass us all the way to the Colorado River."

"Then how are we to stop them?" Eduardo asked. "*They* may want to kill us."

"Use your good sense," Ash said, "if you have any. Move."

Eduardo looked annoyed, but the others moved away, disappearing into the blackness. Quinn nodded to Ash and then moved to a position where he could keep an eye on everyone. He remained in the dark shadows beside his horse, ready to mount and ride in any direction at any moment.

Before long, the people around the wagons settled down for the night; even the crying babies fell asleep. Soon the night sounds filled Quinn's ears. Coyotes howled and yipped and an owl hooted. In his mind, he could picture where each *vaquero* and Ash were. Each *vaquero* was guarding his own horse and a couple of mustangs while Ash guarded the Kilbride horses and Quinn's foal. So Quinn waited, standing beside his horse in the darkness, waiting for anyone to draw near.

Quinn almost missed their approach. An owl had swooped overhead and masked the first whisper of the sound of their moccasins. Quinn strained, but each footfall was almost soundless. If Quinn hadn't encountered Comanches before, he might have missed it. They were the best riders, trackers, and horse thieves.

Quinn heard Ash shout out, "Here!"

Quinn was on his horse and racing toward Ash. The longhorns woke and bellowed. Almost blind in the black night, he swung down from his horse. He landed and pitched headlong into a Comanche brave. The impact of their two heads meeting nearly knocked them both unconscious. But after a dazed moment, Quinn swung a blow where he thought the man's face was. His fist connected with the side of the man's jaw with a satisfying crack. Before he could get in another punch, he heard some shouting, cursing, and gunshots—and it was over. The Comanche melted into the darkness.

Quinn stood, panting. "Ash?" he whispered.

"I'm all right."

Quinn fell silent, listening. The sound of someone very close in the dark triggered Quinn. He shoved his reins into Ash's hand and he dashed forward. Ahead, someone struck a match and a lantern flickered to light, revealing Kilbride. In that moment, Quinn observed one of the Mexicans, running from far ahead, where he should not have been. "Douse that light!" Quinn called out.

"Did the Indians come—" A gunshot silenced Kilbride's voice. The lantern glass shattered. Kilbride yelped. Quinn halted, barely breathing. Would the Comanche make another attempt? Seconds, minutes passed. Quinn finally let himself breathe in deeply. He loped forward to where the lantern had been lit. "Kilbride," he hissed, "were you hurt?"

"No. Did they get any of the horses?"

"I'll check." Quinn went down the line and checked with each of the Mexicans and then again with Ash. They had lost one of Kilbride's mustangs. That was almost as good as it could be. The Comanche would be happy because they had scored one horse. Quinn could be pleased because they probably wouldn't try again. They were smart enough to know they had been lucky to get away with one horse. But as Quinn jogged to report to Kilbride, he began to wonder why one of the *vaqueros* had been away from his post.

* * *

After a sleepless night, Quinn was half dozing as the camp came awake for another morning. Though he didn't open his eyes, he was aware of the sound of voices and the scrape of spoons and the bubbling of coffee and its sharp fragrance on the cool morning air.

A woman began shouting.

He was on his feet with his pistol drawn hurrying toward the commotion. The *vaqueros* and Ash sprang onto their horses to control the startled cattle. Over the bawling of the cattle, the angry voice came again. It was Miss Jewell. An instant crowd gathered around the woman who was glaring and speaking in spiteful tones.

"What's the matter?" Quinn arrrived, still gripping his pistol.

"My silver brush has been stolen."

Quinn stared at her in disbelief. "You're shouting because your brush is gone? Don't you know better than to make loud noises around a herd of cattle?"

Ignoring this, Miss Jewell marched up to him. "It is a sterling silver brush. Someone has taken it."

"Are you sure you haven't just misplaced it, dear?" her mother asked. "You often misplace—"

The young lady turned on her mother. "I know just where it was put last night. My maid returned it with my hairpins and silver comb and silver mirror to my private chest. Everything was stowed away last night. I watched her do it."

"Where was the chest kept?" Quinn asked, wondering who might be responsible. He'd seen all four of the *vaqueros* in and around the wagons. Perhaps this was tied to the *vaquero* running away last night. Was one of the *vaqueros* a thief? Or could a slave be trying to pay Miss Jewell back for some mistreatment?

Miss Jewell folded her arms. "I've kept it in the gig. But when we had to leave that behind, I stowed it in the wagon where I sleep at night."

"Show me," Quinn said, moving forward.

"I told you. It's not there." The lady sounded ready to spit hot coals.

"I believe you. But from looking where it was, perhaps I can figure out who would have the chance to take it."

The girl made a sound of disdain, but gestured toward the wagon. "The chest is there, open, right beside the spot where it was stowed underneath a shelf."

Quinn hoisted himself up into the large covered wagon, and there was the chest, sitting just where she said. "It is near the back of the wagon. Someone could have reached in and gotten it while you slept." And many of the slaves had been up watching for a different kind of thief. Quinn glanced around. Had anyone seen anything?

Dorritt spoke up, "Who would take it?"

Quinn got down from the wagon, keeping his distance from Dorritt.

"I'll bet Reva did it," Jewell accused with an outstretched arm and pointed finger.

"Reva?" Dorritt objected, "Why would Reva steal your silver brush?"

"You're jealous of me," Jewell said. "You probably told your maid to steal my silver brush because you don't have one."

Quinn folded his arms and took a step closer to Dorritt.

"Girls, girls," their mother cautioned them, "let's remember we're ladies."

Kilbride was marching toward them, red-faced as usual. Neither sister paid their mother any attention. Dorritt stepped closer to her sister. "I'm tired of your spiteful behavior, Jewell. You probably did this just to stir up trouble—"

"Enough!" Mr. Kilbride ordered. "If someone has stolen my daughter's silver hairbrush, it will be found and they will be punished. Now you people get back to your work! We need to get moving. Jewell, you look for that blasted brush later! Get dressed and ready to move. We need to get on the road."

For once, Quinn agreed with Kilbride.

Then a slave, hat in hand, approached Mr. Kilbride. "Sir?"

"Yes," Mr. Kilbride snapped, "what is it?"

Cringing, the man looked down. "I think Amos gone missin', sir. It was so dark last night none of us saw him go. Then he didn't come to breakfast. We can't find him nowheres."

Quinn thought Kilbride might have a stroke. Kilbride turned on Dorritt and cursed her. "This is all your fault—coddling these Negroes. Now we know who stole that brush."

Dorritt opened and closed her mouth.

Quinn fought the itch to grab the man by the collar and make him apologize. He tried to swallow down his anger. *I can't do anything. I'd only do her more harm than good.*

Ash spoke up, "Amos might not have run away. He might have been taken by the Comanche. They didn't get all the horses they wanted, but they might have got the boy."

Quinn frowned. "Could be."

Kilbride looked confused like a young boy playing a game he couldn't get the hang of. "Really?"

Quinn nodded. A pall fell over them all.

"Should someone go looking for him?" Dorritt asked.

"No, miss," Ash replied. "It's not wise to venture out alone when Comanches are nearby. Even other tribes try to steer clear of them."

After an unhappy pause, Quinn said, "We better get ready to start out."

"Wait!" Kilbride said. "I think whoever let my mustang be stolen last night will have to repay me for that loss."

Quinn glanced at the man. "No." Kilbride started to bluster and Quinn cut him off, "No, if we five hadn't been on guard, you would have lost every one of your horses and maybe more—"

"Maybe your life," Carlos added.

Quinn turned away. And the others followed him back to their fire and breakfast.

"Fool," Carlos muttered.

"You got that right," Ash muttered in return. "How long will a fool like him last on the frontier?"

Not long. And that was exactly what Quinn feared most. After they reached the Austin settlement, Dorritt would be under Kilbride's protection, which meant no protection at all.

Nine

After the caravan started for the day, Dorritt walked beside Reva near the second ox wagon. In the distance near a clump of oaks, white tail deer scattered, racing away. "Reva, do you have any idea what happened to Amos?"

"No, but I hope he just run off. If those Indians got him . . . Amos never lived out in the wild. I'm scared for him."

Dorritt shook her head. *Dear Father, protect Amos.* She had a pretty good idea why Amos had run off—if he had. Her stepfather had been working himself up to whip someone. And it had been clear to her and the other slaves Mr. Kilbride had chosen Amos as his next victim. So Amos had taken the only action open to him.

Since the gig was beyond repair, a scowling Jewell was now riding with their mother beside the driver of the second ox wagon. Dorritt wondered if Jewell's silver brush had really been stolen or just misplaced. Or more worrying, had Jewell hidden her silver brush for some devious reason? How could one morning bring so much to think about?

"Why you think she pointed her finger at me?" Reva asked.

To continue her campaign to hurt me through threatening you. Could Jewell be that mean? Was taking Reva from her the only way Jewell could think to hurt Dorritt? "I'm not sure," Dorritt hedged. "Jewell never makes much sense to my way of thinking."

"That because you're not spiteful. That girl always get everything she want. And she is never happy."

Dorritt drew in a deep sigh. "Well, she didn't get to stay in New Orleans. I think I'm just tired of all my family. I know that's terrible to say—"

"This child is tired of them too." Reva whispered into Dorritt's ear, "You being a schoolteacher is starting to sound like a good idea."

Dorritt nodded. Then in response to another slave's summons, Reva hurried to help the woman with her baby. Dorritt walked on alone. Even though she faced forward, Dorritt was ever aware of Quinn nearby, herding his cattle and mustangs. She wanted to turn back, walk beside him and talk with him. Her traitorous gaze defied her and she glanced over her shoulder. Their eyes connected. *He is watching me too.* Just this thought sent a thrill through her.

She couldn't stop herself, she looked back again. She couldn't see Quinn. One of the *vaqueros* rode up between them, leaving his companions to work the cattle. He drew closer to her and lifted off his wide-brimmed hat. "*Buenos días, señorita*, I am Carlos."

His speaking to her startled her so, she couldn't reply at first. Then she remembered this *vaquero* Carlos hadn't taunted her. Still, her face grew warm. She nodded and began to walk away.

He dismounted and fell in beside her. "I apologize for my friends' words the first time we saw you. They did not understand why you wanted to learn to fire a musket."

She frowned up at him, wary, fearing he might intend to insult her. "Do you understand now?"

"I understand, *Señorita* Dorritt; you merely wished to be prepared for whatever may come."

Was he sincere? "Apology accepted." She nodded.

"But, *señorita*, you have many to protect you. There are Quinn and Ash. And now there is Carlos. And Eduardo, Pedro, and Juan."

Why was he saying this? As he walked beside her, she studied the man's face. He was handsome and with an aquiline nose from his Spanish blood, high cheekbones from his Indian blood and dark brown—almost black—eyes. He looked to be around the same age as Quinn and was just a few inches taller than she. He was watching for her reaction to him, something she never liked in a person. She nodded again and then began walking faster. Spooked, a flock of prairie chickens squawked and dashed away through the tall grass.

"*Adiós, señorita.*" Carlos put his hat on, mounted his horse, and rode back toward the cattle. What had that been all about? She forced herself to look forward again. Why had he singled her out? She quickened her pace. Was this *vaquero* Carlos an enemy or a friend? *Maybe I've just become suspicious.* But there had been something in Carlos's eyes, more than apology. She had seen his unexpected interest in her as a woman.

* * *

That evening after they had made camp and were eating supper near one of the wagons, Jewell recommenced her campaign against Reva. After walking and worrying all day, Dorritt had little energy left for another battle. She massaged her temples and then took another sip of the hot bitter coffee.

"I know it was Dorritt's maid who took my brush. She's mad at me because I said Reva wasn't doing enough work."

"Let it go, Jewell," Dorritt said, sighing. "Reva does not steal."

"What do you know about it?" her stepfather snapped. "I'm going to get to the bottom of this." He stood up and roared, "Reva! Come here this instant!"

Before she could figure out what was happening chaos exploded around them. The cattle bellowed and began to stampede. As the cattle charged, a few slaves yelled and bolted. The *vaqueros* leaped to their horses. They headed off the cattle, turning them away from the party. Dorritt grabbed her mother, threw her up against the nearby wagon, and pressed her body over hers to protect her. Dorritt stood there panting, unable to move. Then she realized her mother had fainted. Just in time, Dorritt thrust her arms under her mother's and lowered her to the ground so she didn't fall. "Jewell, get mother's vinaigrette with her smelling salts."

Reva hurried up to Dorritt. "Miss Dorritt, what's wrong with your mama?"

Dorritt began to ask Reva for her mother's smelling salts, but her voice was drowned out by the hoofbeats. Quinn galloped up beside them. Looking over her shoulder, she saw Quinn's expression taut with anger. He leaped down from his saddle and put his face in front of Mr. Kilbride's. "When will you people learn? There must be no loud sudden noises around a herd of cattle."

Mr. Kilbride sputtered.

Dorritt raised her voice. "Please, someone get mother's vinaigrette. She's fainted."

Her stepfather shoved past Quinn, ignoring him. "Why aren't you doing what your mistress says?" he demanded of Reva. And he punctuated the question with a slap across Reva's face.

"Don't strike my maid," Dorritt said.

"She's my property and I'll do what I wish with her. She is as useless as you are." Kilbride slapped Reva again.

Outraged words scalded Dorritt's throat, but she had to hold them in. For Reva's sake. If Mr. Kilbride stated out loud he was going to sell Reva, he would never back down. Her heart thumping, she said mildly, "Will someone please get me mother's vinaigrette?" Reva hurried away, her hand pressed against her cheek.

"Did you hear what I said, Kilbride?" Quinn demanded, just behind him.

"You are impertinent." Mr. Kilbride didn't look his way.

"And you are stubborn. No one is to shout, scream, or shoot a firearm when we have cattle to herd. Someone could get hurt. Bad."

Reva returned with the cut-glass vinaigrette in her hand. Dorritt took it from her, lifted its stopper, and waved the small vial under her mother's nose.

Mr. Kilbride drew close and bent on one knee. "Elspeth, are you all right?"

Her mother's eyes fluttered open. "Oh, what happened?"

Mr. Kilbride took her hand in his. "The cattle began to stampede. You fainted."

Her mother clutched Mr. Kilbride's hand. "The loud noise . . . I'm afraid you must learn to speak more softly, Harley." She gazed up at Quinn. "Was anyone hurt?"

Dorritt stayed on her knees, dumbfounded. Her mother had actually said something that proved she was aware of what was going on around her and had scolded her husband. Dorritt and Reva exchanged shocked looks over her stepfather's bent back.

"You mustn't worry your sweet little head over this," Mr. Kilbride said, stroking her mother's hand.

Her mother looked to Dorritt. "Dear, I feel so weak. Would you brew me some tisane tea?"

"Of course, mother. Right away." Dorritt rose and with Reva at her side hurried to where the medicinal herbs were stored inside one of the wagons. She opened the box and lifted out a cloth bag of leaves, aware that the *vaquero* Eduardo had come and was watching her.

"What you think's going on here?" Reva whispered.

"I have no idea." Dorritt hurried away. What had caused her mother to faint? And what had caused her stepfather to show such thoughtfulness?

Watching Dorritt hurry away, Quinn swallowed down his bile and climbed back on his horse. When he reached the end of the caravan, Carlos rode up to him.

"How is the *señora*?" Carlos asked.

Quinn didn't welcome this question. "Mrs. Kilbride just fainted. Miss Dorritt is tending to her." It had not escaped Quinn's notice that Carlos had spoken to Dorritt that morning. Showed his interest in her. "Shouldn't you get back to herding?" The Mexican had the nerve to give him a knowing grin, showing that Quinn's interest in Dorritt hadn't gone unnoticed by Carlos either.

Quinn gripped his saddle horn and wished it were the man's neck. *What did you say to her? And what business is it of mine, anyway?* Quinn was too honest not to recognize his own jealousy. But Carlos had as little chance with Dorritt as he did. So why didn't that make him feel better?

* * *

The next morning was sunny as usual. Quinn sat beside Ash, holding a cup of coffee and staring at the small fire. The Mexicans were tending to their horses, getting ready for the day. It was just about time for Quinn to give the signal they should start. But he had been looking ahead, watching for Dorritt to signal, as was her custom, everything with the wagons was ready to go.

"That Reva is a mighty pretty girl," Ash muttered.

Startled, Quinn looked to his friend's eyes. "I hadn't thought . . ."

"I'm glad to hear that." Ash grinned and took another swallow of coffee. "Besides, you only have eyes for Miss Dorritt."

Quinn's ears burned. If it had been anybody but Ash, Quinn would have denied it. "Miss Dorritt is a lady. I'm just a half-breed scout."

"That's stupid talk." Ash sounded disgruntled. "Your pa wouldn't like you talking like that. He always had pride in himself."

"My pa never mixed with ladies and gentlemen. I don't think less of myself, but I don't want others thinking less of her."

Ash drained his mug. "There is that. But things are changing. She isn't going to be living in the U.S. I remember when he was getting up his expedition Zeb Pike said to me, 'The frontier is the great equalizer.' He said that when some white gentlemen tried to talk him into firing me. Pike was right. On the frontier, it doesn't matter who you were born to be. It matters what you know and can do. You can do a lot."

"Maybe." Quinn noted Dorritt was standing beside one of the Conestoga wagons and looking back at him intently, her signal the caravan was ready to move whenever he decided. He liked the way they worked together. He rose. "Time to get moving."

Ash got up also, smothered fire with dust and poured out the dregs of coffee from his cup on it too. Then he stowed his mug and climbed into the saddle. Quinn signaled the *vaqueros* and wagon drivers and then rode to the head of the train. Quinn tried not to think about Dorritt and her plans to become a schoolmarm in the Austin settlement. He tried not to watch her as she walked beside her mother, who was sitting on the second wagon. He tried not to notice Carlos riding close enough to watch her. The caravan bumped along over the coarse grass of the prairie. Mile after mile.

With a jerk, Quinn realized the wagon with Dorritt's mother on it had suddenly stopped. And there was a commotion of women around it. He rode toward the wagon. When he arrived, he dismounted a way off.

"We have to stop," Dorritt called to him. "My mother is indisposed. Mr. Kilbride!" She waved toward her stepfather.

Quinn wanted to ask her what exactly *indisposed* meant, but merely nodded. Kilbride hustled up and then he called for help. One of the Negroes helped him carry his wife to the back of the wagon, and soon she was inside it, lying down in the narrow wagon bed.

Quinn waited. Everyone waited. Finally Quinn ambled over to the wagon and motioned Reva to come to him. When the girl stood next to him, he leaned over and asked, "What is wrong with Mrs. Kilbride?"

Reva pursed her lips and then said, "She's bleeding. Not a normal woman's flow."

He nodded his thanks and then drew apart. He knew little about such things. He would wait until Dorritt came to tell him what was happening and what needed to be done.

Inside the covered wagon, as Dorritt knelt beside her mother, she held her hand. Only moments earlier, her mother had announced she was expecting. One of the slaves, a midwife, had been summoned. But the only help the midwife had to offer was to prop her mother's feet up higher than her body. After the midwife left, Dorritt tried to absorb the fact that her mother might be pregnant and might be miscarrying. Both were shocking and unexpected ideas.

"It's not unusual," her mother said, "for a woman my age to have a change of life baby. I'm only forty-one you know. I know that sounds old to you, but it isn't too old to have a baby."

Dorritt squeezed her mother's hand. She didn't ask why her mother hadn't told her this earlier in their trip. Gentlewomen usually did not speak about pregnancy. And what could Dorritt have said? She couldn't figure out how she felt about this news. As she glanced down at her mother's skirt, the widening crimson stain was sickening—frightening.

Father, what do I do? Please I don't want to lose her. The possibility of her mother dying made her light-headed. She bent over her mother's hand, gripping it tighter.

"Don't worry, Dorritt," her mother mumbled, "I'm not going to leave you. I'm going to have this child. And it's going to be the son your stepfather's always wanted. Your stepfather knows I really tried to give him a son. But only Jewell survived. I've always been a disappointment to everyone. I didn't give your father a son. If I had, maybe he wouldn't have gone and fought that foolish duel that killed him. My own father wanted me to have born a son. What good are girls he said to me and my sisters over and over. I've been cursed my whole life. It's all my fault that we had to leave New Orleans." Her mother moaned and twisted, panting. "If I'd given your stepfather a son, he'd have had an heir to leave the land to and he wouldn't have gambled so much. Please, God, let this be my son. Take away my shame."

Dorritt tried to follow her mother's heartbreaking ramblings. They sounded almost biblical, like the barren Rachel begging Jacob to give her a son or Sarah unable to bear Abraham a son until her old age. Each of those women had seen not bearing a son as a shame. Evidently not much had changed. Dorritt had never given a thought as to why her mother was always so vague and disconnected. Was she getting answers to some of the questions she'd never thought to ask? "Have you miscarried before?"

"Yes, you're old enough to know now—once before Jewell and twice after Jewell. Then I didn't get with child again." Her mother closed her eyes, panting as if in pain.

Dorritt suddenly felt like a frightened little girl. She wanted to plead, "Mama, don't give up. Don't close your eyes. Don't leave me." She breathed in her tears. *Father, spare my mother. Please. And if it could be, let this baby be born and let it be the son she wants so badly.*

"I want to see my mother." Jewell's voice came from outside, fretful and upset.

"What could you do for her?" Mr. Kilbride snapped, unseen. "The midwife has done what she can and your older sister is more able to take care of your mother than you are. And it's much more appropriate." Jewell tried to argue with him, but Mr. Kilbride with unusual brusqueness told her to go about her business.

Only one time before had Dorritt heard her stepfather speak harshly to Jewell like this. That day in the parlor when they had learned they were moving to Texas. When he'd accused Jewell of not bringing André to the point of proposing marriage soon enough. What had caused this change in Mr. Kilbride? Was it also the hope of a son? An heir?

"Miss Dorritt," Reva's voice came from the rear of the wagon, "I have some tisane tea for your mother."

Dorritt moved to take the cup from Reva. Then she carefully carried the cup and knelt down beside her mother again. "Here, mother, I'll help you sip this. It may be of assisantance." *It may not. But I don't have anything else to do.* Dorritt hated feeling helpless.

Ten

Much later, Dorritt sat opposite Reva at the rear of the covered wagon, each leaning back against the high sides. A delicate, cooling evening breeze brushed her face. It made her feel even more hot and sticky. She longed for a refreshing bath—in vain. Even if there had been a stream nearby, shock and worry had rendered her limp with exhaustion.

When the bleeding had finally stopped, the midwife had come, examined her mother, and said she had not miscarried. With this good news, they had helped her mother into clean clothing. Mr. Kilbride had come in and comforted her. And when he left, she had fallen asleep.

"Mr. Kilbride," Reva whispered, "sure can sweet talk when he wants to."

Dorritt was so tired she only nodded. But dull anger simmered inside her. Why had her stepfather—?

Reva interrupted, putting Dorritt's question into words, "If he knew Mrs. Kilbride was expecting, why did he start us on this journey?"

Dorritt merely shook her head.

"Everything hard enough without this," Reva said with finality. "Now, you lay down next to your mama before you fall out of this wagon sound asleep." Reva tugged Dorritt into the wagon and urged her to lie down in the narrow wagon bed. But would sleep come?

* * *

In the scant moonlight after long hours of waiting, Quinn watched Dorritt's maid climb out of the wagon. He stepped forward and she turned to him. He whispered, "How is Miss Dorritt? Her mother?"

"Both fine. Sleeping." She yawned. "Good night, sir."

Quinn nodded and moved back into the shadows. He knew he should go back nearer the cattle. But he found he couldn't leave. Then someone moved behind him. He listened and watched, thinking he recognized the man's gait and faint jingle of spurs. Was it Carlos? He whispered the man's name, but got no answer. And whoever it was moved away. So Quinn settled himself at the base of a nearby tree to keep watch over Dorritt.

Quinn had seen too clearly how tired, drained she was. He couldn't leave her unprotected in this weakened state. How could Kilbride just walk away from his ill wife and lie down to sleep? An owl hooted and Quinn squirmed against the rough bark of the tree trunk. It was going to be a long night.

* * *

Dorritt woke to the sound of her stepfather's cursing. His loud words pounded her temples like small hammers. She lay quite still, staring up at the arched unbleached muslin top overhead, praying for some strength, some energy. Another dawn. She heard Mr. Kilbride curse again and then the sound of a strong, stinging slap. She closed her eyes, praying for forbearance. She wanted nothing more than to get up, go outside, and slap her stepfather's face. Why must he always make a bad situation worse? Every day their provisions and endurance lessened. Would they be able to start moving again today?

She dragged herself up and scooted nearer her mother. Her mother was lying very still, but she was awake. "Dorritt, will you please go out and ask Mr. Kilbride to come to me? I think if we had a few words, he would calm down."

Dorritt stared at her mother. How could the fact that she was expecting a child change her mother this much? It was as if a rough husk like coconut bark had been pierced and stripped from her mother. Was this the power of hope, of feeling valued? Of no longer feeling shamed? "Certainly. I'll do that right away."

Her mother squeezed her hand and nodded. "I'm going to be all right now. I don't want you to worry about me."

Dorritt merely nodded and crawled on her knees to the end of the wagon where she righted her skirts and scooted down.

Her stepfather came to her immediately. "How is your mother?"

"She wants to speak to you. I'm going to go prepare her another cup of tea and get some hominy grits."

"You do that." But her stepfather was already climbing into the wagon.

Shaking her head, Dorritt walked toward the cook fire. Reva picked up the large coffee pot on a cast-iron trivet and poured Dorritt a cup. "Thank you, Reva. I also need a cup of tisane tea for my mother." Dorritt took a cautious sip of the hot coffee.

When Reva had the cup of tea made, she handed it to Dorritt, who carried it to the wagon. Mr. Kilbride took it from her. He glared at her, but said in a mild voice, "Your mother insists she is able to travel today lying down." He looked away. "Do you think she is well enough to travel?"

Mr. Kilbride asking her a civil question and even for advice

left Dorritt speechless. She swallowed. "If we put more cushion-
ing underneath her so she isn't jounced around too much she
should be all right. A couple of the featherbeds should do it."

Mr. Kilbride nodded. "See to it."

Still taken aback at his civility, Dorritt nodded and then left
to get the featherbeds. Would wonders never cease? As she
turned to get the supplies, she noticed Eduardo standing beside
his horse watching her, studying her. It made her uneasy.

* * *

Late in the afternoon, Quinn was riding near the head of the
caravan. He glanced over just when it happened. The first Conestoga wagon suddenly lurched, its right-front wooden wheel
breaking loudly. This was the third time they'd had a wagon
wheel break. And they had no more to replace it. Quinn rode
up to the wagon and joined the driver in surveying the damage.
Kilbride rode up behind them and dismounted. Quinn frowned
at him. "We're going to have to make do with the remaining
wheel we saved from the gig."

"That gone to make the wagon ride funny," the ox driver
agreed. "But no other way."

Quinn waited for Kilbride to say something rude. And he
wasn't disappointed.

After a moment spent cursing the driver for breaking the
wheel through poor driving, Kilbride ordered, "Then get on with
it. I'm going to go back and sit with my wife."

The driver nodded and said, "Yes sir."

Quinn stepped back and let the slaves begin the work of
changing wheels. It was a tedious and strength-demanding chore.
Quinn glanced around, keeping an eye on what was happening
around him. Dorritt was moving up the caravan, speaking to
the people. With a sudden rush of pleasure, he realized she was
watching him from the corner of her eye.

Then something else caught his notice. Far northward, he saw dust being stirred up and pronghorn antelope scattered. Someone was coming. But who? He didn't move, but tensed and continued watching. Could it be a Comanche war party this time? Or more Spanish or Mexican soldiers? Or bandits? In broad daylight? Or just another party of travelers?

Ash came up beside Quinn, walking his horse, and motioned with his head toward the north. Quinn nodded. And then the two of them ambled toward the rear of the caravan. They halted outside the wagon where Kilbride and his wife were. "Kilbride," Quinn called, "may I have a word with you?"

Kilbride stuck his head out from the rear of the covered wagon, looking disgruntled. "What is it?" he snapped.

Quinn motioned for him to come down and then he pointed toward the north. Kilbride just scowled at him. Quinn motioned for Kilbride a second time. This time the man got down and, huffing his irritation, walked away from the wagon to Quinn.

"Someone's coming," Quinn told him in a low voice. "I'm going to get everyone ready in case it's a war party or something else we don't want to meet up with unprepared."

Kilbride looked staggered. "But we haven't met with any trouble so far."

Quinn shrugged and turned toward the *vaqueros* to alert them. As he passed Dorritt, he paused. "Company is coming."

She nodded.

"If I give the signal, take cover under the wagons with the women and children."

"I'll tell them," she said, and hurried off.

"Quick-witted and she is a very pretty woman too," Ash said.

Quinn ignored Ash. He'd deal with his friend later; tell him to stop saying such things.

Eduardo and Carlos rode up and motioned northward. "You see?"

"Be ready." Quinn swallowed down his dislike of this man. Just because Carlos had taken a shine to Dorritt didn't make him bad. Only smart.

"You think Comanches attack in daylight?" Carlos asked.

Quinn shrugged. "If they think we're an easy target."

"We *vaqueros*? An easy target?" Eduardo grinned. "We know how to fight."

"Good to hear," Ash commented.

* * *

Dorritt stood, looking northward. The approaching party had become identifiable as one similar to theirs, but with only one wagon for the whites and fewer slaves on foot. They had a few farm animals and cattle at the rear. Mr. Kilbride moved forward to welcome them. But Dorritt noticed Quinn, Ash, and the *vaqueros* still remained on horseback with weapons drawn and ready. She felt just as hesitant as they. That the newcomers owned slaves was already a mark against them—to her mind.

"Howdy!" a man on a horse at the head of the other party hailed them. "Where you headed?"

Kilbride responded, "Hello! We're the Kilbrides on our way to the Austin settlement."

"*Whoop!*" the man yelled. "We're the Andersons and we're headed the same."

Within minutes, the Andersons were shaking hands with Mr. Kilbride. Dorritt watched until she was called forward with Jewell. "This is my daughter, Jewell, and my wife's daughter, Dorritt Mott."

Dorritt curtseyed to the Andersons, who looked about the same age as her parents and who had three sons who appeared to be around fourteen to twenty-five and one little girl around ten. Their dress was rough, some homespun and some deerskin. But they spoke good English and observed proper courtesy. Jewell flashed a charming smile at the eldest son. Dorritt kept her place a step behind her sister.

Mr. Anderson looked past her. "I see you got a half-breed and some Mexicans with you." The man's tone was disapproving. "I don't like having half-breeds around. I don't trust anything but whites and good coloreds who know their place."

Dorritt imagined herself slapping Mr. Anderson's face.

"I needed the *vaqueros*," Kilbride said almost apologetically. "My people aren't accustomed to herding longhorns and half-broke mustangs through wilderness."

"Well, no one knows cattle better than Mexicans," Anderson allowed, and spat tobacco on the ground.

"*Gracias, señor,*" Carlos spoke up, his gun still drawn, "for your compliment. We are still trying to discover what it is Anglos know better than anyone else."

Mr. Anderson drew his gun and held it at his side. "I don't take sass from anyone."

"If that means an insult, neither do I," Carlos said with a smile obviously intended to infuriate the two white men. He lifted his musket, ready to fire.

There was a tense silence, then Mr. Anderson's eyes slid from Carlos and he switched his attention to Ash. "Do you let your slaves ride?"

Her stepfather's round face flamed and he muttered, "He's a free black and came along with our half-breed scout." Anderson looked shocked and opened his mouth to speak.

"Quinn and I don't think much of ignorant Anglos, either," Ash interrupted him. "I'm Ash and I'm not pleased to meet you, Anderson."

All the white men swelled with anger. And raised their guns. But froze when it evidently dawned on them they were facing six armed and grim-looking men. And these were men of color who would not hesitate to shoot—a completely new and unexpected situation, no doubt.

Dorritt struggled with her fury. She wanted to lash out at

Mr. Kilbride and Mr. Anderson, but she didn't want to precipitate actual bloodshed. "Mr. Quinn saved my sister, Jewell, from drowning in the Sabine," she declared. "While we were still in Louisiana, he also found us shelter from the hurricane. And he has stood us as friend and guide since that night." Then she glared at her stepfather. "Isn't that right, Mr. Kilbride?"

Her stepfather looked flabbergasted. And sputtered.

"Yes, he has," Dorritt's mother said from the opening in the Conestoga. "Mrs. Anderson, I've been poorly for a few days. But won't you and your little girl come and have tea with me? We will have to make believe this wagon is our parlor or our veranda." The woman, the little child, and Jewell hurried to Dorritt's mother.

Dorritt turned away, still shaking but somehow proud. She hadn't expected the *vaquero* Carlos to stand up for himself like that. *Though I should have. He walks with pride.* She hoped suddenly that there would be many such men in Texas. Men who would stand up for themselves.

"Where are you going, girl?" her stepfather demanded.

"To make the tea," Dorritt replied without pausing.

She expected to hear Mr. Kilbride telling Anderson and his sons what a rebellious and intractable daughter she was. Instead he was explaining that Dorritt's mother was in a delicate condition and Dorritt had been up all night several nights nursing her. That explained her being unusually quarrelsome. Dorritt almost stopped to ask him what his purpose was for saying this. Then it hit her. He was still planning on marrying her off. *I'll run away like Amos and take Reva with me before I marry a son of that kind of man.*

* * *

After dark, the sound of singing drew Quinn to the Anderson wagon. Sitting there, Carlos was singing a Spanish song to the little Anderson girl. Quinn had heard it many times before, "*De*

Colores." Carlos finished singing it in Spanish and began to sing it in English.

> *Painted in colors,*
> *the fields are dressed in colors in the spring.*
> *Painted in colors*
> *painted in colors are the little birds,*
> *which come from the outside.*
> *Painted with colors,*
> *painted with colors is the rainbow*
> *that we see shining brilliantly above.*
> *And that is why great loves of many colors*
> *are what I like.*

The little girl was enjoying the song, swinging this way and that to the music and holding out her skirt as if she were dancing. Mrs. Anderson, Mrs. Kilbride, and Dorritt were nodding to the melody and smiling. Jewell stood beside her wagon farther down, listening. Even Ash and Dorritt's maid were standing in the distance listening. Ash tried to put his arm around the girl and she shrugged away and wagged her finger at him. Quinn shook his head. Was Ash really interested in this girl or just flirting? Ash's first wife had died many years ago, and Ash was nearly forty. Would he take a wife now?

When the song ended, the two mothers applauded. "Thank you, Carlos," Mrs. Kilbride said. "Do you have children of your own?"

"No, *señora*, I have not yet taken a wife." Carlos turned and looked boldly at Dorritt. "But I have a little sister who loves this song."

Quinn burned. Why did Carlos think he could get away with showing interest in Dorritt? Should a Mexican *vaquero* court a lady like Miss Dorritt? No. But Quinn might have to remind himself to press this point on Carlos.

"Well, thank you," Mrs. Anderson said. "Now, Nancy, it's time to get you to bed." Mrs. Anderson held out her hand.

"Please, please, one more song?" Nancy begged.

Carlos hunkered down beside the little girl and pinched her cheek. "You must mind your mother, Señorita Nancy. But I will sing to you tomorrow."

"Promise?" Nancy asked.

"Promise," Carlos said, and stood up, looking around.

Quinn did the same, but Dorritt had slipped away into the shadows. Still Quinn waited until after the *vaquero* paused to greet Miss Jewell and then walked beside the Kilbride wagons, headed toward the end of the wagon train. Quinn moved rearward too. In light of the first touchy meeting between the newcomers, Ash, himself, and the *vaqueros*, he wanted to know what the Andersons and Kilbrides might be planning. So he lingered in the shadows away from the campfire by the Kilbride wagons.

Anderson and Kilbride were drinking whiskey with Andersons' two older sons around the campfire. The youngest son sat whittling by the fire. Quinn worried that these newcomers might egg Kilbride into doing something stupid, just to save his pride.

Anderson was saying, "If you're planning on farming, according to the agreement with Austin, a family can get one *labor* of land. But if a family is going to ranch, the man can get one *sitio* of land."

"How much are those in acres?"

Quinn heard the greed in Kilbride's voice. Glancing away from the fire, he saw Dorritt standing in the shadows by the nearest wagon and listening too. Yes, she would want to know what the Andersons were telling Kilbride. Warm pleasure flowed through him just from her presence. He clamped down on the feeling but he couldn't staunch it.

"A *labor* is one hundred and seventy-seven acres. A *sitio* is over four thousand acres," Anderson said.

"Four thousand acres free," Kilbride said, sounding awed.

"Free? The land's not free," Anderson said.

"It isn't? I heard . . ." Kilbride turned a dark look toward Quinn.

Quinn ignored it and watched Dorritt step back farther into the shadows as if making certain she wouldn't be seen. He hoped none of these men would say anything a lady shouldn't hear. Dorritt was too fine a woman to be in this rough place with rough men.

"It's almost free, sir," the eldest son, Cole, said, "The price of land in Austin's grant is going for one-tenth of the price in the U.S. Just a dollar twenty-five an acre. And we'll be free of taxes for at least the first decade. Thomas, my next younger brother, and I are going to form a 'family' together so we get a larger family grant alongside our father's. And then we can all work it together."

"You can do that?" Kilbride asked.

"Yes, sir," the youngest boy piped up, "it's too bad you only got girls."

The two older brothers laughed. "We're not sorry. Both your daughters are mighty handsome-looking women," Thomas the middle brother said.

"Your stepdaughter Dorritt has a great deal of presence," the eldest Cole added, and then said something Quinn didn't understand to the younger boy. In return, the youngest scowled as they continued to tease him. Quinn gripped his long rifle, forcing himself to remain still. If Dorritt were his, no man would be allowed to bandy her name about.

Then Mr. Anderson interrupted the teasing in a serious voice, "No leatherstockings, no frontiersmen, are wanted. Only men who are ready to work hard and clear the land and make it profitable are going to be welcome."

"I'm glad to hear that," Kilbride said. "We don't want the wrong kind of people ruining such a golden opportunity for the rest of us."

"Exactly so," Anderson agreed.

Quinn moved away, disgusted. He'd already known he would never be wanted in the Austin settlement. So why did it upset him so to hear it said out loud? Then Quinn halted, listening. Was someone moving out in the darkness? Dorritt? He looked for her, but she had moved away. Still, he waited, silent and listening, for a long time. But all he could hear were the men drinking and talking by the fire.

* * *

He stood in the shadows and watched the Anglos drinking. Their words made him blaze with anger. Austin must be in league with diablo, *the devil, himself to get such easy terms to so much land. And no taxes! With that much land, these ignorant Yanquis would become gentlemen,* dueños. *He would remain landless—forced to steal silver from his cousin and from Kilbride's haughty daughter— while these Anglos gained land and wealth with no effort?*

He spit on the ground in contempt of them. His father's people were la Raza, *the descendents of Rome. The Northerners, the Anglos, were invaders, barbarians. He willed himself to cool down. Even barbarians could be useful to a smart man, and he was a smart man. His main goal was in the end more important than all. He wanted his cousin disgraced or dead or both.*

An idea was coming to him, a way to use the Anglos, especially the lovely one with the whitest skin he'd ever seen, against his cousin. It might work. He could make it work for his advantage. If his cousin had found him out as a thief, he must do what he could before he had to run for it.

* * *

The next morning at the back of the Conestoga, Mr. Kilbride slapped Jewell's face. Dorritt, who had just stepped down from the wagon after taking tea to her mother, was so shocked she almost grabbed his hand. Before Dorritt could say a word, her stepfather said in an angry undertone, "You will not make an embarrassing scene for us. One of the servants must have taken your silver comb, and I don't want to hear about it anymore. When we are through with the journey, we will unpack everything, and if I have to strip every slave naked in the noonday sun, I will find your brush and your comb."

"Why do I have to wait?" Jewell snapped, rubbing her face where he'd slapped her.

"I don't want to insult the Andersons—as if we suspected them," her stepfather said. "Now go about your business."

Jewell grumbled but she obeyed.

Trying to figure out if there were any significance to the loss of Jewell's silver brush and comb, Dorritt watched her half-sister stalk away. And she wondered if any of their people might be tempted to do such a thing out of spite. Ahead, Eduardo stepped away from a wagon and Jewell stopped to talk to him. From Jewell's gestures, Dorritt thought she must be telling the Mexican about the second theft—since no one else was available to listen to her indignation. Dorritt turned to find the *vaquero* Carlos once again in front of her. She gasped and pressed a hand to her throat.

"I surprised you. I'm sorry," he said with a slight bow, his hat in his hand.

"*Buenos días, señor*. What can I do for you?"

"*Nada*. I just wished to greet you. *Buenos días, señorita*. And to say again, do not worry about these coarse Andersons. That kind will not prosper in the new Mexico. There are many fine people, fine families here in *Tejas*. You will find friends here."

Dorritt didn't know how to reply to this without encouraging the man, so she merely smiled and walked on. Was he just one of those men who thought themselves a Don Juan and couldn't let a woman go by without being charming? She'd already tagged Eduardo as that; he was always hanging around looking at her. But Carlos too? He didn't seem the type. She shook her head.

As she walked, she suddenly became aware of a loud commotion going on toward the rear of the caravan. Reva was running to her and calling her. "Come quick, Miss Dorritt. Amos sneaked back last night."

Dorritt's heart slid cold and fearful down to her toes. As she hurried, she watched the crowd gather. This was absolutely the worst time for this to happen. The presence of the Andersons would make Mr. Kilbride react in the most extreme manner to show mastery over his slaves to impress these strangers. *Dear Father, what can I do?*

She arrived near Amos. The boy's clothing was ripped and shredded already. Sitting slumped against the wagon, his face looked swollen, as if he had been stung by insects. He looked weak and hungry.

Mr. Kilbride, approached, looking belligerent and carrying his rolled whip in one hand. "Tie him to the wagon wheel."

This was what she'd feared he'd say. Even a strong young male would have a hard time surviving a severe whipping. And then he'd have to ride in one of the wagons or die in his tracks.

Dorritt stepped close to Mr. Kilbride. "I'm afraid if you whip him, at the very least, he'll be feverish and useless for two weeks or more."

"He should have thought of that before he ran away." Mr. Kilbride bellowed, "I said, tie him to the wagon wheel! Now!"

The two ox drivers moved forward reluctantly, turned Amos to face the wagon, and with leather thongs, began to tie Amos's wrists to the top of the wagon wheel. Amos sagged, half kneeling, half standing.

"Mr. Kilbride," Dorritt pleaded softly, "be kind. When we reach our new land, we will need Amos."

"Go to your mother, girl," he ordered. "This is none of your business."

Dorritt stiffened as if an iron rod had been shoved up her spine. *I won't let you scar, torture, and maybe kill Amos just because you want to look like a man to these Andersons.* She inhaled breath for strength and moved to stand between her stepfather and Amos. Drawing the battle line. She folded her arms in front of her, trembling with an intermingling of fear and outrage. "This *is* my business." Her low voice corroded her throat like acid. "The welfare of our people has always been my business." *Mine, not yours. Never yours.*

Kilbride glared at her and all the while darting surreptitious glances at the Andersons. "Step aside, girl."

"No." She stared into his eyes. Implacable.

Her defiance turned her stepfather's jowly face red. "You are meddling in affairs that don't concern you. Now step aside before I have to discipline you too."

"Mr. Kilbride," one of the ox drivers spoke up in a servile tone, "why don't you let me take Amos's place? He just a boy without sense."

"No," Dorritt answered. "There are no slaves in Mexico. And indentured servants may not be whipped." She didn't know if this was law or not, but it was the only justification that came to her seething mind.

"Step aside," Mr. Kilbride said, his voice thick with rage. *"Now."*

"No." Dorritt was shaking, but she was not going to back down.

His face twisted with rage, Mr. Kilbride began to loose his bullwhip.

"You would use your whip, on your own daughter?" Carlos

spoke up from the circle surrounding them, sounding astounded, outraged. "It is not even to be considered."

"Shut up and go back to the cattle, Mexican," Kilbride commanded.

"Fool," Carlos growled, reaching for his gun.

Fear like needles prickled down Dorritt's spine. Had she pushed Mr. Kilbride too far? *It doesn't matter. I'm not moving.* Her hands fisted. Her chin lifted.

"Look around you, Kilbride," Ash said.

Kilbride went on, moving into place to use the whip. Ash repeated himself. Kilbride ignored him. But then Mr. Anderson cursed in surprise, making both Kilbride and Dorritt look around them.

All of Kilbride's slaves—male and female, plus the *vaqueros*, Quinn, and Ash—had circled Kilbride, Amos, Dorritt, and the Anderson men. The *vaqueros*, Quinn, and Ash all had their weapons drawn. And all looked ready to fire.

Dorritt inhaled, tingling with shock. *What have I done? Father, tell me what to do to avoid bloodshed.*

"It looks like we're going to have to make an example of this boy," Mr. Anderson said, drawing his pistol from his belt and aiming it at Amos. "Don't you agree, Kilbride?"

"Yes," Kilbride said with a pugnacious glare.

Amos sobbed, quaking.

White-hot anger gushed through Dorritt's core. She swallowed down the wordless rage, shaking with its force. She backed up farther until her body covered Amos. "No one is going to shoot this boy."

Anderson made a sound of derision and lifted his pistol.

"The first man to shoot will be the first man to die," Quinn's voice came low, menacing. And absolutely determined.

"That is right," Carlos agreed. "I will allow no man to hurt the boy or the *señorita*."

Dorritt's heart was pounding so hard she thought it might burst out through her skin. But she remained absolutely still, poised in front of Amos. Ready for whatever came.

"You're getting above yourself, half-breed," Kilbride snarled, completely ignoring Carlos. "This does not concern you."

Quinn ignored Kilbride. "Put down the whip, Kilbride. And, Anderson, put your pistol back in its holster."

"We don't take orders from the likes of you," Anderson growled.

"Then I guess today is the day you and your sons die," Ash said conversationally.

"*Sí*," Carlos agreed, but in a voice dark with fury. "Mexico would be better off without your kind, men without respect or honor." He spat into the dust, further goading the white men.

Then there was silence. But not a passive silence; it was a festering, expanding hot-air silence which threatened to combust at any moment. Dorritt felt light-headed. *Father, give me the words to say. I didn't want anyone to get hurt today.* But she did not back down, could not.

Everyone remained frozen in place. The minutes ticked by. Why were they all standing here? What actually had started this? Dorritt rubbed her forehead as if clearing her mind. *Father, please.* And then Dorritt knew what to say. *This is all about nothing.*

"This has gone far enough," she said, keeping her voice completely neutral. "No one is going to be whipped. No one is going to be shot. And no one is going to die. We need every hand we have to make a go of this. I've had enough." She turned and began to untie Amos's wrists, though her fingers jerked clumsily with nerves.

Kilbride cursed her.

From the corner of her eyes, Dorritt saw Quinn's jaw tighten and knew one more word might be her stepfather's last. "We're in the middle of the wilderness." She spoke as if she hadn't heard Mr. Kilbride. "We need our guide and our *vaqueros*. And we can't afford to lose any of our people. Amos ran away but he came back. He is just a foolish boy." She raised her voice. "And he's found out he cannot survive in the wilderness, so neither he nor any of our other people are going to try to run away from now on. Amos has suffered hunger, insects, and thirst. And probably sheer terror at times. That's punishment enough. There is absolutely no reason anyone has to lift a whip or point a gun."

"Señorita Dorritt is wise, as well as beautiful," Carlos said with warm approval.

"I must agree," Ash said in a mild tone. "Now, gents, are we going to get started? Or are we just going to stand here all day with our guns pointed each other?"

Eleven

Though her knees felt crushed like storm-flattened grass, Dorritt managed to finish untying Amos's wrists. Then she stood taller while her strength was draining from her limbs. She shivered with weakness. *Please, Father, don't let me faint. Don't let violence break out.*

"Reva, please help me get Amos near the fire. I may need to cauterize some of his bites and cuts." Just speaking these few mundane words, Dorritt found herself panting as if she had been racing.

With cautious steps as if crossing a brook, stone by stone, Reva left the circle around the scene and moved toward Dorritt. "We better get some coffee into him. He look pretty done in."

Dorritt glimpsed the terror in Reva's eyes, which belied her friend's matter-of-fact tone. Dorritt drew a quick breath and continued behaving as if only she, Reva, and Amos were present. "Yes, and I think we better let him ride today in the back of one of the wagons. Let's be quick. The sun is getting higher. We need to get on the trail for the day."

Eyes downcast, Dorritt and Reva half carried Amos toward the nearest fire. No one fired. But the hardest test faced them now. Approaching the circle of people, they came to the Andersons. She and Reva did not look up and did not pause. They just pushed through. Forcing the newcomers to give way.

The Andersons swung away with audible disgust. Their disdain strained Dorritt's nerves like cloth stretched in an embroidery frame. Still, she kept her head down as she and Reva laid Amos down near the fire. Dorritt went on caring for Amos with Reva's help. Staring at the ground, she heard the Andersons getting ready to leave for the day. And was glad. She took a cautious breath.

Muttering hot words, Kilbride stalked over to her. He leaned down and said with palpable menace, "You have ruined our reputation here in Texas. You will pay for this day. I will not forget it."

Dorritt looked up, intense dislike and disrespect gushing through her. *You have ruined our reputation here in Texas. You will pay for this day.* "I will not forget it either."

He raised his hand to slap her for this insolence.

A gunshot rang out. Kilbride jerked around.

"Oh, pardon me," Ash said with exaggerated courtesy, "I misfired."

Kilbride turned and stalked away.

"Sorry to disturb you, ladies," Ash said, pushing back the brim of his hat.

Reva turned and grinned at him. "You didn't disturb me."

"Oh, the lady finally speaks to me. My lucky day." Ash turned and sauntered off toward cattle and horses.

"Well," Reva said in a low voice, the smile in her eyes fading, "we all came through with our skins. I didn't expect that. We're going to have to watch Mr. Kilbride. He'll make you pay. Make us all pay."

"If he can," Dorritt agreed. Her confident words did not reflect her own deep uneasiness.

From the corner of her eye, she watched Quinn wait until all the others had dispersed. Only then did he leave his post, guarding her. He'd been her champion. This gave her a feeling she could not describe.

On this earth she'd only ever had one person who could actually protect her: her father. But when she was a child, he had been killed in a duel and left her and her mother alone. Except for God and Reva, she'd been on her own ever since. And usually there wasn't much Reva, a slave, could do. That everpresent vulnerability suddenly caught her around her lungs, twisting into an awful feeling of being smothered, buried alive, a sensation that had first come that horrible day when she'd lost her father, her family.

That day she lost a father who should have loved her enough not to fight a duel, not to desert her. But she couldn't change the past. She couldn't control the future. She only had today. And today Quinn had stepped forward in front of everyone to protect her. She drew in a deep breath. *He risked his life for me.* So many sensations and emotions bubbled inside her she could not sort them out. Instead, she forced herself to focus on treating Amos's many minor wounds. It was the only way she could hold herself together.

Reva leaned close and whispered in her ear, "What you going to do with that Mr. Quinn?"

She couldn't deny there were times when images flashed in her mind. She was pressed against him and his lips hovered over hers—so close. The power of this fantasy raced through her, lush and strong. Her whole body flushed. Holding it all in, she shrugged and looked away.

Reva clucked her tongue. "You're going to have to face Mr. Quinn. No turning back."

Dorritt nodded, still unable to meet Reva's eyes. *What can I do with him?* But she really didn't want to know, didn't want to face the horrible, wonderful truth glowing inside her. If she faced it, then she would have to make a decision.

* * *

To Dorritt's relief, the two parties had finally set off by mid-morning. The Anderson wagon had pulled ahead, as if distancing themselves from the Kilbrides. Now hours later, the sun was well past its prime. Soon the cool of the evening would begin. As Dorritt had all day, she kept her gaze forward on the wagon. There, in its rear Amos slumped asleep, his head bobbing in time with the jolting wagon. And in the first wagon farther ahead, her other worry, her mother was lying inside on featherbeds and bumping over the faint packed-earth trail of the Camino Real.

But over all loomed the fear of how Mr. Kilbride would retaliate against her, Quinn, Amos, Ash, and Reva. Quinn and Ash could defend themselves. She had only to defend herself. But Reva and Amos were vulnerable. And when it came to dealing with his slaves, Mr. Kilbride knew no shame. Her stomach churned with worry.

From behind, Quinn's calm voice sounded, making Dorritt glance up. She lowered her eyes again, trying to hide a spontaneous smile. Quinn had appeared to linger protectively near her all day. Over and over, her mind repeated his words, "The first to shoot will be the first to die."

As a Christian, the words should have distressed her. But she had never indulged in self-deception. She hadn't wanted anyone to bleed or die. Yet knowing there was someone close who was willing and ready to defend her to the death—altered her outlook, the trend of her thoughts. Joy, fear, uncertainty, and more emotions crested, ebbed, flowed within her. Something inside her had changed this morning. And she knew for certain the difference was irrevocable.

Then movement caught Dorritt's eye and she tensed. Jewell was marching straight at her. Dorritt had been waiting for a reaction. Well, here it came. Falling back and moving away from the caravan so that no one else would hear what was coming, she tried to tighten her defenses, prepare for whatever skirmish Jewell was intent on. But for whatever reason, she found her half-sister less threatening now than she had yesterday.

Jewell finally fell into step beside her and their people had drawn back from them. No doubt afraid of Jewell's lowering brow and stormy expression. *Good, just the two of us.*

"I hope you're happy with this morning's disaster," Jewell snapped. "After the outrageous scene you caused in front of the Andersons, how am I to make a successful marriage?"

Dorritt almost replied that Jewell's father had triggered this morning's high drama. Instead, she quietly voiced something that came to her unexpectedly, "I hope you're prepared to begin handling your father's business affairs here in Texas."

"I—" Jewell halted, looking flustered. "Don't try to distract me with nonsense."

Why did I say that? Dorritt shimmered with surprise at her own audacity, but continued, "It's not nonsense. Before Grandmother Kilbride passed, she taught me how to keep books and—"

"I'm not here to talk to you about foolishness —"

"It's not foolishness, it's reality. When we reach the Austin settlement, I'll show you a ledger and teach you how to keep it." *Why am I saying this? How could I make Jewell do anything?* "I'll also show you how to know how much seed to save or buy per acre of land—"

"Stop this! I won't be distracted. You have damaged our family's reputation."

Dorritt ignored her. *It wasn't I who damaged the family's repu-*

tation. "Keep your voice down. Do you want the Andersons to hear you? Now listen, mother might have taken over management in Texas. But if she carries to term, I don't think she'll be able to handle the business along with a new baby. And she may not return to high health —"

Jewell hands became fists; she halted and stomped her foot. "Stop!"

Recalling Jewell as little girl using the same tantrum tactics, Dorritt fell silent, but walked on. Jewell hurried to catch up with Dorritt.

Jewell's voice was low but urgent. "Why did you do that this morning? Certainly you knew what it would cost us."

Suddenly Dorritt was out of patience. Did Jewell think she had wanted to have her hand forced in front of the deplorable Andersons? "Jewell, I'm sure you won't understand even if I tell you. All your life you've been indulged and petted—"

"And you have resented that," Jewell lashed out, her face pink. "Was that why you did it? To ruin my chances of making a good marriage?"

"I did it because Amos didn't deserve a whipping just to bolster your father's pride."

"Slaves must be kept in order," Jewell said, parroting phrases from her father's mouth. "Runaways must be punished."

"Tell me, Jewell, what's worse than being a slave and being forced to walk through the wilderness of Texas?" Dorritt couldn't keep the rumbling anger from her voice. "I'm just not going to stand by and take whatever nonsense your father wants to dish out. Things are different here and now." *I'm different here and now,* her mind added silently.

"You keep trying to change the subject but I won't let you. Don't you realize the consequences of your defiance this morning?"

Dorritt didn't answer immediately. For once, Jewell had a

valid question and Dorritt considered it. "No, neither of us can know *now* what the consequences will be. But you're right, there will be consequences."

"Are you deranged? The consequences are quite clear. You have made us outcasts." Jewell's lowered voice caught and she gave a half hiccup, half sob. She pressed the back of her hand to her mouth and blinked back tears.

Dorritt considered Jewell, not her words, but her. She recalled seeing Mr. Kilbride slap Jewell and felt a glimmer of sympathy. "The past few days haven't been easy for you."

"What do you care about that? You don't care about me. You never have."

Dorritt glanced into Jewell's stormy brown eyes. "People care about those who care about them," she said with a wry twist.

Jewell's hand flew up, but before it could connect, Dorritt caught her sister's wrist. "You won't get away with that anymore."

"This new arrogance of yours won't last," Jewell hissed. "You shamed my father. He won't forget it. I won't let him."

"As you will." Dorritt flung Jewell's wrist away from her. "But I'm not the one who started this chain of events. Your father gambled away what was left of our fortune. Now we are facing the consequences of that . . . crime."

"All gentlemen gamble," Jewell said, dismissing the accusation. "The Panic did us in."

"That's what your father used as a face-saving excuse." Like a fork scraped over raw flesh, the old resentment lacerated Dorritt inside. "But I'm the one who's kept the books and run the plantation for nearly ten years. I know the truth."

"I don't believe you. You're just trying to shift the blame. I don't understand why you can't see you've not only spoiled my chance to marry well, but also your own."

Dorritt shook her head. "Jewell, you're only fifteen. You have plenty of time to marry. And you can't make me believe you won't contract an advantageous marriage."

"And I suppose you've decided to become our half-breed's white squaw," her sister sneered.

Like a cork drawn from a bottle, this accusation released Dorritt's fury. She couldn't speak. The disrespect shown to Mr. Quinn and herself was appalling. Finally, Dorritt looked into Jewell's gloating face. "I don't intend to marry. I never have."

Her sister made a sound of derision.

"Jewell, you are not me. For a woman, marriage is like letting oneself be sold on the block. I won't do it."

"You're still talking nonsense. No woman willingly chooses spinsterhood. Marriage to any decent man is preferable to being an unwanted old maid."

Now Dorritt sighed and half turned to go the other way. "I am not like you."

"That's right. I'm young and beautiful. You are not. And you will have no choice. If my father persuades someone to marry you, what choice will you have?" Jewell's voice rose. "Are you willing to be known as an ungovernable female? Are you pre-pared to be rejected by polite society? Are you ready to lower yourself to consorting with a half-breed? Are you?"

Her half sister's scornful words sliced through everything else. Jewell was self-centered and willful. But she wasn't stupid.

Am I prepared to cross that line? The thought shivered through her like an unexpected frost. All she had as protection in this world was her status as a decent woman and a cultured lady. "I don't know," she murmured. *I don't know what I'm going to do.* Then she lifted her chin. "Changes are coming, Jewell." *We will all be changing.* Or was she the only one as usual who saw what was coming, what was real?

Jewell stalked off, muttering to herself.

Father, truly what have I triggered? How will it all end? She recited her favorite verse.

> *Delight thyself also in the LORD; and he shall give you the desires of thine heart.*

Reva had said earlier, "No turning back" and it was true. Still, her heart fluttered like a panicked bird caught in a net.

* * *

Quinn watched the caravan quiet down, everyone settling in for another night's exhausted sleep. The Andersons were keeping to themselves, far ahead of the Kilbride wagons. Today though, the miles weren't what had tired Quinn. With every step he took, worry for Dorritt had pecked at his peace. From a distance, he'd watched what he thought must be an argument between her and that sister of hers. All day he'd been more aware of her than ever before.

And he hadn't thought that could be possible. But today it had been as if she were always in front of him. He'd almost breathed in time with her. What was she thinking? Had he helped her or harmed her by threatening her father? After Quinn left them at the Colorado when Kilbride thought Dorritt was again unprotected, would he retaliate against her? Or would he try tonight? In case that proved true, Quinn must stay near. He heard someone approaching and turned, ready for anything.

Eduardo and Carlos were drawing near. "Señor Quinn," Eduardo jeered, "You watch for your lady?"

Carlos gave Eduardo a disapproving glance.

Quinn heard more than just the words; he grasped the thought behind them—that she is a lady and not for the likes of you.

"She's not my lady." *I don't deserve a lady.* Then Quinn straightened. "But she *is* a lady."

Carlos, now glaring at Eduardo, replied, "Everyone sees that.

No one with eyes and ears can doubt the quality of Señorita Dorritt."

Even though Quinn agreed with Carlos, he still didn't like hearing Carlos say the words. "What do you want?" Quinn growled, feeling like a bear with a thorn in its paw.

"Señor Quinn, I thought we would reach the Colorado more quickly. But we have not. And I must reach home in two days," Carlos said.

"You're leaving then?" Quinn asked.

"*Sí*, I go at dawn. I will leave Eduardo and the other two to herd the cattle and help guard the wagon train and protect Miss Dorritt."

Quinn noticed Carlos said, "I will leave . . . ," so it was true. Juan and Pedro took orders from Eduardo and Carlos. But now it was certain Carlos must outrank Eduardo. Quinn offered Carlos his hand. The man worked hard and appreciated the lady and treated her with special courtesy. And for latter reason alone, Quinn should be glad to see him go. "I bid you farewell, then."

Carlos shook his hand. "I'm sure we will meet again."

Quinn didn't like that much, but kept his silence. The two Mexicans moved away. Carlos walked to Dorritt and obviously took his leave of her, bending to kiss her hand as if he were a *don*. Watching from behind a clump of bushes, Quinn tried not to let the sight bother him. After all, Carlos, a half-breed too, had as much chance as he had of winning the lady. Eduardo also bowed over Dorritt's hand and then walked away.

Quinn settled himself on the ground to watch without being seen, waiting until Dorritt was safely in the wagon where she slept with her sister. After everyone else had fallen asleep, he would go and bring her out to talk, just as he'd done that night in Louisiana when she had been sleeping in the loft. Perfectly still, Quinn waited.

Under and around the wagons, the slaves were lying down

now, wrapping themselves in blankets. In the distance, Ash chuckled and made Quinn's gaze seek his friend. Ash was talking very close to Reva in the last of the long twilight shadows. Was Ash really interested in Dorritt's maid or just flirting? Ash liked to flirt. Something Quinn had never even tried. Slowly but surely the camp turned in to sleep one by one. Again, coyotes prowled, yipping nearby, but wouldn't venture closer.

As Quinn waited, Dorritt's face and form came to his mind. She smiled at him. Her teeth were white and even, except for one of the upper ones which overlapped its neighbor. He liked that her lower lip was just a little fuller than the upper. Her mouth always looked soft and appealing. He closed his eyes as if that would help him shut out the improper images rising inside him, not in front of him.

"Mr. Quinn."

Her low rich voice brought him to his feet with his knife at the ready.

Dorritt uttered a soft cry. And pulled back.

"I'm sorry," he whispered, "I must've been dozing." He lowered his knife and swept off his hat.

"I shouldn't have surprised you." She turned to go.

No. Stay. He caught her arm, and the touch unleashed everything he had held back for weeks. He drew her to him. She came willingly and was as soft within his arms as he had imagined. At first, all he could do was process the sensation of her resting against him. The feeling went to his head like too much sun.

Then he gave in to temptation and let himself stroke her hair, that spun sunshine which always beckoned him. He slid his cheek against hers and felt her breath on his ear. "I wanted you to come out," he murmured to her. "I was waiting until everyone fell asleep. And then I was going to come and get you,

Dorritt." He waited to see if she'd tell him not to use her given name.

"Why, Quinn?"

Again, her breath fanned his ear. She'd dropped the mister. He found it hard to swallow. "I wanted to say I'm sorry."

"For what?"

"For threatening to shoot your stepfather this morning—"

She looked up at him, the half-moonlight silvering her skin. "Oh no. I was so grateful. You saved Amos from a terrible whipping."

"But I showed partiality to you, Dorritt."

She looked into Quinn's eyes—so blue even in the half-moon night. He'd said it all with those few simple yet powerful words, "But I showed partiality to you." She wanted to reply, "I don't care." But of course, she did care. Or she should. *I'm so confused. My heart and my mind are at war.*

"I'm sorry," he repeated.

"Don't apologize. You were brave and you can't know how much it meant to me to . . . to have someone defend me." Warm blood rushed to her face. She tried to look away, but his hand caught her chin. He lifted it so she was looking up into those gleaming blue-blue eyes. She found she had trouble drawing breath.

She saw his mouth dip lower, lower. The thrill of an anticipation she'd never known before zipped through her every nerve. His mouth moved downward—relentless but so slowly, so unhurriedly. And then his lips met hers. She gasped, overpowered. Her heart stopped for one beat and then raced.

I have lived for this moment.

The truth of this sang through her. She leaned against him, wanting, needing, to be closer to him. But soon all her awareness centered on where their lips touched and became one. Though her feet still touched the earth, an incredible lightness lifted her. She felt herself softening as if bathed in warm lavender water. He was her only anchor, the only real thing that existed in that moment, and she clung to him.

The long kiss ended at last and she found herself clasped tightly, her cheek against his deerskin shirt. She drew in the scent of him—a mix of deerskin, woodsmoke, and faint honest sweat.

"You smell so good," he said, stroking the back of her hair.

How shameless she was—she'd come to him without bonnet or gloves. And though she'd washed the dust of the day from her face and neck and hands, she still felt as though she'd come to him, to this special moment, unprepared. She wished she had been able to wear her blue silk ball gown and her paternal grandmother's pearl necklace and earrings for him. Foolish, foolish thoughts.

"I shouldn't be holding you like this." He tried to step back.

"No." She clung to him—still bold, unashamed. "Just this once, Quinn," she implored.

He pulled her tighter to him again. "Just this once," he agreed. "I don't want to ruin your reputation. I know what white men think of a white woman who mixes with an Indian."

Though she didn't reply, she acknowledged what he said was true. But she retorted silently, *Yes, but it's all right for white men to take a squaw. All right for a man to take a slave mistress. But their white wives must be pure in their eyes. In their way. While they do as they please.*

"We can't change the way things are," he whispered, so close his lips tickled her ear lobe. "Were the white men in New Orleans all blind? Didn't they see your worth?"

She laughed without mirth. *They thought me "thrifty and good with children."* "I never wished to marry. I never thought I could trust any man that much."

He didn't respond directly to her; he pulled her closer. "I have not sought a wife. I have wandered too far too long."

Dorritt wondered if she could defy the world. But his saying that he'd never sought a wife wasn't a proposal. Her confusion mounted but she pushed it away. She pressed against him and stroked his back, wishing she could penetrate the shirt to his skin. It was a shocking unprecedented desire. But she didn't feel horrified at her own brazenness. *Being close to him feels so right.* She drew in breath and closed her eyes. In her barren and lonely life, she concentrated on this once-in-a-lifetime interlude.

"The world is the way it is." He stroked her hair. And then he stopped abruptly.

"What?"

He pressed a finger against her lips. Then he whispered into her ear, "I think someone is moving in the darkness. Or it might be an animal rustling the grass."

Icy horror sliced through her. The consequences of being caught here with Quinn like this were overwhelming, too shattering to contemplate.

"You must go back now." He thrust her from him. "Go now."

She staggered away from him, her heart pounding with a dull ache. Had she lost her good name? All for a few moments of perfect bliss? She hurried to the wagon, trying not to make a sound, not to wake anyone. When she stepped into the blackness around the rear of the wagon, she nearly cried out. Jewell was standing there, almost invisible.

"Taking an innocent evening stroll?" her sister asked with rich sarcasm. "Dear sister, you must be careful here in the wilderness." Then she turned and walked away.

Dorritt stood there, willing her rioting heart to calm. Had Jewell actually seen her in Quinn's embrace? Or had she merely caught Dorritt coming back and was trying to pay Dorritt back for the scene over Amos? Dorritt closed her eyes and all that came to her was Quinn's exquisite kiss.

* * *

Mr. Kilbride's angry ranting woke Dorritt the next morning. She lay there, wanting to put her hands over her ears, shut out his voice. How much longer could she stand his tantrums and bad humor? But she still had no idea how to separate herself from her family and him. Perhaps the Andersons would tell about her defying her father and coddling a slave and destroy her chance to establish herself as a schoolmistress. The thought should be a distressing one, but she found it wasn't. Why? She had felt different yesterday after Quinn's protecting her and even more different after she'd kissed him. She tried to define what she felt and it was . . . happiness. *I didn't expect to be happy in Texas.* The thought was exciting. She recalled Reva's idea that they might find men of honor in Texas. She'd rejected it, but deep in her heart she'd always wanted love. But love was such a risk. Marriage was till death and could take the little independence she had as a spinster.

But it was just another morning from the sound of Mr. Kilbride. Unwillingly, she opened her eyes and saw she was alone in the wagon bed. Then Reva's face appeared in the opening at the rear of the cloth cover. "Miss Dorritt, you best come. That man all upset again."

Dorritt scrambled toward the rear of the wagon, smoothing back her loosened hair, as she climbed out and down. "What is it?" What was upsetting her stepfather this morning?

Twelve

"The Andersons left early to get away from us," Reva said as they hurried toward the gathering ahead near the first wagon.

There, Dorritt went to her mother, who looked distressed. "Mother, what's this about the Andersons?"

Her mother took Dorritt's hand. Her stepfather put his face directly in front of Dorritt's. "The Andersons left early this morning to get away from us. I told you that you have ruined our reputation here and we haven't even reached the Brazos," Mr. Kilbride accused, spit flying from the side of his mouth.

Quinn took a step closer to Dorritt and she read in it evidence of his protectiveness toward her. This knowledge poured through her like warm butter. *Would she ever be able to erase from memory those stolen moments with him? Did she want to?* Pushing back her uncombed hair, Dorritt wondered who had been the one moving in the dark who had interrupted her with Quinn. Certainly for a time she and Quinn had been completely unaware of what was going on around them. Her face warmed.

"This doesn't surprise me," Jewell said, as if relishing this insult. "I don't know how I'll face the shame Dorritt brought to our family."

Dorritt made herself look directly into her half-sister's eyes until Jewell looked away.

Her mother spoke up, "You'd have thought that they would have had the courtesy to say farewell before leaving us. This is just rude. I don't think you should blame my Dorritt just because these vulgar people have no manners."

Dorritt couldn't form words. Her mother was defending her against her stepfather and Jewell? She couldn't get over the change in her mother. Was it the child she was bearing or the promise of a new start in life? How could just the hope of bearing a son make such a difference in her mother?

Quinn cleared his throat. "Maybe the Andersons had a reason for leaving early. They couldn't have gotten much ahead of us, just a few hours. We might even catch up with them today."

Her mother turned to her husband. "After such rude behavior, I don't really care if we catch up with them or not. And I'm not going to let this upset me."

Looking a bit like a man who had just been forced to swallow a fly, Mr. Kilbride cast a nasty look toward Dorritt. But then he leaned over and kissed his wife's forehead. "Yes, Elspeth, you're right. You don't want to mark the baby." He turned and shouted, "We leave in ten minutes!"

Dorritt helped her mother up onto the ox wagon seat and sat down beside her. Then she turned to accept a cup of coffee from the cook. Soon the wagons began to move. Dorritt could only hope in the haste nothing had been left behind. But then much of the mental baggage she had been carrying all the way from Louisiana had fallen away. Her mother's change of heart, Quinn's protection, and more . . . Texas was beginning to feel

like the place she wanted to be—in spite of people like the Andersons. *"Trust in the Lord, and do good; so thou shall dwell in the
land. . . ."*

* * *

In the afternoon, Dorritt, sitting beside her mother on the bench
of first ox wagon, saw Quinn appear on the southern horizon. All
morning she had told herself to put their private moments out
of her mind. Instead, she found that the memory of their secret
interlude, that stolen kiss, only grew stronger. Now, just watching him ride toward her, she experienced that same breathless
anticipation she had last night as his lips had lowered to hers.
She swallowed, trying to hold herself together against the force
of the recollection. How was she supposed to keep from showing his effect on her?

Ahead, Quinn rode to her stepfather and motioned toward
the horizon. She wondered anew at this change in how solici-
tously her stepfather was treating her mother. She'd never realized how only bearing two daughters had been a cross her
mother bore. What had her mother said when she was in danger
of miscarrying? Hadn't she said that if Dorritt had been a son,
perhaps her father wouldn't have fought the duel that cost his
life? But why? *I have to find out if that's what my mother really
meant.*

Quinn and Mr. Kilbride approached their wagon. "Mrs. Kilbride, Quinn says the Andersons are just a few miles ahead at an
Indian village."

"An Indian village!" her mother said. "Is that safe?"

Dorritt lowered her eyes, fearful that her mother or stepfather would read her tender regard for Quinn. A melting sensation flowed through her, just because Quinn was near.

"The Caddo are peaceful people," Quinn said. "Most of their
tribe has been driven into the missions. The Andersons look like
they've stopped to trade with the Caddo."

"Do these Indians have anything worth our trouble?" her mother asked.

"They are good at weaving cloth and making pottery," Quinn said.

Dorritt hazarded a glance in his direction and felt her face warm. She looked down again.

"Then let's proceed. I would love to do a little shopping out here in the wilderness." Her mother said, and smiled.

Quinn looked at Dorritt. Even his glance had power over her. Quinn turned and rode near the front of the caravan. She bowed her head. Was there no way for them to be together? She tried to imagine a life with Quinn, the wanderer, and couldn't see how she could live that life.

Before long, Dorritt glimpsed the village in the distance. Soon they drew up near the Andersons' deserted wagon outside the prairie village of thatched huts. As if unsure about this rendezvous, their slaves remained close to the wagons. Mr. Kilbride helped his wife down from the wagon, then led her on his arm into the village. Quinn walked just a few steps behind her mother. And Dorritt trailed after him, her arms folded behind her, distinctly wary about encountering the Andersons again.

The Caddo houses, shaped like cones made out of poles covered by rushes and hides, ringed an open green. Dorritt was surprised to see that the houses were around three times as tall as Quinn and that cornfields, already harvested, stretched beyond the village. The Andersons were there, trying to communicate with the Indians, who stood around staring at them with clear mistrust. The Andersons did not look happy to see them. Dorritt noticed Jewell predictably drifted closer to the handsome eldest son.

"Does your scout—" Mr. Anderson cleared his throat and waved his arm toward Quinn. "—speak their language? We can't seem to get them to understand that we want to see what they've got to sell. We'd heard about buying blankets and such from the savages hereabout."

Quinn did not move or act as if he had heard what Anderson said. Dorritt didn't blame him one bit. She felt his presence drawing her toward him and forced herself to stay still.

Her mother spoke up, "Mr. Quinn, I'd appreciate seeing what these Caddo have to offer. Is it of good quality, do you think?"

Once again, Dorritt was surprised at her mother speaking up in front of people and also realizing she should do something to calm the turbulent waters around them.

Quinn looked to her mother, his face softening. "Yes, ma'am." He stepped forward and made some sweeping hand signs. After just a brief pause, the Caddo nodded and smiled, responding in kind. And soon, all manner of pottery, baskets, and feathered trinkets were brought out and displayed.

Dorritt hung back, taking in everything, watching how skillful Quinn was as he translated her mother's questions to the Caddo into the silent language of his hands. He knew so much she thought with unaccountable pride. The thought startled her. But it was true. He could speak English, Spanish, and probably Cherokee, since he'd been raised by a Cherokee mother, and he could speak sign language with his hands. And maybe more languages. He knew about hunting for game, about horses, about cattle, about the Spanish, about the different tribes here, and about this land. And he had been far into the northwest of the barely charted wilderness beyond Texas.

Dorritt stood up straighter. Why didn't people see everything he was? Why did they deem him *just* an illiterate half-breed? In New Orleans, a man was valued for his wealth and his manners and his education. But wealth could be lost and what did manners mean if true courtesy was not behind them? And Quinn was educated, educated in the ways of the West, which were much more useful here.

Peering inside the Caddo house, she noted its neatness and order. Why did people call the Caddo filthy savages just because of their darker skin? She stood straight again and walked around the conical house. Once again, she was aware how differently she viewed this world from the people around her and recalled Maria back in the church at Nacogdoches.

She sighed, wondering how this journey was going to end. Moving on, she halted by a small house attached to the rear of a bigger house. She peeked farther inside and saw pumpkins, cured venison, and corn, all stored there for the coming winter. How could a white person see an ordered village like this and dismiss the residents as uncivilized?

She turned back to watch Quinn where he stood near her mother and Mrs. Anderson, chatting over the pottery. All day she had avoided being anywhere near Quinn. But perhaps that was as noticeable, as incriminating, as staying at his side all day. Dorritt strolled over and acted as if she were interested in the wares for sale.

Her heart jumping at his nearness, she formed her face into a mildly interested expression and spoke the first words that came to mind, "Mr. Quinn, I was wondering if you would give me some lessons in sign language too. I think it might come in handy, don't you?"

Before Quinn could reply, there came an outcry from the distance. The Indian women grabbed up children and began to run. Their men called to them and pulled out guns, bows, and arrows.

"Quick!" Quinn shouted, dropping his long rifle from his shoulder into his hands. "Get to your wagons! Either Comanches or soldiers are coming!" He pushed Dorritt toward her mother. "Run! Run to the wagons!"

Her stepfather was bellowing, "What's happening?" But

though the Andersons didn't like Quinn, they were quick to obey his warning. They were making haste to their wagon and arming themselves.

It was like being sucked into a tornado. Dorritt helped her mother run to the wagon, praying all the way this wouldn't trigger her mother to miscarry. Just as Dorritt was helping her mother into the wagon, she saw uniformed soldiers on horseback, riding toward the village. So out of place in their crisp white and blue uniforms. But of which army—the Spanish or the Mexican? Had the revolution been overthrown? Why were they attacking the Caddo?

Gunfire boomed, sending up plumes of black smoke. Instinctively, Dorritt ducked. Then the soldiers were riding toward the cone-shaped houses, not the wagons. And the Caddo were running for their lives. But how could they outrun horses? Panic welled up inside Dorritt. Was she about to witness a bloody massacre? She wanted to run forward and help, but what could she do? She wanted to cover her eyes with her hands, but she could only stare in horror.

It was all over in minutes. The Caddo fled and the soldiers lit torches and set fire to their houses. Dorritt shuddered—all the food, blankets, hides—gone! What would the Caddo eat this winter? How would they keep their children warm? Then the soldiers rode toward the wagon train. Would they be next— burned out and left in the wilderness? Why would the soldiers burn the village but not pursue and kill the Caddo? It didn't make sense. Dorritt watched the soldiers advance on the wagon train. Emotions were rushing through her so fast she couldn't identify them. She shivered and wrapped her arms around herself. And tried to keep breathing.

Quinn, Ash, the *vaqueros,* her stepfather, and the Anderson men moved forward on horseback in a wide line to meet the commander, bearing down on them. Without words, Dorritt and her mother joined hands. Fear clotted in Dorritt's throat.

The soldiers halted and the commanding officer spoke to Quinn. As before, he did the parlaying in Spanish. Dorritt watched the negotiations, she prayed for protection. She pressed her lips together to keep them from trembling. Would life in Texas be unpredictable like this even after they reached and settled in the Austin settlement? Would they never know peace?

Finally, Quinn turned toward the wagons. And her. From where he was, he gave her the slightest of nods and then, averting his eyes, followed her stepfather back to their party. Dorritt's heart leaped. She wanted to jump down and run to Quinn. But of course she waited with her mother. Her back straight, she folded her hands tightly in her lap.

"Mr. Kilbride!" her mother called out. "What do the soldiers want?"

"They're with the new Mexican army. They say we must go with them to San Antonio de Bexar." Her stepfather sounded disgruntled and goaded. "They're taking us to their commanding officer there to see if we have the right to be in Mexico."

The news hit Dorritt like a flaming arrow. She pressed a hand to her heart.

"Do we have to go with them?" her mother asked faintly.

"It seems to be so," Mr. Kilbride replied, his jaw working.

Unable to stop herself, Dorritt looked to Quinn. He responded with a set expression—telling her silently they must go with the Mexicans, but he would protect her. But seeing what these men had done to the peaceful Caddo, destroying their stored grain and dried meat, blankets, all their wooden-handled tools left her questioning. "Why did they burn the village?" she asked Quinn. "What was the point?"

Something dark was brewing behind Quinn's eyes. He was

coiled like an overly tightened spring ready to snap. *He is as angry as I've ever seen him.*

"Looks like the Mexican soldiers are just like the Spanish," Ash drawled. "They want all the Indians to be in the mission system." Somehow he made these lazy words a bitter accusation.

"But they let the Indians go?" Dorritt pressed him. It didn't make sense.

"The soldiers just keep burning them out—over and over until they finally give up and go to the mission and become peons," Quinn said, tightly controlled outrage evident in every sharp syllable. Suddenly, he looked at her as though she were the enemy. The look made her feel as if he had slapped her face, she put her hand to the imaginary sting.

Then Quinn said something short in Spanish to the *vaqueros.* He turned with them and rode off toward the cattle which had dispersed in the commotion. Quinn didn't look back at her. She sat still, absorbing Quinn's rare show of anger. Had it been at her? She closed her eyes, thinking of soldiers driving her from her home and burning it to the ground. Life in New Orleans had no doubt been cruel, but she had been protected by wealth. But not here.

Mr. Kilbride told his wife he was going to speak to Mr. Anderson. Ash gave Dorritt an unreadable look and rode off toward the cattle too. Wanting to seek out Reva, Dorritt made as if to get down from the wagon, but her mother stopped her with a hand on her sleeve.

"Dorritt, I am very concerned over this. Your stepfather is not a patient man and this could delay us."

Dorritt didn't want to discuss Mr. Kilbride now. She needed to make sense of this. "Mother," she chose her words with care, "why have you changed? When you speak to Mr. Kilbride, you seem so much stronger . . ."

"Yes, I do feel stronger. I feel as if I've awakened from a long sleep—like Rip Van Winkle." Her mother mentioned the recent story they'd read together in New Orleans.

"Why did you wake up? I mean what changed?" She'd had never really talked to her mother like this.

Her mother stared down at her gloved hands in her lap. "Over the past days, I've done a lot of thinking, a lot of remembering. My father wanted sons. He had five daughters. He never paid us the slightest attention. Our mother died. He adopted the orphaned son of a cousin as his heir. Unmarried daughters can't inherit land." Her mother's tone was bitter. "We were all married off as soon as we were of marriageable age. My father made me hate myself for being what I was—a female. And more so as a female who couldn't give her husband a son."

Dorritt considered this. She wanted to say, but why did you do the same to me? Why didn't you love me? A glimpse from her childhood flashed in Dorritt's mind. Her much younger mother was sitting in green grass under a flowering cherry tree, humming and braiding a daisy chain for Dorritt's hair. *You loved me then, but not later.* Dorritt made herself speak truth, "I've always felt all those years ago when father was killed that I lost you too. You were never the same. Why did you change?" Suddenly Dorritt couldn't bear to hear her mother's answer. What if it was her fault? Dorritt muttered an excuse and hurried away from the wagon. She ignored her mother's call to wait, her heart pounding.

As she rushed off, their wagon train, just behind the Andersons started off again. The Mexican soldiers rode on one side along the length of the combined train. Their forbidding presence made Dorritt uneasy, deeply uneasy. She let the wagons move farther ahead of her. There was only one person she wanted to talk to. But Quinn wouldn't thank her for turning to him here and now. She chafed at the scrutiny of so many eyes.

Yet compelled by a force she couldn't resist, she worked her way to the end of the caravan where the cattle plodded.

In the dusty rear, Quinn slid down from his horse and fell into step beside her as if he had been waiting for her. She glanced around. They were alone, the cattle and dust separating them from the caravan. And all the prying eyes.

"Should I be worried about these soldiers?" Dorritt asked.

"I wish I knew," Quinn replied. "With the change of government in Mexico City, Stephen Austin might have lost his right to bring Americans into Texas. I always thought it was a stupid idea, anyway. Inviting Americans into their territory is like inviting a bear into your house." Quinn's voice was derisive.

It even stung her. "You don't have a very good opinion of my people. Or should I say *our* people? You told me your father was an American. That makes you an American too."

Quinn shrugged, looking nettled. "Your stepfather. Mr. Anderson. They don't look at me as an American."

"They wouldn't be the ones to decide." Dorritt paused, a sudden thought hitting her like blinding sunlight. Pulse racing, she went ahead, as reckless as if she had nothing to lose from saying exactly what she felt. "Why don't you buy land in the Austin settlement? You could set up your ranch and breed your horses and raise a herd of cattle. If the Andersons' sons can do it, why not you?"

Quinn gave a bark of a mean-sounding laughter. "Because I'm half Cherokee and because I'm a leatherstocking. They don't want *my kind* in their Anglo settlement. And I'd rather live with scorpions."

She ignored his dark words as bright hope streaked though her. "If you are useful, as you were today at the village, Americans would tolerate you. I mean they'll need someone to speak to the Spanish and speak to the Indians. If they need you, they will let you in. Americans may be many things, but they are always practical about getting what they want."

He sent her a look of loathing. "I don't want to be useful or tolerated. I don't want to have anything to do with them. Maybe my idea of raising horses, breeding mustangs, and thoroughbreds is just stupid. I will never settle down. Never belong anywhere."

"It's not stupid." Why couldn't he see it? It was suddenly so clear to her. "I feel like I'm changing. God is here, working on me. When I left New Orleans, I had hoped that this trip would be His way of setting me free, free of my stepfather. But I—"

"I don't know what you're talking about. What has God got to do with this trip?"

Dorritt felt completely inadequate to answer this. She felt like she was feeling her way through a strange room in the darkness. But with a new, a strange, hopefulness. "I don't know." *I don't.* She lowered her voice, "You have caused me to change for the good. All good gifts come from God, and you have been a gift. You . . . have protected me." *You have kissed me.*

"And in doing so, I haven't made Kilbride my friend."

"God can change us and we can change the way things are—"

He interrupted her, "If God is on this trek with us, I'll believe it when I see some evidence of that."

Feeling inadequate, Dorritt tried again. "You could belong in this new settlement. You could be a man of property—if you only believed that you could. If you had land, people would have to respect you."

"Respect me like they respect your father?" Quinn almost sneered at her. "That's what you don't see. God can't make me want the respect of people who would respect such a worthless man."

Dorritt gripped his sleeve. *Stop it.* "I'm just trying to show you a way out." *A way for us to be together.* "Don't you see that?"

He pulled free. "There is no way out. No way *in*. I will always be outside. Always." He turned away, swung back up onto his horse, and was gone. She stared after him, hurt by his words, yet hurting for him, too.

She pressed her fingers to her temples and then glanced forward. Her stepfather was venting his wrath at the soldiers by snapping his whip behind the first wagon—as if that would change anything.

Ash rode up and swung down beside her. "You all right?"

Looking away, Dorritt brushed away the start of tears. "This awful dust."

"Quinn looked mad."

Dorritt swallowed and cleared her throat. Maybe Ash could help. "I was just trying to open his eyes. Help him see he could have a life here in Texas. Why can't he buy land in the Austin settlement?"

"Because he's half Cherokee." Ash swatted away a fly.

"He could overcome that. He's got skills and knowledge Americans will need to prosper here in Texas. Don't you see that too? Are you as blind as Quinn?"

Ash rubbed his chin. "You might have a point, but I doubt you'll ever get Quinn to see it."

"Why?" She began to feel weak, wrung out like a rag. No doubt a reaction to the sudden excitement that had gripped her.

"Because he doesn't want to be useful. He doesn't want his mother's blood to be overlooked. And he doesn't see in himself what you see in him. He doesn't understand how much a man he is. He needs something someday and soon to show him, prove it to him what he could have—if he was willing to reach out and take it."

Dorritt didn't know what to say to this. She understood a little of what Ash said. But compared to her situation as a spinster, as a man, Quinn could break free. She'd told him how. And he'd rejected it out of hand. She sighed and brushed away a stray hair from her eyes.

"What do you want in Texas, Miss Dorritt?"

His question took her by surprise. But she didn't follow her first inclination and decline to answer. "I want to be free of my stepfather. I want to be a free woman. And I want Reva to be free and with me."

"You can be."

Irritation buzzed inside her. "I can't. I'll never be free."

"That's what you think. Just like Quinn thinks he's not a man who can be landed and respected. But you watch and see what happens. I think soon everything will turn out just right. Yes, soon may come the first day of freedom for many." Without another word, he pulled the front of his hat brim and swung back up into his saddle.

Dorritt walked, looking down at her dusty moccasins. Why did the world have to be the way it was? And why was she always on the wrong side of where power and freedom lay? What did Ash mean that freedom was coming soon? Didn't he know how foolish that hope was? *In New Orleans not so long ago, I thought I was going to be set free. And I was wrong. So very wrong.* She didn't like feeling this way, but Quinn's complete rejection of her words burned like sand in her eyes. God was on this trek with them. She had felt herself changing. Her mother was changing. *Father, show Quinn you are here.*

Thirteen

Kilbride's frayed temper broke at twilight. Quinn had watched Kilbride let the worrying escort of soldiers work him into a fever. The man's voice had become more and more shrill, his motions jerky, as if something were stinging him over and over. And why not? The day before, Dorritt had embarrassed Kilbride in front of the Andersons. And now the Mexican army was forcing him to go to San Antonio, far from the Austin settlement. Of course, Kilbride would want someone to pay for everything going from bad to worse, but who? If Quinn had liked Kilbride at all, he would have had some sympathy for him. But Kilbride deserved no sympathy. And now he proved that in front of God and everyone.

"Reva! Josiah!" Kilbride called near the main campfire. Everyone within hearing turned to watch, even the Mexican soldiers. There was almost a frenzy in the man's tone. He sounded like a man who'd been in bad pain too long and could no longer bear it.

Quinn moved forward, his long rifle at the ready on his shoulder. Everyone gathered around the campfire, just as Kilbride had intended. The man wanted an audience. For what? Was he going to try to hurt Dorritt's maid? And in that way, hurt Dorritt? Quinn's gut tightened, recalling how short he'd been with Dorritt. Yet, there was nothing he could do to stop this.

Looking skittish, Reva walked slowly forward, her nervous eyes on her master's face. Josiah, one of the seasoned ox drivers, slouched forward, his thumbs in his belt. He did not look at Kilbride. Quinn glimpsed Dorritt at her mother's side.

"It's time, Reva, you had a husband," Kilbride said in an oily tone, which made a mockery of kindness. "I've been remiss in not providing one for you. Just because your mistress has never found a man to her liking doesn't mean that you should remain unmarried." He looked at Dorritt as if taunting her.

Quinn saw Dorritt open her mouth to speak. But then she closed it and looked down at the ground. What could she say?

"Josiah, your wife has been dead for nearly a year. Reva is your wife now." Kilbride looked at Reva and gave her a dreadful smile. "I expect a baby within a year. As the Good Book says, be fruitful and multiply." Kilbride chuckled.

Quinn wanted to wipe the terrible grin off the man's face.

Dorritt moved forward, obviously ready to object. But Ash stepped up to Kilbride. "I don't think so."

Kilbride turned away, ignoring Ash.

"Indentured servants cannot be forced to marry. And since there is no slavery in Texas," Ash raised his voice and let amusement creep into his tone, "—you can't force Reva to marry Josiah." Ash repeated this in Spanish so the Mexicans standing around watching would understand too.

Kilbride swung back. "This is not any of your business—"

Ash cut off Kilbride by turning to the Mexican captain, who

had drawn closer to the fire. Ash raised his voice to ask him a question in Spanish. Quinn hid a grin. Leave it to Ash. The captain replied shortly. Then Ash smiled at Kilbride. "The captain agrees with me. You can't force an indentured servant to marry against her will."

Kilbride began to sputter.

"But since you want to find Reva, a really fine-looking woman in my opinion, a husband, I think we can take care of that." Ash turned to Reva. "I was intending on proposing to you tonight and then on buying your indentured paper from Kilbride. I don't like having to propose to you in such a public manner. But, Reva, would you do me the honor of being my wife?"

Silence. Just the lowing of the cattle, nickering of horses, and the crickets could be heard. Then Kilbride exploded, "No!"

Ash ignored him. "Miss Reva, what is your answer?"

"Yes, my answer is yes." Reva came quickly toward Ash and took his hand. "Yes."

"Well, one yes would've done it," Ash drawled with a wide grin.

Quinn heard Dorritt give some sort of gasp and choke. It twisted his insides. He began to move closer to her. Kilbride would lash out.

"I said no!" Kilbride yelled. "I forbid it. I will decide what happens to my slaves!"

Quinn had become used to Kilbride's angry outbursts and red face, but this time the man's whole body shook with his fury. And the man's eyes were wild. Quinn was afraid he would make the mistake of trying to physically attack Ash.

Ash turned to the Mexican officer and spoke in Spanish again. When the Mexican officer responded with a short "No," Ash turned back to Kilbride and Quinn edged farther forward. "I just explained all this to the captain and asked him if slavery is now legal in the new Republic of Mexico. You heard his answer. And I know you wouldn't want to break any laws here in the Republic of Mexico, would you?"

Quinn gripped the butt of his long rifle. Would Ash push Kilbride too far? Quinn kept watch on Dorritt from the corner of his eye.

Ash grinned. "Now, Mr. Kilbride, why don't you get out that metal box with the indentured papers? Then we can prove to the captain here that you're not doing anything illegal, like, say, bringing slaves onto Mexican land. And I'll pay you Reva's indenture sum."

Kilbride did not move an inch. He shook and stammered and reached for his pistol. But Ash was too quick for him. Before Kilbride's pistol cleared his belt, Ash had his pistol out and aimed within inches of Kilbride's forehead.

It was as if everyone drew in the same shocked breath. Quinn heard it and felt it in his own chest. He moved forward and then halted. Ash knew what he was doing. Still, Quinn slid his long rifle into his hands, ready to fire at a moment's notice. Why hadn't Ash let him know what he intended to do? The answer was quick and clear. Kilbride had forced Ash's hand.

"Now, we have a situation here," Ash drawled, staring into Kilbride's wide eyes. "I know you're just concerned for Reva's welfare. You're not really angry with me for proposing to her and for being willing to purchase her freedom. From her indenture, that is." Ash scanned the crowd surrounding Kilbride, Reva, Josiah and himself. "That's right, isn't it?"

Kilbride followed Ash's gaze and stiffened when he realized that not just one gun was aimed at him. Along with Quinn, the Mexican soldiers and the two *vaqueros* were aiming guns at Kilbride. His red face went pasty white, almost gray. The man swallowed and twitched.

Quinn worried the Andersons might push in and cause someone to get shot. But the Andersons had faded away. Then from the corner of his eye, Quinn saw movement. It was Dorritt going to the wagon. His brave Dorritt opened the concealed panel and lifted out that metal locked box. With downcast eyes, she carried it to her stepfather and held it out to him.

Quinn moved forward, ready to strike Kilbride down with the butt of his long rifle if the man lashed out at her.

A great shudder shook Kilbride. But he pushed his pistol farther into his belt and pulled out his chain with the key. With barely controlled hands, he opened the lock and lifted the lid. "You find her paper." Kilbride's voice was rough with fear and fury.

Dorritt turned the box toward herself and then knelt by the fire. She looked at each of the papers in turn and then drew one forth. "Here it is." She rose and handed him the single sheet. Quinn shifted, ready to defend her.

As Kilbride took the indentured paper, his hand shook.

"What is the indenture price?" Ash asked as if he were merely passing the time of day. Ash could do that. It was something Quinn had always liked about his friend—cool under the gun.

His jaw working, Kilbride looked to Dorritt. She cleared her throat. "One hundred and twenty dollars."

Reva gave a little gasp and then pressed her hand to her mouth. Around Quinn, the *vaqueros* and soldiers shifted on their feet, continuing to point their guns at Kilbride.

Still aiming his pistol at Kilbride, Ash grinned at Reva. "Don't worry, honey. You're worth that and plenty more." Ash slowly lowered his pistol, shoved it in his belt, and lifted a pouch that hung there. Quinn heard the clink and rattle of coins as Ash loosed the drawstring of the pouch and searched through his coins.

Then Ash counted out several gold coins into Reva's hand. And then from a pouch hanging around his neck and under his shirt, he pulled out a wad of U.S. and Spanish currency. Then he took all the money and stepped forward to count it out. When Kilbride made no attempt to take the money, Ash dropped it into the locked box.

"I'll take that indenture paper now." Ash held his hand out. As if in a trance, Kilbride gave Ash the paper. "First," Ash said, "I need you to sign that and add a note saying that I have redeemed Reva on this date." Kilbride just stared at him dumbly.

Quinn gripped his long rifle tighter. Would Ash be able to pull it off? Or would Kilbride break and do something dangerous and foolish?

Again, Dorritt knelt beside the fire, reached into the lockbox, and drew out a small bottle of black ink and a quill. With concern, Quinn noted her hands trembled as she trimmed the quill point and opened the bottle of ink and dipped the quill. She handed the pen to her stepfather, and Ash laid the paper in his palm.

"That won't work," Dorritt said, and she lifted the metal box, shut the lid, and held it underneath the paper as a writing table. Kilbride paused. But then he scribbled on the page.

Ash looked down and nodded with satisfaction. Then the Mexican captain approached the fire and spoke to Ash. Ash nodded and motioned Dorritt to offer the lockbox, paper, pen and ink to the captain. "The captain thinks he should sign it too to make it official," Ash explained.

After the captain wrote his signature, Ash blew on the wet ink as Dorritt took the pen back and put away the writing implements. Ash folded the indenture paper and tucked it into the pouch, hanging around this neck. "Well, now that concludes our business." Ash turned to Reva and held out his hand. "Come along, wife."

Reva hesitated, casting a glance at Dorritt.

Dorritt noticed this and pulled herself together. She couldn't spoil Reva's first moments of freedom—even if her own heart was breaking. "Go ahead, Reva." Each word plunged like a knife into Dorritt's heart. She drew breath with difficulty, shivering with it. "I wish you and your husband every happiness."

Reva ran to Dorritt, throwing her arms around Dorritt's shoulders. "I don't want to leave you," Reva whispered.

"Go." Dorritt struggled with the physical pain of wrenching loss. "Go and be glad. I am."

Reva turned away then and went to Ash, tears trailing down her cheeks. Ash put his arm around her shoulder and drew her away, through the surrounding Mexican soldiers. "We'll be going off aways to talk in private," Ash said, pulling politely at the brim of his hat. "I have a lot to tell my bride."

Dorritt could not move. She knew she should get away from Mr. Kilbride before he came out of his trance. But she was entranced too, frozen in despair. Reva was free and Dorritt was glad. *But I'm still in bondage.*

She looked across at Quinn. What had Ash said before? That Quinn needed to see he could be someone? She almost wished it was Quinn declaring her his wife and taking her away with him. *And she'd never thought that about any man before.*

But now Quinn, who still appeared startled, did not look as if he were going to take any action tonight. Though she could not feel her feet, Dorrit walked to the wagon and stowed the lockbox. And then started to wander away. She had to be alone now. Her movement appeared to release the others. Every slave quickly disappeared into the twilight shadows before Mr. Kilbride could light on a scapegoat to vent his wrath upon.

Feeling detached, Dorritt put one foot in front of the other, her arms dangling. *Mr. Quinn can't see his way to freedom. What had he said?* He needed to see evidence that God was on this trek. Well, hadn't they just witnessed a miracle? But she'd always thought that miracles made a person happy. *I must not begrudge Reva. I am happy for her. It's just the shock.*

But her stepfather's sharp low voice halted her. "Not so fast, young lady."

Dorritt froze where she stood. She had not realized he'd followed her.

Taking her shoulders in his hands, he swung her around to face him. "Don't think I haven't been watching you, Little Miss Know-It-All. You stay away from that half-breed."

She pressed her lips together. So here was her stepfather's revenge. But he couldn't know Quinn and she had shared a kiss the night before. He couldn't know what she felt for Quinn. *Because I don't know—exactly.*

Then Mr. Kilbride tightened his grip on her shoulders making her flinch. "You will not disgrace your family any more than you already have. We are going to be highly regarded in Texas. And if you do anything that interferes with that, I'll disown you no matter what your mother says. We'll cast you out into the streets."

"Take your hands off Miss Dorritt," Quinn said, looming up out of the darkness.

Dorritt gasped, suddenly fearful. Her stepfather's eyes looked wild, as if he had been pushed beyond endurance. She didn't want to witness physical violence.

Kilbride released her and swung around to face Quinn. "And you keep away from her. My stepdaughter is not for the likes of you."

Dorritt struggled to hold back her angry words. The disparity between the two men was so clear in her mind. An honest, good man, Quinn. A dishonest, foolish man, Mr. Kilbride.

"I know that," Quinn said. "But that doesn't mean I won't stop you from hurting her."

"I wasn't hurting her. I was just reminding her of her duty to her family."

Quinn challenged him, "It seems to me that she knows her duty to her family. Do you?"

Her mother's voice interrupted, calling, "Mr. Kilbride! Isn't it time we turned in for the night?" Kilbride glared at Quinn, then turned and marched away.

Quinn and Dorritt were left facing each other. She found she couldn't speak. She waited to see what he would say to her. He said nothing. When she could bear the silence no longer, she murmured, "Good night, Mr. Quinn." She wished he would stop her. And hold her in his arms again. All things were possible with God, but only if one believed it. She wandered to the edge of the encampment and headed out farther, wishing to be as far away from everyone as possible. Oddly disjointed, numb as though she had been beaten but not yet feeling the pain from it. She tried to put it all together—God, Reva, Ash, and Quinn.

Quinn watched Dorritt stagger away, looking like a flower wilting in the hot sun. He started to follow her and then stopped himself. *I can't do anything for her. And if I try, I could end up just harming her more.* Kilbride had just proved Quinn's attraction to Dorritt had not gone unnoticed. And Quinn wouldn't make Kilbride go through with his threat of disowning Dorritt. A woman alone on the frontier couldn't make it. Dorritt needed her family such as it was.

The Andersons from a distance had also missed nothing of tonight's show and Quinn wouldn't go to Dorritt, wouldn't give them or Jewell gossip to use against her. He moved away, thinking about how lucky Ash was to have rescued Reva. But only Reva's being a slave had stood between them, and money had taken care of that. No amount of money would ever be able to break the barrier between Dorritt and himself. How could he ever give her the elegant life she deserved? Quinn walked the length of the wagon train to the campfire at the rear and eased down, sitting cross-legged.

Carrying two cups of coffee, Eduardo wandered up and sank down beside Quinn. Eduardo handed him one cup of coffee and began to sip his own. "Your friend knows how to get what he wants."

Quinn nodded and took a swallow of the hot bitter brew. He hoped Eduardo didn't expect conversation. But for once, the man didn't. They drank their coffee in silence; Quinn stared at the flames, which looked unusually bright all of a sudden. His eyes were tired. He blinked.

"You seem very sleepy," Eduardo said, taking the empty cup from Quinn's hand. "Why don't you just lie down for a short *siesta*? I'll wake you when it is dark and your turn for watch."

Quinn could barely nod. He found himself sliding down onto the coarse grass. His eyes shut. *What's happening. . . ?*

* * *

Unable to face anyone, Dorritt waited for the camp to go to sleep. She sat on the earth and fanned away the few mosquitoes. Images from the recent drama kept flashing before her eyes. She kept seeing Reva walking away from her. *I've lost Reva.* The sounds of the large encampment behind her took a long time to fade into slumber and quiet. Still, she made no move to go to the wagon. There was no comfort to help with this loss. Not even tears or prayers would come.

Then out of the darkness, Eduardo approached her. "*Señorita* Dorritt, Quinn has asked me to come and get you." He offered her a hand and helped her up. She walked beside him, wondering what Quinn would have to say to her, barely aware of walking. Perhaps Quinn would tell her where Ash had taken Reva. She and Eduardo had gone quite a distance when it dawned on Dorritt that they had walked away—not toward the encampment. She was far from the others now. She halted. "Where is Quinn?"

Before she had time to cry out, Eduardo caught her in a tight embrace with his hand clamped over her mouth. "I regret this indignity, *señorita*. But this is for your own good. Carlos would not want me to wait any longer. Who knows what your stepfather might do to you after Ash has taken your maid? I must protect you." The sardonic tone he used belied his words and her fear leaped up like flames. She tried to break free and could not. Through tightly shut lips, she screamed into his hand— without making a sound. Fear made her dizzy. She struggled. Eduardo held her with ease, his grip like a tightened noose.

And then Juan was there, tying a tight gag in her mouth while Eduardo tied her hands in front of her. Then he led her away by her bound hands quickly, so quickly that she could not stop or refuse without falling on her face. Stumbling after him, she tried to question him around her gag, but could not.

"Do not fear. This is all for your good," Eduardo murmured, still with that ironic twist.

My good? What will they do with me? Help me, Father.

Then Eduardo asked. "And Quinn?"

"*Sí,*" Juan said.

What did that mean? Tears wet her gag. What had they done to Quinn? What was going to happen to her?

Eduardo murmured. "Don't cry. I'll take good care of you." And then he chuckled.

Fourteen

Late the next morning to the distant sound of orders given in Spanish, Ash with Reva at his side sauntered into camp. Mrs. Kilbride crept out of the wagon and looked around. Ash steered his bride away. They'd come to camp to claim her few possessions. As they passed Kilbride's lady, Amos came to her. "Mistress, I can't find Miss Dorritt."

"What do you mean?"

"I been up and down the line and I can't find Miss Dorritt. The cook sent me to look for her because she didn't come out of her wagon . . . for breakfast." Amos rotated his hat in his hand. "I went to the wagon but she gone. I can't find her, mistress."

Ash halted. *Miss Dorritt gone?*

Mrs. Kilbride looked around the camp and so did Ash. The ox driver Josiah, the man Mr. Kilbride had last night tried to make marry Reva, came up behind Amos. "Mistress, two of the *vaqueros* are gone. And Mr. Quinn too."

Quinn too? Ash changed directions and moved toward Amos and Josiah.

"What?" Mr. Kilbride barked from behind his wife. He climbed forward out the back of the wagon.

Both Amos and Josiah jumped backward to keep out of his reach. "Master," Amos said, keeping his eyes on the ground, "I can't find Miss Dorritt."

"And two of the *vaqueros* and Mr. Quinn are gone, sir," Josiah repeated.

"Look harder," Kilbride barked. The two servants nodded and left him, moving quickly.

Reva's eyes widened and Ash took her to Mrs. Kilbride. "What has happened to Miss Dorritt?" he asked.

"I don't know," Mrs. Kilbride replied. "Reva, please go get Miss Jewell and bring her here. She might know where her sister is."

Reva bobbed her head and took off. Ash eyed Kilbride and then squatted down by the fire, accepting a cup of coffee from the cook.

Very soon, Miss Jewell appeared with Reva. "What's this about Dorritt disappearing?" Jewell snapped.

"We can't find your sister," Mrs. Kilbride said. "Or Mr. Quinn and two of the *vaqueros.* Have you or any of the Andersons seen them?"

Jewell laughed.

"*Jewell.* This is no laughing matter." Mrs. Kilbride sounded shocked.

Jewell changed expressions, looking suddenly dour. "I'm sorry, mother. I didn't want to say this. But I saw my sister and the half-breed scout kissing the other night. Evidently she has run off with him."

Mrs. Kilbride pressed both hands to her open mouth. "No, I don't believe it."

Ash didn't either. Quinn would never leave without finding

Ash—even on his wedding night—to tell him what was going on. Something wrong had happened here. A sick feeling erupted in Ash's empty stomach.

"I'm so sorry to hurt you, Mother." Jewell tried to look contrite, but failed. "But I saw what I saw. And now she's gone and he's gone. Doesn't that prove I'm right?" Mrs. Kilbride began to weep.

Frowning, Reva moved to stand next to her husband. Ash rose and put an arm around her shoulder. He whispered to her, "Quinn would never leave without telling me."

Reva looked up at him and nodded in agreement. "Miss Dorritt neither."

Juan approached them and swept off his large hat. "*Señor and señora*, I stay," he recited in a singsong voice. "Pedro and Eduardo go. I herd cattle. At San Antonio, I leave. I take pay to Carlos and Eduardo."

"Why did the two Mexicans leave?" Kilbride asked.

Juan shrugged. And repeated what he already said. Then he said, "*No hablo inglés.*" He bowed his head and turned to walk away.

This sounded fishy to Ash. Had the two Mexicans made away with both Quinn and Dorritt? But how?

Jumping down, Kilbride reached out and grabbed Juan's shoulder. "Where did the other two *vaqueros* go?"

Juan shrugged again and pulled away. "*No hablo inglés.*"

"Do you know where my daughter or Mr. Quinn has gone?" Mrs. Kilbride called after him.

"*No hablo inglés.*"

At a silent appeal from Reva, Ash stopped Juan and put the questions to him in Spanish. But Juan couldn't or wouldn't tell him more. All he said was Pedro and Eduardo had gone ahead on business. Juan was to finish the herding job, collect their pay, and join them in San Antonio. Ash wasn't satisfied but couldn't think how to get the truth from Juan—if Juan knew the truth.

The Mexican officer approached them. *"¡Vamanos! ¡Adelante!"* He motioned with both hands in a forward sweep. He repeated the two words again. And then he clapped his hands. The meaning came clear. It was time to set forth.

Ash stood, gazing around, trying to get some idea of what had happened last night after he took his bride far from camp. Someone had taken advantage of his being distracted. But who?

Both Kilbrides tried to go after the Spanish captain to change his mind. "We can't leave. My daughter is missing," Mrs. Kilbride pleaded.

When the officer shook his head, she called out to Ash and waved him to come to them. "Mr. Ash, please won't you tell him our daughter is missing? We can't just leave her."

"¡Captain! ¡Por favor!" Ash explained the situation rapidly to the officer but the captain gave him a curt denial.

Mrs. Kilbride raised her voice as if it would make her words understandable to the Mexican, saying, "My daughter, Miss Dorritt, is missing."

"No importa," the Mexican officer who looked nettled replied. *"¡Vamos!"*

"We can't just leave without her." Mrs. Kilbride's voice held an edge of hysteria.

Ash then turned to Mrs. Kilbride. "I'm sorry, ma'am. He won't change his mind. I think he's angry that the four of them got away without any of his men noticing. He's not going to go look for them."

"But—" Mrs. Kilbride started.

"¡No importa!"

Mrs. Kilbride tried once more, "Mr. Ash, please ask him—"

The officer slipped his musket from his shoulder and aimed it at Mrs. Kilbride. *"¡Vamos! ¡Vengan!"*

The two Kilbrides looked at each other, both bewildered. But what choice did they have?

Worried, Ash led Reva away to the wagon where Dorritt had slept. She climbed inside and lifted out the small cloth bag that contained her possessions: a change of clothing, a comb, and a few handkerchiefs. When she was standing beside her husband again, she asked, "How're we going to find Miss Dorritt?"

"I guess I better do some tracking." The camp around them was alive with running and shouting as the wagon train got moving once again. "I must go and gather up our cattle and mustangs. Then we'll wait until this bunch leaves. I've got to take time to find Quinn's or the Mexicans' trail."

"Miss Dorritt would never go off with Quinn without telling me first. She wouldn't," Reva repeated.

Ash nodded. "I don't need convincing." He saw she was very worried. "You and Miss Dorritt are close, aren't you?"

"Yes, she's not like any other white person I know. I mean when we're with other people, she treats me like a slave. But when we are alone, we're just friends. We been together since we we're babies. She's special, my Miss Dorritt. I can't be happy, Ash, if something bad happen to her."

Ash tucked his free hand around his wife's waist and squeezed her to him. He knew how she felt. The thought of losing Quinn caused an ache deep in him.

"Don't worry. I'll do the best I can." But he didn't say how big Texas was and how easy it was to make someone disappear in the empty miles.

* * *

Quinn was first aware only of the overwhelming smell of horse. He couldn't open his eyes. He tried and tried but they wouldn't open. Thoughts, voices whispered just beyond the reach of his mind. *What? What?* Someone was speaking or were they singing?

Then he realized something covered his face. But how could that be? He tried to reach up and take it off and there was only a tug. Something tight bound his wrists together. He tried to pull his wrists apart, break the binding. He couldn't and then he found that when he jerked his hands, it caused a tug at his ankles.

Then it all came together. He was trussed up and lying with his belly over a saddle. His wrists were tied together and connected by leather thong to his bound ankles. He had a rough cloth sack over his head. And his nose was bumping into the side of a horse's belly.

For a few moments he checked and rechecked to see if this was real. He swallowed and swallowed until he had enough spit to speak. "Where am I?" *Why?*

"*Ah*, Señor Quinn, you have come back to life."

Quinn recognized the man's voice, but could think of no reason why Eduardo would do this to him. They weren't friends, but what had he done to make this Mexican angry? "Eduardo?"

"*Sí, Señor.*"

"Why am I trussed up like this?" Quinn knew he should be angry, but he still only felt as if it couldn't be real.

"Because you must have time alone, time to consider your life." Eduardo's tone was mocking.

It sparked Quinn's temper. "Untie me. *Now.*"

"No, Señor Quinn, I do not think it would be smart for me to untie you. I think you are very angry with me and you are not a man that should be made angry."

"Then why did you do this? It's crazy."

"No, not *loco.* Everything makes sense. Some people have plans. I have plans. It all makes sense. But only to me. For once I know everything and I will make everything work for me."

Quinn held himself very still. Anger poured through him like molten lead. But he couldn't let his rage master him. He must be able to think. Clearly. But the feeling of being helpless, something he hadn't been since he was a small boy, filled him with rage. He closed his eyes and breathed in and out slowly. He willed himself to be calm. How had this happened? He searched his mind and he saw himself taking a cup from Eduardo. "You put something in my coffee."

"*Sí*, an old mixture of herbs and of the poppy. We had to. Even with Ash away and busy with his new bride, you are not a man to be taken by surprise."

We? Who was in on this with Eduardo? The answer was easy. There were four *vaqueros*. Carlos had left earlier. Had that been part of the plan? Quinn listened hard. But he could only hear the footfalls of two horses, no more. He wanted to ask where they were going. Why. But he didn't want to give Eduardo the chance to mock him more. What day, what time was it? He couldn't have been out for more than the night. How far had they come? And in what direction? He had questions, but no answers.

"Don't worry. Señorita Dorritt is safe with Carlos."

Quinn went still. They had kidnapped Dorritt too? Fury strong enough to make him capable of murder welled inside him. Anger at Eduardo and anger at himself. In a flash, he saw himself and Dorritt together yesterday. He'd been short with her. He'd told her, "They don't want *my kind* in their Anglo settlement. I'd rather live with scorpions." He'd pulled away and left her. Without a kind word.

"*Mi primo*, my cousin Carlos, must always have the best of everything. So you must not worry." Eduardo continued mocking Quinn. "*Sí*, Carlos has great respect for your beautiful lady. Or now his lady, *su bonita doña*." Eduardo chuckled, taunting Quinn. "Don't worry"

Quinn clamped his lips together. This man would pay. And Carlos. They would regret the day they were born. *I will find you, Dorritt. As soon as I break free. I will.*

* * *

Sitting in front of Pedro on his horse, Dorritt stared straight ahead. She was no longer bound or gagged. They were deep in the wide open land of Texas. There was no one to appeal to and nowhere to run. On and off, a stray tear would trickle down her face. Many times in her life, she had felt powerless. But not as hopeless, as vulnerable as she felt now.

It was still unbelievable. She kept thinking, *I will wake up from this nightmare.* But the hot sun beating down on her shoulders, the smell of a horse, and the feeling of Pedro sitting so close behind her refused to be discounted. It had happened. The Mexicans had kidnapped her. Why? She was afraid to ask questions now because what sane reason could have made the *vaqueros* do this? And with her small Spanish vocabulary, she couldn't question the man behind her.

They reached a small grove of live oak trees. He swung down from the saddle, offered her his hands, and urged her down from the horse. As she tested her cramped legs. Pedro said, *"Siesta. Agua. Un vaso de agua."*

He led her into the shade of the oak trees and motioned her to be seated. She arranged her skirts around her modestly and folded her hands in her lap, trying to hold in her despair. Soon he brought her a cup of cool spring water. Then he walked away from her and seemed to be troubled about something. He spoke to himself in barely audible snatches—sounding worried and angry. What was he deciding? Whether to kill her or not?

She drank, still holding back tears and not giving in to the terror that wanted to shake her. *Dear heavenly Father, help me. Help Quinn find me.* A traitorous tear trickled down her cheek. For the thousandth time, she relived those few precious moments she and Quinn had shared. The strength of his arms as he'd held her and the feel of his firm chest supporting her.

She pressed her lips shut and drew in breath, forcing away the tears.

Then Pedro came to her and spoke more Spanish, but Dorritt only caught *"pronto,"* which means "soon," and Carlos's name. Questions filled her throat. She swallowed them down. Everything was too bizarre. What was this all about? Would she ever see Quinn again? She had no doubt he was looking for her. But her heart froze. Had something happened to him too? *Oh no, Father, protect him.*

Fifteen

Quinn's head must have been split in two. And he couldn't get two halves back together. He opened his eyes to total darkness. He was lying on his back on earth, not across his horse's back. His throat was so dry he had the feeling it might nearly have sealed. "Ed . . . Ed . . . Eduardo?" Then he remembered. Some time earlier Eduardo had struck him unconscious. After two days of riding slung over a horse, Eduardo had stopped and given him some water. And then the blow to the back of his head had come.

Slowly, Quinn moved to sit up, causing his head to threaten to explode, and he felt he might be sick. He sat still until the giddy feeling stopped. Slowly, he lifted both hands and took the sack off his head. He looked around the deep, shadowy interior. He felt for a wall. His hand touched the thin poles that made up a *jacal*. Slowly, he eased against the wall and leaned his head back. He closed his eyes again and drew in deep breaths, smelling warmed sand, stale air, and his own sweat.

Where had Eduardo left him? The darkness told him it must be nearly full night and his wrists and ankles were still bound. Degree by degree, his eyes caught a little natural light as it sifted in through the slits between the poles and holes in the thatched roof. A tall round gourd jug became visible, outlined by the bright moonlight. He reached for it, sniffed it and then gulped almost all the warm water. So Eduardo did not mean for him to die of thirst here. What had been the point of kidnapping him, after all?

They wanted me out of the way. Because I was the only one who could have stopped them from kidnapping Dorritt. Quinn took in another deep breath. Eduardo had brought him two day's distance from the wagon train. He needed to get outside and look to the stars and try to figure out which direction he had been brought. He wasn't a man who gave in to despair. But he was mighty close now.

He began working at the bindings on his wrists. He knew with time he could wet and stretch the leather and free himself. But first he wanted to look at the stars. In spite of his aching head, he got down on his belly and snaked toward the door. Would it be fastened? He pushed against it and it swung open. Fresh cool air bathed his face. He crawled out. He rolled onto his back, and after the dizziness passed, he gazed up at the stars overhead. It was a clear night, no clouds with a nearly full moon rising.

Then the head of his horse loomed above him and a big soft tongue licked his face. "Hey there," he murmured. He reached up with both hands and stroked his horse's nose. Nearly weak with gratitude, he realized he had been left with water and his horse and with bindings he could work free of. So what did that mean? He rolled a little onto his shoulder and reached out to make sure he was right. Yes, Eduardo had hobbled his horse so his mount could not stray. He stared up at the sky, his horse moving away to graze on the high grass. One by one, Quinn picked out the stars in the sky and found the North Star.

Without a sextant, not even a compass, it would be difficult to know exactly where he was. But he knew from his father that in central and eastern Texas there were many rivers and all flowed from west to east toward the Mississippi. The wagon train had crossed the Brazos and was heading for the Colorado when the Mexican soldiers had taken it into custody. On the way here, Eduardo had passed a couple of creeks, but perhaps one had been a river they'd crossed at a narrow ford. In two days, Quinn couldn't have been taken off Texas territory, so if he went north he would reach one of those rivers. And going along those rivers always led to towns or ranchos. Maybe San Antonio. And he knew Ash and Dorritt's family would be heading there too, under Mexican guard.

Morning would come. And he would have worked the leather off his wrists and ankles. He would find food and then he would mount his horse.

Then out of the blue, Dorritt's words came back to him—*I feel like I'm changing. God is here. . . . All good gifts come from God . . . you have been a gift.*

He regretted his bitter reply: *If God is on this trek with us, I'll believe it when I see some evidence of that.* It was awful being apart from her. Not knowing what Eduardo might have done to her was worse. He gazed up at the spangled sky. *God, the God Dorritt trusts, are you here? Protect her. I will find her. And if anyone had harmed her, I'll make them pay.*

* * *

Two long days and two endless nights, Dorritt carried in the pit of her stomach constant sickening fear. She found it hard to keep anything but water down. Added to this was enduring endless hours in the saddle. She was accustomed to walking, not riding on horseback mile after mile. The country she'd been forced to cover was uninhabited and the landscape unfriendly. After the first day, they had left the rolling prairie behind them and for the past day had crossed a more arid, rugged land of washes, high grasses, twisted mesquite, thorny catclaw, and prickly pear cactus. Nearing another nightfall, she swallowed down tears from the pain of the raw skin and aching muscles from the saddle. Then she saw on the horizon a scattering of buildings. They looked to her as if made of some kind of smooth stucco with elegant arches for doorways.

"Rancho Sandoval," Pedro said, motioning toward it. He had spoken so rarely that his voice made her jump. *Rancho Sandoval? What was that?* Her body cried out for freedom from the crowded saddle, from the reek of Pedro's and her own stale sweat. But what would happen to her here? What would she face next? She banished the tears that were trying to start. Clamping her quivering lips together, she tried to bring up her reserves of courage.

In the distance, indistinct people had ventured out of the house and other buildings and were gazing at them as if trying to see who they were. From the way they were reacting, it was clear they had not been expecting her.

And then a man, dressed in dark Spanish clothing, hurried across the yard, mounted a fine horse, and started toward them, picking up speed. As he drew closer, Dorritt recognized him. He was Carlos—Carlos dressed as a gentleman. "Señorita Dorritt, how is it that you are here?" he called to her.

His question so unexpected, so at odds with the terror of the past few days, unleashed long-suppressed tears. She covered her face with her hands to hide them, choking back her sobs, now wrenching her smarting, weary-to-death body.

Reaching them, Carlos snapped off several sharp questions in Spanish to Pedro, who answered in brief sullen syllables. Carlos

made a hissing sound filled with anger. *"¡Eduardo, lo pagarás!"*
He swung toward her.

She drew back from him.

He held out an open palm. "Don't be afraid," he said in a kind
voice, as if coaxing a stray cat. "I regret this. I . . ." He fell silent,
frowning. "Come. I will make you welcome." He slid from his
horse and with great gentleness helped her down from Pedro's
horse. He dismissed Pedro with a curt wave of his hand. *"Más
tarde.* Later."

Carlos was dressed as a gentleman in sleek navy blue trou-
sers and a short jacket with a snowy white neckcloth tied with
neatness. He would not have looked out of place in the parlor
back at Belle Vista. Nothing made sense. She looked away from
Carlos, wiping her face with her hands. "Where am I?"

Not mentioning her weeping, he asked, "Do you wish to ride
or walk?"

"Walk," she murmured, and then staggered against him. "Where
am I?"

He offered her his arm and then slapped his horse's rump.
It took off toward the house ahead. "Señorita, this is my home,
Rancho Sandoval."

She heard the tenderness and pride in his voice. With difficulty, she began to walk, gripping his arm. And as he led her
closer to the house, she understood the pride. Backlit by the
setting sun, which was trailing magenta, pink, gold, and charcoal
ribbons across the sky, the large hacienda looked like a Spanish
painting. Involuntarily she said, "How lovely."

Carlos looked at her with frank approval. *"Gracias,* I knew
you would love it. You are a woman who was born to be a *doña,
a dueña."*

She regretted the spontaneous words that had slipped through
her lips, so she tried to show no response to his reply. She knew
what the word *dueña* meant. She'd lived around New Orleans

Creoles, who were descendents of Spanish and French colonials. She knew the ladies of Spanish descent were often referred to as *doña*, and *dueña* roughly translated to "lady" and "landed lady."

As she walked, she worked at not moaning aloud her pain and uncertainty. Even though the term *dueña* gave her some idea of his intention, she's still feared to ask Carlos precisely why Pedro had brought her here. Now she understood clearly what she had only guessed before—Pedro as well as Eduardo—took orders from Carlos. So even though Carlos had not physically brought her here himself, he must have had something to do with her being kidnapped. *But why?*

However, Carlos did not offer to tell her and she was afraid to ask. If she asked and received an answer, an answer that might terrify her more, it would make this all too real. And she had all the reality she could handle at the moment—just being here in this strange place with this man who was almost a stranger to her. Defenseless. Alone. Exhausted from riding two days with little rest and drained from constant worry.

Sun-darkened Mexicans came forward, looking confused at her arrival. If somehow Carlos had intended her to be brought here, how could she not be expected? As he helped her walk, Carlos spoke in rapid Spanish to the crowd of *vaqueros*, peons, and servants. Then he waved his hand, calling their attention to her. "This is Señorita Dorritt, *nuestra huésped*, our guest." The Mexican men bowed with their hats pressed to their chests, and the Mexican women bobbed shallow curtsies. Carlos asked, *"Dónde está Alandra?"*

"Ya duerme," a large-hipped Mexican woman replied.

Who was Alandra? Dorritt lurched against Carlos, her fatigue suddenly weakening her knees. She staggered and it brought a tidal wave of loud, fast Spanish. Carlos swept her up and carried her through the shadowy house into a large bedroom. There, Carlos squeezed her hand, kissed it, and bid her, *"Buenos noches,*

Señorita. Please do not worry. I will unravel this, and please believe that you are safe here."

At Carlos's command, two Mexican women took charge of her, urging her to sit in a lovely dark chair. It had been so long since she sat in a chair, even saddlesore, she sat down with a feeling of wonder. She clasped the wide plain arms, the wood smooth and cool under her palms. Another woman came in with a silver tray with a silver tankard of creamy hot chocolate and a dish of sweetmeats. Dorritt sipped the warm sweet brew and revived. She smiled and said, *"Gracias."* The women bowed and retreated from the room.

The other two women carried in a large elegant bathtub and filled it with buckets and buckets of water. And before she knew it, they had stripped off her wrinkled, grimy clothing and settled her into the metal tub. Heaven, it was heaven. A bath with rose-scented soap. Behind her, the younger woman washed her hair, rasping her scalp and then rinsing and rinsing. It was pure delight that drew all worry and tension from Dorritt's scalp and neck.

When this was done, the older woman gestured toward two buckets of rinse water. She went on to point to a jar of rose-scented cream on a small bedside table and on the bed, already turned down, several white fine linen towels, and a nightgown of the most delicate white cotton lawn. Then the two women bid her, *"Buenos noches, Señorita,"* bowed themselves out, and shut the dark wood and solid-looking door behind them.

"Gracias. Gracias," Dorritt called softly to them and then lay back against the tub and just enjoyed the feeling of water around her. Had it been just over a month that hip baths had been a daily occurrence, not an impossible luxury? She tried to make sense of what this all meant but her mind moved like a rusty hinge. Even though she didn't know what was happening, seeing Carlos again had moderated her fear. She had formed a good opinion of him previously from his politeness and even

gentlemanly ways. He'd even sung songs to the Anderson girl. And here and now, his reactions had been genuine as his surprise at seeing her arrive. Though she did not know what *"¡Eduardo, lo pagarás!"* meant, the way Carlos had said it sounded as if Eduardo should be afraid.

Finally she rose still unsteady, rinsed herself, patted herself dry, anointed herself with the rose-scented cream, and slipped on the gown. How marvelous. Still her sense of physical well-being warred with her nagging uncertainty. And her sense of loss. Would she ever see her mother again? Reva? Quinn? Why had she been brought here? And why did Carlos work as a *vaquero* when in fact he was a *caballero*, a gentleman, and a *dueño*, a landowner?

The last golden rays of sunset were about to fade and leave her in darkness. She approached the high imposing bed, also of polished dark wood. A bath, a clean nightgown, a chair, a bed. Luxuries. She smoothed her hand over the fluffy feather pillows, the cotton blanket, and the muslin sheets, starched and pressed just like at home. This place was pure bliss; it was like coming to a home she'd never known.

She breathed out a long, deep sigh. Then in gratitude, she dropped to her knees beside the bed on the wooden floor. She tried to pull her thoughts together, but her deep fatigue, pain, and bewilderment made all but the simplest prayer impossible. *Heavenly Father, I don't know where I am, but you do. You have brought me to this land, this place. Protect my family, Reva and Ash, and Quinn.* Then she slid between the sheets, resting her head on the feather pillow, and she was dreamlessly asleep.

* * *

Quinn awoke in the *jacal*, thirsty and sore. He passed his dry tongue over his parched lips. Some time in the early hours of morning, he had finally worked off his bounds. His wrists and ankles were chafed, but they were free. He sat up and looked around the inside of the small hut. There was nothing inside it, but the jug and him. Lifting the dried gourd jug, he resisted drinking the last of the water. He needed to find a well or spring or creek near here. There might be, and his horse would need water badly. He stood, still feeling the painful knot the size of an egg at the back of his head. Another matter he *would* take up with Eduardo with his fists. As soon as he could find him.

Quinn stepped outside and looked around. They had left the prairie behind. So he knew he'd traveled south. South of the prairie was drier, higher grass and fewer trees. But over the three days since he'd been drugged, how far south or west had he been carried?

Quinn's horse came to him, nickering. Quinn poured some of the water from the jug into his cupped hand and the horse licked it up. He repeated this slowly so as not to waste water until he had drained the jug. Then he rubbed his horse's nose and apologized for not having more. Just before Quinn mounted, he noticed a flash of silver among the low grass. He went over and knelt down and found his knife stabbed into the sand. And then he noticed around the corner of the *jacal*, his saddle. A coincidence? Not likely. So he'd been left a jug with water, his mount, his saddle, and his knife. Then he heard it—the faint trickle of fresh water over rocks. A spring! No wonder there was a *jacal* here. It would be a sign to travelers there was water nearby.

He found the spring in the side of the ridge, trickling between rocks. He drank the cold water until his teeth felt numb. Then he made a shallow rough trough out of scattered rocks and dry grass. He brought his horse and let him drink. Finally, he saddled his horse and turned it toward where the North Star had been the night before. Well, he'd been left all he needed. But either way, he would make Eduardo sorry, make the Mexicans pay. Carlos had not concealed his interest in Dorritt.

Where had they taken her?

His empty gut burned. He started north, looking for any creek that would lead him to the nearest river. Images of Carlos touching Dorritt's hair, holding her in his arms tormented Quinn. Maybe Dorritt was too good for Quinn, but she was also too good for the Mexican *vaqueros*. *I did everything I could to protect her. But, in the end, I couldn't.* Images of her being abused, hurt tormented him. *Also now her reputation would be sullied, which would do another kind of damage to her.* His outrage gave him strength. *I'll find you, Dorritt. And they'll pay. All of them.*

* * *

The next morning Dorritt awakened and stared into a strange face. It was a pretty little Spanish girl of around five years, with dark hair and eyes, smiling down on her. Dorritt blinked, not trusting her eyes.

"*Buenos días*, Señorita Dorritt."

Dorritt pushed herself up, her muscles screeching, no. "*Buenos días.* Who are you?" How stupid. The child wouldn't speak English.

"I am Alandra Maria Inez Sandoval, *hermana de* Carlos Benito Juan Sandoval." The child curtseyed.

"Oh, my, you are a clever girl. You're so little to speak English."

Alandra grinned and turned back and forth, making her navy blue ruffled skirt swirl out.

Then Dorritt remembered the Spanish word *hermana*. It meant sister. "You are the sister of Carlos?"

"*Sí, sí,* he is at *el desayuno*. Breakfast." The little girl took her hand and tugged it. "*Venga, por favor*. Come. Please."

Dorritt stayed in the bed. "Please wait. I need to dress."

The little girl nodded with enthusiasm. "*Sí, sí, vístase.*"

The large-hipped Mexican woman who had helped her the night before bustled into the room, speaking rapidly in Spanish. She waved the little girl out, bobbed a curtsy to Dorritt, and helped her dress. The dress and undergarments Dorritt was given to wear were a bit old-fashioned and a little too large. But it felt so wonderful to be wearing something clean and pressed that Dorritt overlooked these shortcomings. She smoothed her hands over the deep blue cotton as she looked down at it. This was the dress of a lady, not a servant.

Here in this room she almost felt safe, could almost forget she didn't belong here. But this was just one part in what must be the large *hacienda* of Don Carlos Sandoval. She recalled arriving here last night and finding that Carlos was a man of property, not a humble *vaquero*. Of course, he had never behaved as if he were just a vaquero. She should have recognized that in the way he bowed and spoke in a cultured voice. His disguise as a *vaquero* had been good, but there had been many hints of his true identity.

As if thinking of him had somehow summoned him, Don Carlos Sandoval appeared in the doorway, dressed as the landed gentleman he was. "*Señorita*, Dorritt, you look lovely this morning."

Dorritt looked at him, her mouth going dry. When would she get enough courage to ask him exactly why he'd had her brought here? Could she trust what she was seeing now? Could she trust this man's courtesy as genuine?

"I hope your night was comfortable. I have a few minutes to sit with you at breakfast before I begin my rounds." He offered her his arm.

Though gripped by a feeling of moving in a waking dream and apprehensive of what might happen if she did not take his arm, she complied. He led her through a house, which startled her with its elegance. Paintings of highborn Spanish ladies with mantillas and patrician-looking Spaniards, polished dark wood and leather furniture in a spare but elegant style, brass candelabras and sconces, finely-slatted shutters closed on what must be the east side of the house, deflecting the heat of the morning sun. Again, she could not hold back her honest reaction. "Your home is very lovely," she murmured.

"I am very proud of it. My father and mother came here from Mexico City over thirty years ago. It was a complete wilderness, and out of it they made this." He waved his hand as he led her into the central courtyard of the house.

"Oh, how beautiful." The sight of the red petunias and cactus blooming in the partially roofed courtyard forced the words from her.

Carlos beamed at her. "Please be seated, *señorita*." He clapped his hands and a young woman who addressed him as "Don Carlos" came out, bearing a tray with a pewter platter of ripe melon, a kind of flatbread, and scrambled eggs. "The bread is called tortillas," he said. "It is different from the yeast bread you are accustomed to, but I think you will like it."

Dorritt nodded and helped herself to the platter while the young woman filled a cup with fragrant coffee, mixed with chocolate.

Don Carlos also accepted a cup. "I ate much earlier." He dismissed the girl with a nod.

For a few moments, Dorritt sipped her coffee and then took a bite of ripe melon. Its juice ran down her chin and before she could, Don Carlos caught the juice with his starched white linen napkin. She looked into his dark eyes and then she looked away, shaken. Only Quinn had ever looked at her that way. She only wanted Quinn to look at her that way. Not this man who'd become an enigma.

"Did you pass a comfortable night?" he asked.

"Need you ask?" She smiled though her lips trembled. His very ease of manner frightened her. "A bed after weeks of traveling with a wagon train?"

He nodded.

She took a deep breath, drawing of all her courage, preparing herself, to ask him exactly why he'd had her brought here.

Another Mexican entered the courtyard. Hat in hand, he hurried to Don Carlos and spoke in urgent Spanish. Don Carlos looked displeased and rose. "Excuse me, please, I must attend to business." He bowed over her hand and then hurried off with the Mexican still speaking rapidly beside him.

As if she had been watching, little Alandra hurried out from the house and scampered over to Dorritt. She sat down in the seat Don Carlos had just vacated. "I sit with you, *señorita*. You are *muy linda*, much pretty."

"So are you, Alandra."

The little girl wrinkled her nose at the compliment. "My brother said you *simpática*, nice."

Dorritt merely smiled at this.

"You be good *esposa* for my brother."

Dorritt recognized the Spanish word *"esposa."* She sat as if petrified, as cold wave after cold wave of fear washed through her.

Sixteen

Enduring the hot afternoon of his new freedom, Quinn finally came to a creek. His horse was the one who really found it, sniffing the air and then heading straight for the shallow water. Mesquite, tall grasses, and stunted cottonwood trees twisted around the creek bed. While his horse drank slow and long, Quinn waded out into the calf-high creek and then lay down and let the cooling water flow over him. It was so good to wash away the sweat and dust of days on the trail.

Finally, Quinn led his horse out of the creek, hobbled him, and then went upstream to a place with a rapid current flowing. Only then did he bend down to drink. It wasn't icy Colorado mountain spring water, but it slaked his thirst.

He used his bandanna to scrub the sandy grit from his face and neck. Then he lay back on the grassy bank to let his buckskins dry while he watched his horse drink and graze, drink and graze. The relief of drinking fresh water and the comfort of lying in the shade, clean and cool and no longer thirsty, chafed his raw guilt.

Each day that had passed had fueled his concern for Dorritt. He tried to close his mind to what might be happening to her. No matter her inner strength, she was a defenseless woman in a strange land in the hands of dishonorable men with no friend at hand. He scrubbed his face with his palms as if he could scrub away the horrible images in his mind. He knew what lawless men were capable of. *I can't think of that now. I have to stay steady. Find her.*

Lying there in the shade of the cottonwoods, he once again went over everything Eduardo had said to him those two painful and humiliating days Quinn had traveled trussed up with a sack over his head. He had Carlos's family name: Sandoval. He remembered there was a family, a wealthy family of the name Sandoval south of San Antonio. Not much to go on.

He stood and retrieved the water gourd jug he'd brought with him. Today he'd made it to the first thing he needed to succeed. He had found a creek and a creek would lead him to a river and the river would lead him to people. He hoped he would reach San Antonio on the San Antonio River. If not, the only other settlement was Santa Dorotea farther south and east. He knelt and filled the gourd, his hands cooling in the running water. He doubted these wealthy Sandovals would be closely related to Eduardo or Carlos, but every family had its black sheep. But maybe they would tell them how to find these two.

He clicked his tongue and his horse ambled over. Quinn hung the filled gourd on his saddle horn. Then he gathered up the bridle, mounted, and headed eastward along the creek. *I'll find you, Dorritt. And if anyone has hurt you . . .* Anger scorched through him. He tightened his control. Emotions clouded a man's judgment, but brought back sharp memories. For one instant, Dorritt's silky hair slipping through his fingers. The thought that some other man might be touching her—He stopped right there. Even though they had never exchanged words of love, Dorritt would be depending on him to find her. Because he had protected her, she'd said she honored Quinn as a good gift from God. Whether that was true or not, Quinn wouldn't fail her.

*　*　*

From a distance late that afternoon, Ash and Reva, both on horseback, watched as the Anderson and Kilbride parties along with the soldiers arrived in San Antonio and drew up to the imposing adobe walled fort called the Alamo. For the month of October it was still hot, and he'd spent too many years up north. Ash wiped his perspiring face with the red bandana from around his throat. He wondered, with only a speck of interest, what would happen to the Anglos now. After no luck tracking Quinn or Dorritt, Ash had turned back and caught up with the wagon train. "I know you're worried, honey," Ash said, his own jaw tight from tension.

"I know you did your best," Reva murmured in a defeated voice.

"We're not beat yet, Reva." He touched her soft shoulder. "Just because each trail broke up doesn't mean anything bad has happened to your lady or my friend." His own failure felt like a thorn dug in deep, close to his heart. "If Eduardo and Pedro wanted Miss Dorritt and Quinn killed, they didn't need to take them far away." *And we would have found their bodies.*

"I believe that. But my heart doesn't feel it. For so long, it's only been just Miss Dorritt and me. We could never count on her mama or Mr. Kilbride or anyone. We just had each other and God."

"That sounds like Quinn and me after his father passed. But Quinn and me always set a place where we'll meet up if we have to part on the trail. This time it was San Antonio. As soon as Quinn gets free, he'll head to here."

Reva nodded. "I'm worried that Miss Dorritt might have been hurt. But even if nothing bad has happened and we find her, I don't want anybody here knowing Miss Dorritt has been alone with maybe three men and no chaperone." Reva's voice caught and she had to swallow. "If this gets talked about among the white folk and people believe it, there will be nothing left of her good reputation. It won't matter she didn't go willing. Something like this always marks the woman not the man. She'll be branded 'soiled.' And she'll never be free of it, not if she live to be a hundred."

Feeling as sad as his bride sounded, Ash nodded and urged her mount forward but kept track of the cattle surrounding them. He knew if anyone dared to speak against Dorritt, Quinn would call that man out and kill him. But would that help Dorritt's reputation? No, Reva was right. It was the way of the world. A man played and the woman paid.

Just as Ash was going to move his wife and cattle along, he noticed the Mexican captain. As if he were the King of Spain, the Mexican captain motioned for Mr. Anderson, his two adult sons, and Kilbride to enter the stockade of the fort with him and his troops. Still surrounded by Mexican soldiers, the four Americans walked into the Alamo, stiff and straight. Left with the three wagons, Mrs. Anderson, her daughter, Jewell, and Mrs. Kilbride looked apprehensive, watching their men being marched into the walled fortress.

"Ash," Reva murmured, "I don't really care what happen to Mr. Kilbride. But he married to Miss Dorritt's mama." She appealed to him with her worried expression.

He sighed for effect. "I had to go and marry a softhearted woman."

Grinning, Reva smoothed her palm along his cheek. "Maybe the soldiers here will have seen Miss Dorritt."

Ash kissed her palm. "You're right. They might have word of

her or Carlos or Eduardo. You follow me and then wait outside the walls."

Reva nodded, and the two of them nudged their horses toward the large fortress with many buildings and a stone mission church whose arches were high above the adobe wall. "It sure a big place," Reva said, sounding impressed.

Ash slid from his horse, helped his wife down, and handed her the reins. Then he walked to the sentry post. After he had explained to the soldier who he was and why he wanted to enter, he was allowed to go in as far as the courtyard. The three Andersons and Kilbride had been left standing in the hot afternoon sun in the large courtyard of the fortress, guarded by two soldiers. The captain must have entered a building, probably the *commandante*'s office. The four Americans glanced sideways at Ash, who'd paused beside them.

"What are you doing here?" Kilbride growled.

Ash folded his arms, looking straight ahead. "My bride doesn't want anything to happen—" he kept his tone even "— to the man who is married to Miss Dorritt's *madre*."

"We don't need help from the likes of you," Anderson said.

"You already speak Spanish, then? My, my, that only took a couple of days for you to learn. Guess you don't need me." Ash made as if to move away.

The oldest Anderson son, Cole, spoke up, "Wait. Please, will you be our interpreter?"

Ash glanced at the red-faced man who sounded as if the words had been wrenched from him. "That's what I came here for."

Anderson started to object. But then the second son spoke up too, "We need him, Pa. We could end up in jail here or sent to prison in Mexico City. Pride is well and good, but right now we need somebody who understands these people and their language."

Ash grinned. Necessity and fear could make a man admit

weakness. "I'm glad to see that one or two of you has some sense. It never occurred to you that if you moved to Texas, you'd have to deal with Spaniards and Mexicans?"

Cole replied, "We needed cheap land to start over, and how many Mexicans are there in Texas? Pretty sparse. We planned on sticking to ourselves at the Austin settlement. Let Austin handle all the Mexicans and Spaniards." His opinion of dealing with these "lesser" people came across all too plainly.

Just then the Mexican captain stepped outside and motioned toward his two men to bring the Americans forward. When Ash explained his role, the five of them trooped behind the captain into the *commandante's* office.

The *commandante* was obviously a Creole *rico*, treated as a nobleman here. He was most likely one of the descendents of the Canary Islanders, who had settled in Mexico along the San Antonio River Valley. His European heritage showed in his pale skin and blue eyes. Ash greeted him with formal politeness, removing his hat and holding it to his chest and bowing low. He turned to the Americans and said, "Hats off and bow."

The Anglos hesitated, but then removed their hats and made the slightest of bows toward the *commandante*. Ash could see Kilbride's jaw working the way it did when he was about to blow up in anger. Ash didn't think Kilbride had enough sense to know how much danger he was in here, but Ash couldn't help that.

The interview did not last long. Ash explained to the *commandante* why the Andersons and Kilbrides were in Texas. The *commandante* did not think the charter that Moses had obtained and then passed to Stephen Austin after his death would be valid in light of the change in government. He commanded the Americans to stay in San Antonio until he received notification from Mexico City. He said in two days his regular courier would be heading south to Mexico City and he would add to the papers a request to the government for a decision at that time. Then he dismissed Ash and the Americans.

When Ash explained this to the Americans he warned, "If I were you, I would just bow and leave now. It's best not to object directly to the *commandante* and certainly not to counter him this first time. You need to think this over and find a way to persuade him to let you leave San Antonio. We have a saying here in Mexico, '*Obedezco pero no conformo*, I obey but do not comply.' Now smile and thank the *commandante* for his time."

Kilbride lost his temper. "Thank him! We should have been with Austin by now!" He threw his hat to the floor. "I won't stand for this!" he roared. "You have no right to stop us!" He charged the *commandante*.

One of the soldiers struck Kilbride over the head with the butt of his musket. Kilbride hit the floor hard, unconscious. The *commandante* waved his hand and gave an order, "*¡Llevele al cárcel!*"

The two Mexican foot soldiers each picked Kilbride up under a shoulder and dragged him out. The Andersons, looking stunned and disbelieving, did not move. Ash motioned for them to follow him.

Outside as they walked across the courtyard, followed by another pair of the soldiers, Cole asked, "What's going to happen to Kilbride?"

"He got himself thrown into jail," Ash said, not feeling sorry at all.

"For how long?" Mr. Anderson asked, sounding hollow.

"Don't know. This isn't the United States. We don't have laws I've heard you got protecting a man's rights. Or maybe we do now if we have a constitution." Ash shrugged. "But that doesn't matter here and now. Kilbride could stay in jail for months."

"Whatever possessed him to act that way?" Cole asked.

"The man's a jackass," Anderson said.

"I couldn't have said it better myself," Ash agreed.

Anderson looked like he wanted to put Ash in his place, but swallowed the words.

Ash shrugged and walked back to his wife. Reva started to ask him questions, but Ash shook his head at her. She quieted and the two of them rode through the plaza, Reva leading the mustangs by a rope, Ash herding the cattle before them.

Outside of the plaza, Ash followed the San Antonio River until he came to a jumble of *jacales*. Near the first one, he slid down from the saddle and called out the common frontier greeting, "Hello, the house!"

An older Mexican woman came to doorway and called back, "What do you want?"

He moved nearer. "Don't you recognize Dulcy and Emilio's son?"

"Ash! You have come home!" More exclamations and shouts of welcome came as other family members came out of the other doors: "¡Hola! ¡Saludo!"

His aunt invited, "Come in, come in. Let your cattle graze in the fenced pasture near the river." Everyone stared at Reva but waited for Ash to introduce her.

Two young boys herded the cattle away to the rough pen. Ash turned to Reva. "This is my father's family's land. They speak some English."

"You didn't tell me you had family here." Reva looked worried.

"Just my aunt, and some cousins." Then he introduced Reva, and they were overwhelmed with women and children who drew them into the largest *jacal*. On a bench against the wall, he and Reva sat side by side.

His aunt sat beside them as the younger woman hurried to offer them coffee and tortillas: "The men are still in the fields for the day, Ash. They will be excited that you have returned."

Ash sat back and listened to the women question Reva about

herself and their marriage. His bride looked pleased by her warm welcome. Finally, he rose. "I need to go into the cantina and find out if anyone has seen Quinn."

Reva looked around at his many relatives and whispered, "Do I have to stay here by myself? I've never been in a strange place and on my own before."

"Novia—" Ash caressed her cheek. "—my bride, the only reason I am leaving you at all is the fact Quinn is the best friend I have in the world. And you love your Miss Dorritt. Quinn and your lady would do the same for us."

"I'm sorry. I know you have to do what you have to do." She rose and rested her head upon his chest.

He stroked her back and kissed her forehead. "If I don't come right back, don't worry. You're family here. Just take care of the cattle and get to know my cousins."

She nodded. "I'll do what you say."

Ash's aunt said, "We take good care *tu novia*, Ash."

Outside, Ash swung back up into his saddle and headed into San Antonio to the cantina. Back in the plaza, he noted the wagon train had moved to the far end of town to set up camp. He tied up his horse and sauntered into the cantina to make his inquiries. When he walked inside, the first person he saw was Eduardo.

* * *

"I go San Antonio. I see *baile en la plaza mayor,*" Alandra chattered on.

Dorritt sat with the little girl in the shady courtyard of the hacienda in the warm afternoon. In this pleasant setting in the company of this cheerful child, most of her fear and doubt had ebbed. But some still lingered like a low fever. Had she really been kidnapped and brought here? Why? When could she ask Don Carlos what this all meant?

"Señorita?" the little girl prompted.

Dorritt smiled and stroked Alandra's black silky hair. How could Don Carlos mean her ill and yet leave his sister, this delightful child, in her company? "What is a *baile?*"

"It is dance. The *señoras—*" Alandra pantomimed sitting on a bench "—on *los bancos. La música* starts, *señoritas* choose the *caballeros.*" Again, Alandra pantomimed the choosing of partners.

"The women do the choosing?" Dorritt remembered the many times at New Orleans balls where she'd usually sat watching the other young women dance. If it had been her choice to make, would she have sat out the dances? Or would she have approached one of the men and let him lead her to the floor?

Quinn's face popped into her mind. Its effect on her was like being caught up in a strong wind. She imagined herself in Quinn's arms and he was leading her into a waltz. The feeling expanded inside her, forcing her to face how much she missed the quiet and trustworthy man.

"*Sí,*" Alandra said with a twirl, "afterward the gentlemen take *señoritas* where there are *los pasteles,* sweetbreads, and *café.* When I am old, I go to *bailes.* And dance the fandango. Like this." The little girl struck a pose, one arm curved over her head the other arched in front of her as she leaned her head back.

Dorritt had seen the fandango danced in New Orleans. She smiled and clapped her hands. "I'm sure you will be a lovely dancer."

Over the past hours, Dorritt had spent a lot of time with Alandra. Yet since morning, she had seen little of Carlos. Not for the first time, she wondered if this was on purpose.

Alandra began dancing nearby and clapping her hands and clicking her heels. Dorritt watched with pleasure. Her brain, however, kept working. If Don Carlos finally spoke with her, what would she say to him? *Why have you brought me here? When can I go back to my family?* The possible answers to those questions still haunted her.

Alandra tugged Dorritt's hand and said, "Dance with me?" Dorritt laughed and rose, clapping her hands over her head too. This shady fragrant courtyard and Alandra didn't fit with a man who would have her kidnapped. If Don Carlos was a *caballero*, a gentleman, why had he ordered her taken by force? The code of honor among the Creoles was as strict as the American's and not lightly broken. No young *señorita* was ever allowed out without an older lady chaperone. To steal a maiden from her family would not even be considered by a Creole gentleman. So why had Don Carlos ordered her kidnapped? Had he? She'd been terrified for two days and then upon arriving here, welcomed and pampered. *Dear Father, why am I here? How can this be part of your plan?*

Alandra called out with sudden excitement, "*¡Mi hermano!* I show Señorita Dorritt how we make fun in Texas. I tell about *bailes* and dance."

"*¡Excelente!*" Don Carlos bent over Dorritt's hand. Then he swung Alandra up into his arms. "The heat of the day is past and I have been neglecting you dreadfully. I was wondering if you charming *señoritas* would like to put on your riding habits and go for a ride with me."

Dorritt's nerves tightened. So now they might talk? Had the time come for her to find out why she had been brought here? She faced him, drawing her courage close around her. "If Alandra would like to, I would."

"*Sí, sí*, I want to ride *mi poni*. Señorita Dorritt, I name her *Pimienta*, Pepper. She has *vivacidad*."

"*Sí*, she has spirit," Don Carlos agreed.

Dorritt smiled though her neck tightened. "I must meet Pimienta then." She offered her hand to Alandra. "Come let us put our habits on." She did not bother to question Carlos about whether or not she had a riding habit. If he had asked her to don one, then she would find one on the bed in her room.

As she and Alandra walked into the house to dress, she promised herself if Don Carlos did not tell her of his own accord, she would ask him to tell her why he wanted her here. *I will face the truth—with you beside me, Father.*

* * *

Ash looked over the crowded *cantina*, willing his anger to cool. Eduardo sitting there as innocent as a babe galled Ash. He wanted to grab Eduardo by the throat and choke him until he told him where Quinn and Dorritt had been taken, but Ash couldn't act rashly. While Eduardo could be well known here with many friends, after years away in the north, Ash was little known. At the bar, Ash ordered his ale and kept his back to Eduardo.

"Is that you, Ash?" Eduardo's voice hailed him in Spanish.

Ash slowly turned, still resting one elbow on the bar. "Eduardo, we meet again."

"*Sí*, where is your friend Quinn?" Eduardo taunted.

So Eduardo wanted attention, wanted Ash to ask him about Quinn. "You saw him last, didn't you?"

Eduardo laughed. "*Sí*, I did. Do you want to know where I left him?"

Ash gazed at Eduardo. What was the man up to? Did he think he wouldn't have to answer for what he had done? Ash answered smoothly, but with iron in his heart, "Quinn can take care of himself. Wherever you left him, he'll find you. If I were you, I would watch myself. Quinn does not take a joke very well."

"*Ah*, you think I play a joke on Quinn. No, I took him because he was interfering with my cousin Don Carlos Sandoval's plans for a certain young Anglo woman. *Mi primo*, you know, always gets what he wants."

"Sandoval is your cousin?" Ash's jaw tightened in surprise.

"*Sí*, he is Don Carlos Benito Jose Sandoval *de* Rancho Sandoval."

Ash had of course heard the name Sandoval, a wealthy *dueño*.
He sipped his ale. "So you are the cousin of Sandoval?"

"Yes, my cousin grows lonely on his rancho and wanted some
feminine *compañia*." Eduardo leered at Ash.

Counting to ten silently, Ash took a long drink of his ale. He
did not want to talk any more with Eduardo. At least not here
and in front of everyone.

"How is your bride, Ash? Or have you lost her already?"

Ash raised one eyebrow. "I think Eduardo you've had too much
to drink. My bride is safely where I left her with my family."

"And where is her mistress, Señorita Dorritt? Or should I ask
who is she with?" Eduardo chuckled in a nasty way. "The pretty
Señorita Dorritt seems to be exactly what my cousin was looking for. Such lovely white skin and long golden hair. I am sure
they are getting along very well together at his rancho." Eduardo's voice was thick with innuendo.

Ash left without a word. Heading back to Reva, he wondered
why Eduardo was making trouble for his cousin, a wealthy and
powerful man. What game was the man playing and why?

* * *

In the late afternoon sunlight, Dorritt rode sidesaddle beside
Carlos. Alandra bounced along on her little pony Pimiento just
in front of them. Dorritt wore a hat with a rakishly tilted brim
and a well-made black riding habit that was just like the other
clothing. Had Carlos been married? Were these the clothing of
his late wife? The possibility pained Dorritt. When would she
have a moment to question him—away from little ears?

She gazed over the vast and striking savannah of Rancho Sandoval. When she'd arrived, she had been exhausted and terrified
and it had been twilight, the shadows concealing the rancho
and its setting. But now everywhere she saw signs of a well-
managed ranch. Outbuildings and fences in good order. Peons

living in neat *jacales*. A large paddock of fine-looking horses. Indeed, the horse she was riding was a sleek white Arabian. In New Orleans, she'd always been mounted on the horse nobody else wanted to ride.

Then they began climbing up a gentle slope to the highest ground. When they stopped, she gasped. The sight of the acres and acres of savannah with thickets of mesquite and cotton-woods in all directions took her breath away. A large scattered herd of Longhorns dotted the grassland. And in the distance, sleek pronghorn antelope leaped over the rust-colored foliage— fleet and elegant. Once again, she couldn't hide her reaction. "It's beautiful."

Don Carlos turned to her with a bright smile. "*Sí*, it is beautiful. And it is mine. My rancho is many acres—over seven thousand."

She gasped silently again. Rancho Sandoval was vaster than she'd guessed. And this man who had masqueraded as a humble *vaquero* was its master. She wondered how she had overlooked all the hints that he was a *caballero*. His manners, his excellent English, the confidence that was a part of him.

"Alandra," he said, "why don't you see if you can find some pretty rocks to take home? Give me your pony's reins to hold for you."

The little girl eagerly slipped from her pony and handed her big brother the reins. She began wandering away, looking down at stones. Dorritt stiffened her nerve, ready now to ask why—

But Don Carlos spoke first. "Señorita Dorritt, I was very, very surprised when Pedro brought you here. Shocked, in fact. Do you believe that?"

Dorritt looked quickly toward him. "Yes, yes I do. You looked as surprised as I felt." Was he going to explain without her having to ask?

Don Carlos drew in a deep breath as if he had been holding it. "I was so shocked at first I did not know what to do except make you welcome and see to your comfort and safety."

She heard in his voice the absolute sincerity, which, after all, had shown to be true. She'd been treated as an honored guest, not a prisoner here. Now she also grasped why during the past hours, Carlos had stayed away from her. He had been confused about how to handle the situation. "Carlos . . . Don Carlos, you and everyone in your household and your sister have made me very welcome." But she must face the truth and ask for it. "I know you were surprised when Pedro brought me. But I know he works for you. Why did Pedro bring me here—if you had not ordered him to do so?"

Don Carlos's face changed. His mouth pulled back as if ready to snarl. "I questioned Pedro and he just did what he was told to by Eduardo, even if he didn't like it. I thought I'd left you safely guarded."

"You told the other *vaqueros* to protect me?" she said.

"Yes, this is the wilderness and there are so many dangers." Don Carlos's face hardened. "But you could not have been in such danger that you needed to be brought here. They frightened you and put you in danger for no reason." Don Carlos's voice hardened. "I have been wondering also how Eduardo got you away without Quinn or Ash noticing."

"I wondered that myself. But the night I was taken, Ash married Reva and bought her freedom. They were distracted and Ash might not have known until morning." She worried her lower lip, trying not to feel the pain of abandonment. "You don't think something has happened to Ash and Quinn, do you?"

"I do not know what to think." Don Carlos threw up a hand as if defeated. "Quinn is wary and wise of the ways of the frontier. I know he would have protected you with his life. Since he didn't, does that mean Quinn must have been . . . ?"

Hurt? Disabled? Killed? Dorritt's heart squeezed painfully. "None of this makes sense. . . ."

"Can you give me any idea of why my cousin Eduardo might for some reason think you were in danger? What else happened after I left to come home for Alandra's birthday?"

"That's why you left us?"

"Yes, I had promised her I would be home for her birthday. But we were delayed with the wagon train."

Dorritt nodded. A big brother hurrying home for his little sister's birthday. She should not be surprised. It was obvious here and now he loved this little girl. "Nothing much happened till we came to a Caddo village. A troop of Mexican soldiers rode in and burned it." Dorritt swallowed, suddenly emotional at the memory of the screaming of the women and children.

"*Señorita?*" Don Carlos asked in a caring tone.

"I'm fine." She raised a hand, and gripped her reins tighter. "The Mexican captain challenged our right to be in Texas and decided he would take us all back to his *commandante* in San Antonio. That same night, Ash married Reva and I was kidnapped. My only guess is that the wagon train has continued on to San Antonio."

Don Carlos's face twisted. "What we really need to know is why my cousin Eduardo had you kidnapped and brought here."

"Eduardo is your cousin?" *I never trusted Eduardo.* This bubbled up from deep inside her. Just as the man beside her had given her clues of his true nature, Eduardo had always had a way of looking at her and speaking to her that should have alerted her that he was a sly creature. "Why didn't you tell us who you really were?"

Don Carlos looked into her face, imploring. "This has been an unusual year for me. I rarely go along on cattle drives north to Natchitoches. And then on our way home, I saw your caravan in Nacogdoches. I decided to travel with your party incognito because I wanted to make sure of my opinion of the Anglos. I wanted to know if I was right in thinking it a mistake in letting them into Texas."

Dorritt couldn't blame him. Who would want Mr. Kilbride as neighbor?

Don Carlos gave a wry smile. "Anglos expect Texas, the new Mexico will be just like home, like *los Estados Unidos*. But we were a Spanish colony. And when have the English and the Spanish ever agreed on anything? Americans settling in Texas will be like adding oil to water. Anglos do not blend in. Anglos conquer."

Dorritt nodded. "You are very perceptive. They are coming because they want the land. And once they have the land, they will want more."

"I want Texas and the rest of the new Republic of Mexico for Mexicans. Not Spaniards. Not *angloamericanos*. I cannot understand why Mexico City ever allowed this Austin scheme. Except that they were desperate to find someone, anyone, who would settle here in *Norte Tejas*."

Dorritt remembered Quinn's words. "Quinn said inviting Americans in was like inviting a bear into your house."

Don Carlos laughed out loud. And nodded. "Señor Quinn is nobody's fool."

She sighed. "But we have drifted from speaking about our situation—"

Don Carlos's face darkened. "Eduardo has brought shame on both of us. It is most improper for you to be here without a chaperone, such as your mother. I do not know what I can do to protect your reputation. But I will do everything in my power."

Dorritt watched Don Carlos, as he gazed at his sister, playing. How would they ever sort out this mess and get her back to her family safe and untarnished?

He turned to her. "I have given you today to see how we live here at Rancho Sandoval. What do you think of my home?"

Though Dorritt hadn't expected this question, she thought over what she'd witnessed the past today. Carlos's house was a happy one. It was hard to know precisely how she knew this. But even though she could speak so little Spanish, there was no anger or fear in the voices and faces of the servants, the *vaqueros* or the peons. There was laughter and singing and smiles. And Alandra, though obviously a little spoiled, was well mannered and obedient. This told her a great deal about Don Carlos Sandoval as a master, as a brother. "Yours is a happy home."

Again, his bright smile. "Except for one thing. Rancho Sandoval needs a *doña*."

The face of the man in New Orleans who had wanted Dorritt to marry him because she was frugal and good with children flashed in her mind. Was this just going to be another case of a man who needed a wife to make his life easier? Is that why Alandra had said Senorita Dorritt would make Carlos a good *esposa*? "Is that why I'm here, Don Carlos?" She couldn't keep the stiffness out of her tone. "You need a woman to take care of Alandra and run your household?"

"I did not have you brought here," he said gently. "Eduardo did it. But Eduardo knew I did want you here."

"Why?" She gazed into his face, ready to weigh his answer.

His features softened and his voice was low, caressing. "Because *estoy enamorado de ti*. I have fallen in love with you."

Seventeen

Dorritt found she could not breathe and looked away. No man had ever said these words to her. She'd thought she would never hear them. She'd even denied she wanted to hear them. But here she was on a rise in Texas overlooking thousands of acres beside a man who was a good master and a good brother. And this man had said the words she'd secretly yearned to hear.

What could be her reply? She found she no longer feared him but she was unsure of her own heart. She knew she had feelings for Quinn but he had rejected trying to change. He didn't seem willing to make room for her in his wanderer's life and he hadn't come after her, despite his previous protection. She couldn't have imagined ever having these feelings for any man. And now someone, a gentleman, felt this way about her, Dorritt, the unwanted daughter. Her feelings capered and tumbled inside her. Was it possible that she had found what she had thought impossible? Could she have found two men who were worthy of love—Quinn and Don Carlos?

She wished Reva were here. She needed someone to help her figure this all out. Dorritt slid from her horse. "If you fell in love with me, I still don't understand why you didn't reveal yourself to me before you left."

Don Carlos had slipped from his horse too. "Let me explain. After you had settled in with your family north of San Antonio, I had intended to court you. I am acquainted with your *familia* but you do not know mine. My father was a Spaniard whose family had lived in Mexico City for three generations. I think you will understand me when I say Spaniards in Mexico looked down on mixed-blood Mexicans like me because we *mestizos* came from Spaniards that intermarried with Indians."

Dorritt could think of no comment. She nodded.

"My father, a Spanish pureblood Creole, fell in love with my mother, who was a *mestiza*. His family was absolutely opposed to their marriage. But my father married her, anyway, and went to the governor and requested a land grant north of the Rio Grande. Since the governor wanted people who would move north, my father's request was granted. He paid a nominal fee for the land and hired people who wanted to move to Texas with him. And that is how Rancho Sandoval came to be."

Dorritt asked him a question that had bothered her, "Whose clothing am I wearing?"

"My mother's. She outlived my father for several months but died soon after Alandra was born."

It was as if the tension in her midsection relaxed. This man did not see her as a convenient replacement for a late wife.

"My father never regretted his decision to marry *mi madre*. He told me never to marry until I found a woman I truly loved. He said if I married anyone who was just a good match, I would never be happy. I am nearly thirty years old. And you are the first woman whom I have loved." He frowed and shrugged as if defeated. "And now because of Eduardo, I cannot court you as I'd intended."

Dorritt did not doubt for one second that he was being completely honest with her. Yes, a woman coming alone to the home of an unmarried man she was not related to would provide a juicy scandal for everyone high and low who heard it. She gazed again over the wide open horizon, the lush grass undulating with the wind like waves, the unnumbered cattle; a herd of antelope darted in the distance. Then it hit her. A release, a sense of transformation shuddered through her every nerve. Inside her, more tight little knots were unraveling. And her mind was thinking brand-new thoughts and her heart was feeling newborn emotions. This land was so big. Her thinking must expand to fit this new place.

And Dorritt liked that Don Carlos was putting no pressure on her. He loved her but he was not telling her she must marry him to protect her reputation. He was respecting her as an equal, not a weak woman to be ordered around. She took his hand. "I do not know. I have never considered marriage." She let go of his hand and watched Alandra hopping after a locust. How could she explain? "You say you had parents who loved one another and made a life for themselves. That is not what I have learned from my mother." Sadness closed her throat. "I have only ever wanted to be free, free of my stepfather, free to live life on my own." Saying this aloud and to a man liberated her further. Her lungs expanded.

"I see. Forgive me, but I eavesdropped on your conversation with your maid about living alone and running a school. That is an estimable goal. But I think I could make you happier. I said the first night you arrived here you were born to be a *doña*, a grand lady who oversees a *hacienda grandiosa*."

Dorritt gazed at him and then at the vast grassland. "Maybe I have been wrong," she murmured. "Maybe I can have a different life here, can trust a man with my heart."

At a question from Alandra, Don Carlos went to his little sister. Then returning to Dorritt, he said, "I know you have been intrigued by Señor Quinn and perhaps . . . more."

She pursed her lips and tried to smile. "You are very perceptive. I have a great deal of respect for Mr. Quinn and he is special to me." She looked away. "But he has never said anything to lead me to believe he wants more than friendship with me." He kissed you, her mind insisted. But what was a kiss? It said nothing of Quinn's intentions.

Watching his sister as if giving Dorritt room to speak her mind, Don Carlos nodded.

"Don Carlos, I need time to consider your proposal. I need to see Mr. Quinn and talk to him and find out if he does have feelings for me. I need to go back to my family." Her heart lurched. "I don't think my stepfather or half-sister miss me, but I know my mother must be worried. And in her delicate condition . . . Will you take me to San Antonio?"

"Of course, I am sorry. And we do not want your mother to be distressed any more than she already is." His voice became harsh. "But most of all I regret that Eduardo did not treat you with the respect that you deserve." He took her gloved hand. "But I will do everything in my power to show you are a lady of honor. And I will let no one—no one—show you disrespect."

His fervent promise moistened her eyes. Someone cared about what happened to her. "Thank you. I do not hold you responsible. But I'm very afraid Mr. Quinn will hold the kidnappers responsible."

Don Carlos's jaw hardened. "I hold them responsible also. They will pay for what they have done."

Again Dorritt gazed at the vast ranch before her. Could she

actually marry and be happy? Could she have a life vastly different than one she'd ever dreamed of? She now understood a little of why God had allowed her to be brought here. But the situation was so tangled and her heart ached for Quinn. *I have feelings for Quinn. But do I have a future with him?*

* * *

For two days, Quinn followed the creek to the river, which turned out to be the San Antonio. And now, ahead he saw the walls of the fort, the Alamo. Grim tension held sway over him. Finally, he'd reached the town where he hoped to find his friend Ash and the Kilbride wagon train safe and sound. But that did not bring him much nearer finding Don Carlos Sandoval, Eduardo, and Dorritt. Weary as he was, he felt the anger rise in him again, hot and fierce. Eduardo would pay and so would Carlos.

He came upon the wagon train first just beyond the plaza. Before he could even call out, Mrs. Kilbride hailed him, "Oh, Mr. Quinn, where's my daughter?"

Her question stopped in his tracks. "Ma'am, she isn't with me. From what I understand from Eduardo, both Miss Dorritt and I were kidnapped at the same time."

"Then why don't you know where she is?" Mrs. Kilbride hurried forward with her hands clasped tightly together.

"Eduardo took me someplace different than he sent Miss Dorritt. Did all the *vaqueros* leave at the same time—when Miss Dorritt and I were kidnapped?"

Cole Anderson had come forward and answered for her, "Juan stayed to herd the cattle. So you're saying Eduardo took you one place and the other *vaquero* took Miss Dorritt to another place?"

"Yes, that's exactly what I'm saying happened." Quinn's irritation flared like sparks. "Have you seen Eduardo or Juan or my friend Ash here in San Antonio?"

"Juan came with us. And since then, we've seen Eduardo and

Juan from a distance. And your friend Ash helped us when we first got here—"

Mrs. Kilbride interrupted, "Mr. Quinn, they put my husband into jail."

Quinn couldn't deny that hearing Mr. Kilbride was in jail did not disturb him; it did not even surprise him. "He tried to tell the *commandante* what to do, right?"

"Yes," Mrs. Kilbride said. At the same time, Cole burst into laughter. Mrs. Kilbride turned an angry look on him. "This is no occasion for levity."

"I'm sorry, ma'am," Cole apologized, holding back his laughter. "What we couldn't figure out, Quinn, is how Eduardo got the jump on you."

That grated inside Quinn. "They drugged my coffee."

"That's low," Cole said. "I'd be happy to help you teach those Mexicans a lesson."

"Looking to get thrown into jail too?" Quinn quizzed.

Cole propped his hands on his hips. "No, what I want to do is get out of San Antonio and meet up with Austin on the Colorado. Can you help us with that?"

"I doubt it. You've seen my friend Ash?"

"Yes, he is at the other end of the San Antonio. He and his new wife are staying over there with some other colored folk."

Just where I thought he'd head. Quinn touched the brim of his hat and turned to leave.

"Mr. Quinn," Mrs. Kilbride called after him in a troubled voice, "won't you help find my daughter?"

He mounted his horse. "Ma'am, no power on earth will stop me from finding her." His own words goaded Quinn—deep and hard.

He rode through town barely aware of the people around him. In a few days, a week would have passed since he and Dorritt had been kidnapped. He knew if people heard of her kidnapping, they would assume her virtue had been compromised and her reputation would be ruined. He'd been so careful not to let his feelings, his regard for her cast a shadow over her name. And now this. He approached the *jacales* where he knew Ash had family and called out, "Ash!"

His friend came out of one of the *jacales* and shouted, "I knew you'd turn up! A man can't get rid of some fleas!" When Ash reached him, he embraced and pounded him on the back. "You look like you could use a square meal." Ash called over his shoulder. *"Tia, por favor, prepara la comida. ¡Tortillas y frijoles para mi amigo!"*

Then Reva ran out and hugged Quinn. "I'm so happy." She burst into tears. "But where is my lady?"

Quinn allowed her to hug him and then pulled away, unused to this type of greeting from a woman. "I'll find her. Don't worry. And Eduardo will pay and so will Carlos. Carlos is a Sandoval."

"I know. He's *the* Sandoval," Ash agreed, waving Quinn toward the door. "I'd heard of him but not seen him much. And I didn't recognize him dressed like a common *vaquero*. Though those silver spurs should have told me something. Anyway, I've seen Eduardo in town." Ash's mouth drew together like the mouth of a leather purse. "I didn't want to take matters into my own hands until I found out what happened to you. So I've just been watching him."

Quinn burned but forced himself not to turn immediately back to town. He needed food, water, rest, and time to think this through. "I need to know all that happened after I was kidnapped. Everything."

"Don't worry. I paid close attention."

Soon inside the windowless *jacal*, Quinn sat on a bench at a small pine table and began eating some spicy and delicious beans wrapped in a tortilla. The green chilies burned his throat, but he was glad to taste something with flavor. He had eaten saltless fish and small game on the trail. It was good to eat food again that a woman, a good cook, had prepared. He watched and listened to the kitchen chatter. Ash's bride Reva appeared happy with her new family and in return, the family looked pleased.

Ash had it all. A family, a new bride. Quinn closed his eyes a moment and imagined what it would be like after a trip or a day's ranching to come home to Dorritt and eat food she'd prepared and then hold her soft body close, breathe in her fragrance. He stopped himself and concentrated on tasting the peppery *frijoles* and on how to find Dorritt.

* * *

Quinn awoke with a start. He lay on the dirt floor on a hand-woven wool blanket. After his meal, he had lay down just to take a nap. But now he awoke and morning light was flowing in through the open door. He had fallen into a deep sleep and had slept the night through without even changing position. He knew that meant he had really been too tired to think straight or to do anything. But it still griped him. Dorritt was out there somewhere. She needed him. And he needed to find her.

Nearby, he heard Ash get up, making a rope bed shift and creak. "You awake, Quinn?"

Quinn rolled over and faced Ash. "Yes, why didn't you wake me up?"

"You were too tired to do anything but sleep. Now, my sweet bride will make us some coffee and eggs and we'll figure out how to find Miss Dorritt."

"I was thinking of finding Juan or Eduardo or both and beating them until they tell us what we want to know." Quinn sat up and began rolling up his blanket.

"I think that makes pretty good sense. In fact, I'll kind of feel disappointed if they answer us right away and we don't have to beat them up."

"Make them tell and then beat them up anyway," Reva added, coming back inside.

Ash looked at his bride with fake surprise. "Oh, dear, I married a bloodthirsty woman."

Quinn gave a half smile. The words were lighthearted, but his intention wasn't.

After breakfast, Quinn and Ash left Reva and headed into town. The dusty *cantina* was quiet as was the plaza. Ash asked the unshaven barman if he knew where Eduardo or Juan were putting up. The man said he didn't know; then he tried to mine gossip from them. *Who was this* señorita *that Don Carlos Sandoval was "entertaining" at his rancho?* Quinn bit his tongue from telling the man off. He hurried out and caught up with Ash, walking into the morning sun.

"Do you think that he was talking about Miss Dorritt?" Quinn asked Ash in a low voice. He hoped both that this was the answer to where Dorritt was and that it wasn't true. Dorritt with Carlos is what he'd feared, hated. But if it were true at least he'd know where she was.

"Could be. Think we should just get ready and head for Rancho Sandoval?"

"I don't want to go off half-cocked. Eduardo could have planted this story just to get us out of town. I want to question him before I do anything. Let's see if there's anyone else who knows where Eduardo is."

Several fruitless hours later, the two of them headed back to Ash's *jacal*—no wiser than they had been when they left after breakfast. They'd discovered that Eduardo and Juan had been seen in San Antonio on and off over the past few days, but no one knew where they were staying. And Ash and Quinn had not found them at any of the houses or shops around the plaza.

"Do you think they've gone back to the Sandoval ranch?" Quinn asked, his patience thin as a single hair.

"Might be. If we can't find Eduardo, we may just have to head there and see what we can find."

Quinn nodded, trying not to give into gloom. It didn't help that he kept imagining Don Carlos touching Dorritt's hair and face. Each time this image came, he wanted to put his hand around someone's throat and squeeze.

After a midday meal with Ash's large family, Quinn and Ash headed back to the *cantina*, where they hoped to find Eduardo. If they had no luck this afternoon, they would prepare and leave in the morning for Rancho Sandoval. They walked into the *cantina*, which was now full of men. Eduardo turned and said in Spanish so all could hear, "*¡Hola, amigos!* We meet again."

Quinn nearly launched himself at the man who'd kidnapped him and now taunted him with an insulting grin.

Ash gripped Quinn's shoulder and muttered, "Don't let him goad you. We need to find out where Dorritt is. Without making a big fuss about what may have happened to her and bandying her name about more than it has been."

Quinn knew the truth of each of Ash's words. But it was hard not to just start swinging his fists. Still, he kept his face closed and his tone cool. "We do indeed meet again, Eduardo. Are you happy to see us?" Quinn spoke in English, not wanting the whole town to hear what they were saying.

Eduardo chuckled in an unpleasant way.

Quinn noted that every man in the *cantina* was giving them their full attention. Just what he did not want. "Why don't we step outside where we can speak more privately?"

Eduardo laughed out loud and then replied in Spanish, "I don't think so, *mi amigo*. You are not happy with me. But you cannot blame me. Whatever happened to you and Señorita Dorritt was on my cousin's orders."

All other conversations had stopped. No one was even trying

to look as if they weren't following the conversation between Eduardo and Quinn.

"That is what you say," Ash said. "But I will want to talk to your cousin myself. It's easy to put the blame on him when he's not here to defend himself."

Eduardo shrugged as if he were totally unconcerned. "What blame? My cousin enticed a pretty woman to come and stay with him at his rancho. Why is that worthy of blame? She is an Anglo and perhaps she thinks he will marry her. But my cousin is proud. He would never have serious intentions toward anyone not of Spanish birth."

Quinn was so angry he actually saw Eduardo through a red haze. "If you dare to speak another word against the lady, I will beat the truth out of you."

"Eduardo," Ash said evenly, "I can't figure out your aim. Something isn't right here. And I don't mean just because you kidnapped Quinn. What deep game are you playing?"

This finally prodded Eduardo. His face grew red and his hand drifted toward the pistol shoved into his belt. Then he stopped himself. He took a deep breath and tried to laugh. "Game? I am playing no game. Don't you think I know what I'm doing?"

Before Quinn could speak, he heard from outside the sound of voices calling out greetings, the noise of hooves and the jingling of harnesses. Chairs scraped back as everyone stood and headed toward the door. Everyone except for Eduardo, Ash, and Quinn. Before Quinn could reach Eduardo, he heard from the front of the *cantina* in Spanish: "It is the carriage of Don Carlos Sandoval!"

Eighteen

If what Eduardo had said was true and Dorritt was with Don Carlos, then Quinn might see her here and now. At least, he'd come face-to-face with Sandoval. The desire to shove everyone out of his path to the plaza hit Quinn like a Gulf shore wave. But he held himself back. His heart thundering, he sauntered out at the rear of the crowd. Ash stayed at his side. Just as Quinn stepped beyond the *cantina* into daylight, Don Carlos Sandoval opened the door of his large, sleek black carriage. It was hard to believe that the *vaquero* he'd never quite trusted was in fact a very wealthy man.

A Sandoval outrider jumped down from his horse and lowered the steps. Then Carlos reached out to take the hand of a little girl.

A little girl? And from her features obviously related to Sandoval. Quinn halted in midstride. He hadn't been expecting to see anyone but Don Carlos and perhaps Dorritt.

The little girl wore a dress of red cotton and bonnet to match. Grinning, she hopped down: step, step, step to earth. Then she turned back and called, *"Baje las escaleras, por favor,* Señorita Dorritt."

If Quinn had been threatened with instant blindness, he couldn't have looked away. *Yes, please come down the steps, Miss Dorritt.*

Dorritt came into view, framed by the carriage doorway. Her smile seemed forced. All in black—gloves, bonnet, and dress—she looked even paler than usual. As she accepted Don Carlos's hand and let him help her down the three steps, Quinn felt the touch of Dorritt's hand as if it pressed his own. He clenched his jaw, trying to hold in that imagined contact.

Then she looked up, straight into Quinn's eyes. Their gazes connected. For one moment, she stared into his eyes with frank honesty, imploring him—for what? He tried to read the message there, but so many thoughts were jumping in his head he couldn't focus. Nothing he saw made any sense.

"¡Muy queridos amigos! My dear friends, may I introduce the lady I hope to marry, Señorita Dorritt Mott." Carlos lifted Dorritt's hand high and turned her one way and then another.

The men around him looked surprised and confused. This made it a certainty—in Quinn's mind—that over the past week Eduardo had been busy gossiping against Dorritt. Certainly not been speaking of her in a way befitting a lady who Don Carlos Sandoval, one of the largest landowners in Texas, would consider marrying.

Although these words shocked Quinn, he had to allow one instant of relief that no physical harm had befallen her. Then, like a volley of musket balls, raw emotions ripped through Quinn. After all his worry, he was thrown off balance at seeing her safe, not in dire straits. He was furious at Sandovol for putting her on display as if he owned her. And a sinking disappointment gripped Quinn's insides as he tried to grapple with the fact that she was with a man like Don Carlos—he who had everything to offer a lady. Quinn's hands curled into fists. What was going on here?

Here in the plaza, Don Carlos was letting everyone know his opinion of Dorritt. His words and manner said she was without question a lady worthy of marriage and respect. *I should be happy for her. It is what she deserves. She would make a man like Don Carlos an excellent wife.* This thought deepened his misery.

"Señor Quinn," Don Carlos called to him, "later we must speak. *Por favor.*"

Startled, nettled, and confused, Quinn managed a polite pull at the brim of his hat and then he stalked away, head down and fast. *Yes, we will talk, Sandoval.* He heard Ash call his name, his footsteps hurrying after him. But Quinn didn't slow or turn. Until, suddenly, a thought came to him.

He halted, considering it. He looked around for Eduardo and Juan. They were nowhere to be seen. Eduardo had not come out to greet his cousin. Why was that? Was he unwilling to see Don Carlos? Had he slipped away, fearing a reckoning? But from whom—Quinn or from Don Carlos Sandoval? Or perhaps both?

Dorritt watched as Quinn rushed away. Her heart strained to follow him. But she had duties to perform first. Would she be able to make Quinn understand that nothing had happened to her? That Don Carlos wasn't responsible for her being kidnapped? How to untangle this knotty situation? She fought the desire to hurry after Quinn. Perhaps pursuing him would be futile. He hadn't come for her. And she needed to reassure her mother. But their reunion would include her stepfather and half sister and wasn't something Dorritt looked forward to. She looked up to Don Carlos, who was smiling at her though his eyes were troubled. "Will you escort me to my mother at the wagon train?" She had glimpsed it on their way into town.

"Of course." He offered her his arm.

And she held out her hand to the little girl. "Alandra, come. I will take you to meet my mother."

"Is she *simpática*?" Alandra skipped at Dorritt's side.

Dorritt's saddle-sore muscles still pulled as she walked. Would her mother be *simpática*, nice? Or distant and confused again? "Yes, she is nice to little girls," Dorritt hedged.

She needn't have worried. The moment her mother saw Dorritt coming, she rushed forward. "Thank God, you're safe! Oh my Lord, you answered my prayers!" She began weeping.

Dorritt hurried ahead and accepted her mother's embrace. "I'm fine, mother." Feeling guilty over her uncertainty about her mother's welcome, Dorritt tried to smile, but failed. "I'm sorry you were worried. It couldn't be helped." Dorritt smoothed her mother's salt-and-pepper hair back from her pale and haggard face. Evidence of her mother's pregnancy was visible with a thickening around her mother's normally slender waist. "You should be sitting down."

Dorritt helped her mother over to the wagon train, where a few straight-back chairs had been unloaded. Her mother sank into one and Dorritt sat on the one beside her.

"Where were you, Dorritt?" her mother asked, wiping her tears with a crumpled handkerchief. "I was so worried."

"I'm sorry about that. I was kidnapped and taken to Rancho Sandoval, which is south of here and is the home of Don Carlos." Dorritt motioned to him to come forward.

"Wasn't he one of our *vaqueros*?" her mother asked in a confused voice.

Don Carlos bowed before Mrs. Kilbride. "You must accept my

apologies for that innocent deception, Señora Kilbride. I let you
believe I was a simple *vaquero*, instead of a rancher. Pedro, Juan,
and Eduardo work for me. As for your daughter's kidnapping—"
Don Carlos looked pained "—there must have been some mistake made due to poor judgment."

Dorritt thought her mother looked preoccupied. And little
Alandra was hopping on her toes with anticipation. "Mother,"
Dorritt said, "this is little Alandra, Don Carlos's sister."

Alandra made an extravagant curtsy and then bobbed up.
"Hello, Señora Kilbride."

Her mother wiped her eyes and nose and smiled. "Hello, little
girl."

"I am called Alandra," the little girl pointed out and proceeded
to lean against Dorritt. Dorritt took the hint and lifted the little
girl onto her lap.

"Señora Kilbride, where's your husband?" Don Carlos asked.
"I wish to apologize personally to him."

"Oh." Her mother looked harrassed. "My husband is in jail
here in the Alamo. He let his temper get the best of him. I don't
know what to do or how long they will keep him."

Then Jewell appeared, striding forward, followed by Cole
Anderson. Jewell's eyes sparkled with spite. "So, Dorritt, you've
returned."

Jewell's tart taunting words did not surprise Dorritt. She did
not attempt to reply.

Don Carlos bowed to Jewell, but went on speaking with their
mother. "You say that Señor Kilbride has been arrested? On
what charge?"

Jewell evidently recognized the quality and style of Don Carlos's gentleman's clothing. Her eyes widened. She glanced to
Cole, who merely shrugged.

Dorritt knew it was beneath her to take any pleasure in disconcerting her sister, but she couldn't help herself. Trying to hide a smile that wouldn't stop, Dorritt stroked Alandra's back and ignored Jewell.

Cole Anderson spoke up, "Kilbride got excited when the commandant said we had to stay here until Mexico City confirmed we have a right to be in Texas."

"You are dressed very fine, Carlos," Jewell said, obviously not following the conversation.

"Señorita Jewell, we meet again." Don Carlos bowed to her once more.

Dorritt spoke up, "Sister, Don Carlos Sandoval isn't a mere *vaquero*. He owns Rancho Sandoval south of here." Dorritt couldn't resist adding, "His ranch covers nearly eight thousand acres."

Jewell opened and then clamped her mouth as if being forced to swallow some horrid medicine. She glared at Dorritt.

"And I am *su hermana*, his sister," Alandra added.

Dorritt chuckled. "Yes, this is poor, shy little Alandra."

Cole smiled at the little girl. "My little sister is out picking wildflowers. But she will be happy to see Carlos again."

Nodding, Don Carlos smiled indulgently at his little sister. "Señora Kilbride, if you will allow, I will leave Señorita Dorritt and my little sister with you. Soon I will go and speak to the *commandante*. I know him and will find out if anything can be done for your husband."

"Oh, would you?" Mrs. Kilbride took Don Carlos's hand between both of hers. "I would be so grateful. Dorritt disappearing. The soldiers making us come here, and then . . ." She pressed her handkerchief to her mouth.

"Don't be sad." Alandra jumped down from Dorritt's lap. She began petting Mrs. Kilbride's shoulder.

"I will join you at the inn, Señorita Dorritt." Don Carlos turned to Mrs. Kilbride and Jewell. "You must allow me to secure accommodations for you also. Little Alandra wants to stay with your daughter, but I'm sure Señorita Dorritt would want her mother and sister to be comfortable as they wait upon events."

"What happened to you, Miss Dorritt?" Cole Anderson asked as if he'd been holding this back with effort. "We were concerned about your safety."

"It isn't clear yet why Eduardo kidnapped me," Dorritt said, choosing her words with care. "But Don Carlos is innocent. He was shocked to see me show up at his ranch and has shown me only the most gentlemanly regard and courtesy."

"My brother is *muy enojado,* much angry with Eduardo," Alandra said with audible disapproval.

Jewell looked irritated that she wouldn't be able to use the kidnapping against Dorritt. But Dorritt's thoughts had already drifted back to Quinn. She had observed him toward the rear of the crowd when she'd alighted from the carriage earlier. But he had not approached her. Why? Perhaps hearing Don Carlos state the hope that she'd become his wife, Quinn had believed that she'd already agreed to marry Don Carlos. Still, his rejection stung. During those terrifying miles after she'd been kidnapped, she had allowed herself to imagine their reunion. In her heart of hearts, she'd anticipated a scene that included an ardent embrace, vows of eternal love, and fervent kisses. Yet Quinn had never spoken to her of love. . . .

Dorritt rose and offered her hand to the little girl. "Don Carlos, I think I'd like to go to the inn now."

* * *

Inside Ash's shadowy *jacal,* Quinn stood, ready for this clash. At the sound of Don Carlos's greeting to Ash, Quinn had moved into his fighting stance, so he could draw his knife or pistol with ease.

Don Carlos halted just inside the door. "I didn't come to fight, Quinn."

"Too bad. I feel like fighting." Quinn shifted on his feet, ready to spring. "You have much to answer for."

"I don't blame you. My cousin Eduardo has served me an ill turn. He kidnapped Señorita Dorritt, the lady whom I have fallen in love with and wish to marry."

Unhappy with these words, Quinn didn't let down his guard. Was Don Carlos telling him the truth? Was Eduardo the one responsible for everything?

"You were telling the truth then," Ash asked, entering behind Don Carlos, "when you told everyone you intended to marry her?"

Don Carlos lifted his chin. "*Sí*, I was. I'm in love with the *señorita*."

"Where is my mistress?" Reva asked from the bench.

"At the inn," Don Carlos said.

"Ash, I'm going to find my Miss Dorritt, if that's fine with you." Ash nodded and Reva left.

"Señor Quinn, I am at a loss to know why Eduardo did what he has done. When I left the wagon train to go home, I told him to *protect* Señorita Dorritt until she safely arrived at the Austin settlement. That was my order to him. Do you have any idea why Eduardo had Señorita Dorritt kidnapped?"

Quinn was still weighing and measuring each of Don Carlos's words. The man sounded as if he were speaking the truth. Quinn glanced at Ash. His friend nodded once. Quinn relaxed his stance. If Ash thought Don Carlos was telling the truth, Quinn would give the man a chance to be heard. "Eduardo drugged and kidnapped me too."

Don Carlos let out a sound of shocked anger. "That explains why you didn't go after Pedro and rescue Señorita Dorritt."

"Sit down and let's talk." Ash waved toward the small table and reached for the coffee pot hanging in the small hearth.

Uncertain and unconvinced, Quinn watched and waited,

holding back all the anger that still dug its spurs in to him. "Don Carlos, tell us what you know."

"You know more than I," Don Carlos spoke as if holding tight to his own anger. "Three days ago, Pedro arrived at my ranch with *la señorita* in front of him on his horse, saying that my cousin told him to bring her to me. I cannot tell you how shocked, how incensed, I was. Can you tell me why you think my cousin Eduardo would do this?"

Ash's features twisted with concentration. "You say that Eduardo is your cousin. How well do you two get along?"

Don Carlos made a sound as if he were annoyed. "Eduardo has always been of a dark nature. He sneers at life."

"How long has he worked for you?" Quinn asked.

Don Carlos sat down at the bench. "When we were both still children, he came to our family as an orphan. He is two years older than I, the son of my mother's oldest sister. My parents raised him as a member of the family."

"But now he works for you?" Quinn asked. Ash finished pouring out three cups of coffee and sat down.

"Yes, Eduardo is family but he is related to my mother, and so not an heir of my father. He has long acted as *my* foreman at the ranch. I have often thought . . ." Don Carlos's voice faded.

"Sounds just like a situation that can breed envy," Ash said with a sideways glance at Don Carlos, "if a man has a jealous nature."

Quinn could always count on Ash's skill of sizing people up. He was rarely wrong.

Don Carlos pressed his lips together in a firm, displeased line. "I have done as my parents did. I have treated my cousin as family. But since his family had nothing to leave, he inherited nothing. I have paid him well, but he likes to spend it drinking, gambling, and visiting *bordellos* in Laredo or Santa Fe."

Beginning to believe Don Carlos, Quinn sat down beside Ash.

"If damaging my or the *señorita*'s reputation was his intention, he has failed." Don Carlos looked determined. "If Señorita
Dorritt will consent, I will marry her. I don't care what anyone
believes. I know the truth."

Silence hovered over and around them. Quinn chewed on
Don Carlos's intention to marry Dorritt, tried to choke it down.
Couldn't.

Then Don Carlos looked Quinn in the eye. "I believe you are
my rival for the hand of *la señorita*. Is that true?"

* * *

In her small but neat room at the inn, Dorritt heard a soft knock
on her door. Who was it? She got up from the bed where she lay
beside a napping Alandra and opened the door. Her heart soared.
"Reva, oh, my sweet Reva!" Dorritt threw her arms around her
former maid. "Oh, how I have needed you."

Reva hugged her back fiercely as if trying to communicate
the same feeling with her intense response. "I was so worried."
Reva wept onto Dorritt's shoulder. "I was so afraid I never see
you again."

Dorritt shed a few tears too and then drew Reva into her
room. She glanced toward Alandra, who was deep in slumber
and motioned toward the two chairs near the window. "Sit
down. We can talk softly without disturbing her."

"Is she Don Carlos's sister?"

"Yes, how did you know?" Dorritt's eyebrows lifted.

"Ash, my husband—" Reva blushed "—came back today and
told us Don Carlos had brought you and his sister to San Antonio."

"Where is Ash?" *And Quinn?*

"He is with Don Carlos and Quinn at Ash's family's place,"
Reva said.

Dorritt found she couldn't speak.

Reva nodded firmly. "I just heard Don Carlos says he love you and want you to be his wife. But Quinn love you and you love him. What are you going to do?"

Dorritt was caught by Reva's declaration that Quinn loved her. She couldn't reply.

"Well, which is it? Which man are you going to marry—Don Carlos or Mr. Quinn?"

Nineteen

Reva's question pierced Dorritt's heart like an arrow into a bull's-eye. She sprang up from her chair and paced with quick, jerky steps to the door. *What am I going to do about Don Carlos, about Quinn?* "You know I have never thought to marry." *But my life has changed and I must also. But how can I let myself trust a man? What if I'm wrong?*

Reva came and urged Dorritt back to a chair by the window. There Reva gripped Dorritt's hands between hers. "Don't put me off. I see you want to marry. You want to marry Quinn. And don't you try to tell me different."

With surprise, Dorritt gazed into the smooth caramel-colored face of her lifelong friend. She'd always thought of Reva as her friend first and her maid second. But now Dorritt realized that before she had always been the leader in every conversation. Reva's direct words and honest contradiction revealed her own new confidence, her freedom from bondage. To Dorritt, it was startling and vaguely troubling. *Have I without meaning to always disrespected Reva, just like everyone else?* It was a dark and sobering thought. Among many others crowding her mind.

Dorritt wilted into her chair. "Quinn was there, Reva. There when I arrived in Don Carlos's carriage in the plaza and he didn't talk to me." Dorritt's disappointment pooled cold and clammy in the pit of her stomach. "He has never spoken of love to me." *Even when he kissed me.*

Reva sat down opposite her again. "The whole time he was with our wagon train, I watched Mr. Quinn. He stayed near the stock, did his work. But he always had one eye on you."

The new Reva had opinions and stated them. Dorritt felt as if Reva was leading her across a precariously swaying bridge, *not* following her as she always had before. Her maid . . . no, her friend . . . was pulling, forcing, her take one step after the other. Dorritt hung her head. "Just being attracted to me, watching me, doesn't mean that he wants . . . that I am . . . that we . . ."

Reva sat and sighed. "You're right. In some men that watching you could mean a lot of different things. But not with Mr. Quinn. I study him and it wasn't just that he always looking toward you, but *how* he looked at you. He got deep feelings for you."

Dorritt examined each word Reva said, held each up to the light of honesty. *But he has never revealed these deep feelings to me.* Dorritt's hands fisted and she pressed the two fists tightly together, knuckles to knuckles. "I have deep feelings for him."

"Well, I'm not the one you should be telling." Reva had the nerve to sound amused.

If I do, will it matter? Dorritt reached over to the nearby bed and smoothed the stray hair from Alandra's cheek as she slept—looking so innocent, untouched by life. "You may be right," Dorritt whispered, hearing the words but not really feeling them. "But it is not easy to change the way a person, the way I have thought all my life." *The way Quinn has thought all his life.*

"I know you right about that." Reva poked Dorritt's arm. "Ash had to change his way of thinking. Do you think it was easy for Ash to ask me to marry him in front of everybody like that? That it was easy for me to say yes with you standing there looking like someone about to kill you?"

"Reva, I wanted you to be free. You just never told me that matters between you and Ash had gone that far."

"I know you want me to be free, but how could I tell you? Ash never say before that night that he wanted to marry me."

"He hadn't?" Hope flickered in Dorritt's heart, a tiny bright spark. Could it be the same way with Quinn and her—he felt but hadn't put those feelings into words?

"No. Ash liked me, but he kept thinking maybe he's too old for me. And maybe I wouldn't want to marry him. But then your stepdaddy tried to make me marry Josiah. That made Ash speak up right quick. And now the same thing's happen to you and Quinn."

Dorritt blinked. "What? I don't understand."

"You do too." Reva shook her head at Dorritt. "Eduardo kidnapped you and now Don Carlos want to marry you. That's just like your stepdaddy trying to make me marry Josiah. You're going to marry either Mr. Quinn or Don Carlos. Two men who see you, see how fine a woman you are. Now you've got to make up your mind which man you choose."

Quinn had appeared in Dorritt's life just when she needed him, a gift from God. And he occupied the deepest, most secret place in her heart. But right there beside it was her fear of allowing any man to control her life. Bondage—that's what marriage had always meant to her. And now Don Carlos had offered her his heart and his name. And he was a good man, a settled man, while Quinn the wanderer remained silent. Everything was so mixed up. Dorritt looked at Reva, who had just been freed from slavery because Ash had redeemed her. Reva didn't feel enslaved by marrying. Instead she'd become free. It was easier for Reva to marry—

"I know what you're thinking—it easy for me. You thinking I married Ash because he bought my freedom—"

"No." Dorritt didn't want to cast a shadow on Reva's happiness, her marriage. Agitated, Dorritt popped up again and looked out the window. "Facing this decision is hard for me. But you're right. My life, my situation has altered." Still, the word *altered* had the power to start cold liquid fear dripping into the pit of her stomach. Was she brave enough not just to love, but to also marry, to trust a man, to give up her independence?

Dorritt gripped the wooden sill, looking out the window. "My situation is much more complex than a simple decision of which man to marry, Reva." Dorritt thought about her last conversation with Quinn and his quick rejection of her suggestion he buy land in Texas. Would Quinn be able to change the way he thought? The way he lived? Invisible bands tightened around her breast, making it hard to breathe. Why did everything have to be so complicated?

Reva got up and hugged Dorritt from behind, resting her chin on Dorritt's shoulder. "You are a smart woman. I know you make the right decision."

Dorritt patted Reva's hand around her waist. When Reva said she must return to Ash, Dorritt led Reva down the stairway and outside. There in the cool shade under the front porch, Dorritt took Reva's hand. "I need to speak to Mr. Quinn alone. Can you arrange that?"

"I don't want anybody to see you coming with me." Reva looked concerned. "But I come for you tonight after everyone asleep. I come to the back door here and take you to our *jacal.* Quinn's staying with us."

Dorritt squeezed Reva's hand. As Reva walked away, Don Carlos appeared walking across the plaza and stepped in from the blinding sunlight and met her there. "*Señorita*, where is Al-andra?"

"Asleep." A jumble of emotions flocked around Dorritt's heart. She fell silent with guilt. This man loved her. This man wanted to marry her. And tonight she was going to sneak away to see his rival. "I should check on her." Dorritt turned away.

Don Carlos stopped her with a gentle hand on her elbow. "If you need anything, you will tell me, no?"

No doubt if she asked him to, Don Carlos would take her to Quinn himself. But she could not ask this of him. It struck her as a cruelty to do so. So she merely nodded, hoping she didn't look as guilty as she felt.

* * *

Dorritt watched the last golden rays of the autumn sun finally dip below the horizon. Then she slipped downstairs and out the back door of the inn. Over her head and shoulders, she wore one of the dark shawls that had belonged to Don Carlos's mother. Ash, along with Reva, waited in the shadows for her. She looked up at him in surprise.

Ash pulled at the brim of his leather hat. "I decided I should be your escort too, *señorita*. We don't know what Eduardo might do if he came upon you two women alone."

At the memory of Eduardo clapping his hand over her mouth, overpowering her, Dorritt shivered in the warm evening air. She nodded and Ash led her and Reva swiftly and quietly through the back ways of San Antonio and then along the river to his family's land. When they reached their hut, Ash motioned for her to wait just behind him, obviously shielding her from view. Had Reva and Ash kept her coming a secret? That possibility tightened her nerves more. Then Ash called, "Quinn."

Dorritt waited, nearly holding her breath. Ash stepped aside, and there was Quinn in front of her. And he did not look happy to see her. Only wearing his buckskin breeches and moccasins, he held himself stiffly and his eyes were stormy. But even his air of remoteness tempted her nearer; she moved toward him.

"It's time you talked things over with Miss Dorritt." Ash said no more, but walked past Quinn into the *jacal.*

Night sounds and a warm breeze sighed around Dorritt. By the light of the crescent moon and of stars piercing the ebony sky, she drank in the sight of Quinn, so lean, tall, and confident. As always, he ignited all her senses, sharpening every sound, every breath. "We need to talk." It was difficult to say those few words. She kept her features deceptively composed. When he didn't reply, she cleared her throat. "I didn't know that you had been kidnapped at the same time that I was." Would this start him talking?

"I should have protected you." Quinn's voice sounded rusty, as if he hadn't spoken much that day.

Dorritt shook her head, still moving closer to Quinn. "That's not what I meant. I feel responsible for your being kidnapped. If you had not been a threat to Eduardo's plot, he would not have bothered you." She halted in front of him now.

Quinn dismissed this with a wave of his arm. "What Eduardo did is not your fault. And he is going to pay—"

Dorritt interrupted, taking his upper arms in her hands. His skin was warm and his muscles hard under her palms. "I don't want to talk about Eduardo now. In fact, I think when he kidnapped me, he did me an unexpected favor."

Her words and her touch visibly took Quinn aback. His hand rose but stopped in midair. Had he nearly caressed her cheek? "What do you mean by that? He frightened you, made your family worry. He tried to ruin your reputation."

Dorritt drew herself up. "I'm not concerned about my reputation." *Not in the way that I was before.* She drew closer; it was as if the air around them was charged with her awareness of him. She didn't have to touch him to feel his presence. Quinn refused to look her way, to make this easier for her. She wanted to shake him. Instead, she turned and walked toward the river, hoping to draw Quinn away from anyone who might be able to overhear them, wanting him alone to hear her. And if she could cause him to come after her, that would tell her something of his feelings for her.

Stopping, she spoke quietly, "Yesterday, Don Carlos took me to the highest rise on his ranch. He told me about his parents and how they fell in love in Mexico City and married in spite of family opposition and how they had come to that place nearly thirty years ago."

She sensed Quinn following her and continued speaking into the darkness, "As I gazed over his acres, I began to see that I had still been thinking about my life, about me as I had lived and had been thought of in Louisiana. But Louisiana is the past. Texas is the future, my future. I cannot be bound by the old ideas, by the old me. And then I knew I must make a decision." She turned to face Quinn. The sound of river water trickling over rocks was loud in the silence between them.

In the low light, Quinn halted behind Dorritt. She turned to face him. Not wanting to look at her beauty, which always made him weak, he stooped to sift through the earth and pebbles at his feet, fighting his desire to draw her into his arms. Dorritt was a danger to him, to what he knew as reality.

"And now you must make a decision too." She put a hand under his arm and tugged him until he rose and faced her. She brushed her hand over his hair down to his cheek.

Her touch, each stroke of each finger, had such power over him. He tried to make sense of her words, but couldn't. Close to her, he caught her sweet fragrance on the breeze. He straightened up fully. "What are you talking about? What decision?"

Her face burst into a smile, as powerful to him as watching a dawning sunrise. "That's why I had to talk to you alone. You need to make a decision because you see—" she inhaled deeply, "—I have fallen in love with you."

Quinn jerked as if he had been punched. "You, I—"

"Don Carlos gave me the strength to say that out loud to you. They are the words he said to me." She clasped Quinn's hand, drawing it up and pressing it to her heart. "I thought I would never hear those words from any man. But that was the old me, not the Texas me."

His eyes lowered, Quinn tried to remove his hand from her soft palm. "Don Carlos will be a lucky man to have you for his wife."

She didn't let him pull free. "I love you, not Don Carlos. Doesn't that mean anything to you?" She paused. "Do you love me?"

Why had she said those words? Pulling free, he turned his back to her. "I can't love you."

She moved around him and came face-to-face with him again. "That isn't the question, Quinn. *Do* you love me?"

His heart pumped blood in great swells that washed through him. He looked over her head and wouldn't reply. He should have gone after Eduardo this morning immediately after Don Carlos had arrived. He'd let his anger cloud his judgment. But no more.

She shook his arm. "Why can't you tell me you love me?"

Her touch and nearness tempted him. Quinn grimaced, swallowing the words he couldn't say. "I'm not for the likes of you."

"That is not Texas thinking," she objected, clinging to his arm. "I have already told you you could buy land. You could have your own ranch. You could breed cattle and your horses. And we could have a life together. A good one I think. I hope."

Hadn't they already covered this? Why did she think Texas was so different? She was wrong. A cloud moved and let faint moonlight flow down, lighting her face. Quinn shook his head, resisting the desire to bend down and taste her lips. "Everyone would look down on you because you had married a half-breed."

"Not if I lift my chin proudly. And Don Carlos has Indian blood too, but because he has seven thousand acres, do you hear anyone calling him a *mestizo*?" Dorritt's rich voice that always affected him rose. "If you make a success of your ranch, it will be the same for you. Or I should say we make a success of *our* ranch? I have run my stepfather's plantation for almost ten years. I know how to manage land, how to run a plantation. A ranch can't be much different, just cattle instead of cotton."

"You're talking crazy." Very well, if she insisted, he would tell her all the reasons he shouldn't love her. "I'm a half-breed. I'm unlettered. You're a white lady, an educated lady. And we both know me—a leatherstocking—would never be welcome in an Austin settlement. And I'm nearly thirty. Life on the frontier is short. Both my parents were gone very young. I'm a bad bet all around."

Dorritt moved till they were almost touching. "Why are you being so stubborn? If we decide not to let what *others* think hold us back, keep us as we are, we can have it all. A good life together, perhaps children, and something to leave them when we die. Since you force me to, I will sacrifice the last of my pride. All you have to do is say I love you too and let's start our life together."

He brushed past her and started walking away, everything in him clamoring for him to turn, take her into his arms, and speak the words she wanted to hear.

She pursued him and grasped his arm once more. "Was that kiss nothing to you?"

"It was just a kiss." *Why are you putting us through this?* He lifted his shoulder, shaking off her hand. "You should marry Don Carlos. He is wealthy with a good reputation. He can give you the life you deserve."

"I may marry Don Carlos," she said fiercely. "But only if you cannot love me. Only if you remain a coward."

He kept going.

She hurried forward and planted herself in front of Quinn yet again, as if daring him to brush past her. "*Stop.* Think what you are doing, what you're throwing away. Do you think that I go around casually telling men I love them? Is that what you think?"

"No, that's not what I think. I have already said what I know. Just because you think in a new way, do you think the whole world has changed? It hasn't. I am still the same half-breed I was in Louisiana." He tried to go.

She stood her ground. "Yes, you are. But we can't let what was true in Louisiana hold us back here. In Louisiana, I allowed myself to see myself as less than I am, less than God made me. And you can't let—"

He tried to go around her. She moved with him, blocking him.

"Quinn, you allowed yourself to see yourself as men like my stepfather see you, not as God does. But should you, should I care what small, empty men like him think?"

Quinn made a sound of disgust. "I can't believe you're talking to me like this. This is not how a lady talks."

"I won't let you throw that word in my face. I'm a Texas woman. And this is how a Texas woman talks to the man she loves. I love you. I want to be your wife. But you have to be fearless too. You have to begin thinking notions big enough for this land, big enough for us to be together."

"Marry Don Carlos." Quinn brushed past her toward the *jacal.* "Ash, bring Reva! We'll see Miss Dorritt back to the inn."

Dorritt tried to answer him but he turned his back as the other two joined them outside.

With Ash and Reva, Quinn walked Dorrritt to the inn's back door and waited until she went inside. He'd not dared to look at her face on the way, but then by the faint light falling from the inn windows, he glanced into her face. Her expression cut him— he'd seen happier faces on dead men.

From the inn doorway, Dorritt watched Quinn walk away. Ash and Reva hesitated near her as if wanting to talk. Dorritt couldn't bear it and turned away—and found Don Carlos waiting for her just inside the inn. She gasped in surprise.

Caught coming in after visiting Quinn, Dorritt did not know what to say to Don Carlos. She stuttered a guilty incoherent explanation; then closed her mouth.

He gazed at Dorritt without any expression except polite concern. "*Querida*, I do not think it is wise for you to be outside after dark."

Dorritt had heard him call Alandra *querida*, and so she knew it must be a word of endearment. His using it touched her, and deeply. She owed him the truth. She looked him in the eye. "I had to speak to Mr. Quinn. Alone. But I did not go unprotected. Ash and Reva escorted me to his family's land and then they and Mr. Quinn saw me back here."

Still looking only respectful, Don Carlos bowed. "I would have wished you to have taken *tu madre* as your chaperone. May I see you to your room now?"

She was grateful he did not ask for more of an explanation. She reached for his arm. "Yes, please. I am very tired." She walked beside him until just outside her room. "I take it that Alandra is staying with friends tonight?" When he nodded, she asked, "Have you found Eduardo?"

Don Carlos frowned. Then he leaned over and kissed her forehead. "He has evaded me today, but my outriders have been searching for him. We will find him. Do not let him trouble you. I will take care of Eduardo."

"Oh, please, I . . . ," she stammered, his kiss flustering her, "please don't do anything dangerous." She touched his sleeve. *I wouldn't want anything to happen to you. You're a good man.*

In answer, he merely bowed, kissed her hand, and then urged her inside her room. There, she stood in the darkness, letting her eyes become accustomed.

Dorritt sank down onto the chair by the window and looked down at the moonlit plaza. Her emotions had twisted her midsection into a ball like a bundle of damp clothes waiting to be pressed. Tonight by the river, she had taken the most fearless step of her life. She had exposed her very heart to Quinn. And what had been his reply to her honesty? Nothing but evasion. She closed her eyes and breathed deeply, feeling the pinch of anguish tight around her lungs. *I will give him time. Before I despair.*

* * *

Back at Ash's place, Quinn tried to walk past Ash and enter the hut. But Ash waved Reva on inside and then caught Quinn's arm. "Hold up. I've got a few words to say to you."

"I've had enough talking for one night." Quinn tried to brush past Ash again.

Ash stopped Quinn by blocking his path.

Ash crossed his arms. "When did you turn coward?"

Quinn bumped up against Ash, trying to make him back down. "Just because we're friends, don't think you can get away with calling me names."

"Are we friends? Do you look down at me because I'm *de color quebrado*? Of mixed blood?"

The question irked Quinn, gripped him like a fist around his throat. "Of course I don't. Why would you ask me something so stupid?"

"Because you're *acting* stupid. Your pa didn't see you as something less because *tu madre* was Cherokee. And he never let anybody show disrespect to her or to him or you. Why do you?"

Was everyone but Quinn blind? "Nothing I do or say will change the way *ricos*, Creoles, or the Anglos think of me. I am *mestizo*, I am a half-breed."

Ash made a sound of disgust. "*¿No comprendes?* Don Carlos Sandoval's just like you. He's a *mestizo* just like you are. But do you hear anybody calling *him* that? Anyone here throwing his mother's Indian blood into *his* face?"

Quinn stared at Ash, as he took this in. He'd never thought of Don Carlos in those terms. Dorritt had said the same. *He's a half-breed too.*

Ash went on, "Maybe the Creoles would call him *mestizo* in Mexico City or New Orleans. But this is Texas. And here Don Carlos is respected—why? Because he owns land. Here land is wealth. Land is power. That's why the Anglos have come to get the land, the power. Why can't you see getting land can work for you too? Land would make men respect you. We talked about buying a few acres and raising horses. But why not a *sitio* of land, thousands of acres? Like the Andersons want? Why not you too? And most of all, having a woman like Miss Dorritt as your wife would make other men respect you."

Quinn heard Ash, but all he could think of was Kilbride's scorn in every look, every word he'd ever said to Quinn. "I'm not interested in the respect of men I don't respect."

Ash shook Quinn's shoulder. "Are you interested in having a life with the woman you love? You fell in love with a lady, not an Indian, or a *mestiza* or a *mulatta*—a white lady. That means you have to give up wandering, buy some land, and give her the life an educated lady deserves." Ash pushed Quinn away from him. "And when you do, you'll be a man no one dare disrespect. The only thing that's stopping you is you think too small." Then Ash turned to walk inside.

But the voice of Don Carlos hailed them in the darkness. "Señores Quinn and Ash, may I have a word?"

Quinn wished he could become invisible. Why did everyone—want—to—talk—tonight? "It's late," he growled.

Don Carlos's face was cast in shadow by the scant moonlight.
"My two men think they have found where Eduardo was staying
in San Antonio. But he has vamoosed. Tomorrow early I intend
to go after him. I plan to start out at daylight to track him and
bring him back to face trial for kidnapping Señorita Dorritt."

A man like Don Carlos might be able to get Eduardo pros-
ecuted. But Quinn wasn't about to be left out of this hunt. "I'm
going with you."

* * *

As he and Juan fled San Antonio, Eduardo was grateful for the
pale moonlight. He was certain his cousin had spent this day
looking for them, so they had nearly a day's ride as a head start.
Regret simmered in Eduardo's gut. He wished he'd kept his
mouth shut in San Antonio. When Pedro had sent word that
he'd gone back on their deal and decided to take the *señorita* to
Carlos instead of holding her in the place he'd been told to, he
and Juan should have cleared out of San Antonio.

But he had set up everything so carefully. He had been confident that as soon as Quinn had made it to San Antonio, he would
hear the gossip Eduardo had started about Señorita Dorritt and
Carlos. And if Quinn confronted him, he would continue to
insist that Carlos had told him to have both kidnapped.

Then Eduardo planned to disappear and Quinn would have
hunted Carlos down. Even if Carlos had denied ordering the
kidnappings, how could he prove it if there was no one as a witness? In the best of all possible outcomes, Quinn would have
killed Carlos.

Even if Quinn hadn't killed Carlos in a duel, there would
have been a scandal. And his proud cousin would have been embarrassed and the *señorita's* reputation would have been under
a cloud for the rest of her life. It would have even stained her

children. That would have gained Eduardo some satisfaction. But Quinn had not believed Eduardo's lies about the woman. And both Quinn and Ash had come looking for Eduardo. And now Carlos too.

"I can't ride all night," Juan complained from behind Eduardo.

"I can. If you want to face my cousin or Quinn, stop here and go to sleep," Eduardo snapped. "If you think they aren't preparing to hunt us, you're a fool."

Juan muttered something under his breath.

Eduardo blazed with anger. Everything was always against him. And now he was running for his life. He dug his heels into his horse and picked up the pace. Juan grumbled and Eduardo ignored him. Life never went his way. Well, he wasn't going to give Don Carlos Sandoval the satisfaction of dragging him back to face trial at the Alamo. Never.

Twenty

In the graylight just before dawn, Dorritt, restless and wakeful, stood at the window in the inn and looked out over the plaza, still sleeping. She glimpsed motion below and heard the sound of horse's hooves on the packed earth. Two horses came into view. Quinn was on the first and on the other was Ash with Reva, riding behind him. Shock rippled through Dorritt's tired mind. And instant fear. Something was happening. Then leading his horse from behind the inn, Don Carlos walked into the plaza and hailed the other men in a low voice.

Dorritt didn't wait to see more. They were going to hunt Eduardo! Pulling on her wrapper, she raced down the stairs and out the front door. "Wait!" she called. "What are you doing?"

The three men stared at her but didn't reply. Don Carlos mounted his stallion as Ash helped Reva down. Reva came directly to her. "Now don't make a fuss. The men have to find Eduardo—"

Dorritt tried to interrupt.

Don Carlos held up his hand. "Eduardo knows I would not let him go unpunished for kidnapping and lying about you or me. And that Quinn would never let the fact he'd been drugged and kidnapped go unpunished—"

Dorritt held out her hands to him. "But why do you have to go? Won't the commandant at the Alamo send soldiers—?"

Don Carlos cut her off, "Here law-abiding men enforce what is right. We will bring my cousin back to face a trial for what he has done—if he doesn't prefer death."

Dorritt closed her eyes. All she could think of were the long rifles the three men wore slung on their backs and the pistols in their belts. She went toward them, one hand still held up, beseeching. There would be bloodshed. And it might be Eduardo's but it could be Quinn's or Don Carlos's or Ash's—

Don Carlos said, "*Señorita*, Eduardo has brought this on himself."

"Why did Eduardo do this?" she asked, her hand falling, her spirit sinking.

Reva put an arm around Dorritt, stopping her.

"One can never know what another man's thoughts are. But as I think over the past, I see my cousin's envy as I never recognized it before." Don Carlos gathered his reins more tightly.

In the early morning coolness, Dorritt made a cautious guess. "He's envious because you are the *don* and not he?"

"It must be so."

"But why now? You say he's envied you for years?"

Don Carlos lifted one shoulder. "Now that I realize that Eduardo has been my enemy and not my trustworthy cousin, I remember things that I ought to have noticed before. I think Eduardo has been stealing from me when he went on cattle drives to Louisiana. He tried very hard to dissuade me from going this time. And I was surprised when the price we got for our cattle was so much higher than in the past. I set it down to market changes, but now I think I was gullible to trust Eduardo with so much money. Maybe he feared I would take action against him. I just don't know."

Don Carlos sucked in air as if it pained him. "Who knows what has been going on inside Eduardo's heart since we were children together? When I learned that he had kidnapped you, I saw at last that he was not the cousin I thought I knew. I must have been blind not to see his *resentimiento* toward me. I should not have kept him at Rancho Sandoval as my foreman. I should have given him land far from me and let him be on his own. But I did not see him as I do now." Don Carlos turned the head of his horse toward the south.

"A man's heart is deceitful above all things," Dorritt whispered the scripture.

"Unfortunately. My men will stay here protecting you. We will return as soon as we can. Buy whatever you need here. Just say my name." Don Carlos pulled the brim of his hat toward Reva and Dorritt and then started away.

Dorritt looked up into Quinn's face. Why didn't he say anything? Speak to her? But the determination in his face was unmistakable, unshakable. She pleaded with him with her eyes, yet he said nothing. And Dorritt was reminded of the first time she'd seen him in Natchitoches. He was closed to her again, a stranger again. She wrapped her arms around herself, not against the early morning chill, but the one emanating from Quinn.

"Well, let's go to where Eduardo was staying and pick up his trail," Ash said, breaking the heavy silence between Quinn and her. He waved good-bye to Reva.

Reva waved at the men as they rode away.

At the sound of their going, Dorritt's heart stopped, a weight like a huge boulder pressing down over it. Her fingers actually tingled with shock. She sucked in air. She had to move. She had to stop them.

"Come on." Reva took her arm and was leading her back inside.

"We should have stopped them," Dorritt said, pulling against Reva.

"They are gone already."

For a moment, Dorritt closed her eyes and drew in a breath that felt jagged in her throat. In less than two months, Dorritt's life had been flipped upside down like biscuits turned out of a pan. "I don't want Quinn, Ash, or Don Carlos risking their lives. How can we stop it?"

"We can't," Reva said flatly, leading Dorritt inside and up the steps. "The men will do what they want no matter what we say. And frankly Eduardo deserve to be shot. He kidnapped you. He kidnapped Quinn. He is trying to hurt his own cousin, his own blood. He deserve to be shot."

Dorritt stared at her friend in the gray light of dawn, growing brighter and brighter. "Reva, I can't believe you're standing there telling me that you want someone to die. I don't want Quinn to murder—"

"They are not going to hunt Eduardo down and kill him. Don Carlos said that he would bring Eduardo back to face a court." Reva continued standing for herself, her new freedom revealing itself.

Hanging her head, Dorritt couldn't help showing the hurt that came with Reva's lack of support. "But, Reva, what if Eduardo won't come back, what if he fights and . . . someone is killed?"

Reva leaned closer to Dorritt, speaking in a low fierce tone, "Then Eduardo will be the one to die and it will be his own fault."

Twenty-one

The October sun was high and fierce. Quinn walked beside his horse, following the intermittent trail that Eduardo and Juan had been unable to mask while escaping San Antonio. After leaving Dorritt and Reva at the inn, Quinn, Ash and Don Carlos had gone to the abandoned *jacal* where Eduardo and Juan had been squatting since leaving the wagon train. They found Eduardo was heading westward, leading them deeper into the rugged country west of San Antonio, not south. The grasslands directly south wouldn't give the outlaws any cover. Quinn had come this way years ago. Ahead on horseback, Ash slowed. He pointed down at the trace of a hoofprint in the dust and coarse grass. Nodding, Quinn mounted his horse and the three of them rode on.

His eyes alert for anything out of the ordinary, his mind took him back to the night before. Dorritt's beautiful face in the moonlight—so passionate, so sure of her love. For him. Riding just feet away was the man—the gentleman—who could give her everything she deserved. Quinn imagined Dorritt in Don Carlos's arms. The image galled him, fired his jealousy just as it had during those three days when Quinn had believed that Don Carlos had ordered Eduardo to kidnap Dorritt.

In the distance far to his right, Quinn thought he saw a glint of something. He slowed and wondered if he had imagined it. He then rode forward, letting his mind go back to a story about the Osage his father had told him beside a fire one night on the trail. Eduardo might think he was smart. But Quinn knew his father had been smarter. Quinn would keep an eye out—maybe Eduardo had heard that story too.

Once again, Quinn's memory forced him to see Dorritt's pale skin and warm eyes. A fine woman, an educated lady, Dorritt had told him she loved him. *I can't believe it.* Again he caught the barest sound of a strange horse stepping on rock. Whose horse?

Now not even the memory of Dorritt's declaration of love could distract Quinn from the plan developing in his mind. *I watched you for weeks and I know you too well, Eduardo. Know men like you too well. Small men who envy larger men.* Quinn moved closer to Ash and began speaking out of the side of his mouth. Ash knew the Osage tactic too. The secret was not letting Eduardo suspect that they knew what he was up to.

* * *

The long day had finally ended, and Quinn, Ash, and Don Carlos sat around the fire, sipping hot coffee and chewing dry tortillas and spicy pemmican. Though the October days were just as warm as September's, the sun did sink below the horizon earlier now. Something Quinn was very glad of tonight. This chase might end tonight—if he was right. It was hard to keep the conversation going when what the three of them wanted to discuss couldn't be mentioned out loud.

"So, Don Carlos, what do you think of us Mexicans being a republic now?" Ash asked.

Ash always amazed Quinn in that he never thought anyone outranked him, yet he was never disrespectful. It was an interesting combination. To be at ease with himself and everyone, high or low.

"I am uncertain. I am not unhappy to be free of Spain, but I doubt anything will change here in Texas. And I make it a habit to stay away from Mexico City. There is so much deceit and—" Don Carlos waved his hand in a showy way "—play-acting. Everyone wears a mask." Don Carlos made a face.

"I know what you mean. I went to Mexico City when I was young. I had to go to the big city and see it for myself." Ash shrugged. "Once in a lifetime was enough for me."

Quinn listened to them but more to the night sounds, the crickets and the wind through the few cottonwood trees. The waiting was the hardest. Because it gave him time to think of Dorritt. He forced himself to think ahead. Ash was married now and would settle down with Reva, probably near his family around San Antonio. *What will I do? After we bring Eduardo in for trial, I will leave, find my mother's clan. Among the Cherokee, I can find peace, breed my horses, and maybe find a woman to marry.* The now cold coffee in his cup was bitter, but not as bitter as this thought. He looked up and was glad the moon was shrouded with a veil of clouds.

* * *

The attack came in the darkest, coldest hour of the night. Two shots came from the cover beyond the shadowy cottonwood trees. Quinn was ready. He fired at the exact spot where the musket flash had flared. Then he swung his long rifle back onto his shoulder. He pulled his pistol and tomahawk from his belt and ran toward the place. Another flash, another shot. Someone grunted.

In the faint moonlight, Quinn saw movement. He fired his pistol and the shadow jerked. Another shot boomed and Quinn felt the shot slice his cheek. He hit the ground and rolled. He quickly reloaded. Then he stilled, listening for any telltale sound. None came. The night sounds came back to normal. Quinn waited. Waited.

Finally, Don Carlos called out softly, "Have they gone?"

Quinn eased up, listening. "Yes."

"Then come here. *Por favor.*"

Something in his voice brought Quinn to his side fast.

"You were right, *mi amigo*," Don Carlos said with an effort to hide his pain, "two of us would have died. He shot our bedrolls, the ones you made us crawl out from on the side away from the fire."

"It's an old Osage trick." Quinn wished they dared blow some life into the embers of their fire. But what if Eduardo hadn't gone far and doubled back again?

"You're hit. The shoulder?" Ash kept his voice low.

"*Sí.*"

Quinn and Ash knew how to treat gunshot wounds. They worked together packing the wound with cloth and bound it tightly to stop the bleeding.

Quinn caught Ash's eye in the scant light. And he didn't like what he read there. Don Carlos's wound wasn't clean-through; the ball was lodged. They'd need a doctor, and the only one was back at the Alamo. If only they could have been sure that they'd hit Eduardo. Whatever they decided, they'd have to wait till morning.

Twenty-two

At last morning came, and after searching the area and not finding Eduardo's body, Quinn knew what had to be done. The three of them sat in the cover of spiny shrubs and cluster of mesquite trees around a very small and clean fire with hardly any smoke. Don Carlos looked gray with pain, his eyes looked feverish, and when he moved, he winced. Ash made coffee and and passed out sea biscuits and dried meat. Quinn sipped the steaming coffee and then told Ash, "Don Carlos has to have that shoulder looked at."

Ash said, "Yes, I'm taking him to San Antonio."

"I am sitting here and can hear you. I am not a child," Don Carlos objected.

Ash shrugged. "That's right and you know I'm right. That ball has to be dug out and you need to be in bed, getting good care."

"But what about Eduardo?" Don Carlos asked, his face twisting as he took cautious breaths. "Are we to let him go free?"

"I'll go on alone," Quinn said. "And let's not waste time argu-ing. Ash will take you back to San Antonio. I'll go on. After Ash delivers you to the army surgeon at the Alamo, he can always pick up my trail and catch up with me—"

"I don't like it," Don Carlos said. "Eduardo is treacherous. He can't be trusted to fight fair. Look at last night. He sent Juan ahead to leave a trail. Then he doubled back. He followed us just as you thought and would have killed us in cold blood." Don Carlos grimaced with pain.

"Eduardo is a snake," Quinn agreed. "But I'll track him. You'll—" He held up a hand to stop Don Carlos. ". . . help us most by going back with Ash without fuss. I won't crowd Edu-ardo and won't let him take me by surprise. I'm a better tracker than he is. And I won't make the mistake of thinking he wouldn't pull any lowdown trick he could think of." *And it will be a relief to be hunting on my own.*

Don Carlos looked as if he were chewing stones, but finally he nodded. "It goes against what I want to do, but *sí*. I'll just end up slowing you down."

Soon Don Carlos and Ash were mounted and heading north. Quinn sat drinking the last of the now cold coffee. It was not long after dawn. *If I were Eduardo, what would I try next? Would I give up and just try to lose the tracker behind me in the rugged country to the west? And then when I'd lost them, head south? Or would I try to ambush the tracker one more time?*

He sucked in the last few drops of coffee and rose. He kicked dust over the fire and made sure no ember remained. Even if Edu-ardo tried to hide his trail, Quinn was certain he could still track him. He saddled his horse and swung up to start the hunt again.

The country became more rugged as the miles passed. Dor-ritt's tender smile and golden hair kept coming to Quinn. He couldn't shake off remembering her. Her words came back to him: "In Louisiana, I allowed myself to see myself as less than

I am, less than God made me. And you allowed yourself to see yourself as men like my stepfather see you, not as God does."

How could her words come back so clear? Why didn't she realize that the Creator who lived behind the sun had nothing to do with whether they could be together as man and wife? How could she know the God who was so far, far from humans? *I am who I am. I know what I can do. I know that I will die and leave this life. God directs the sun and wind, and the times of planting and reaping. He is not close. He is far from us.*

Still Dorritt's voice, the low rich voice that did things to the back of his neck when she was near, came again in his mind as if he'd just heard her, "You see yourself as men like my stepfather see you, not as God does." He shook his head. He wanted to believe her, but how could he? He must keep his mind on the trail. Nothing else.

* * *

It happened around noon. When Quinn saw the stream and the sheltering cottonwoods and willows in the distance, he recognized the trap Eduardo might set for him. He stopped in the cover of the rise and primed his long rifle and made sure of his pistol. There were two of them—Juan as well as Eduardo. He'd need two shots to take them. He nudged his horse around the rise and he dismounted. On his belly, he settled behind some rocks left over from a slide. He had a clear view of the stream, surrounded by the low bushes and cottonwoods that always thrived around creeks.

He lay still and settled in to wait. A stone was pressing against his breastbone, so he shifted until it didn't push against a bone. Waiting wasn't anything Eduardo would be able to stomach. That's why Eduardo had tried to ambush them last night. Eduardo wanted it over, to be free of looking over his shoulder.

The bright sunlight sparkled on the water and also picked up the glint off a musket, or was it a spur? Whatever it was exactly,

Eduardo would have been sorry to know Quinn had glimpsed it. Barely breathing, Quinn waited. Juan and Eduardo would become more and more nervous the longer the time they remained still hiding in ambush. So Quinn waited, waited—silent and without moving.

Finally, they gave in. And Eduardo and Juan did what he'd waited for them to do. They slipped out of their hiding places around the stream—where they had been ready to ambush him again.

"Throw down your guns!" standing, Quinn roared.

The two turned toward him. Then they dived toward their horses.

Quinn let his flintlock bark. Eduardo shouted. Their horses were screaming—plunging. Then Quinn reloaded his long rifle. He aimed for Eduardo again, but the man's horse danced in front of him. Quinn ran down the slope. He fired again. Eduardo staggered and went down. But he raised his long rifle. The shot hit Quinn on the right side. Quinn jerked but then fired his pistol and lost his footing. He tried to catch himself.

His head struck a rock. He stared up into blue. The thought that he should protect himself floated in his head but he couldn't move. Then he heard footsteps approaching. *No.* He looked up into Juan's darkly suntanned face. Fear like he'd never known shot through him—fiery lightning. He still couldn't move. Couldn't speak.

Creator of all, he's going to kill me. Please. No.

The memory of Dorritt's face the first time he saw her blazed across his mind. He stared at Juan, refusing to close his eyes to death. Juan stared at him a long time. Quinn remained tense but unable to move. *I'm helpless. God, help me.* Juan picked up a rock and brought it down. *He's going to smash my skull. No. No.* The blow, pain. Blackness.

* * *

Quinn opened his eyes and stared up at the blue-gray sky, the sun low on the horizon. At first, he couldn't draw his thoughts together. The sun was warm on him. His horse snuffled as he chewed grass nearby. A terrible thirst finally pulled Quinn into conscious thought. *Am I dead?*

Then the pain hit him. No, he was alive. And hurting. He sat up slowly and looked down at the site of the pain—his right thigh on the outside, high near the hip joint. Blood had flowed freely and was still oozing out onto the earth. He tried to examine the wound, but he was light-headed. He sat very still until the world stopped swirling around him. But where were Eduardo and Juan?

He looked down the slope to where they had been. They had gone. Why? Why hadn't they finished him off? He recalled Juan standing over him with a rock. *Why did he just strike me unconscious? Why not kill me? I was helpless.*

Quinn slowly got to his hands and knees, taking time so he wouldn't lose consciousness again. Finally, he managed to stagger to his feet and grip his saddle horn. He leaned into the horse and he let it walk him down the hill, Quinn favoring his right side.

Around the creek, he saw where the other two horses had been. There was blood on the ground—a lot of blood. He closed his eyes and recalled the flash of time that the firing had taken. Yes, he had seen Eduardo jerk and stagger. *I hit him. He shot me. Juan came to me on the slope.* Quinn relived that awful moment when he saw death coming and he couldn't move.

Why didn't he kill me?

Quinn couldn't come up with a reason. He gazed around, but the facts could not be denied. He was wounded. Eduardo was wounded or dead. Eduardo and Juan were gone. And Quinn must return to San Antonio. He couldn't continue the chase alone, wounded. If he did, he'd end up vulture bait.

He sank down and drank deeply of the cool water. Then he eased into the rapidly running creek and washed the blood off his leg in the cool water. If he didn't, the scent of blood would draw scavengers to him, revealing his presence for miles. Back on the bank, he tried to pad and then tie his bandana around the wound. He managed, but it was in an awkward place. He filled his water skin. Then using the strength of his arms and the saddle horn, he hoisted himself up and swung his wounded leg up into the saddle. The pain made him screw up his face and break out in a cold sweat. He sat in the saddle, panting with the pain. He hated to give up the hunt, but his dying out in the wilderness wasn't going to bring Eduardo to justice.

Quinn turned his horse back toward the northeast and hoped he'd make good time before he became too feverish and perhaps delirious. Why hadn't they killed him? It didn't make sense.

* * *

In the Alamo infirmary, Dorritt sat beside Don Carlos and heard him revive, drawing in a shallow breath. Candles glowed in the darkened room. She bathed his forehead with cool water.

He opened his eyes. "Am I dreaming?" he murmured.

"No, you're in the Alamo, safe. You've been unconscious for several hours." She ran the soft worn cloth wet with water and vinegar over his face.

"What has happened?" he asked, gasping between words.

"The army surgeon removed the shot from your shoulder. It was very deep. You're lucky. He said it missed your heart and lungs. But you are feverish and will need careful tending."

"Not lucky. I am blessed. I had hoped that the next time I saw you I could tell you that I'd brought my cousin to justice. I'm sorry." He caught her hand.

His grip was weak and it grieved her. She blinked away tears and fought to keep her voice even. "You mustn't say that. I'm glad you are safe and I'll make sure you get the best of care. Ash left immediately to go back and join Quinn on the hunt. You just close your eyes and rest."

He pressed the back of her hand against his cheek. This sign of his love for her wrung her heart. *He's such a good man, Lord. Please bless him. Let him recover fully. And please bring Quinn back safely with Ash whole too.*

She drew her hand from Don Carlos's and wet the cloth again. She bathed his face and continued praying. She'd fallen in love with a man—something she'd never thought she'd do. And all because this man Don Carlos had declared his love for her. But Quinn, the man she loved had refused to see her as a part of his future.

She drew in a deep breath, trying to shake off this burden of despair that kept trying to crush her. *This is Texas, not Louisiana. I'm a Texas woman now. And I believe that God brought me here for a reason.* Yet her heavy heart was dragged down with worry. It was hard to cling to faith when the man she loved was out hunting an evil man and perhaps being hunted in return. *I will have faith and not be daunted by these small thoughts. The Lord will give me the desire of my heart. Please.*

* * *

Ash had set out immediately after delivering Don Carlos to the surgeon at the Alamo. He'd only had time to kiss his bride and tell her he had to go back. With each mile, Ash had hoped that Quinn had already caught the dog Eduardo and would meet him along the trail they'd made on the first leg of their hunt. He knew that Quinn would come back via the same trail they'd forged on the way from San Antonio. So now at dawn, he was drinking the last cup of coffee by the morning fire when he heard a horse coming. He reached for his rifle, and then eased back into the few low shrubs around his makeshift camp.

He recognized Quinn's stallion immediately and sprang forward, still clutching his gun in case this was more skullduggery. But it was only Quinn. When Ash saw the blood caked down the side of the horse, he swallowed an oath. "Quinn!"

His friend lifted his head. "Ash." His voice sounded weak.

Ash grabbed the horse's bridle and asked, "What happened?" And he did a quick survey of the bloody bandage wrapped tightly around the top of Quinn's thigh. It looked as if it were keeping more blood from flowing. *Good.*

Quinn blinked. "I shot Eduardo. And he got me. Passed out. Juan didn't kill me."

Ash didn't ask any more. "Can you stay in the saddle?"

"Think so."

But Ash didn't like what he saw. He went back to the fire, lifted the kettle, and poured the strong dregs of the coffee into his cup and put it into Quinn's hand. "Drink this. And I'll get on my horse." Quinn drank while Ash quickly stowed all his gear into his saddlebags and mounted his horse. "I'll get you back to San Antonio as fast as I can." And then they were heading northeast again, and Ash was praying that the bandage would hold till they reached the Alamo.

* * *

Quinn awoke in a dark room. He blinked and tried to think how he'd come to be here and where here was. Then he remembered; he'd wounded Eduardo. The fiery pain in his thigh forced the memory of his own wound on him. Then he heard a soft voice. It was Dorritt's voice and he felt his spirits lift. All he could think of was the feel of her soft mouth on his. That kiss had been the best moment of his life. He almost called to her and then he heard another voice—Don Carlos's.

"I'm glad Ash found Quinn so quickly," his rival said. "Quinn loves you, I know it."

Quinn tried to think why Don Carlos would say this.

"Doesn't that bother you that I have feelings for Quinn? You've proposed marriage to me."

Her words plunged like a sword into Quinn's heart. How could mere words cause more agony than a bullet tearing flesh?

"I see the attraction between you two. But I think I will win you for myself. In the end. After Eduardo has been dealt with." Don Carlos's voice was soft—Quinn could hear the love in each word.

"Could you be happy with me as your wife, even knowing I had loved another man?"

Quinn remembered how Dorritt demanded that he be honest with her. But he had been unable to tell her he loved her because he had nothing to offer her. The memory of turning away from her scored him like razor-sharp claws.

Don Carlos replied, "A woman can love more than once in her lifetime. A man dies and his widow remarries. Does that mean she did not love her first husband? No. Does that mean she loves her second husband less? No. Quinn is a good guide and *vaquero*, a good man. But if he lets you go, after time passes, I will still want you for my wife. Because in the end, it all comes to this—*Estoy enamorado de ti*, I love you."

The sword plunged into Quinn again. He bit his lips to hold it in and tasted his own blood. *I love you, Dorritt, but.* . . . Then Dorritt came to his side and he lay very still with closed eyes. He heard Reva's voice, "You go on back to the inn to rest now, Miss Dorritt. Ash is waiting to walk you there."

Dorritt replied, "Quinn still hasn't regained consciousness. I'm worried." Her low voice curled around his heart.

"He's weak and needs care and time. He'll be all right. Don't you worry. Now go sleep."

Quinn heard Dorritt leave and in spite of the fever still burning his face, he felt colder than he had before. Reva came over and felt his head. He played possum, not wanting, really unable, to talk to anyone. Then he felt himself sinking into unconsciousness again.

When he opened his eyes again, it was very quiet. Still dark with a little candlelight.

"So you finally come back to us," Reva said, standing over him.

He tried to speak, but his lips stuck together. Reva left and was back with a dipper of water. She lifted his head and trickled water into his mouth. When the dipper was empty, she brought another. The water revived him and he could think again. "Dorritt?" he asked and then regretted it.

"Your lady is at the inn getting some sleep. She'd stay here round the clock if I didn't make her go to the inn at night."

Your lady. "How is Don Carlos?"

"He's hurt pretty bad. The surgeon had to dig out the ball and it was in deep and lodged in the collarbone. It was nasty. The doctor won't tell us what his chances are. Just says he needs careful nursing. And he'll get that. How're you feeling?"

"Rough."

Reva felt his forehead with the back of her hand, her cool hand. "Your ball went straight through, so we just had to clean the wound. The surgeon put a couple of stitches in it and then Dorritt and I fomented it, to draw out the poison. We'll do that again come morning. For both of you."

Quinn couldn't stop himself from speaking—the puzzle came again. "Juan didn't finish me off."

Reva pulled over a chair and sat at his bedside. "Tell me about it. Ash didn't know too much."

"It was another ambush, but I had already figured out Eduardo . . . would try to finish me off and then his run would be less dangerous. Eduardo isn't very clever. I just thought where would I . . . be most exposed to attack and that's when I'd stop for water. So near the next creek, I hunkered down under cover and . . . waited them out." He panted slightly with the exertion of forcing out words. *But I have to tell someone, make sense out of this.* "When I didn't come and didn't come, they finally broke cover. I hollered for them to put down their guns. They fired. I fired. I know I wounded Eduardo. But then I fell and . . . hit my head. I couldn't move or talk for a time. And Juan came and struck me senseless with a rock. I can't figure why Juan didn't just shoot me."

Reva bathed his hot face in the vinegar water and Quinn listenend to the only other sound, Don Carlos's labored breathing. "*Señora*, I can't figure out why they didn't just finish me off."

"Maybe Juan's not a murderer. Or maybe God didn't want you dead. He wanted you alive."

Quinn grimaced. He remembered asking God for help when he thought his end had come. But didn't all men do that? How could God be so great he could create everything and yet be close enough to hear a man's final words? It didn't make sense. "God is far from us—beyond the sun."

"I know how you think. But no, God's right here. I didn't think that for a long time. Miss Dorritt always pray that if we trust God, He would give us the desires of our hearts. But I thought they were just pretty words, not for a slave like me. And when we heard that we were going to Texas, I say maybe we can be free in Texas and find men with honor there. But I didn't really believe my own words. And I know Miss Dorritt thought that idea of men with honor was crazy. But then I met Ash and he bought my freedom and married me. And that was my desire—to be free and married to a good man."

Quinn thought about all this. The fever burned like the noontime sun in the desert. Did God really care enough to do that? Was God close, not far away?

"And I think you better stop telling Miss Dorritt you can't love her. And get busy and propose. Or you'll lose her to Don Carlos," Reva scolded.

He winced at the pain her words caused. "He has more to offer her—"

"If you think that matter to Miss Dorritt, you're loco. She would be happy in a *jacal* with the man she loves. She's been rich and she wasn't happy. You better get enough guts to claim Miss Dorritt and be quick about. I think that's why God didn't let them kill you. You have another chance now to make Miss Dorritt happy. You are the desire of her heart, and I don't think you should be so stubborn."

Don Carlos moaned and Reva turned to him.

Quinn stared at the shadows on the ceiling. If only his mind wasn't mush, he could figure out what to do.

* * *

Six days later, Don Carlos insisted on going home. With the help of Don Carlos's outriders, Ash had just finished bathing both men, who'd been propped up on chairs. Trying to avoid their bandages, Ash had doused them with buckets of warm soapy water and several buckets of cold rinse water. Quinn felt almost human. His fever had broken last night and he had been able to eat something like a normal breakfast. Ash dried and helped Quinn pull on a clean pair of breeches over a fresh bandage and set him back on the chair. Then he helped Quinn into a clean shirt. Quinn still wasn't supposed to walk without help, and his hip ached with a pain that nearly brought tears to his eyes if he moved wrong.

Ash went over to help one of the outriders, who was dressing Don Carlos so he could be carried out to the carriage. "Señor Quinn, I want you to come to my hacienda too," Don Carlos said. "You will receive much better care from my servants than here."

"Yes, and Miss Dorritt is going to the hacienda too to keep Alandra company. She already insisted that Quinn must come too," Ash announced.

"She did, did she?" Quinn's voice came out gruff, but hearing these words lifted his heart. Dorritt still wanted him. His mind had been busy over the past six days, trying and trying to make sense out of his escaping death. He'd survived when he should have died. And that meant something. "I need to talk to Miss Dorritt before we go."

The room went very still.

"I'll take you to her," Ash said. "And by the way, Don Carlos has offered me the job of being his foreman in Eduardo's place. And now that I'm a married man and ready to settle down, I took it. Reva and me will be at Rancho Sandoval too." Ash grinned.

"Good. That's good news." Quinn thought of all the years Ash had been his companion. And it made what he had to do easier.

"Come on. A little sun will be good for you." Ash helped Quinn stand.

Light-headed, Quinn leaned against Ash and let him support his right side so that he didn't have to put weight on the right leg. Outside, Ash left him on a chair under the covered porch of a nearby building. Even with constant pain, it was good to be outside in the sun and see men walking around and feel the fresh breeze on his face. Quinn couldn't recall ever feeling this weak. Or hopeful. Or uncertain.

Then Dorritt was walking toward him and her beauty made his lips numb. His heart moved inside him as if trying to go to her even if he couldn't. He tried to push himself up.

"No!" she called out and hurried forward. "Don't try to stand."

He let himself relax back onto the chair and she was there, touching his face, checking for fever. Her soft palm tempted him. He longed to turn his face farther into her softness and kiss her palm. "I'm better," he mumbled. Ash brought a chair over for Dorritt and then walked away.

"You are one strong man, Quinn." Dorritt fussed with his shirt collar and lifted his wet hair over his right shoulder. "But you still need to heal."

Her touch nearly made him forget to say the words he'd nerved himself to speak. First he had to see if she'd changed. "How is Don Carlos doing—the truth?"

Her face drew down with worry. "He is going to have a long convalescence. The ball was deep and the surgery was dreadful. I wanted him to stay here until his fever has fully broken, but he wants to be home. And I can't blame him. The day trip may tax him, but he will recover faster at home, I think. I hope. And his little sister was brought back today from friends and will go home with us."

Her words spoke of honest concern and friendship, not passion.

Quinn cleared his throat. Now that the moment had come it was hard to get the words out, and this setting was hardly the right one—curious soldiers glancing at them while walking nearby and the sun beating down on the fort courtyard. "Will you . . . marry me?"

Silence. His face burned as if the fever had returned. He waited in an agony of uncertainty. Had he waited too long?

Then she took his hand. "Of course I'll marry you. But why have you changed your mind?"

Her hand in his gave him the courage to put the rest of what he was feeling into words. "I can't really see my way forward. To marry and settle down was never in my plan. I just wanted to raise a few fine horses. But then I saw you in New Orleans—"

"You saw me there?" She turned to him with wide eyes.

"Yes, at the August horse race. You were there and dressed so fine and walking so tall. I had never seen a woman as special as

you before. I couldn't forget you, and then I saw you in Natchitoches, and found out that you were the daughter of the man
who cheated me out of ten head of cattle and two mustangs. I
had gone to the race looking for a horse to buy, but your stepfather said, 'Why not gamble for the horse?' "

She stared down but did not drop his hand. "I'm his *step*-
daughter, not his blood."

This made him smile. "Yes, you are nothing like your stepfather."

"Tell me why you see your way to marry me now?" She kept
her eyes lowered.

The words flowed out of his lips, "Because they didn't kill
me. And Reva said I'd better stop being stupid and marry you.
Because I said I wouldn't believe in God being close unless I saw
some evidence. I'm still wondering how a powerful God can be
concerned about me. I'm not important. But only God could
have saved me—I was unable to move or even speak and Juan
could have killed me easily."

His words sounded paltry to his own ears, and yet he couldn't
stem their flow. "But if you are really sure you love me and want
to marry me, I want it too. I still don't want to settle near Anglos.
And I still don't know if I can be all that you deserve, but I'll do
my best. I can't let you go. It's that simple—I can't let you go
out of my life." There, he'd said it all. He felt weak from all the
words.

Smiling, Dorritt squeezed his hand. "Yes, I want to marry you.
And it will be hard to be separated from my mother, especially
before the baby's born, but it's normal for a daughter to marry
and leave her mother."

Quinn sat there with Dorritt's hand in his, thinking that it
had all been so easy and yet so hard. And he was still so weak
that he didn't feel up to traveling to Rancho Sandoval. And how
would Don Carlos take his plans to marry Dorritt? Would he

still welcome him now that Quinn was marrying the woman he loved?

Dorritt rose.

"Where are you going?" He didn't like her leaving him.

"I'm going to go get my mother and the priest and we'll marry before we leave. I don't know when we'll be back here. We might as well marry while my mother can act as our witness."

He stared at her. "All right." What else could he say? And of course now that the thing was settled, his tall lady wouldn't hem and haw. She would manage everything just right. It's one of the things about her he loved most.

And the wedding took place right there on the steps of the Alamo church, with many soldiers looking on and little Alandra holding Dorritt's hand. Mrs. Kilbride was there, weeping into her handkerchief while Jewell scowled and Mr. Kilbride watched from the jail window. The Kilbride slaves had also come to the wedding in the fort courtyard, standing at a respectful distance.

Dorritt didn't like to leave them, but she hoped her mother would look after them and protect them from Mr. Kilbride. Though slavery was against Mexican law, Dorritt knew there was little chance to free them. There was work to be done and not enough people to do it on the frontier. The Mexicans would say there was no slavery, but they kept the Indians uneducated and poor as peons working the land. So no one in charge would challenge Kilbride's indenture papers. Changing this situation was too big for one woman. And Dorritt knew that.

After a tearful farewell between Dorritt and her mother, Don Carlos and Quinn were helped into the carriage. Everyone else would ride on horseback to Rancho Sandoval. Reva sat proudly behind her husband.

With little Alandra sitting in front of her, Dorritt was mounted on Jewell's mare. Her mother had given Jewell's mare as the family's wedding gift to the newlyweds. Jewell had been cross about this but hadn't made any public scene over letting the mare and Quinn's foal go. Maybe Jewell was growing up a little. Maybe Texas was stretching her heart and mind. Or maybe life seemed a bit more uncertain with her father still in prison and their being kept in San Antonio.

Leading one of her husband's mustangs, Dorritt rode out of the town and turned back to wave to her mother and sister. Then she turned toward the southwest and her future.

Epilogue

That night

With a feeling of unreality in the hacienda at Rancho Sandoval, Dorritt sat down on the edge of her bed back in the same elegant bedroom as before. And same as the first time, it was twilight and she'd just finished her bath. The servants had moments ago removed the tub. The tile floor was cool under her bare feet. And her wet hair was wrapped in towels. *This is real. I am here at Rancho Sandoval.*

This is my wedding night. She drew the damp white linen towels from her hair and began to dry and finger comb her long straight hair. The dark wood door opened and her husband entered with the help of one of the servants. Her pulse jerked in her veins and her heart galloped while she sat so still.

Quinn's hair was damp. He'd wanted to wash the road dust from him also. He wore only his buckskin breeches. And though he favored his right leg, he moved silently; she did not even hear his bare feet padding on the tile. He did not walk to her, but to the window where he sat on a bench there, looking out while the servant left, closing the door behind him. "I can't believe everything that has happened over the past week."

"Nor can I," she whispered as if someone were eavesdropping on them. Her throat was thick and her voice felt unsure.

"Don Carlos is a good man," her husband said. "I will do what I can to help him while he is ill."

Don Carlos is a good man and so is my husband. I am Señora Desmond Quinn. And proud to be so. "I hate what Eduardo did and tried to do," Dorritt said, moving to her husband's left side on the bench.

Quinn put his arm around Dorritt. "Don't worry. Eduardo has a bounty on his head. He will not go free. "

"Quinn, why did Eduardo try to wound his own cousin? Don Carlos was good to him."

"Some men despise goodness in others. And being treated good by someone he resented—" Quinn said, and shrugged. "That probably made Eduardo hate him more than if Don Carlos had treated him shabbily."

"What do you mean?" She gazed into Quinn's blue eyes, seeing the righteousness there. His smooth tanned skin begged her silently to touch him.

"Eduardo couldn't show his anger out in the open. He depended on Don Carlos and hated him and hated himself for not breaking with Don Carlos."

She gave into temptation and stroked Quinn's cheek. *This is my husband. I can touch him.*

Dorritt could no longer think of Eduardo and all the evil he had been capable of. She stared at her husband, his long golden-threaded hair and bare chest silvered in the moonlight. She thought, *I have married a beautiful man.* An unseen force drew her still nearer to him. His skin was silk under her palms as she slipped them up his arms to his shoulders and then rested her cheek against his chest.

He kissed the top of her head and ran his fingers through her hair from scalp to end. "We will help Don Carlos to get well."

"Yes. We won't let Eduardo upset us. Or spoil what we've been given." Then she whispered,

> "Delight thyself also in the LORD; and he shall give thee the desires of thine heart.
> Commit thy way unto the LORD; . . . And he shall bring thy righteousness as the light. . . .
> Rest in the LORD and wait patiently for him: . . . For evildoers shall be cut off: but those that wait upon the LORD, they shall inherit the earth."

Quinn murmured, "That is about the Creator?"

"Yes. He's kept his promises." *To Reva and me. Thank you, Father.*

Quinn cleared his throat. "He kept me alive. So that we might have a life together."

She looked up into the honest blue eyes she loved. "Yes, God is faithful."

He lowered his lips slowly, slowly until she thought she might die if they did not claim hers soon. Then he was kissing her and whispering, "I love you, my bride."

Tears slipped from her eyes as she let his love envelop her. *I am married yet both loved and free—the true desires of my heart.*

Historical Note

The land called Texas in 1821 was an interesting locale. This time period in the West is really transitional between the colonial days and the American West. What most of us think of as the Wild West began after the Civil War. In the 1820s through the 1830s, Americans were for the first time moving west of the Mississippi in large numbers. It's hard to believe, but after America gained its freedom and set up its Constitution, the frontier was the Northwest Territory, which encompassed the eastern Midwest. For example, Illinois became a state in 1822. Abraham Lincoln was twelve years old when Stephen Austin got a land grant to bring three hundred Anglo families into Texas, a state in Mexico.

Spain agreeing to let *angloamericanos* into their territory was an act of desperation. They could not draw anyone in numbers from Spain or Mexico who wanted to move north of the Rio

Grande. And Spain realized that it could not hold onto the land if they could not populate it. So the last Spanish governor of Mexico agreed to let Moses Austin, and upon Moses' death, his son Stephen to bring Anglos into Texas. Of course, the truth was that Americans had already been filtering into Texas in small numbers for years. Spain didn't have the troops to keep out the American squatters. So the Spanish invited Americans who were already coming into Texas. Spain did this so they wouldn't lose Texas to the Americans. Which, of course, was completely illogical.

Spain tried to prevent the Americans from changing Texas into an Anglo colony by insisting settlers agree to convert to Catholicism, not bring in slaves, and pledge allegiance to Spain. Of course, the Anglos had no intention of doing any of that. As Cole Anderson said, the Americans thought they would just keep to themselves and be Americans in everything but what they called themselves.

The Mexican Revolution of 1821 actually took place in Spain, when liberals took over and ousted the king. Padre Hidalgo had led the peons in a revolt in 1811 but had been executed and the revolt crushed. But with the overthrow of the king, Mexico announced its independence and formulated the first, very liberal constitution of Mexico. The liberal Constitution of 1824 was welcomed by the *angloamericano* settlers in Texas, since it set up a federal system and constitutional freedoms just like in the United States.

But the Mexicans had no tradition of self-government, and the Constitution of 1824 would soon be scrapped in favor of dictatorship and central control. And this is what led to the Texas Revolution of 1836, with its famous call, "Remember the Alamo!" And this turbulent time is what Alandra Maria Inez Sandoval will face when she comes of age.

I hope you enjoyed reading the first book in my Texas Star of Destiny series. I took the title of the series from the Texas state song, which interestingly was written in 1829, seven years before Texas broke away from Mexico. As Don Carlos Sandoval said, "Anglos don't blend in. They conquer."

I love to hear from readers. Please drop by my website: www. LynCote.net or e-mail me at l.cote@juno.com.

Blessings,

Lyn Cote

Discussion Questions for
The Desires of Her Heart

1. The status of women has changed a great deal over the past two hundred years. Compare and contrast the life of a woman of 1821 and the life of a twenty-first century woman.

2. What is the biblical view of the status of women? What does Scripture have to say?

3. Read in 1 Samuel 16 the account of Samuel anointing David as the second king of Israel. What does this tell us about how God judges people?

4. Have you ever been forced to trust in God in difficult circumstances? How? And what did you learn about trusting God? Why is it so hard to trust God at times?

5. Dorritt, her mother, and Reva all were liberated in Texas. What triggered each of them to begin to behave differently, in a freer manner?

6. Racial prejudice was rampant in 1821. Why did this trouble Dorritt? What did Maria tell Dorritt she possessed that others lacked?

7. Go to any concordance and look up the word *trust*, then choose a few verses about trusting God and write them down. Trusting God means surrendering to His will for our lives. What do you need to surrender to Him and trust Him with in your life?

8. Which characters were your favorites and why?

9. Psalm 37 was Dorritt's life scripture. What is yours?

10. Quinn didn't believe God cared about him personally until he came face-to-face with death. Why do you think this was?

LYN COTE married her real-life hero and was blessed with a son and daughter. She loves game shows, knitting, cooking, and eating! She and her husband live on a beautiful lake in the northwoods of Wisconsin. Now that the children have moved out, she indulges three cats—V-8 (for the engine, not the juice), Sadie, and Tricksey. In the summer, she writes using her laptop on her porch overlooking the lake. And in the winter, she sits by the fireplace her husband installed with the help of a good neighbor during their first winter at the lake.

Lyn's inspirational novels feature American women who step up to the challenges of their times and succeed in remaining true to the values of liberty and justice for all. The story of America is one of many nationalities and races coming together to forge our one nation under God and Lyn's novels reflect this with accurate historical detail, always providing the ring of authenticity. Strong Women, Brave Stories.

Lyn loves to hear from readers, so visit her website at *www.LynCote.net* or e-mail her at l.cote@juno.com.